THE ULTIMATUM

"Nancy Moser is a gifted storyteller. Her characters stay with you long after the last page."

KAREN KINGSBURY, BESTSELLING AUTHOR OF
One Tuesday Morning

"Strong characters, costly choices, eternal consequences. How far is each of us willing to go to share the love of Jesus with a lost world? In *The Ultimatum*, Nancy Moser looks at that question in a heart-stirring way that challenges readers to examine the depth of their own commitment to Christ."

CAROL COX, AUTHOR OF *TO CATCH A THIEF*

"I loved this book! *The Ultimatum* by Nancy Moser kept me up until 2 A.M. Nancy did a wonderful job of portraying the conflict that can happen when Christ moves into only one half of a marriage partnership. I've been telling all my friends about this fabulous read!"

COLLEEN COBLE, AUTHOR OF *WITHOUT A TRACE*

A STEADFAST SURRENDER

"This gripping drama will challenge your own spiritual journey—what I love best in a novel!"

CLAY JACOBSEN, AUTHOR OF *INTERVIEW WITH THE DEVIL*

"Once again, Nancy Moser manages to weave drama, a bit of suspense, and spiritual challenge into an entertaining whole, complete with a surprise ending."

JANELLE BURNHAM SCHNEIDER, AUTHOR OF *RIVER OF PEACE*

THE SEAT BESIDE ME

"Nancy Moser delivers a fast-paced, absorbing story in *The Seat Beside Me*. I didn't want to put it down!

ROBIN LEE HATCHER, AWARD-WINNING AUTHOR OF
RIBBON OF YEARS AND COAUTHOR OF *THE STORY JAR*

"A powerfully dramatic story that forces the reader to wonder, *How many times have I been spared?* After reading *The Seat Beside Me,* you will never sit by a stranger without the realization that every encounter is God appointed."

VONETTE ZACHARY BRIGHT, COFOUNDER,
CAMPUS CRUSADE FOR CHRIST

THE INVITATION

"A fascinating tale of four different people who are called together for a mysterious purpose. Through their intriguing story and the suspenseful ending, Nancy Moser sends her own invitation to the reader, asking us to consider how God can use us—and all ordinary people—in the most extraordinary ways."

FLORENCE LITTAUER, SPEAKER AND AUTHOR OF
PERSONALITY PLUS AND *SILVER BOXES*

THE QUEST

"*The Quest* mirrors a bit of Frank Peretti's books as we see the battle for good and evil come to the forefront."

CHRISTIAN LIBRARY JOURNAL

THE TEMPTATION

"Nancy Moser deftly melds page-turning suspense with engaging characters and solid biblical truth. Along with the two prequels, *The Temptation* deserves shelf space with spiritual warfare classics like those of Frank Peretti!"

CINDY SWANSON, PRODUCER/HOST OF *WEEKEND MAGAZINE*
RADIO SHOW, ROCKFORD, IL

THE
ULTIMATUM

[A Novel]

NANCY MOSER

Multnomah® Publishers *Sisters, Oregon*

THE ULTIMATUM
published by Multnomah Publishers, Inc.

© 2004 by Nancy Moser
International Standard Book Number: 1-59052-144-7

Cover image by Steve Gardner, His Image PixelWorks
Background cover image by Getty Images/Jerry Gay

Unless otherwise indicated, Scripture quotations are from:
The Holy Bible, New International Version
© 1973, 1984 by International Bible Society,
used by permission of Zondervan Publishing House

Other Scripture quotations are from:
Holy Bible, New Living Translation (NLT)
© 1996. Used by permission of Tyndale House Publishers, Inc.
All rights reserved.

Multnomah is a trademark of Multnomah Publishers, Inc.,
and is registered in the U.S. Patent and Trademark Office.
The colophon is a trademark of Multnomah Publishers, Inc.

Printed in the United States of America

For information:
MULTNOMAH PUBLISHERS, INC. • P.O. BOX 1720 • SISTERS, OR 97759

Library of Congress Cataloging-in-Publication Data

Moser, Nancy.
    The ultimatum / by Nancy Moser.
        p. cm.
    ISBN 1-59052-144-7 (pbk.)
    1. Hostage negotiations—Fiction. 2. City and town life—Fiction. 3. Sacrifice—
Fiction. 4. Robbery—Fiction. 5. Kansas—Fiction. I. Title.
    PS3563.O88417U45 2004
    813'.54—dc22

                                2003026157

04 05 06 07 08 09 10—10 9 8 7 6 5 4 3 2 1

To Shari, Linda, Judy, Teresa, Carl and Loraine,
Pastor Stan and Emily…and all the lovely people of the
Cornerstone Baptist Church in Exeter, Maine.
Your faith, friendship, and prayers are an inspiration.
I may be a midwesterner by birth, but through you,
Maine has won my heart.

NOVELS BY NANCY MOSER

The Ultimatum (sequel to *A Steadfast Surrender*)

A Steadfast Surrender

The Seat Beside Me

The Sister Circle

'Round the Corner

Time Lottery

THE MUSTARD SEED SERIES:

The Invitation

The Quest

The Temptation

If you have any encouragement from being united with Christ,
if any comfort from his love, if any fellowship with the Spirit,
if any tenderness and compassion,
then make my joy complete by being like-minded,
having the same love, being one in spirit and purpose.

PHILIPPIANS 2:1–2

One

My dear brothers, take note of this:
Everyone should be quick to listen,
slow to speak and slow to become angry,
for man's anger does not bring about the righteous life that God desires.

JAMES 1:19–20

JERED MANSON RAN FOR HIS LIFE.

His lungs ached.

He glanced behind. The guy was still after him.

Maybe he should give up. Stop running. Let whatever happens, happen. But just as Jered let the thought in, he got a break.

Just as Skimmy, Scummy—whatever he was called—ran across the street toward him, a van drove in the way. The sound of hands slamming against its side merged with a honk. Shouted words.

Jered took advantage of the distraction and darted into an alley. An open delivery truck was parked like an invitation. He hurtled inside.

But it was nearly empty. No place to hide. And when the truck's owner came back, he'd surely make a ruckus. *"What you doing in there? Get out of my truck!"*

By then Scummy would have caught up, he'd hear the yelling, and Jered would be dead.

All for a portable CD player.

Way back during the first block, Jered had nearly dropped it, given up the loot in the hopes that Scummy would be satisfied and not come after him. But from what Jered had heard about Scummy, retrieving the goods wouldn't be enough.

During the past three months Jered had learned that revenge was the motivating factor on the streets. *You do me bad, I do you.* It didn't need to make sense. Logic and reason had nothing to do with anything. Honor did. The street's form of honor. It didn't help that Jered was skinny, looking more wimpy than tough.

A lady walking on the sidewalk at the end of the alley hesitated and pulled up, as if she saw someone coming.

Scummy?

A half-closed dumpster stood across the alley. He jumped down from the truck, crossed the alley, tossed the CD box inside the dumpster, hauled himself up and over the edge, and fell into the garbage. He couldn't reach the lid to shut it and didn't want to risk the noise, so he scrambled under the half that was closed, pulling the garbage around him as cover.

Within seconds he heard footsteps and huffing.

He froze.

He held his breath.

The footsteps came close, and Jered heard a leap onto the back of the delivery truck, a few steps inside, then a jump down. More steps. Far. Then near.

When Scummy kicked the dumpster, Jered stifled a yelp. He clamped his hand to his mouth to hold his heart inside.

With a few cuss words, Scummy moved on.

All was quiet.

Except Jered's heart. He tried to take deep breaths but didn't dare gasp. It was a full minute before he could trust his body, when he didn't have to consciously think about his heartbeat or getting his next lungful of air.

Only then did he let his muscles relax. But as they did, he sank deeper into the trash. A black garbage sack was sliced open, and the rancid smell of rotting Chinese food hit his nostrils like a slap. Jered hadn't noticed the smell before. He'd been too busy surviving. But now...

He covered his face with his hands, against the smell, against the stress, against the reality of where he was and what he'd become. He heard his dad's voice in his head. *"Jered, what* are *you doing in the trash? Stupid kid! Don't you have any sense?"*

Sense had nothing to do with it; survival, everything. Survival was the king he bowed down to every morning as he hoped to make it through another day, as well as the king he worshipped every night when he was still alive. Actually, now was a time to celebrate, for he *had* survived. Again. This time.

Enough of this. He rubbed his tears angrily and climbed through the garbage to the open side of the dumpster. The fresh air was cool—in all forms of the word. He set the CD player on the lid and rearranged some sacks so he could get high enough to climb over the edge. As soon as his feet hit the ground—

"Whatcha doing there, kid?"

It was the delivery man, back at his truck.

Jered brushed off his jeans, knowing the dumpster was *not* responsible for their dirtiness. "I lost something inside." He picked up the CD player.

The man walked toward him, disbelief clear on his face. "Food can't be very good in there."

"I wasn't searching for food."

The man dug a bill from his shirt pocket and handed it to Jered. "Here. Go get yourself something to eat."

If Jered had any pride left, he would have argued. He took the bill. "Thanks. 'Preciate it."

The man nodded and they parted. "Take care of yourself, okay, kid?"

He was doing his best. He really was.

Annie McFay ran for her life.

She stepped onto the front stoop, zipped her jacket to her chin, and began running—toward something or away from something; she wasn't sure.

Running was her sanity, her time alone when she had to think things through. The fact it was helping her lose the ten pounds she'd put on since she turned thirty was another factor. Working at the Plentiful Café, where low-cal was as foreign as tiramisu, did *not* help her waistline. People expected down-home cooking at a small-town diner, and that's what they got.

Out of habit, at the end of her driveway she turned right, heading toward Steadfast's town square. But after three strides, she changed her mind and ran in the opposite direction. She'd be around people soon enough. She had to be at work in less than two hours. Until then...

When she found her rhythm, she let herself zone in on her problem: She had no idea what to do with her husband, Cal. With his disapproval. More than anything she wanted him to understand what a difference Jesus was making in her life, how much better she was feeling about everything—except her marriage.

Why couldn't he see that her newfound faith was not a threat to what they had? If anything it would make it better. Cal was a good man. She could hardly wait to see the better man he could be with Jesus behind him, backing him up.

She grabbed a deeper breath that had nothing to do with physical exertion. Its vapor flew past her cheek and slid through her ponytail.

How could a decision seem so right, so good in her own mind, yet seem wrong and bad in her husband's?

She heard Cal's voice in her head: *"Don't go overboard about this religion stuff, Annie-girl."*

Overboard? Moi?

Annie sidestepped a puddle and acknowledged her penchant for jumping into new projects with too much gusto and not enough stick-to-itiveness. Could she help it if her paintings never looked as good as the ones by that TV guy, Bob Ross? The eighty-five dollars' worth of art equipment wasn't really going to waste. Ten-year-old Avignon—Avi—was playing with it. The fact Avi seemed to have more innate talent than her mother was something Annie would rather ignore.

Another puddle. Another thought. Could Annie help it if she was horrible at the telemarketing she'd tried to do from their home? Hey, she'd readily admit *that* was a mistake. It was hard to cold-call when she herself hated to receive such calls.

Then came the mamba lessons, the needlepoint kit she'd started and set aside, the How to Speak Italian tapes (just in case they ever traveled to Tuscany), and the handy-dandy donut maker she'd bought from a shopping channel.

The truth was, she liked to flit from project to project, never landing long. She meant well. It was all part of the cost of finding herself. Finding her talent, her purpose. Finding out why she *was*.

What Cal refused to understand was that Jesus was helping her do just that. Not that she had it all straight yet, but ever since she'd invited the Lord into her heart, she felt as if she finally had a shot at answering the purpose question.

Wasn't it natural that she wanted to share her newfound hope with her husband? Together, they could discover what's what.

Truth be told, Cal was a bigger flitterer than she was. But unlike her projects, his forays were often pricey. *"You gotta spend money to make money, Annie-girl."* Yeah right. Prove it.

His goal followed the ever-popular get-rich-quick scenario. If, along the way, he found some inner truth, whoop-dee-do. But if not, he didn't seem to mind. And there was another motive behind Cal's schemes. One that he would never admit. Cal *wasn't* searching for his purpose, but he *was* searching for a way to make his father proud. The fact Fergis McFay had died soon after they were married—Annie had never even met the man—was a detail that seemed beyond Cal's ability to embrace.

Any comment Annie had made toward that effect—"You don't have to keep trying to please him, Cal. He's gone. And you please me plenty, so ease up"—was met with a look that screamed at her ignorance and warned her to leave it alone.

So be it. If Cal wanted to waste his time trying to gain brownie points from a dead father, who was she to stop him? As the queen of quirkiness, Annie had no latitude in judging the oddities of others. So for the most part, she let Cal try to get rich quick and was there to catch him when he failed. Which was always.

Pooh. What was money anyway? As long as they had enough to pay their bills, celebrate Christmas in a decent fashion, and take an occasional trip to Kansas City or Saint Louis for a weekend, Annie could have cared less how many zeros were behind the dollar amounts in their bank accounts. You can't take it with you—as her recent ten thousand dollar inheritance from her mother had proven. Sometimes Annie wished they hadn't gotten that money. It only added fuel to Cal's entrepreneurial fire.

A dog barked as she ran by a house, and she detoured across the street. Rehashing the past was getting her nowhere. Nor was complaining. After ten years of marriage, she and Cal were a good complement to each other. She liked to cook; he liked to eat. She liked to dink around the house; he liked yard work. She liked country music, and he liked the pretty female singers. In most areas of their lives, their corresponding interests drew them together like two magnets finding their mates.

Until a certain Man had turned their magnets around, repelling one another...

Annie ran between Steadfast's tiny hospital and the elementary school on the edge of town, stopping to catch her breath at the ball field. The ball field had been the location of her transformation. Had she meant to come here this morning?

The last time she'd stood in this spot it had been covered with a big white tent. A revival had come to town in August, and her friend Merry Cavanaugh, the librarian, and Merry's beau, Ken Kendell, the police chief, had invited all three McFays to join them. Posters were all over town for the Praise Show, even in the window of the café. Word of mouth had popped with excitement.

And Annie *had* been curious. A "praise" show? *Praise* was not a word she associated with religion. She had few memories of church as a child, but most revolved around eating cheap store-bought cookies as the adults stood around and talked, or being told to sit still during a sermon from a man whose face got way too red when he yelled at them. The best part of church was getting a new pair of patent leather Mary Janes every year. She loved how the shoes made a funny sticking noise when they touched.

Praise? Please. It was not in her churchgoing memory bank. And yet, Merry and Ken had been persistent. Excited. So what could it hurt? When Annie had suggested to Cal that they accept the invitation, he'd been adamant against it. "No way. You're not getting me in there with a bunch of fanatics."

She asked him to explain, but he shut up, shaking his head. Nohow. No way. And though that should have been the end of it, for some reason Annie had felt compelled to add, "I think Avi and I will go. If that's okay."

Cal had raised an eyebrow and flipped a hand. "Knock yourselves out. Work yourselves into a praise-the-Lord tizzy."

Tizzy was not exactly what happened, but the Praise Show did get something working in Annie that night. She'd felt a stirring unlike anything she'd ever experienced. And a joy. And a longing for what Merry and Ken obviously had, as they sang and raised their faces toward the sky. Even Avi had been moved. She'd taken hold of Annie's arm and looked up at her with excited eyes. "I like this, Mama. I want this."

Exactly what "this" was hadn't been clear at first, but the main speaker began to lay out what they were offering, telling about God sending His Son to earth, Jesus dying on the cross because He loved the world that much, taking the rap for everybody's sins... And then the raising up to heaven part being a promise that we'd live in heaven someday if only we believed He was who He said He was. How could Annie *not* believe? How could she say anything but yes to someone who'd done all that—for her?

When they invited people to come forward to make it official, she looked down at Avi, and Avi looked up at her. "Let's do it, Mama. Let's go."

And so they did.

At the memory, Annie sank to her knees, right there in the field. Was this the spot where it had happened? She looked around. It was pretty close. And she knew it was the perfect place to do what she should have done the moment she'd started worrying.

She scanned the field. No one was around. It was way too early. The sun was just starting to come up on the horizon amid a blaze of pink and steel blue. The sun. The Son. He'd changed everything for her then. He could help her now.

"I want Cal to know You, Jesus. Show me how to reach him."

She tried to think of more to say, but these few words had expressed what was directly on her heart better than a hundred that beat around the bush or sounded eloquent. With an "Amen" she stood and headed home.

She was doing her best. She really was.

Two

Wisdom is supreme; therefore get wisdom.
Though it cost all you have, get understanding.

PROVERBS 4:7

ANNIE SET THE PLATES before her customers. "One Plentiful Pancake Surprise and one Sausage Omelet Supreme. Dive in, gentlemen." She pointed at their empty coffee cups. "You stocking up on caffeine for the winter, boys? Back in a jiff with another refill."

As she headed for the coffeepot, she spotted Cal enter the Plentiful with Bailey Manson, the owner of Steadfast's gourmet Bon Vivant restaurant. Leaving last night's latest Jesus argument behind, she blew her husband a kiss that turned into a wave. He winked and pointed to the counter. She nodded, and they took a seat. Every time she saw Cal she was struck by his manly-man, lumberjack looks. The latest movie heartthrobs had nothing on her hubby.

She grabbed the pot and made the rounds, chatting and laughing along the way but also glancing at the two men. Not only did Bailey not fit with the Plentiful crowd—in his black pants, turtleneck, and jacket he looked like Annie's image of a la-di-da Hollywood director—he also didn't fit with her husband, who was wearing his staple of jeans and a red plaid flannel shirt Annie had tried to throw away twice. Yet it was more than their appearance.

Though there were no social hoity-toitys in Steadfast, Bailey held himself as high up as he could, nose ever-reaching. Why? She hadn't a clue. Annie would rather be one of the gang than all alone like Bailey, looking down at the party going on without him. Lonely business, feeling better than.

The two men had gotten to know each other the past couple

months while Bailey added on to Bon Vivant. Cal had a home improvement business, though in truth he was a glorified handyman, and Bailey's addition was his first big job where he was hired to be the general contractor and coordinate other workers. It was definitely a step up from putting in a few kitchen cabinets or building a deck.

Annie would never say this to her husband, but she still didn't know why Bailey had hired *him*. And now, she couldn't imagine Bailey allowing himself to become chummy with the hired help. Yet here they were, laughing and chatting like best buds.

She headed to the other side of the counter, hooking a finger in a couple mugs along the way. "Coffee, gentlemen?"

Cal took the mugs. "Fill 'er up, Annie-girl, and bring us two cinnamon rolls, extra frosting."

When Bailey shrugged, Annie got the rolls. She tried to give Cal a what's-up? stare, but he never looked at her. She wanted to grab his face and make him look, make him catch the question she was trying to fling at him. It was almost as if he was avoiding her eyes...

"Order up!" Donald, the owner, cook, and chief bottle washer, had the voice of a bullhorn that could not be ignored.

Annie got busy, yet every chance she had, she looked at the men. They ate with their bodies angled toward each other, their free hands emphasizing their words. They talked more than they ate. Ooh, yessireeny, something was definitely brewing.

At one point, Dottie, the other waitress, leaned close, cocked her head in their direction, and whispered, "What's up with that odd couple?"

"I don't know, but I'm going to find out." Annie wiped her hands on her pastel uniform, shuffled her shoulders, and took a deep breath in an exaggerated preparation for battle.

"Ha! Go get 'em!" Dottie said.

Annie made a beeline toward the dynamic duo. Their rolls were only half eaten, and their coffee mugs were nearly full but steamless. She poured two fresh cups as a way to ease into their world. She shoved Cal's plate an inch closer. "My, my, gentlemen. What's got you so caught up that you're forgetting to eat?"

Cal swiveled his stool to face her. "Opportunity is knocking, Annie-girl."

"Pounding down the door," Bailey said.

She suffered an inner sigh. "Sounds noisy. Care to share?"

"Bailey's got an idea that could make us tons of money. Make us—"

Cal stopped talking when Harold Shinness edged up to the counter.

Bad timing, Harold. Bad timing. "What can I get you today, Harold?"

"I represent the library bunch, Miss Annie." He nodded toward the Steadfast Library across the square. "Four cinnamon rolls, please. Merry and I want ours normal, Ivan doesn't want any frosting, and Blanche says she'll have his portion added onto hers."

Annie smiled. "I've never seen a woman with such a sweet tooth. Grab a stool. I'll get 'em for you."

Harold sat next to Bailey. "Morning, Bailey. Cal."

Both men nodded, but it was clear they weren't comfortable in Harold's presence. They didn't know what they were missing. Sure, Harold had gone through his weird stage after the death of his wife—only talking in quotes from Shakespeare, scurrying around like a half-witted recluse—but he was back to normal now. Or as normal as Harold could be. He was a sweet old guy, but unfortunately, "sweet" was not a trait Cal cared about. Annie could only assume by their not-so-subtle shunning that Bailey felt the same. Men could be as shallow as cookie sheets sometimes.

The real proof they considered Harold a nonentity was when they continued their conversation as if he weren't even there.

Cal talked while Annie placed Harold's rolls in a hinged container. "Bailey's got this idea to open another restaurant."

"Steadfast's already got two. What do we need with more?"

Bailey lowered his voice. "No offense, Annie, but this place can hardly be considered a restaurant. It's a diner, plain and simple."

"Yes, it is. And it serves plain and simple food and does a good job of it. Any extra padding in the waistlines of Steadfast is Donald's doing."

Bailey leaned back, unconcerned. "The Plentiful has home cooking, no atmosphere, and uniforms out of a seventies' waitress sitcom."

Annie looked down at her pink *Alice*-style attire. "At least my name isn't Flo." She pretended to fluff her hair, but it was pulled into a ponytail. As a redhead, pink was *not* her best color.

"My Bon Vivant serves the other end of the eating spectrum with gourmet food in an elegant setting."

"And cummerbunds. Don't forget the cummerbunds."

He ignored her. "What I'm proposing is to fill the needs of the middle ground. Open a restaurant that has the atmosphere of home, with the food you'd like to eat at home but never have the time to fix anymore."

"Bailey, you're not listening. We have home cooking here."

"Most of it's fried. People can't eat that every day. And some, like me after my heart attack, can't eat it at all." As if to prove his point, he shoved the rest of his roll away. "I'm talking healthy home cooking. The cooking of the new century." He slapped a hand on the counter. "If we're successful, people will never want to eat at home."

Harold raised a hand. "Excuse me, is that a good thing?"

Bailey blinked at him. "It's certainly not bad."

Harold raised an eyebrow. "But does Steadfast really need such a place?"

"Need has nothing to do with it." Bailey grinned and quoted Kevin Costner in that baseball movie. "If we build it, they will come."

"Yeah," Cal said. "Nobody likes to cook anymore. Nobody sits around the table at dinner. They—"

"We do." Annie felt herself blush. "Sometimes." *Do TV trays count?*

"But if we made it homey enough, people could come and sit at *our* tables and eat together." Cal's eyes widened. "Hey, we could even have televisions going so people would really feel at home."

"It's an interesting thought," Bailey said.

Harold's head shook back and forth. "That's one word for it."

Bailey swiveled his chair to face him. "You have a better word?"

Uh-oh. Annie stepped forward with Harold's order. "Ten dollars, please."

Harold slid off the stool and fished a crumpled bill from his pocket. He turned to leave.

"I'm waiting for an answer."

"Hey, Bailey. Take it easy…"

"I'm just asking."

"Ask nice."

"I thought I did."

They all looked at Harold as he slowly turned to face Bailey. He held the box of rolls with both hands and looked at the floor a full five seconds. Then he raised his head and nodded once. Wisdom shone in his old eyes. And compassion. "What people want and what people need are two different things."

"They don't have to be," Bailey said.

"But they are. I have no doubt the kind of restaurant you describe would be a success—monetarily. But maybe you need to ask yourself whether it would be a success morally."

Cal let out a huff. "How did morals get into this?"

Harold's voice remained soft. "Any time you tamper with the framework of family life, you risk ruining something sacred."

Bailey tossed his hands in the air. "For pity's sake, we're giving them good food in a nice setting."

"You're taking them away from hearth and home during one of the few moments of the day when busy families come together to talk."

"They can talk at the restaurant."

"It's not the same."

Bailey's smile became smug. "And who are you to say anything? You don't have a family. You never had any kids."

"Bailey!" Annie couldn't believe his rudeness.

She had never witnessed the kind of love Harold had shown for his wife when she was alive. Annie didn't know the reason why they'd never had children but sensed Harold held a deep pain regarding that fact. And Bailey should talk. His wife had left him years ago. And a few months previous his son, Jered, had run away.

Bailey continued, "It always galls me when people who don't have experience talk as though they know more than they possibly could. They should mind their own business; that's what they should do." He turned his stool toward the counter with a backward flip of his hand.

Cal turned away, too.

Harold stared at their backs, his face drawn, yet amazingly not with anger but with sorrow. Annie's impulse was to hug him, comfort him. She looked at Cal and Bailey. They were thick as thieves again, oblivious to the pain they'd caused.

As Harold turned toward the door, Annie hurried around the counter. "Let me get the door for you." She followed him outside. "I'm sorry, Harold." She nodded toward the two men inside. "I like what you said. I agree with you."

His smile was wistful. "Protect what you have, Miss Annie. Don't let anyone tear it apart."

She watched him cross the square as long as she could before the October cold forced her inside.

Annie went back to work with Harold's warning ringing in her ears.

Bailey and Cal stood outside the Plentiful Café next to Cal's truck. Rust spotted the fender, and the hokey sign on the door—*Cal's Home Improvements* with the phone number on it—was a quarter-inch off plumb. Bailey had noticed it the first time he saw it, and it made him question the precision of Cal's building capabilities. How plumb was his construction work when he couldn't even get a stupid ad painted on straight?

But had it stopped Bailey from hiring him? Not that there was much choice in Steadfast. Inane little town. One heating and air company, one electrician, one building contractor, but three plumbers. Curious.

It was true he could have gone to nearby Eldora to get bids. After all, he'd used an Eldora contractor to build Bon Vivant ten years previous. Unfortunately, those bridges were burned and the ashes scattered. Bailey was sure the construction grapevine in Eldora had had a field day listening to his last contractor exaggerate their differences. And in no way did they appreciate the distinction between being deemed "difficult" versus "discerning." He wanted what he wanted when he wanted it. Was that such a ridiculous request?

Cal droned on about college football. Mindless drivel. Bailey nodded dutifully, though he could have cared less whether Kansas or Kansas State won, lost, or fell off the face of the earth. He didn't have time for sports. He was an entrepreneur. The fact he had to lower himself to sports small talk was an unfortunate game he had to play to achieve his objective.

And his objective was to get Cal's help on the new restaurant. Cal's work on the addition to Bon Vivant was winding down, was acceptable, his prices reasonable, and his character gullible. If Bailey handled it right, he could get Cal to invest Annie's inheritance.

Cal had never leaked the exact amount but had implied it was a hefty sum, which meant it *had* to be close to six figures. Once he had the money, he'd get Cal to do the construction work at a discounted partner-price, leaving Bailey to run it and deal with the proper apportioning of the profits. What Cal didn't know about the restaurant business was in Bailey's favor. Ignorance could indeed be bliss—and be used to Bailey's benefit.

Cal opened the door of his truck and got in. Bailey forced himself to concentrate for the final good-byes.

"I sure appreciate you coming to me with this project, Bailey. I won't let you down."

Bailey put on his best buddy smile. "I knew you'd be the one to ask. We'll talk more later." He shut the door, gave a two-fingered salute, and walked to his silver BMW parked across the street—safe from other door-dinging vehicles.

Cal beeped his horn as he drove by.

Bailey gave him a parting smile. *Sucker.*

"Sucker!"

The kid bolted like a sprinter. Jered didn't understand why until he unfolded the wad of bills. Only three ones folded inside a five. "Hey! I told you twenty! You owe me—"

The kid paused at the corner of the alley. "Don't you know nothin', man? You don't give the goods till you get the cash. Are you dumb, or what?" He ran away.

"Are you dumb, or what?"

Jered shoved the eight bucks into his pocket. He *had* been dumb. This time. But the kid had moved so fast. He'd shoved the wad of money in Jered's left hand and plucked the CD player out of his right hand in one motion. All that work stealing it in the first place, running for his life from Scummy, hiding out in a dumpster for eight lousy bucks? *Was* he dumb? If so, he was getting smarter every day. Street smarter.

He went back to his truck. His home. His world.

A too-sweet smell hit him as soon as he opened the door. He looked at his stash of food on the floor of the passenger side and heaved a rotting apple out the window. What was left? A box of generic Ritz-type crackers, a half loaf of bread, a can of beans, and some bologna. He was sick of bologna sandwiches. Yet every time he complained, he reminded himself of the harder time he'd had when the weather was warm. He hadn't been able to keep meat and cheese then. His menu had increased tons when the colder temperatures of October rolled in.

But his income had not.

He *was* willing to work, but it was hard getting a decent job without decent clothes. He hadn't thought to pack when he took off from Steadfast three months ago. He'd gotten outta there pronto, afraid he'd caused his dad's heart attack and mad at his dad for helping that sickly sweet orphan Sim.

Talk about a con job. Sim comes to town, holes up in the library attic, and wins the heart of the town. What a scam. And his dad had been as big a patsy as anyone. Letting her stay at *their* house. Playing games with her. Treating her special, as if she was more important than...

Jered ripped his stocking hat off and barreled it into the windshield, leaving his too-long, greasy hair plastered against his head. When he'd left home he made the huge mistake of not thinking long-term. He stuffed a few clothes into a backpack and headed to Kansas

City. But two T-shirts and a second pair of jeans didn't cut it for job interviews at any job beyond the first one he'd had scrapping out construction sites.

Plumbers, framers, electricians—nobody cleaned up after themselves. And why should they when grunts like Jered could do it for them? He'd only kept that gig three weeks till his back gave out and he got a nail in his foot.

Everything he earned went for gas and food. He wouldn't have money to buy new clothes until he had a real job, and he couldn't get a real job until he had decent clothes.

What'd they call that? A catch-22?

Nothing was working out as he planned, and Kansas City had been a bust. Right off Jered hooked up with some people who were into drugs. He'd even tried some. But never again. Hinky stuff and hinkier people. Nope, drugs weren't his scene.

Kansas City was a good place to hide, but it was too big. He'd grown up in Steadfast, population 3,386, and was used to dealing with the likes of his buddies Moog and Darrell. A couple six-packs, banging a few mailboxes, and throwing stuff at old Harold—that was the extent of their bad doings. Things were too heavy in KC. He didn't like being scared all the time.

So he left. He hadn't planned on ending up in Eldora, just twenty minutes from Steadfast—and his father. It was almost as if his truck had driven with its own mind. But once he'd seen the city sign, he felt better. More in control. More...

He looked around the alley. In control? Ha. He still lived in his truck, still scrounged for food, was still afraid. He still didn't have a job, and peddling what little he had guts enough to steal wasn't something he was good at.

Then what was?

He opened the glove compartment and got out his music. Scraps of his compositions. Nothing finished. Just some junk he *had* stuffed into his pack before leaving. Luckily, finding new paper to write on was easy enough. The trash was full of it. He used the backs of used paper and wrote and wrote—as best he could. He really needed his guitar. Why hadn't he brought his guitar with him?

He pictured where it stood in his room behind his door—unless his dad had sold it or given it away. It was a good possibility. Bailey Manson, fancy restaurant owner, didn't care about his son *or* his son's music. In fact, he'd been totally against it, calling Jered's dream to be a somebody in the music world "absurd and impractical."

I'll show him.

Jered laughed at the thought. "Oh yeah, I'm really showing him, aren't I?"

His voice ricocheted around the cab of the truck. Such a lonely sound. Only one thing would make the feeling go away.

Jered locked the doors, positioned his backpack as a pillow, spread his T-shirts over him as a blanket, and lay down to find oblivion.

Annie picked up the phone. "Plentiful Café, this is Annie. Whatcha hungry for?"

She listened a few seconds then hung up, whipping off her apron. "Dottie, cover for me. I gotta go!"

Dottie was hanging her order on the clip-turnabout in the kitchen pass-through. "What's going on?"

Annie grabbed her purse. "Avi fell on the playground. The school nurse said she needs stitches. They'll take her across the street to the ER, but I'm heading there now."

She didn't wait for permission.

Annie ran into the ER of the Steadfast Hospital, her eyes darting, searching for her daughter.

The receptionist stood and pointed to the right. "Avi's in there, Annie. She's fine."

Annie had to see for herself. She found her daughter lying on an examination table. A doctor was sewing up her knee. A slightly pregnant nurse invited her in. Annie's stomach grabbed at the thought of seeing a needle puncture skin, so she avoided looking at the wound and moved beside Avi, taking her hand, scanning her face.

"Hey, sweet-apple, how you doing?"

"I'm okay."

"She'll be just fine," said Dr. Grant.

The nurse looked up from the work and smiled. "She's quite the brave girl. Not one tear."

"I *did* cry at school," Avi said.

Annie stroked her long strawberry blond hair. "It's okay to cry. You don't always have to be brave."

"She's not a crier?" the doctor asked.

"Never has been." Annie flicked the end of Avi's nose. "Even as a baby when I'd check to see if she was wet or hungry, she'd look right back at me with a crease on her little brow, as if studying the situation."

"Mama says I'm low maintenance."

The nurse laughed. "That's a good thing to be."

Dr. Grant stood erect. "There. That's that then. Susan will finish up here." He patted Avi's knee. "You take care of yourself, little lady. Don't run so fast next time, okay?"

He left them, and the nurse got bandage supplies out of a cupboard. Annie nodded at the nurse's belly. "When are you due?"

"March."

"Is this your first?"

"Biologically, yes. But I also have a fifteen-year-old daughter. Technically she's my niece, but her parents were killed in a car accident so she's mine now."

"How awful. I mean, it's nice you've found each other."

Susan nodded. "Sim's a great kid. We just moved here in time for her to start school. Hey, she's a great babysitter. I'm sure she'd love to sit for Avi."

"Sim! I've met her!" Avi said. "Over at Cassie's house. Cassie's sister is fifteen, too."

Annie realized she and the nurse hadn't really met—which was strange in a town the size of Steadfast. "I'm Annie McFay."

"Susan Kellogg. Glad to meet you."

"Likewise."

"Now let's get a bandage on this."

"Can I see the stitches first?" Avi asked.

Annie put a hand to her midsection. "Ugh! Leave me out."

Susan laughed. She helped Avi sit up, and the girl studied the medical handiwork as if the wound belonged to someone else. Annie listened to Susan's instructions but was heartily glad when the bandage was secured. She helped Avi to the floor.

As she walked them out, Susan said, "Would you and Avi like to come to our house tomorrow afternoon? A few friends come over every Saturday, and the women have a Bible study while the kids hang out. Sim usually does some craft with them."

Avi yanked at Annie's sleeve. "That sounds fun, Mama. And you don't work tomorrow."

Annie thought of her run—and her prayer. Maybe she'd get some advice on how to reach Cal. Merry had been asking her to go to *her* Bible study for a month now, but with Cal's attitude Annie hadn't wanted to risk it.

At Annie's hesitation, Susan said, "Hey, don't worry. We don't force anyone to believe anything. It's just a time a few of us can get together and talk about life, which naturally means letting in some God-talk." She smiled. "Can't rightly have one without the other, can we?"

It sounded perfect. "I'll be there."

"Super. Come at one-thirty. I'm making my famous death-by-chocolate brownies. You like chocolate, don't you?"

Avi's hand shot up. "I do!"

"Then it's settled."

Okay then.

Even though Annie didn't feel much like cooking, she had to. There was a point to be made and an argument to win through creating a wonderful family meal they would eat together—around the table. Proof to Cal that Bailey's restaurant idea was off the mark.

She'd just shut the oven after checking the lasagna when Cal walked in the kitchen door, hung his jacket on a hook, and headed toward the front of the house to go upstairs to change. He was tracking in mud. "Shoes!"

He looked behind him. "Oops. Sorry." He backtracked, undid his work boots, and put them on the back stoop.

Cal never forgot his shoes. Ever. "What's up? Bailey drain your brain today?"

He didn't answer. When he came back in, he avoided her eyes. *Two times in one day?* He stepped toward the oven. "What do I smell?"

"Lasagna." Like a game show hostess she took a step back, revealing a tray of garlic cheese bread on the counter. "And for your dining pleasure, you also get bread. And salad. With a grand prize of apple cake."

He nodded once, but his brow was tight.

"Hey, babe. What's wrong?" she asked.

He blinked twice, managed a smile, then kissed her cheek and pulled her close. "I'm starved." He kissed her again.

She nudged him away. "Go get cleaned up. Dinner will be ready in fifteen minutes."

He unbuttoned his shirt. "Where's Avi? How's her leg? You never called me back."

"Sorry, I got busy. She's doing fine. She's up in her cubby reading."

"Isn't it a little cold in there?"

Annie had thought the same thing. The unfinished storage space off of their bedroom closet was Avi's hideaway. The fact she could barely stand up inside didn't matter. It wasn't a standing-up space; it was a close-the-door-on-the-world snuggling-up space, a playing dolls space, a place to think and dream dreams. "Avi assured me she'd be fine. She has blankets and all those pillows. And her lamp. She's quite cozy."

"How'd the stitches go? Was she upset?"

Annie put a hand to her chest. "Our Avi? Upset? Surely you jest?"

"She's a tough one."

He headed for the stairs. Annie watched him go. Toughness ran in the family.

❧   ❧   ❧

It happened in slow motion.

With a move right out of a Frisbee game, Cal's plate of lasagna left his hand and slid onto the edge of the counter. But the weight of the uneaten food worked against it, and the plate teetered on the edge, then fell facedown onto the kitchen floor. The thickness of the lasagna absorbed most of the shock, saving the plate from destruction. Most of the plate. One chip fell away, a blue triangle against the white of the floor.

Annie found her voice, even as her hands lunged helplessly and too late. "Cal!"

"You started it. I come home, hoping for a peaceful—"

Annie pointed to the mess. "I'm not the one who overreacted. I made an innocent comment about how this meal is proof that what Harold said at the diner today was—"

"I can't believe you're taking Harold's side over mine."

They'd been over this. "Just because you're my husband, doesn't mean I have to agree with every make-it-rich scheme you come up with."

He emptied his glass in the sink, the ice cubes rattling. Annie was glad when he set the glass down safely. "Who makes the real money around here? Me or you?"

She hated this point. "That's not—"

He took a step toward her, his voice louder. *"Me* or you?"

"You. But I don't think—"

"You bet you don't think. I'm the man. I'm the one who's trying to better our lives."

"And I'm not?" She looked at the fallen lasagna. Certainly he could see that a nice meal made their quality of life better.

"I'm talking important stuff here. Financial stuff."

Why did everything always go back to money? She lowered her voice. They could both give as good as they got, but luckily, it was usually over quickly as long as one of them made the first move toward retrieving calm. If it was usually her, so be it. "Our lives are fine just the way they are, Cal."

His arms swung wide, encompassing the room. "You want to be stuck in this old house forever, Annie?"

"This house has character. It's fine."

"It's not fine, and you know it. If I did the work that needed to be done on this house, I wouldn't have any time to do my real work—"

"Fixing up other people's houses." As soon as she said it, she wished she could take it back.

He took a breath in, then out, then in. "I'm trying to lift us out of this middle-class mediocrity."

Mediocrity was not a Cal word. "Where'd you hear that phrase? From Bailey?"

He shoved a chair, making it topple, then headed toward the front of the house.

"Get back here and clean this up!" she called after him.

So much for calm.

Cal stomped up the stairs. The bedroom door slammed. Annie's chest pounded and her mind swelled with biting comebacks. How dare he ruin her beautiful dinner? How dare he not allow her to have an opinion about his misguided restaurant idea? Hooking up with Bailey was a huge mistake. Couldn't he see that? All Bailey cared about was status and money and walking around like the rest of Steadfast was gum on his shoe. He never did anything for anybody without getting something—

She held in a breath. *Bailey is using Cal just like all the other con men have done. Otherwise, why the sudden interest in treating him like a partner instead of a peon?*

She looked at the ceiling, toward the master bedroom. She had to tell Cal! In fact, she would take great pleasure in telling him. She glanced at the mess on the floor. Cal deserved to be taken down a peg. Two pegs. She'd douse his fire but good.

Annie took two steps toward the stairs when a thought hit her: *Your words are fire. All it takes is one spark...*

She pulled up short. *Huh?*

Shhh.

Shhh? No way.

Enough.

She shook her head against the treasonous thoughts. It wasn't enough. She still had things to say.

Be silent.

Annie put a hand to her chest and tried to get her bearings. This argument with Cal was not over. There were points to be made. Good points. Jabbing points. She tried to remember the idea that had fueled her anger. She held her breath a moment, searching for it in her memory bank.

It was gone. *Something about Bailey... What was it?*

A few more seconds of heavy thought brought up nothing.

What gives?

The sound of the TV blared from the front room. The familiar sound she'd heard a thousand times cut through whatever was left of her anger.

But I want to be mad! I deserve to be mad. God, don't I deserve to be mad?

She glanced at the fallen lasagna and the broken plate, hoping to get stirred up again. She was shocked to find they had no power over her anymore.

How odd.

She grabbed some paper towels. Ten minutes later the floor was clean, the broken plate washed and dried. Annie sat at the kitchen table with a bottle of glue and the broken piece. She read the directions on the glue to make sure it would work on the plate.

Cal stood in the doorway separating the kitchen from the front hall. "I wondered what happened to you."

I've been cleaning up your mess; that's what happened to me. Somehow the words remained unspoken. She shrugged her answer.

Cal took a step toward the table. "Can you fix it?"

"I hope so."

He took the bottle of glue and read the label. "This won't work on stoneware. I have some glue in the truck that should work." He kissed the top of her head.

And that was that.

Three

Starting a quarrel is like breaching a dam;
so drop the matter before a dispute breaks out.

PROVERBS 17:14

BAILEY SHUT OFF THE ENGINE and angled the rearview mirror for one last look. He adjusted his hair, then left his car to enter the Steadfast Library.

He took the steps two at a time, hoping—if Merry happened to be looking outside this fine Saturday morning—that he looked nonchalant and virile. A man with purpose. *All that from a few strides up the step?*

Such deliberate plotting was silly, but Bailey couldn't stop himself. He was who he was... Or was he who he hoped to be? It was confusing. But what he hoped to be was Merry Cavanaugh's boyfriend.

He went inside and deliberately did *not* look toward the front counter where he assumed she would be working. Instead, he turned to his right and saw the mural on the wall. The last time he'd been in, that old man Ivan had been messing with it, trying to restore it to its 1930s glory.

The mural was complete now, a rural Kansas scene of soft hills, groves of trees, lush farm fields, and winding streams.

"Not bad, eh?"

Bailey turned to find Ivan standing close, his hands in his pockets. "You did this?"

"Don't sound so surprised. I'm not good-for-nothing. Not yet."

Bailey took another look and was greeted with a flash of memory: Ivan had placed a block of red tiles where blue was supposed to be. He searched the mural. There was no such grouping now. Obviously,

Ivan had realized his error and rectified...

Then he knew. He'd had help from Steadfast's new resident mosaic artist. "Claire Adams did this, didn't she?"

Ivan's arms crossed. "She most certainly did not."

Bailey raised an eyebrow. "She didn't help?"

Ivan hesitated. "Fine. Maybe she helped a bit."

"Ah-ha."

Ivan flipped a hand at him. "Move on. I don't have time for this."

The statement was ridiculous. As far as Bailey knew, in his pre-mural existence, all Ivan did at the library was read magazines and hang around with his crony Blanche.

Bailey allowed himself to turn toward the counter. Merry was busy helping a little boy check his books out.

Ivan grinned. "Oh, I see. Oh, yes, I see quite fine what's going on here."

Bailey felt himself blush. "I thought you didn't have time?"

"Oh, I have time for this."

"For harassing me?"

Ivan shook his head, looking way too smug. "For watching the doings of a love triangle."

Triangle?

Bailey wanted to ask for details but wouldn't give the old man the satisfaction.

"You *do* know she's been dating Ken for two months now, don't you?"

Bailey's mind leafed through his file of Kens. There was only one. "Ken Kendell?"

Ivan pointed a finger. "You didn't know, did you?"

There was no way for Bailey to save face *and* get information. He pulled Ivan into a stack of books. "Fine. You win. Bring me up to date."

Bailey endured the look of satisfaction on Ivan's face. "It all started when Ken and the Steadfast police got involved looking for Sim's relatives a few months back. Since Sim was staying with Merry most of the time..." Ivan wiggled his eyebrows as if Bailey was sup-posed to fill in the blanks.

"They've gone out on dates?"

"Tons."

"Define tons."

"In the teens. Maybe twenties."

Tons. This was not possible. Bailey had been interested in Merry ever since she moved to Steadfast the previous March. Surely she wouldn't choose a boring cop over his status as town entrepreneur.

Ivan took his arm. "Ken even had a birthday party for her."

Birthday? When was that? Had he missed her birthday?

It didn't matter. While Bailey had been playing hard to get, while he'd been consumed with the addition to Bon Vivant, Merry had moved on and gotten seriously involved with another man. He felt like messing his hair and pulling his shirt out of his pants, a ridiculous notion—and something he would never do. But to know that all his primping, all his prep work to make himself irresistible to Merry was for nothing...

"They're not engaged or anything," Ivan said. "But Blanche and I did have dinner with them over at Merry's the other night, and—"

Bailey raised a hand. He rebelled at the very idea of showing his true feelings to this old coot. His broken heart would *not* be the next item of gossip around the Steadfast grapevine. "You'll have to excuse me, but I have an appointment." He turned to leave and nearly ran into Merry.

"I thought I saw you over here." She glanced at Ivan. "What are you two doing, whispering in the stacks? Conspiring to take over the library or something?"

Bailey saw Ivan open his mouth to speak and racked his brain trying to think of something to say before the old man blurted out something embarrassing.

"We were talking about Jered," Ivan said.

The two men exchanged a glance. It was not a subject Bailey wanted to talk about. If only he could rewind the last five minutes, he'd never come into the library at all.

"Have you heard from him?" Merry asked.

Bailey looked at his watch. "I really have to go."

Merry put a hand on his arm. "Bailey..."

He was a sucker for her eyes. He let his shoulders drop. "I haven't heard from him."

"Have the police found anything?"

You should know. You're dating one. "He's been put on the missing children's network, but so far, nothing."

"I'm sure he's fine, Bailey. He's almost eighteen, isn't he?"

"Next week."

She pulled her hand away. "Oh, my. Away for his birthday. But he's always been independent. Hopefully, he's gotten a job and is living in a little apartment somewhere."

"He had free room and board here. At home."

"Maybe he's pursuing his music."

Bailey stifled a laugh and glanced at the exit. Yet the music thing, it was a possibility. Just after Jered had run away, Bailey received a phone call from a Jamison Smith from Hiptone Records, wanting to get in touch with Jered. Sim had been the one who'd pulled a few strings in that direction, and Merry had helped Jered look up how-tos about getting started in the music business on the Internet, and...

And what did you do?

Ivan was talking, but Bailey hadn't been listening and wasn't about to start now. "I really need to get to the restaurant."

Merry took a step back. "But you just got here. Did you find what you were looking for?"

Not exactly. No. Actually. Not at all.

Eldora was still new to Jered. At least the back alleys were new. He'd grown up going to Eldora for things Steadfast lacked, but he'd been too young to frequent the bar-restaurant scene. He did so now because they had great garbage—as long as you didn't have to hide in it.

Thank God for health regulations. He couldn't believe the amount of food these places tossed out. In Kansas City he'd discovered Mexican places were the best because they usually served free chips with meals, and if a customer didn't finish the bowl, they had to throw them out. Thrown-away chips kept him alive.

He parked in back of the Palamba's Bar and Grill. No one was around. Lucky for him the dumpster was overflowing, so garbage bags were set handily on the ground. He grabbed two bags and tossed them in the back of his truck. He'd take them off-site to sort through them. He was going back for two more when a big guy with a goatee and a long ponytail came out the back. Their eyes met and Jered froze.

The man didn't say anything. He just leaned against the building and lit a cigarette. Jered waited a few seconds, then decided to finish his work. He tossed the final two bags in the back of his truck and hurried to the driver's side.

"You have a thing for other people's garbage?"

Jered dropped his keys. "They don't want it. It's garbage."

The man sauntered toward him, puffing his cigarette, his eyes narrow.

Uh-oh. "Hey, it's just garbage. Don't get bent out of shape." Jered stumbled into the truck, fumbling the keys a second time as he tried to start the engine and close the door at the same time.

The man halted the door with a hand and grinned. "The boy has an attitude."

"I'm no boy. And my attitude is my business."

"But you want *my* garbage."

Jered looked at the building. "You own that place?"

"And everyone in it."

It was Jered's turn to smile. "What's that supposed to mean?"

The man shrugged and put a black boot on the truck's running board. He wiped a smudge of dirt off the toe. "So what you going to do with the garbage?"

"What do you think?"

The man took a drag of his cigarette and let the smoke out slow. "You're either a narc looking for drug paraphernalia—in which case I'd say, 'Have at it, you won't find a thing.' Or you're a runaway kid who's aching for a meal." His eyes skimmed the interior of the truck. "A kid who's been sleeping in his vehicle, living off scraps." He put his boot down. "A kid who hasn't had a shower in way too long."

Jered knew he was ripe and his hair greasy. "Yeah, well, my butler quit."

The man laughed.

"No crime in being on the road, is there?"

"Homeless."

Jered hated to think of it that way. "It's not a crime."

"No, it isn't. But it's a dumb thing to be if you have alternatives."

Jered laughed. "Funny, I don't see any alternatives lying around."

The man squinted at him. "Sure you do. They're all over the place, just waiting for you."

"Yeah, right."

He raised an eyebrow. "Hey. It's no butter off my toast if you don't take an opportunity that's offered you."

Jered's throat was dry. He managed a swallow. "What opportunity?"

"Kitchen work. If you're interested."

Jered tried not to look too eager. "I might be."

"What's your name, kid?"

He thought about lying, but if the guy was giving him a job... "Jered. Jered Manson."

"I'm Jinko Daly."

Jered smiled. "Jinko?"

The man shrugged. "Better'n some. Worst'n most." He pulled out a wad of bills, peeled off two fifties, then handed them to Jered. "Here, Jered Manson. Go to the truck stop and get yourself a shower, then get a haircut and a couple decent-looking shirts. Be back here at six, and we'll see what happens."

Jered loved the feel of real money in his hand. But it wasn't normal for someone to give a stranger a hundred bucks. "I can't take—"

Jinko pushed the money back. "Let's call it an advance on your services."

Jered eyed him a moment. "Kitchen work, right?"

Jinko laughed. "You've seen too many movies, kid. But you *do* owe me."

"What makes you think I won't keep driving?"

Jinko speared him with a look, flicked his cigarette away, and walked back to the building.

⊰⊱   ⊰⊱   ⊰⊱

"But you're usually home Saturdays," Annie said.

Cal stood, drinking the last of his coffee. "Not today. I have some errands to run. Lots of errands. In Eldora."

"What sort of errands?"

He set the mug on the counter. "Construction stuff. Just stuff."

She opened her mouth to ask, *What kind of stuff?* then stopped. She held her coffee cup beneath her chin. She needed to shut up. She'd told Susan that she and Avi would come over for the Bible study. If Cal was around, there was no way he'd let them go. Maybe his absence was a good thing.

Yet she hated being secretive.

But he gave her no choice.

She heard the kitchen door open and realized if Cal had been saying anything, she hadn't been listening. "Bye," he said. "I'll be home late afternoon."

"See you then."

Annie took a sip of coffee. It was cold. Very cold.

Susan's face was a poster for surprise. "Welcome, welcome!" she said as she let Annie and Avi inside.

A cute teenage girl, who had to be Sim, came out to meet them with a little boy about three at her heels. Another teenager and a girl Avi's age appeared close behind. "Hey, Avi. Come into the kitchen. We're making pumpkins out of Styrofoam balls."

Avi was off in a puff of air, leaving Annie alone. She felt like calling, "Come back!"

Susan hung up her coat. The house had "new" going for it, but it lacked the character of the McFay's older home. Beige walls, beige carpet, white woodwork. The furnishings looked new, too, and were only the basics. A picture of a mother and child walking in a meadow hung by the door. Very feminine. Pastel colors. In fact, all the accessories were feminine. No sign of a man's influence at all.

Interesting.

Susan led her into the living room.

"Surprise!"

Annie's jaw dropped. "Merry?"

Merry laughed. "Don't look so shocked. I've been trying to get you to come to my Bible study for weeks."

"But I didn't know your Bible study was *this* Bible study."

"One and the same."

It was then she noticed Claire Adams, the town's resident mosaic artist. Claire scooted over on the couch and patted the cushion. "Merry's wanted to call you ever since Susan said you might be coming, but we thought it would be more fun to surprise you."

"You certainly did that." Annie looked at the final woman, recognizing her as the receptionist at the ER, but she didn't know her name. "The hospital, right?"

The woman sat forward on the wing chair and reached across the coffee table to shake Annie's hand. "Stella Morrow, whose job is admitting patients but not admitting anything that will get me into trouble. Nice to meet you for real. How's your daughter's leg?"

"It's doing fine."

Merry added more information. "Stella is the mother of the two girls and the little boy in the kitchen. The girls are Callie and—"

"Cassie." Annie nodded. "I've met Cassie before. She's in Avi's class, right?"

Stella nodded.

"And your boy...?"

"Is a handful," Stella said. "Yup. Zack's mine and proof that there's definitely a difference between boys and girls. Lord have mercy." She sighed deeply as she set her flowered coffee mug on the table.

Susan pointed to two carafes. "What can I get you: hazelnut coffee or peppermint tea?"

"Hazelnut. Anything hazelnut," Annie said. "Black."

"Why doesn't the Plentiful serve flavored coffees?" Merry asked. "That's *the* thing, you know."

"Which explains why we don't do it. Donald has a mother-complex: He only believes in recipes his mom used."

"No fruit smoothies or quiches for him, eh?" Claire said. "You'll have to settle for orange juice and eggs over easy."

"Nothing wrong with that," Susan said. "Home cooking is comfort food."

Stella put her hands on her ample middle. "As you can see, I've done my share of being comforted."

Their laughter was the laughter of shared experiences. Annie felt right at home.

"Actually, we don't do restaurants right now," Stella said.

"Why not?"

"Zack is a terror. I order him grilled cheese, and he suddenly wants a hot dog. And he always spills. The last time we ate out, he made such a fuss I ended up yelling at him, right there in front of everybody. I completely lost it."

"Happens to the best of us," Susan said.

Stella shook her head. "Not like I did it. We'd all gone to Kansas City for a weekend. My husband was so embarrassed, he virtually yanked Zack and me out of our chairs, threw some money on the table, and hightailed it to the van. That's when we really got into it. We yelled and screamed at each other all the way home. Poor Zack sat in the back crying, and the girls cowered in their corners. The odd thing was how the argument turned. It didn't end up being about Zack's eating habits at all. It's as if every bad thing my hubby and I had ever done to each other was tossed into that car." She shuddered. "It was awful."

Claire crossed her legs. "My ex and I were champions at taking one beef and making it into an entire pot roast."

Merry laughed. "What did you just say?"

Claire shrugged. "You know what I mean."

Susan raised a hand. "Order up some pot roast here, too. My ex, Forbes, and I were good at keeping things roasting. We rarely had a calm moment. My hardest lesson was learning how and when to keep my mouth shut. Not fan the flames."

Flames. Fire. Annie felt her stomach catch. She knew exactly what these ladies meant. She'd experienced it just last night.

Stella pointed at her. "You're nodding. Fess up."

Had she been nodding? She hadn't meant to nod.

Susan spoke. "Come on, Annie. Share. You're among friends."

Annie took a moment and found it to be true. "It happened last night with Cal. I was just about to let go with some really good zingers when these words came into my head, like I was thinking them, but not, because they weren't like anything *I'd* think of."

"What were the words?" Stella asked.

Annie was surprised but glad she remembered the gist of them. "The thought was that my words were fire and that all it took was one spark. Something like that."

"Ain't it the truth?" Stella said. "Burn, baby, burn."

Susan took a Bible off the coffee table. "I think there's a verse like that." She opened it up to the back, then flipped through a couple of pages. "Should I look up *spark* or *fire?*"

"Try *spark,*" Claire said.

A few seconds later Susan drilled her finger into a page. "Here! James 3:5: 'The tongue is a small part of the body, but it makes great boasts. Consider what a great forest is set on fire by a small spark.'"

"Whoa," Stella said.

Annie shook her head. "This is weird."

"No, it's not," Claire said. "It's wonderful."

"SOP," Susan said.

Annie did a double take in her direction. "SOP?"

"Standard Operating Procedure. It's God. It's how He works, how He speaks to us."

Annie shook her head again. "God wouldn't speak to me. I'm too new to all this, too..." She couldn't finish.

"Nonsense," Claire said. "New, old, He talks to us—whether or not we're listening is the question. He's constantly trying to get our attention."

Annie stopped her mug halfway to her mouth. "Well, it worked. I shut up. I didn't say what I was going to say."

"And the argument ended soon after, right?" Susan asked.

"Well...yes, it did." Annie was astounded by that fact. "You mean, that was God? Directing me?"

Stella laughed. "And that was you listening. Way to go, girl!"

"You must be more open to Him than I was." Merry's voice was quiet. "It took a plane crash for Him to get through to me."

Claire reached over and put a hand on Merry's knee. "Oh, Merry."

Annie let the moment register. She'd known Merry had lost her husband and son in a plane crash, but it had never occurred to her... Was Merry's view of the tragedy correct? Had God been trying to get her attention?

Merry waved her hands next to her head. "Goodness sakes, I do know how to bring down a group, don't I?" Her smile was forced. "Let's move—"

There was a crash in the kitchen. "Mom!"

Stella rose. "Zack strikes again!"

Susan rose with her. "How 'bout some brownies? I feel the need for a chocolate fix, right, ladies?"

Annie hung back, wanting to be the last to leave the Bible study. She was not the only one hesitant to go.

Avi pulled at her sleeve. "Do we have to go, Mama?"

"'Fraid so, sweet-apple."

Sim came to the rescue. "I'll go out to the car with you, Avi."

The girls went outside, leaving Annie and Susan alone. They carried the carafes to the kitchen.

Susan shook the one for the coffee. "One more cup?"

"No thanks."

"So how'd you like it? Them?" Susan asked.

"They're nice ladies. I knew that before and feel it even more so now."

"None better."

"And they..." She handed Susan a plate for the dishwasher.

"They?"

"They're so real. I always thought a Bible study would be about being...perfect or something. But it's not about that at all. You all made me feel so welcome. As if I belonged."

"You do belong. We're not great scholars here. We're just a bunch of friends who share what we know about the Lord, try to do better, and find out more."

"But they talked about the verses as if they were talking about a recipe."

Susan smiled. "Recipe. That's a good one. The Bible is full of God's recipes for life. Something for every taste bud, no matter what you feel like eating."

"What amazes me is that it fit with what's going on in my life. I had the argument, then I come here and hear the verse that fits. That's so cool."

"You bet," Susan said. "And now that you've seen it once, be prepared to see it again. And again. And again."

"Really?"

Susan laughed. "I love the look in your eyes. The notion excites you, doesn't it?"

"Yeah, it does."

Susan put an arm around her shoulders and squeezed. "Welcome to the sisterhood, Annie. Now that God's got your attention, there's no way He's going to let you go. Ready or not, here He comes!"

He had *her* attention, but what about Cal's? "I didn't bring it up today, but I'm having trouble with Cal regarding my faith. He just doesn't understand, and every time I try to tell him, explain..." She sighed. "It comes out wrong. All wrong."

Susan took Annie's hands in hers. "Been there, done that, sister. With Forbes I pushed and yelled and argued and pleaded—"

"Did it work?"

"Nope." Her hand moved to her pregnant belly. "In fact, I think my faith was a big part of his leaving me. Leaving us."

Annie put a hand on her own belly. "Oh, dear. I don't want that."

Susan rushed to explain. "It's not a given. It doesn't have to be that way. Yet I often wonder if I'd been more subtle, kind, and loved him into the arms of the Father, if Forbes would have responded differently."

"Sounds a bit gushy and weak, if you ask me."

Susan shrugged. "And who knows if it would have worked? The truth is, God does the calling, one on one, and our spouses have the choice to answer. Or not. Forbes chose not. At least for now."

"But I want Cal to have what I have, to—"

"Feel what you feel? I know. But nobody likes to be bullied into believing. Not even if it's for his own good." Susan sighed. "I wish I could be more help."

The feeling was mutual.

Cal came home earlier than he planned. He'd spent the entire day moving boxes and furniture. He wished he could tell Annie the truth, but it was out of the question.

He'd been able to sustain it all these years with little work. Just a few "errands" slipped into a day. Annie had never caught on. The lie had been a part of his life so long, it was like a layer of skin, something he didn't have to think about, something that could remain covered.

But now, everything had changed. Now he'd have to make more false errands, more trips to Eldora. The odds of keeping the secret were tilting against him, and it would take some heavy-duty manipulation to make things balance again.

If only other things were the same. But Annie's quest for Jesus was an additional factor that threatened everything. He couldn't count on her to act or react the same as she always had. Or to even keep the same schedule.

The truth was, lies did not fare well amid change.

Neither did he. Any time the rules of their marriage changed, his nerves percolated like one of those old coffee machines his parents had, with the coffee bubbling up in the clear lid. Yes, indeed, his nerves were percolating something fierce lately.

And so he'd come home early to seek "normal." He lived for normal. He needed normal like a blind man needed sight. Even if their normal wasn't perfect, it was something he tried to hold on to, a baseline from which the rest of their lives could be measured. Between Jesus and the lie...it was going to be tough.

He took his boots off on the stoop, went in, and hung up his jacket. She wasn't in the kitchen. "Annie?"

"In here."

He went into the front room. Annie and Avi were eating popcorn, watching a movie. Avi scooted closer to her mom, making room for him on the couch. "Come on, Daddy. Sit. We're watching *Lion King*. Even you like that one."

Yup. Even he liked that one.

He took a seat, grabbing onto normal.

It didn't take Jered long to master the art of dishwashing. Though Jinko hadn't specified what was meant by kitchen work, Jered had hoped it involved being a waiter or helping the cook or something. He'd gotten all cleaned up and dressed in the new clothes he bought with the money Jinko had given him just to wash dishes?

Whatever. A few days working a crud job would at least get him some money. Too bad he was already a hundred in the hole. He *had* thought about skipping out, but the idea of Jinko being mad at him... It wasn't that Jinko was a threatening type of guy, but the man had an air about him that hinted one didn't mess with Jinko Daly. Didn't cross him. Not more than once, anyway.

Jered's stomach growled. He hadn't eaten anything since morning, and the constant smell of beef and beans and cheese teased his stomach to the point of pain. Jinko had said he could have a break. Now would be good.

Jered turned to Vasylko the cook. Vasylko had some Russian last name Jered couldn't remember, nor pronounce without seeing it written down. He was a recent immigrant. Where he'd learned to make Mexican food was probably a story in itself.

"How do I go about getting something to eat?" Jered asked. "I'm starved."

"What you want? Taco? Encheelada? Brito?"

Jered liked his accent. "Yes."

Vasylko raised a spatula. "Ha! The boy hungry. Watch out!"

Bonnie, one of the waitresses, winked at him. She was about thirty and reminded him of his friend Merry Cavanaugh back home. "He's a growing boy, Vasy. Heap him up a big plate."

Vasylko did just that, and Jered hoped he could eat every bite as insurance against a later hunger. "Where do I sit?"

Bonnie pointed to the main room. "Usually you can slip into a back table or eat at the bar, but not tonight. Never on Amateur Night."

"What's that?"

Bonnie pointed to a plate she'd just picked up. "Vasy, darlin', they didn't want any rice, just beans."

"Mne tak zhal." He scooped the rice into a huge pot and replaced it with a large scoop of refried beans. "Musical fruit. Ha ha."

Jered stepped closer. "Amateur Night?"

"Every Saturday. Any musician who wants to play for the audience gets a chance. One song. First come, first play."

Jered's heart did a double flip. "Anyone?"

Bonnie flashed him a look. "Oh, no. Don't tell me. You're a musician."

"I try to be. I want to be."

She lifted a huge tray of food. "Then go stand in the back, eat your dinner, and take a listen. Some of them aren't bad."

Vasylko shuddered and made some Russian sound.

Bonnie smiled. "And some are horrible."

The opening notes of "Jailhouse Rock" started. An Elvis-wannabe sang. He was only half bad.

Jered took his plate into the main room. Bad or not, it didn't matter. They were playing music. They were getting a chance.

And so would he. Finally, so would he.

Four

*You will seek me and find me
when you seek me with all your heart.*

JEREMIAH 29:13

JERED SPRAYED THE TRAY OF DISHES and shoved them into the dishwasher. Last Saturday while working the dishes, he'd listened intently to every musician during Amateur Night, alternating between thinking they were good or imagining himself doing better.

Five days thinking about it but doing nothing. His dad had always accused him of being all talk and no action. Was he right?

Every time Jered tried to think of what he'd sing and how he'd sing it, reality jerked him back. Though he'd talked about composing and being a musician for years, he'd never had guts enough to perform for anyone. Except for an occasional song sung to his buddies Darrell and Moog—usually while they were all drunk—he'd never dealt with an audience. Never had to worry if they'd clap or boo.

And Saturday night had proven... Jered felt bad when the boos drowned out the singing. Not that the singers didn't deserve it—some shocked Jered with their gumption. Didn't they know how bad they were? The fact they stood up, thinking they were good when they weren't, scared him to death. Would it be the same for him? *Did* he have any talent? Or was his dad right?

Vasylko sang some Russian song from the stove. Now, *he* had a voice. It reminded Jered of the Russian voices singing in one of his favorite movies, *The Hunt for Red October.* Rich and mellow. If someone with a voice like Vasylko didn't sing on Amateur Night, who was Jered to think he should take a shot?

Maybe he should be satisfied with what he had.

Or not.

The dishwashing job wasn't as bad as the construction one he'd had, but it was still grunt work. Jered was beginning to feel like a poster boy for a Stay in School campaign, an example of the see-what-happens? consequences. It was a mindless job, and when he wasn't thinking about Amateur Night he thought of his friends back in Steadfast. Where were Darrell and Moog hanging out since he'd left with his truck? Was Moog playing football? Was the team winning? *Go Spartans!*

He was missing his senior year in high school, his chance to be at the top of the heap, big man on campus. He wasn't there.

He was here. Washing dishes.

Go home.

He scrubbed a pot as if the act would make the idea go away. Because he couldn't go home. There was nothing for him in Steadfast.

And there's something for you here?

He scrubbed harder.

Forget school. The only reason he'd go home would be to see how his dad was doing. After causing his heart attack by arguing with him last summer, Jered had called a few times, but as soon as his dad answered, he'd hung up. Just the fact his dad *did* answer proved he was okay, didn't it?

Back in Steadfast, Jered would hang out and down a few beers. But he could do that anywhere. His music was the difference. At home he'd worked hard on his music, always in private, during times when his dad was gone—which were plenty. Theoretically, since leaving home he had the freedom to work on his music anytime.

Not that he did.

He really needed his guitar. Since coming to Eldora, he'd thought a lot about sneaking back home to get it. He would pick a Saturday night when his dad was busy at the restaurant, slip in under the cover of dark, and get lots of stuff. Who needed money for clothes? He had a room full of clothes, just waiting for him.

Unless his dad had packed it all away...

He concentrated on the dirty pot and fought the intense urge to heave it across the room. But then he'd be fired, and he needed this job for reasons beyond money, and even beyond the lure of Amateur Night.

The job was proof things were looking up. Thanks to Jinko Daly.

After Jinko had hired him, he'd offered Jered the use of his garage to sleep in. He had a camping cot out there—and a lot more. The garage wasn't used to house a vehicle but to store stuff. Lots of stuff. Some old. Some new. A stack of new DVD players (still in their boxes) sat in the corner. Jered didn't ask why.

Best of all, the garage had a toilet in the corner and a shop sink. Gross-looking things, but they worked. And really best of all, Jinko had allowed him the use of the shower in the house—if he didn't make a mess. Where the garage was a pit, the house was spotless. Jered's dad had been a clean freak, but Jinko was worse—or better, depending on your view. It's like there were two sides to the guy.

So Jered rearranged things in the garage to make himself a home. He cleared a space for sleeping and another for composing. Now that he had room to play, he *really* wanted his guitar. He'd even found a cracked mirror and set it on some shelves, reminding him of his dresser and mirror back home. To top off the room, he wedged a photo in the corner of the mirror, a picture of him and his dad taken in better times. To look at it was to feel homesick, but *not* to look at it made him feel worse. Home sweet home.

He rinsed the dirty pot, his mind merging the present with other times when he'd helped his dad at Bon Vivant. He'd given his dad such a hard time about helping. If only he'd been—

A slap hit him on the back. "How things going, kid?"

"I want to play at Amateur Night." *Where did* that *come from?*

Jinko laughed. "Bonnie mentioned you were a musician-wannabe. Why didn't you tell me sooner?"

Jered shrugged.

"You've got to be aggressive if you're going to make it in the business. You can't sit back and wait for someone to give you an engraved invite."

"I know."

"Have you performed much?"

"A bit."

"Which means none."

Jered shrugged again. Why did Jinko always see through him?

"I'll expect you Satur—"

"I need my guitar."

"So?"

He started scrubbing another pan. "It's at home."

Jinko leaned against the counter, and Jered felt his eyes. "Ah. And where is home?"

"Steadfast."

Jinko snickered. "You didn't run very far, did you?"

"I was in Kansas City awhile."

"Then why did you come here?"

Jered started to shrug but stopped himself. He needed to be more assertive. Definite. "I didn't like the drug stuff I found there. And the town was too big."

"I hate to burst your balloon, kid, but there are drugs going on here in Eldora, too, *and* in Steadfast."

"I know. But it's not the same."

"You're right. It's not."

Jered stopped washing. "You from here?"

Jinko looked away. "Pretty much." He adjusted the cuffs of his black shirt over a gold chain at his wrist. "So when do we get your guitar?"

We? "Uh...I'm not sure. It would mean..."

"Going home. Technically sneaking home, correct?"

"Well, yeah. I wouldn't want my dad to see me. Or other people in town."

"Then we'll go at night. And I'll drive. They won't recognize my car."

This was not what Jered had in mind.

"When's your dad gone?"

"He owns a restaurant, too, so evenings—"

Jinko's eyes flashed. "Which one?"

"Bon Vivant. It's a fancy—"

"I know it. I've been there. I've probably seen your dad. Fancy dresser with lots of hair?"

Jered smiled. "That's him."

Jinko nodded and stroked his goatee. "What do you know?" He slapped the counter. "Let's do it tonight. Nine, give or take. Your dad should be working then, right?"

"He's always working."

"Quit complaining, kid, quit complaining."

Annie approached the customer seated in the corner. He'd been reading the menu over and over—which was odd. Usually people chose their food quickly, the thought of meat loaf or fried chicken feeding an emotional as well as physical need. "Afternoon, sir. I haven't seen you in here before."

"Just passing through."

"Then welcome." She readied her order pad. "You having a hard time making a choice?"

The customer sighed deeply. He closed the menu and handed it to her, pushing his chair back. "I'm afraid I'm going to have to leave. I'll pay something for the water..."

"What's the problem?" She'd never had this happen before.

He put his hands on his thighs, his face sheepish. "This is going to sound silly—after all, I expected this to be a home-cooking type diner—but my doctor said to watch my cholesterol and fat and—"

Ah. "How about I get Donald to broil you up a chicken breast and put it on a bed of pasta with a little red sauce? We'll rustle up some steamed green beans and carrots to go with it."

His eyes brightened. "And bread. I *could* have one piece of bread."

"How's a hard roll sound? Strawberry preserves instead of butter."

He sat up to the table. "I'll take it."

"Coffee? Decaf?"

He smiled. "You're good. Very good."

She winked at him. "Only on Thursdays."

A half hour later, the chicken-breast customer walked behind Annie as she was refilling iced tea for another table. He whispered, "Thank you, dear lady."

She did a double take. "Glad you enjoyed it."

"I left something for you."

A tip. Probably a good tip. "Thanks. Have a great day. Come see us again."

"Oh, I will."

The bell on the door announced his exit.

A few minutes later, Annie went to clear his table. There, on top of a ten-dollar tip, was a clean napkin. On it was written a message: *You are His light to the world. Shine brightly. Read 1 Corinthians 13:4–8. God bless you.*

Dottie looked over her shoulder. "What you got there? A love note?"

"Nah, just a nice tip."

Annie slipped the note into her pocket.

Cal came in from work and kissed Annie on the cheek. "Evening, Annie-girl. Have I got a surprise for you."

"Oooh." She loved surprises. "Just a second." She pricked the last potato and put them in the microwave, pushed the buttons, and turned around.

Cal whipped out a check, holding it with two hands. Annie had to move close to read it. "It's for $1583. From Heartland Insurance."

Cal grinned. "I know."

"Didn't they already pay you on that truck claim?" Oscar from the hotel had gone through a stop sign and rammed into Cal.

"Fifteen hundred and eighty-three dollars."

"Why did they pay you twice?"

He rolled his eyes. "They don't realize they've paid me twice."

"It's a mistake."

"In our favor."

"But you can't keep it."

He yanked the check away. "I sure can."

It was a true statement. "You *shouldn't* keep it."

"Since when?"

She had no answer. Her thoughts zoomed back to another time.

Another mistake in their favor. She hadn't said a thing then. In fact, they'd gone out to dinner to celebrate. Why was this different? There was only one answer.

Jesus.

Cal folded the check in half and put it in his pocket. "I'm going to take a shower."

"Cal..."

He stopped at the kitchen door. "Why'd you have to ruin it, Annie? Why?"

Oh, dear. How could she ever please both the men in her life?

Bailey sat at the kitchen table and stared at the navy sweater in the gift box. Today was Jered's eighteenth birthday. How odd to have presents but no one to give them to.

Jered, where are you?

Bailey pulled his other present close and leafed through the pages of the guitar book. Notes and staffs and fingering charts. They could have been written in Sanskrit for all Bailey could make of them. He enjoyed music but had never learned to read it, and certainly had never learned to play an instrument. Was that why he found it so hard to support his son's dream of a music career?

The fact Jered never finished anything he started is the reason. The fact he never played, never practiced...

He suddenly thought back to their argument last summer, the one that had sent him to the hospital for an angioplasty. It was the last time he'd seen his son. He remembered Jered's words: *"I don't sing in front of you because you don't want to hear me sing."*

That wasn't true. Not exactly. He hadn't wanted to encourage an impossible dream. He wanted to protect his son from hurt.

Jered's words shot back at him. *"But I am hurt! I'm hurting now."*

The look in his son's eyes had torn into Bailey's soul. But that was only the beginning of the end.

"I want you to love me." Jered's words had been plaintive. A cry.

"I do—"

And his final words full of hate. *"Don't lie to me!"*

Bailey shuddered. He'd collapsed to the floor, Jered had run out, and Sim had shown up and saved him.

If only I could see Jered again. I'd make him know that I do love him. I do.

Bailey closed the guitar book. Why hadn't he bought such a gift before?

Because Jered didn't care about my *dream. He didn't care about Bon Vivant.*

Bailey knew the thought was petty. Tit for tat was probably frowned upon in the father-son handbook.

Easier said than done.

He looked at the card. *Happy birthday, son. May all your dreams come true.* At least it was an attempt to say the right thing. Bailey pulled a pen from his shirt pocket and signed it. He wanted to write *I love you,* but the words would not come out. *Come home, Jered?* Why was it so hard? In a desperate spurt, he simply wrote, *Dad.*

He set the card on the guitar book, and the book on the box containing the sweater. A birthday pile for Jered.

Only Jered wasn't here.

Jered kept changing songs as they drove. To have a six-CD player in a car... His truck only had a radio, and a poor one at that.

"You must be a fiend with a remote control," Jinko said. "Land on something, okay? I feel like I'm playing *Name That Tune.*"

Jered finally chose Bruce Springsteen. He settled into leather seats that cupped his back. He was tempted to mess with the seat adjustment buttons but didn't. He'd never been in a Mercedes before. "I love the smell of a new car. My dad gets a new BMW every five years."

"Which explains your taste in rusted-out clunker pickups?"

"He made me pay for it. It's all I could afford."

"Don't let what you can afford stop you, kid."

Jered looked at him. "What's that mean?"

"We're close to town. You want to duck down as I drive through?"

Jered had never thought of going that far. "Do you think it's necessary?"

"Hey, it's your hometown, kid. I'm just your wheels."

Jered scooted down in his seat until his sight line skimmed the bottom of the windows. He was glad they were tinted. The city sign came into view: *Steadfast*. How weird to be on this side of the sign. A visitor. An intruder. How odd to see the holes in the sign that he, Moog, and Darrell had made with their BB guns. And yet it was also comforting. Evidence of his existence. *Jered was here.* Once.

"Where to?"

Jered gave Jinko directions to his house, on the way passing the town square, the library, the Plentiful Café, and the parking lot behind the hardware store where he and his friends had drank their beer, talked, and hung out.

"Turn right here," Jered finally said. "Four houses down. On the right."

"We'll drive past once. You look and see if anyone's home."

"There's just my dad."

"Whatever."

Just my dad. But was it true? Or had his dad rented out his room, or given it to Sim? After all, it was Sim who'd saved him. Poor orphan Simmy, in need of a dad and trying to steal his.

Jered felt a swell of anger. *She can have him. I don't—*

As they passed the house, another emotion swelled as he saw the porch where he'd made forts and played trucks. He'd jumped from those steps at age four, breaking his front tooth when he'd landed hard. The upstairs window belonged to his room...

If he had a room anymore.

"A light's on in the front room," Jinko said.

"Dad leaves it on when he works late. The car isn't there. He's gone."

"Want to park and walk, or risk being out front?"

It was a toss-up. If he pulled into the driveway, Jed Connally in the house on the left might see and get suspicious. But if they parked a block away, more neighbors might see him walking by, carrying his guitar and gear. He'd rather risk one neighbor than many. "Pull into the driveway, way up, by the garage."

Jinko followed directions then turned off the car. "Make it quick."

"Aren't you coming in?"

"Nah. I'll let you visit memory lane alone. But don't wallow in it. Five minutes. Tops."

Jered nodded and got out, making the car door close with a soft click. He used his key on the kitchen door and was assailed by the smell of home. It was indescribable but distinct. The scent of his dad intermixed with the smell of oak woodwork and past meals. Would his dad be able to describe a particular scent as Jered's?

He did not turn on a light. Luckily, the moonlight cut a slice through the room, lighting the blue counter, the blue-and-white-checkered cookie jar, and the kitchen table and its bowl of fresh fruit. He grabbed an apple, taking a huge bite. As he did so, he noticed a box on the table with a green envelope on top.

An envelope with his name on it.

His head whipped around to the calendar that hung behind the kitchen door. Thursday. October 23. *It's my birthday!*

His heart threatened his throat. His dad had remembered his birthday—even if Jered hadn't. He pulled the card from the envelope. The front had a scene of a farm pond with a man and a boy fishing. *Happy birthday, son* it said in a fancy cursive. He opened the card: *May all your dreams come true.*

But as appropriate as the sentiment was, it wasn't the card's words that made him reach for the chair. It was the single word written in his father's awkward scrawl: *Dad.*

That was it? He just signed it *Dad?* He didn't say *Come home* or *I love you.* Not even, *Love, Dad.*

He shook his head, feeling ridiculous for wanting more. His dad couldn't give more; didn't he realize that by now?

Suddenly, sobs took over in waves that made him choke. He raked his face, hating the tears.

He noticed the presents in the box. The navy sweater didn't thrill him, but the guitar book—its very presence spoke volumes.

Jered started when he heard the kitchen door open. "Time's up, kid. Let's get going."

Jered swiped the tears and cleared his throat. "I'll be out in a minute." He was glad when Jinko left. He set the presents and the card back where he'd found them. *Happy birthday, dear Jered, happy birthday to you.*

He pushed the pity party aside and went upstairs. He found an old bag in the hall closet and filled it with clothes and toiletries. He took his Walkman, a few CDs, some staff paper and pencils, and on the way out of the room, his guitar from behind the door.

Once downstairs, he lingered in the front room a moment. How many times had he sprawled on that couch watching TV or videos? When he was little he and his dad would watch the movie *Willow* over and over. His dad liked Val Kilmer's character, Madmartigan. He liked the two Brownies, Rool and Franjean, who kept getting in trouble. He took a step to the left. Yup. There was still a red stain on the rug where he'd spilled cherry Kool-Aid.

It's the past. Move on. Move on.

His feet felt rooted. Planted deep. The only way he would be able to move was if someone plucked him from this spot like a weed.

A weed in a place it did not belong.

He closed his eyes and willed himself to move, pulling away from the memories. Once one muscle moved, another followed, and he was back in the kitchen.

He was worn out. He stuffed another apple and a banana in his bag. His eyes locked on the presents. He couldn't take them. He couldn't. He—

He snatched the card and ran out the door.

"You're quiet," Jinko said.

Jered leaned on his hand and continued to look out the window at the dark fields flying by. So little could be seen. Only the brush up close had any detail, any form. Everything beyond was a black mass. Scary. Unknown.

"Come on, kid. You got your guitar. That's what you wanted, isn't it?"

Jered spoke against his hand. "It's my birthday."

"Your—? Why didn't you say something? We can stop back at the restaurant and I'll buy you a drink. Or...how old are you anyway?"

"Eighteen."

"You look older."

"I'm not." *I'm just a kid.* He suddenly sat up. "I'm not older. I should be hanging out with my friends, sneaking into movies, going out on dates, spending money on computer games, not food."

"You can still do all those things."

Jered snickered. "Everything's changed."

"So what?"

He sneaked a look at this man beside him. The dim light of the dash made odd shadows on his face. "So I should still be doing kid things. Fun things."

Jinko slammed on the brakes and pulled onto the shoulder, nearly toppling the car in the ditch.

"Hey! What'd you do that for?"

Jinko slammed the gear into Park and faced Jered. The look in his eyes made Jered lean hard against the passenger door.

"Poor little Jered. You want to go home to Daddy? Go sit around the table and play Monopoly and drink Kool-Aid? How old did you say you were? Ten?"

It was like déjà vu. Jered and his friends had kidded Sim with much the same words when she'd been staying with his dad. Suddenly her comeback became his. "I like Monopoly. I will always like Monopoly."

Jinko shook his head. His face and words softened. "Look, kid. You were nearly out of the house anyway. So you bumped it up by a few months? That took guts. That's not the action of a kid."

"It's not?" Jered hated the pathetic tone of his voice.

"Of course it's not. You've got a job. You have a place to stay."

Some job. Some place to stay. "I don't want to be a dishwasher all my life or live in someone else's garage."

"Oh, you won't; you won't." Jinko put the car in Drive and pulled onto the highway. He flashed Jered a wink. "I have plans for you. Opportunities."

"What kind of opportunities?"

"You'll see. Don't worry about a thing. I'll take care of you, kid. Just stick with me."

Bailey flipped on the kitchen light and tossed his keys and the zippered bag of restaurant receipts on the desk. It had been a good night for a Thursday. The last customer hadn't left until eleven o'clock. In fact, it had been so busy Bailey hadn't had time to eat anything.

He opened the refrigerator and took inventory. Not much to choose from. Funny how he served such luscious food at the restaurant but ate so simply at home. But of course he had a chef at Bon Vivant. Sanchez was one of the best in the business. At home he only had himself.

Bailey made a decision and carried the milk to the table, where he poured a bowl of Cinnamon Life cereal. *Cold cereal. Some hotshot restaurateur you are.*

He ate standing up, leaning against the counter. The pile of presents for Jered reminded him what day it was. If only Jered had been around so Bailey could have given him his sweater, his guitar book, and the—

The card was gone.

Bailey set the bowl of cereal down hard, the milk slopping over. He wiped his wet hand on his pants and searched for the card. He pulled out chairs, looked on counters, all ridiculous moves but nonetheless necessary.

His eyes locked on the fruit bowl. It was half as tall as it was before. At least one apple and a banana gone.

Jered! The thought gained a voice. "Jered! Jered?"

Bailey raced into the living room, then up the stairs. *He's asleep in bed, exhausted from his journey. I'll barge into the room, and he'll sit up all sleepy-eyed and say, "Hi, Dad, what you yelling about?"*

But at the top of the stairs Bailey saw that the door to Jered's bedroom was open, and he knew the *Father Knows Best* ending would remain relegated to TV sitcoms.

He stopped short at the edge of the doorway, his toes the only part of him brave enough to venture into the inner sanctum. His heavy breathing cut through the silence of the empty house. His next word was a whisper. "Jered?"

He received no answer, and his head started a series of small shakes.

Then a smell hit him like a slap. It was faint, more a hint of some aroma past than an actual scent. But it was distinctly Jered.

"You were here."

Bailey stepped into the room, flipping on the light. The tail of a T-shirt was caught in a closed drawer, a familiar sight when Jered lived at home. His CD tower revealed gaping spaces. A hanger was on the floor of his closet. He'd come.

And gone.

Bailey's legs buckled. He headed for the bed but stopped himself before sitting. The bedspread was tight and smooth. Jered hadn't lingered. He had not sat on the bed, drinking in memories.

He had come. And gone.

He had made another choice to leave, to be anywhere but here.

Bailey's strength left him. He sat, tipped over, then scooted up on the bed. He pulled Jered's pillow to his chest, giving it the hug he could not give his son.

Five

*For the Son of Man came to seek
and to save what was lost.*

Luke 19:10

Annie waved at two regulars as they left. Bob and Bernie. Two Country Classics Supreme and two coffees every Saturday morning for six years. "You tell Dorothy I'd love a couple of pumpkins from your garden, Bob."

"Will do."

She went to clear their table, ready to pick up the three five-dollar bills that were the payment plus tip every week. The men took turns paying. But this time something was different. Under the coffee cup were two five-dollar bills and a twenty.

Had Bob gotten extra generous in his old age?

She looked out the window at him toddling across the street to his truck, his arthritis making his knees stiff. No way. He and Dorothy lived frugally on his pension. His Saturday breakfast with Bernie was a splurge.

Keep it. He'll never know.

Memories of her conversation with Cal burst in unannounced.

"It's a mistake."

"In our favor."

"But you can't keep it."

"I sure can."

"You shouldn't keep it."

"Since when?"

Since now.

She ran out the door. "Bob!" He was getting in his truck. She hurried across the street.

"Goodness sakes, Annie. What's the commotion? And where's your coat? It's freezing—"

She showed him the bills. "You left me too much. You put a twenty down instead of a third five."

He fanned the money. "Well, what do you know? You're right."

"The difference will buy you and Bernie another breakfast when it's your turn again in two weeks."

"Indeed it will. Indeed it will." He handed her back the two fives and dug out his wallet. "Dorothy's been hounding me to get new glasses. Guess this proves she's right. Again." He handed her a third five, then another. "This extra's for you. For your honesty."

She gave it back. "No, Bob. I don't need that."

"But you did something good. You need to be rewarded."

She closed his fingers around the bill. "I have been. Believe me, I have been."

Annie didn't walk back to the Plentiful, she strutted.

Bailey sat on his front porch swing, bundled in a jacket against the October cold. Leaves skittered across the yard, and a few braved the steps to sweep by him. There one second. Gone the next.

He was going crazy. He spent the previous day moaning about Jered's secret visit. He'd heard it said that a burden shared was halved? A good concept, but hard to put into practice when he had no one to share it with. No one to sympathize or help or comfort or advise.

Yesterday morning he'd thought of calling Jered's friends, Darrell and Mag, Mig...what was that kid's name? But he didn't. What if Jered *had* seen them? Talked to them? What if *they'd* had real contact? He couldn't handle the contrast to his own there-but-not-there experience. Stupid kid. Why did Jered tease him so? Either be back or be gone, but none of this in-between.

He'd thought about gaining some comfort by going to the library to talk with Merry, but he couldn't. She wasn't a possibility anymore, not since she'd hooked up with Ken. He'd even considered talking to Sanchez his chef, or Stanley, his head waiter at Bon Vivant. Yet the fact he didn't know anything about *their* personal lives stopped him.

Why would they want to hear about his?

By afternoon, he'd had the phone in his hand, ready to call Claire Adams, but he hung up before dialing. Claire was a smart one—too smart. She'd had him pegged from the first moment she came into Steadfast. Besides, now that she'd moved her mosaic studio here and had accepted a huge commission for a hundred-foot mural in some Kansas City church, she was probably too busy to talk to him.

Or was she too successful?

A long time ago Bailey had accepted the fact he preferred being with people who were under his station in life. True peers made him nervous.

Then there was Cal. Cal was an upright sort of guy. He might even have some decent advice for Bailey. But theirs was a new relationship—a business relationship. Best not to muddy the waters with dirty laundry.

Which left...no one.

How was it possible for him to live in Steadfast his entire life, bring up six brothers here, go to school here, get married here, get left by his wife here, bring up Jered here, start a successful business here, and not have any friends? Many acquaintances, but no friends.

He swung forward and back, forward and back, his hands stuffed in his pockets, a lump on a swing. A worthless—

He spotted Sim riding her bike down the street in his direction. Before he realized he'd made a decision, he was at the top of the steps. "Sim!"

She saw him, waved, and pulled into his driveway. "Hi, Bailey. I haven't seen you in ages."

"I've been pretty busy."

She nodded. The breeze flipped her hair in front of her face, and she anchored it behind an ear. "I saw the addition to Bon Vivant. It's pretty cool."

"Thanks." Now that he had her attention he wasn't sure how to broach the subject.

"Have you heard from Jered?"

Thank you, Sim! He moved closer. "So you haven't seen him?"

"No. Have you?"

Bailey looked past her, taking a breath. "Not exactly. But he *was* home Thursday night."

Sim's eyebrows rose. "How do you know?"

He risked a glance to her eyes. "Things were missing. He got his guitar."

Sim bit her lip. "Does that mean he's doing something with his music?"

"I don't know."

"I hope so." She did a double take. "Oh. I'm sorry. I know you don't approve."

Does everyone *know my inadequacies as a parent?* He tried to think of something that would sound good. "I just want him to be happy."

She didn't respond.

He remembered something. "I never thanked you for contacting that man from Hiptone Records about Jered."

"He called?"

Bailey nodded. "Soon after Jered ran away. Jered's supposed to contact him."

"Does he know?"

"I haven't had a chance to tell him. If he would have stayed around the other night, I would have—" He let the statement die. *Would* he have told Jered about the Hiptone call?

Sim adjusted the pedals. "I gotta go. I'm picking up Avi McFay to come to our house for Bible study. Her mom's working."

It was needless information.

"Let me know if Jered calls," Sim said. "Tell him I'd really like to see him. Tell him my mom and I are praying for him."

Prayer making a difference? Talk about a pipe dream.

Annie washed the pots and pans. All during dinner she'd wanted to share with Cal about her experience this morning at the diner—the overpayment and how she'd handled it so well. She was well aware that he'd just been handed a similar situation with the insurance company and had handled it badly. Annie longed to discuss it with him because she knew her reaction was God's doing, not her own. There was an excitement in that. An excitement she wanted to share.

But the timing had never been right. Cal talked about the finish work on Bailey's addition, and Avi told them how Indian corn was grown. There was little chance for Annie to bring up her good deed, nor was she sure she knew how to word it.

Cal came up behind her at the sink and nibbled at her ear. "And how was your day?"

The perfect opening.

Annie wiped her hands on a towel and turned to face him. "Actually, I had a nice thing happen. Bob and Bernie were in for breakfast—"

"That's nothing new." Cal played with her hair, tickling her cheek with its end.

"But then Bob overpaid me. He made a mistake and put down a twenty instead of a five."

His eyes caught hers, then looked away. "Maybe he was making up for all the lousy tips they've left in the past."

She sidled away from him. "They tip fine. It was a mistake." She grabbed a cloth and began wiping the table. "I ran after them and gave it back."

Silence.

"They were very appreciative."

Silence.

"Bob even offered me an extra five as a reward for—"

"For being so perfect? For showing up your husband because he kept the insurance overpayment? Is that why you're telling me this story?"

"No, no..."

"Why else would you tell it?"

"You asked me how my day went." Lame. Very lame.

"And this is the only thing you could think of to share with me?" He shoved a chair into place with extra force. "Does it feel good being holier-than-thou, Annie? Does it make you feel better than me?"

He stormed from the room.

She fell into a chair. *What have I done?*

Annie came back to the kitchen from outside, carrying a mug of hot chocolate she'd made for Cal. He was in the garage, sorting through his extra lumber and making as much noise as possible. He hadn't wanted her peace offering—or her apology.

She stood at the kitchen window and looked out at the garage, her mind blank. What else could she do to make amends?

Avi came to her side. "What's Daddy mad about?"

"I brought up something I shouldn't have."

"Did you say you're sorry?"

She nodded, then noticed the mug in her hand. "You want some hot chocolate, sweet-apple?"

"Sure."

"Sit at the table," Annie said absently.

Avi did as she was told. She was such a good girl.

At least one of them was.

Jered leaned over the toilet, wanting but not wanting to throw up. He heard the door to the restroom open, then a hard tap on the stall door.

"Get out here, kid. Stardom awaits."

Jered got to his feet. "I don't think I can do—"

"Get out here now!"

His stomach did a different type of roll. He opened the door, and Jinko pointed at the spot in front of him. Jered moved into place, bracing himself. He looked at the floor.

Jinko chucked him under the chin, forcing his face upward. "You'll never know unless you try, kid. Who knows? Maybe you're the next Elton John or George Harrison."

Jered managed a smile. "George is dead."

"Which is what you'll be if you don't get out there. Now."

Jered nodded and took a deep breath. He hoped once he got in front of the audience his nerves would calm down and he'd do fine.

It was time.

He sat on the stool up front. All those faces, looking at him. Some *not* looking at him, chatting as if he weren't even up here. Bonnie the waitress gave him a wink and a thumbs-up, and he spotted Vasylko peeking out the kitchen door. And then there was Jinko, standing in the back with his arms crossed as if Jered better do good or else. Why was it harder performing in front of these people he knew rather than strangers?

He cleared his throat, set his fingers on the strings, and began. What did he have to lose—except his dignity, his pride, and his dinner?

Jinko hoped once Jered got in front of an audience his nerves would calm down and he'd do fine.

He should have let the kid barf his brains out in the restroom. His first strums on the guitar were tentative, and his voice wobbly. Jinko could tell there was a good voice behind it. Somewhere. But it sure didn't come out.

The crowd was merciless—as was their due. Amateur Night was entertainment plain and simple, and the audience thrived on booing the bad acts more than clapping for the good ones. It was all part of the game.

The kid couldn't take it personal. But he did. He finished and fled. Bonnie detoured close and told Jinko, "Poor boy. Go find him."

He had no choice. Sure, it would be awkward, and he'd have to play the comforting father figure for a few minutes. But after that, Jinko could move on to more important things.

After all, he finally had the kid just where he wanted him.

Jered sat out back behind Palamba's, next to the dumpster. He wanted to get in his truck and leave, but he left his keys in his guitar case, and no way was he ever going back in there.

His song had been a disaster, a nightmare come to life. It's like his stomach had sent a lump into his throat that wouldn't let his voice come out.

Which didn't explain his hands. His hands—his fingers—had betrayed him entirely. They rebelled and became weak and useless, unable to hold the simplest chord—or find it in the first place.

People had laughed. And booed. Some had looked away nervously, as if unable to witness such a total bomb. He should have run from the stage during the first stanza, but he stayed and finished, hoping beyond hope that he'd get his act together and offer a few decent notes to the world.

No such luck.

He banged a fist on the dumpster and stood. Enough of this. He'd leave. Move on. None of these people ever needed to see him again. And who needed a truck? He'd walk. Hitchhike. Jinko could have his stuff as payment for his debt.

Suddenly Jinko appeared at the corner of the building. Jered ducked, but too late.

"There you are, kid."

Jered started walking.

"Stop!"

Jered took two more steps, then stopped. He owed Jinko a goodbye. He turned around, stuffing his hands in his pockets.

Jinko came toward him, lighting a cigarette as he walked. He stuffed the pack and lighter in his shirt pocket. He stood before Jered, smoking, eyeing him.

"Go ahead. Say it. Tell me I blew it."

"Big-time. What happened?"

Jered kicked a pebble aside. "Everything left me: the chords, the words, the notes. I knew them all—I've been practicing hard—but they weren't there when I needed them."

"You let nerves win."

"I didn't have much choice."

"Sure you did, kid. You can't let your emotions take over. You have to show them who's boss."

Jered snickered. "And how was I supposed to do that?"

"Quit trying to please other people. Live for yourself."

"I'd love to."

"Then do it. If you're always worried what other people are thinking or feeling, you'll drive yourself crazy. You have to get the mindset that you're better than the rest. Do what you have to do—what you *want* to do—and let other people worry about themselves."

Jered wanted to believe what Jinko was saying; it would feel good to believe that way. But to do it... That was something else.

Jinko took him under his arm. "You go back to my place and—"

"I can't. My keys are inside. In my guitar case." He shook his head adamantly. "I'm not going back in there."

Jinko pulled out his keys. "Take my car. I'll bring your truck later."

Jered looked at the keys in his hand. Keys to the black Mercedes. For Jinko to trust him with his car...

Jinko tossed the cigarette and ground it dead with the toe of his boot. "When I get home, we'll have a little talk about some of those opportunities I mentioned. We gotta get you some confidence, kid. And I have just the thing."

Jered would take it. Whatever it was.

Jered lay on the cot in Jinko's garage, looking at the ceiling joists but not seeing them. Over and over he replayed his performance at Amateur Night. The horror of what *was* intermixed with what he wished had been. If only. If only. He hated those two words.

I should go home.

You are home.

My real home. Steadfast.

Go home as a loser? A failure?

He turned on his side, hoping the movement would nudge the direction of his thoughts. It worked, and another dialogue began, starting with Jinko's words: *"Quit trying to please other people. Live for yourself."*

Easier said than done. I still want to do my music, but I need to make a living—and not as a dishwasher.

But Jinko had an idea, opportunities. He had "just the thing."

Jered heard the whirr-clunk of his truck's engine. He jumped off the cot, wanting to pull himself together. He didn't want Jinko finding him all mopey. If he wanted to be of any use to his boss, he had to at least pretend to be strong.

Jinko opened the garage door without knocking. "Come on."

"Where we going?"

"You'll see."

Jered had no idea why Jinko insisted on using Jered's truck but thought better than to ask questions. Especially ten minutes later, when Jinko pulled onto a dirt and gravel road and shut off his lights.

"How can you see to drive?" Jered found himself whispering.

"I know the way."

The way to where?

About a quarter mile up, Jered could make out a grove of trees, a black blob against the night sky. Nothing good could happen in such a place at two in the morning. Nothing legal.

If only they'd left Eldora and headed toward Steadfast, Jered would have considered jumping out of the truck and making his way home. But they'd headed in the opposite direction. There was no home close. None.

Besides, Jinko was his friend. He'd been nothing but nice. He wouldn't lead him astray. He'd talked of opportunities.

"Here we are."

The road widened to a clearing, to a place where a farmhouse had once stood. A set of concrete steps led to nothing, marking its place. A dark van sat to the left, hidden in the darkness except for the reflection of the moon off the back bumper.

Jinko swung around and backed up to it, then shut off the truck. "Come on."

Jered's imagination took off. *He's going to shoot me and put my body in the van.* But he shoved such a ridiculous notion aside and followed Jinko's instruction.

The normal sounds of night were absent. Any cicadas or birds had moved elsewhere for the coming winter. The only sound was of their shoes crunching against the gravel, and the sound of Jered's arms swishing against his nylon jacket.

He held his arms still as they walked toward the van.

A man appeared from the driver's side. Jered couldn't see any details of his face but could tell his form was bulky—with muscles, not fat. Without a word the man opened the back of the van and Jinko opened the tailgate. They started moving boxes to the truck.

"Help," Jinko said.

Jered did as he was told until the truck bed was full—full of boxes of booze.

"Get in, kid."

Jered walked to the passenger side but turned enough to see Jinko hand the man something. Payment?

Jinko got in, and they backtracked the way they had come. Jered had a ton of questions, none of which he dared ask.

Back at Palamba's, Jered helped Jinko unload the booze. He shut the tailgate. "You drive us home, kid. I'm beat."

As Jered pulled away, Jinko leaned his head against the back window of the truck, clasped his hands over his middle, and closed his eyes. *Isn't he going to say anything?*

Apparently not. Though it was only a five-minute drive, Jinko snored. Back at the house, he woke up when Jered shut off the engine. They both got out.

Jinko lingered a moment, dug a hand into his shirt pocket, and pulled out a bill. He held it with both hands. It was a fifty. "This is yours tonight, for the use of your truck. Next time, when you do it by yourself, this will be a hundred. *Comprendé?*"

Jered took the fifty. Not bad for an hour's work.

Jinko reached into another pocket. "And here's a pager so I can get ahold of you." He showed Jered how it worked.

Cool.

Jinko headed inside. "See you in the morning."

You bet.

Annie hated when they went to bed mad, so she had only dozed. But now, suddenly, for some reason, she was wide awake. She sat up enough to see the clock over Cal's shoulder: 3:16. Ridiculous to get up this early, but what choice did she have? She slipped out of bed and tiptoed downstairs after checking on Avi.

Fine. I'm up. What should I do now?

She stood in the front room. She could watch TV, but she'd have to keep the sound so low she wouldn't be able to hear it—especially when the furnace kicked on. She could read a book. She had a stack a foot high she'd been meaning to start. Just last week Dottie had given her a romance she said she just had to—

Annie looked toward the kitchen. She had another book.

She flipped on the kitchen light and retrieved a pocket Bible from the cupboard where she kept the good dishes. After Merry had given it to her last August, Annie created this hiding place, knowing Cal would never find it.

What an odd attitude. Why did she feel the need to hide the Bible from her husband? It was the most popular book in the world. Nearly every family had one—whether they ever read it was another matter. Even Annie had one. Somewhere. She'd lost track.

She remembered the note the customer had given her the day before. First Corinthians something. She hadn't had time to look it up.

Until now. In the middle of the night.

She retrieved the note from her purse and read it again. *"You are His light to the world. Shine brightly. Read 1 Corinthians 13:4-8. God bless you."* She'd heard Jesus called "the Light of the world," but this man said *she* was His light. She'd received the note after doing a nice thing. So was she supposed to be His light by being nice? Doing good deeds?

Not making your husband feel bad.

The verses. Maybe they'd clarify everything. Annie sat at the table and ruffled through the delicate pages of the Bible until she spotted 1 Corinthians at the top of a page. She found chapter 13 and took a deep breath. *Okay, God. Help me here.* She read:

> Love is patient, love is kind. It does not envy, it does not boast,
> it is not proud. It is not rude, it is not self-seeking, it is not eas-
> ily angered, it keeps no record of wrongs. Love does not

delight in evil but rejoices with the truth. It always protects, always trusts, always hopes, always perseveres. Love never fails.

Annie held the pages against her chest—which had started to pound. Wonderful words she did *not* live out. She was *not* patient and kind. Their argument had started because she was proud and self-seeking. And certainly she was easily angered. She and Cal both were. And they both had a habit of keeping vast records of past wrongs to bring up at opportune moments. The kind of love described on this page was so...so...

Perfect. Was it even attainable?

And Cal wasn't perfect either. It wasn't *just* her fault.

But did that matter? Maybe if she learned to love this way, Cal would come around. Like Susan had said, maybe she could love him into having a faith. Maybe he'd see the good influence of Jesus in her life and want it for himself. Wouldn't that be wonderful?

"You are His light to the world. Shine brightly."

That was it. That was the key. If she believed in Jesus, she had to be His representative, shine *His* light to the world. To Cal.

She looked over the love verses again. These words were not a suggestion; they were a goal to be worked toward, and hopefully attained.

She closed her eyes, willing it to soak in. Such profound truth. *God, help me love this way.*

It was a start. A good start.

Cal felt Annie get back into bed. She'd been up an hour, reading some skinny navy-blue book in the kitchen. When he'd found her gone, he snuck downstairs, peeked in, and saw her. But what was she reading? What could keep her up for an hour in the middle of the night?

He waited until the rhythm of her breathing was deep and steady. He slipped out of bed for the second time and returned to the kitchen. The book was gone. He backtracked to the bookshelf in the front room. No skinny blue book.

Her purse.

It was hanging on the coatrack. No book. He checked her coat pockets. Not there either.

Cal looked around the kitchen. Where would she hide a book? He opened the cupboard that held the cookbooks, but it wasn't there. The desktop was as messy as always. Nothing new had been added.

Then he remembered her secret hiding place up with the good dishes. He'd found a fifty-dollar bill there once by accident and had never said anything. If she wanted to have a place that was hers alone, fine with him. He had his own hiding place. His own secrets.

He opened the cupboard and saw the book on top of the stack of plates. Bingo. He picked it up. *The New Testament, Psalms and Proverbs.* A scrap of napkin marked a page. On it was written a message: *"You are His light to the world. Shine brightly. Read 1 Corinthians 13:4–8. God bless you."*

Cal's heart began to race. Who'd given his wife this note? And when did she get the Bible—a Bible she was reading in the middle of the night? What was with that?

He'd find out. Right now.

Cal took a couple steps toward the front stairs, then stopped. Maybe confrontation wasn't the way to go. Not yet. Still too many unknowns.

He put the Bible back on the plates. He'd keep an eye on Annie, that's what he'd do. He'd be on the lookout for any more strange stuff. *Then,* he'd put a stop to it.

Yes, indeed, he'd watch her, watch her real close. This wasn't going to happen to him. Not again.

Six

*This is how we know who the children of God are
and who the children of the devil are:
Anyone who does not do what is right is not a child of God;
nor is anyone who does not love his brother.*

1 JOHN 3:10

FOR THE FIRST TIME, Annie awoke on Sunday morning and thought about going to church.

Up until now, she'd believed she could be a good Christian on her own, without the benefits of a congregation. But after experiencing the sisterhood of her Bible study—she really hated having to miss it yesterday because of work—and the love insight of 1 Corinthians, she knew *alone* she was weak. Bonded with others, she could find the strength to do this right. She'd made enough mistakes.

According to their habits, Sunday was for sleeping in, for reading the paper at the kitchen table while eating orange cinnamon rolls. Leisurely family time. And yet...

Annie had always felt a little nostalgic seeing a car pass, full of a family dressed for church. It conjured up feelings of her youth and of idyllic TV shows such as *Father Knows Best* and *The Donna Reed Show.*

It made her think of housewives who wore heels and a string of June Cleaver pearls to clean the kitchen, an organdy apron protecting their full skirts. Women who donned makeup even when they weren't going out in public. Mothers who made rolls from scratch, not from a tube, and never once licked their fingers when the frosting just happened to make them deliciously sticky.

Whatever. That kind of perfect wasn't *her,* and certainly, in the whole scheme of things, those kinds of details didn't matter. At least not now. Not yet. She had bigger issues to deal with.

She slipped on her robe with the frayed hem and the permanent stain on the sleeve, tied the belt, and headed downstairs to pop that tube of rolls. She looked forward to licking a little frosting.

Cal came down soon after.

"Morning," she said.

"Morning."

After ten years of marriage she was good at reading the nuances in his voice. And this time his tone indicated forgiveness. When he sat at the table to read the paper she hugged him from behind. He patted her hand against his chest.

Thank You, Jesus.

Avi appeared in the kitchen just as the rolls were in their last minute. She sat at the table, ready to eat. "Funny papers, Daddy."

He glanced up. "Please?"

"Please."

She got her funny papers, setting them against the lazy Susan so she could read *Ziggy* and *Garfield.*

Annie cleared her throat. Avi looked up. Cal did not. "Them that don't help, don't eat," Annie said, knowing with utter certainty that June Cleaver had never said this line.

Avi pushed herself away from the table, got out three plates, and set a napkin next to each. As she poured the orange juice, she sang a song. "'Seek and ye shall find, knock knock, and the door shall be opened. Ask and it shall be given, and the love come a-tumblin' down.'"

Cal glanced up from the front page. "Where'd you learn that?"

Annie seconded the question. "Where *did* you learn that?"

Avi set a glass of juice at her father's place. "Sim taught me. At Bible study."

Since she'd brought up the subject... "I'd like to go to church this morning, Cal."

The air left the room.

Cal let his arm drop, scrunching his newspaper against the table. His head shook back and forth.

"It'll just be for an hour," she said. "You're welcome to come with us."

Oops. Wrong thing to say. Cal looked at her. "You could have fooled me."

"I don't underst—"

Cal shoved his chair back, making both of them jump. He strode to the china cupboard and yanked out the hidden Bible. He shook it in front of her face. "I found your stash, Annie."

She couldn't believe his choice of words. *Stash? You dare to call the Bible stash?* Her heart raced and words of defense lined up, ready for battle. Then she glanced at Avi. The poor thing looked confused. *Join the club.*

She put a hand on their daughter's hair. "Why don't you go upstairs, sweet-apple. Put on your navy dress."

Avi was only too willing to leave the room. Annie found herself praying. *Help, please help...* Maybe if she downplayed the moment? "Sit, Cal. Eat your rolls while they're hot." She was glad her voice sounded calm. She sure didn't feel calm.

The hairs on the back of her neck prickled as she waited for him to move. Finally, he did, tossing the Bible on the table. It knocked over his orange juice.

Annie grabbed the book, but the napkin-bookmark sopped up the liquid, drawing it into the pages. She rushed to the counter, to a towel. The leather cover was quickly cleaned, but the pages—those beautiful wispy pages...stained. Stuck together.

Cal got up and retrieved a second towel, cleaning up his mess. "Sorry. It was an accident." He lifted his newspaper. "Oh, great. It's all over my paper."

The comparison between a throwaway newspaper and her Bible pushed reason aside. Annie tossed the towel at his back, clutched the Bible to her chest, and walked toward the front of the house.

He came after her. "Where you going?"

She headed up the stairs. "I told you. To church."

When he put his hand atop hers on the railing she stopped. "Don't do this, Annie."

"Don't do what?"

"Don't let God come between us."

She let out a breath. "He's not."

Cal snickered.

She looked down at his hand lying on top of hers. She faced him and placed her other hand on top of the pile. "If anything, believing in Him will make me love you more. Better."

Head shaking, he jerked his hand free. "You're wrong. I know you're wrong."

The way he said it... "How do you know?"

Cal put his hands in his pockets and walked back to the kitchen.

Once Avi and Annie were in the car, Avi asked, "Why is Daddy so mad about the Bible? Sim calls it the Good Book. Why would he be mad about you reading a good book?"

"I have no idea." She backed down the driveway but hesitated at the street.

"Where we going, Mama? What church are we going to?"

"Again, I have no idea." Details, details. Annie was just relieved to be away.

"That's okay. We'll find one. I know we will."

They found one. Or rather, they found Merry. And Susan and Sim. Avi spotted them getting out of their cars in a church parking lot. Annie couldn't believe their luck. They pulled into the lot.

Avi bolted from the car. "Sim!"

Annie hoped her face wasn't a billboard of the argument she'd just had with Cal. She got out of the car.

But as soon as the women were close, she blurted out, "Cal and I had an argument! About God."

"Oh, my," Merry said. "That's a big subject."

"Yeah, well, it certainly pushed Cal's button." She turned to Susan. "I tried not to push. But he found the Bible I'd hidden in the dishes and—"

"You hid your Bible?" Merry asked.

Oh, dear. Had she messed that up, too? Tears threatened. "I didn't want to upset him by blatantly reading... And all I did this morning was say I wanted to go to church, but he came unglued."

She felt Susan's hand on her shoulder. "Sim, take Avi into Sunday school. Bring her with you if you want, or let her go with the fifth graders. Her choice."

Avi touched her arm. "Mama? You all right?"

Annie could only nod.

"Your mom will be fine," Susan said. "You girls go ahead. We'll be in in a minute."

The parking lot was full of people. "Can we get in my car please?"

Merry took the front seat and Susan got in the back.

"Do you need a tissue?" Susan asked.

Annie nodded and pointed to the glove box. Merry handed her one, and she dabbed her eyes. "I feel like such a fool."

"For arguing with your husband?"

"For crying in a parking lot."

Susan gave her shoulder a pat. "There are no boundaries for tears. Want to tell us what happened?"

Yes, she did. Annie told them the details. "Why is he so anti-God? I can understand him being a little unnerved by my suddenly reading the Bible and such, but I want our life to be better. Not worse."

Susan sighed. "The more you tell me, the more he sounds like Forbes."

Annie angled in her seat to see Susan in the back. "You said that the other day. Tell me more. I need to know."

"I'll preface it by saying that Forbes was the extreme. I've never seen a man so antagonistic toward faith. He believed in himself, period." She put a hand on her pregnant belly. "He gave me an ultimatum. Him or God."

"Oh, dear."

Susan rubbed her belly, as if comforting the child. "He's a very bitter man. I would have stayed with him and worked through it, but he wouldn't do it that way. It was all him or nothing."

"That's not a very fair choice for him to ask you to make."

"Fair has little to do with a lot of choices, Annie." Susan looked at Merry. "You're quiet."

Merry looked out the car windows. "We should be going in." She turned to Annie. "You'll be okay. Just come with us. You're doing the right thing."

She certainly hoped so.

Cal couldn't stay in the house. The empty house.

He got in his truck and headed out—to where, he didn't know.

That was a lie.

As soon as he turned onto the highway leading to Eldora, he knew where he'd end up. Twenty minutes later he pulled into the parking lot of Friendly Acres Retirement Village. A fancy name masking the truth. It was a nursing home. Plain and simple.

Cal turned off the engine and sat in silence. He hated keeping secrets from Annie, but he had no choice. A ten-year-old lie was hard to undo. Lying had been a huge mistake. Yet, surely if he came clean, she could forgive him.

He put his hand on the door handle. She might be able to forgive him for the lie, but never for the reason behind the lie.

Life was complicated. And totally unfair.

"Dad?"

His father roused from his sleep. "Huh? What?"

Cal gently moved his father's feet to the side and sat on the ottoman. "I thought you'd be in the church service this morning."

Fergis McFay cleared his throat and pushed himself straighter in the chair. He adjusted the oxygen tube in his nose. "I'm not going ever again. They're wrong. And that pastor; I heard he's been divorced. I'm not taking no preachin' from a man who's sinned against God."

Sorry I asked.

His father's eyes were fully awake now. "Why aren't you in church? You still a heathen?"

"I try to be a good man, Dad."

"No trying to it. You be a good man, or God will strike you down. You just watch."

Cal wanted to leave, yet his father was a flame and Cal the moth, flying too close yet unable to stay away from the burn. The hurt. He'd moved him into this nursing home a week ago, after his father's health had gone bad because of the emphysema. And now the doctors said he had the beginnings of Alzheimer's and couldn't live alone in his apartment anymore. Cal *had* to move him. Cal *had* to pay for him.

But with what?

He thought back to the insurance overpayment. Yes, he'd kept it. But not for himself. He needed it to pay for his dad's care. If only he could tell Annie that.

But he couldn't.

Because she thought his father was dead.

Fergis rambled on about heathens and hellfire. Cal had to change the subject or suffocate under the words. "I might be starting a new project, Dad. A friend and I—he owns a fancy restaurant in Steadfast—he asked me... It's a great honor, really. We want to open a restaurant for families and—"

"Humph. What do you know of families? Never been married. Never given me a single grandchild." His eyes flashed as if he enjoyed opening old wounds. "'Cept the one who was a bastard. Seducing that good Christian girl to sin. You should be ashamed of yourself!"

Cal stood and took a step toward the door. "Treena's gone, Dad. You know that. And the baby's—"

"You are a sinner, boy. You must repent or be damned!"

A nurse stepped into the room. "Goodness sake, Fergis. What's going on in here?"

"I was just leaving." Cal pushed past her into the hall, his wings suitably seared.

"Mark my words, boy. Once a sinner, always a sinner!"

Cal gripped the steering wheel. His entire body pressed forward. Toward home. Away from the condemnation of his father.

Fergis McFay had always been a judgmental man, but in the past year or so, as his health had failed, he'd gotten worse. And now, with the unpredictability of his memory, Cal's past with Treena came up far too often.

Treena, a good Christian girl.

And now Annie.

Cal pushed harder on the accelerator. It couldn't happen again. It couldn't. He wouldn't let God take the woman he loved away from him.

A siren blared. He looked in his rearview mirror. A cop.

He checked the speedometer. He was going ninety-three.

Great. Just what he needed.

He slowed, pulled onto the shoulder, and waited for the policeman to come to his door.

"Cal?"

He looked toward the voice. "Ken. Hi."

"Hi, yourself. I thought it looked like your truck, but I couldn't imagine any reason for you coming from Eldora on a Sunday morning."

"Errands. That's all."

"You always drive ninety when you're coming home from errands?"

"Sorry. I was..." *Upset.* "...thinking about something."

"Next time you have such thinking to do, pull over and do it from a parked position, okay?"

"Yeah. Sure." Ken started writing him up. "Ah, come on, Ken. Don't give me a ticket."

"I don't want to, and if you were going a few miles over, I'd give you a warning. But over ninety? Cal, that's ticket material, friend or no friend."

He knew Ken was right. "Fine. Hand it over."

"Let me see your license, please."

He finished the ticket and gave it to Cal, who tossed it on the passenger side of the seat. "Can I go now?"

Ken squinted at him. "That depends. You okay? Want to grab a cup of coffee or something? I'm a good listener."

Cal turned the ignition. "I just want to get home."

"A good place to be, Cal. A good place to be."

❧❧   ❧❧   ❧❧

The service was nearly over, and Annie felt like a sponge, absorbing everything. She'd read the notices in the bulletin about bake sales and pizza parties for the Sunday school kids. A trip to a pumpkin patch and various rehearsals and meetings. Hometown stuff that made her feel warm inside.

She'd gone through the stand-up/sit-down stuff, and Merry had shown her where the various responses were in the hymnal. Annie loved the mellow sound when everyone read together, as if the people were aware of the texture of their seatmates and adapted their voices into a rich weave of words.

She was amazed at the Scripture readings, which reinforced everything she'd gone through the past months. And she listened to the sermon, eager for something to hit her over the head.

But it didn't.

The message that God had a plan for everyone's life was good, but it seemed like frosting on the cake of her thoughts.

And yet, it was perfect. Being hit by a thunderbolt that would make her understand everything in a flash would have been nice but wasn't practical. God didn't work that way.

Did He?

For the closing hymn Annie expected to hear the strains of the organ. Instead, she heard a drum set. And an electric piano. As everyone stood she strained to see the musicians up front. A third person on electric guitar joined in. Susan pointed to an insert in the bulletin that had music printed on it. People started singing—and moving to the music.

It was impossible not to move. She looked at the insert. The song was by a woman named Twila Paris.

The joy of the Lord will be my strength
I will not falter, I will not faint
He is my Shepherd, I am not afraid
The joy of the Lord is my strength!

The couple beside them clapped in sync, not needing to look at the music. The choir swayed like gospel groups she'd seen on TV. A few people raised their hands above their heads, their palms up, as if wanting to catch something.

Something from heaven?

Annie's throat tightened, making singing impossible. She let the music envelop her. Her chest cavity seemed to expand to the point of aching. But it wasn't a bad feeling. She was full of joy. The sheer glory of it all. The words melded with the attitude. Giving. Offering. Receiving.

She closed her eyes and let it in. And as she did, the prominent line of the song broke through: *"The joy of the Lord is my strength."*

Joy.

Joy of the Lord.

Strength.

Then a ticker tape of thoughts...*Joy* in *the Lord. Joy* from *the Lord. Strength* in *Him. Strength* through *Him.*

She felt Susan's hand on her arm and opened her eyes. "You okay?"

Annie put a hand to her mouth and realized a decision had been made. "I want this."

"You want what?"

The tears came out of nowhere. "I want this...this joy."

Susan put an arm around her, pulling her close. She whispered in her ear. "Since you already have Him, it'll come. I promise."

Annie nodded. Oh, my. She hoped it was true. With this kind of joy anything was possible. Anything.

When Jered woke up at eleven, he saw Jinko's car was gone. And he was glad. Jered still didn't know what he'd say to him about the shipment of booze in the middle of the night. Who was he to butt into Jinko's business? He didn't know anything about running a restaurant and a bar. Maybe the whole thing was legit. Maybe this was the way every restaurant got their shipments.

Yeah right.

He couldn't think about it. Fifty dollars and a pager had bought his silence.

Jered gathered up some clean clothes and headed to the house to use the shower. He had to be at work by noon. At the last second he backtracked and grabbed his pager. Just in case.

And good thing, too. Because on his way upstairs it vibrated in his hand. He looked at the display and recognized the number of Jinko's cell phone. Jered detoured to a phone he'd seen in the kitchen and dialed. This was kind of cool. It made him feel important.

The phone connected and Jinko answered. "You're up."

"I'm going to take a shower."

"Hold off a few minutes. I need you to do something for me."

"Sure, but I'm supposed to be in to work at noon and—"

"Forget that for now. Come in when you can. This is more important."

Jered spotted a pad of paper and a pen. He sat at the kitchen desk. "Shoot."

"I'm expecting someone at the house. I was going to be there, but two waitresses didn't show, and I can't leave. You'll have to handle it."

"No problem." This felt good. Real good.

"His name's...never mind; you don't need to know his name. He's a tall guy with a black beard. When he comes to the door, open the garage for him and let him take ten of those DVD players I've got stacked in there. Nothing else. Just ten DVDs. *Comprendé?*"

Jered's stomach grabbed, but he tried to ignore it. "Is that it?"

"He'll give you some money."

"How much?"

"Five hundred. Cash."

Five hundred?

"Get the money first, then let him load the boxes. Ten. Just ten."

Jered had learned that lesson the hard way. "But what if—?"

"What if nothing. I need you to do this. Act strong. Act tough. Pretend you know what you're doing, and it'll flow. Act like a wimpy loser, and you'll have problems."

"I'll...I'll be fine."

"I know you will, kid. That's why I'm trusting you."

"When's he supposed to come by?"

"Within a half hour. Just hang around in the house. Help yourself to whatever's in the fridge. I'll make it worth your while, kid."

Another fifty? "Don't worry about a thing. I've got it covered."

Jered hung up. More boxes changing hands. He'd wondered about the DVD players in the garage. Boxes in, boxes out, money in, money out. Must be the way of the world.

Jered opened the refrigerator and made himself a sandwich from some cold cuts and cheese. He found a bag of chips in the pantry. He wandered through the house as he ate.

Jinko had nice things. Expensive things. Leather couches, modern-looking statues made of glass, an entertainment center full of shelves and drawers and stocked with a widescreen TV that was at least a forty-eight-incher. DVD player, VCR, Bose sound system. Not bad. But best was a grand piano. Jered ran his hands along the keys. He wished he could play like Billy Joel or Elton John. That would be so cool.

But it wasn't just the things that were nice. The place was clean. Beyond clean. Even the magazines on the coffee table lined up. The cord to a pair of headphones displayed a perfect circle. The DVDs were in alphabetical order. Obsessive. Yet in a way it made sense. The order of the house matched the order of the man. Jinko may have worn slightly funky clothes—he seemed to prefer all black with a heavy necklace—but he was always perfect. Not a ponytailed hair out of place. Same with his car. Same with Palambas.

After finishing his sandwich, Jered picked a fallen crumb from an Oriental rug. He started in on the chips, opening drawers and cupboard doors as he strolled. Most were what he expected: more DVDs, CDs, some cassettes.

But one drawer was more interesting. It was full of jewelry. Rings, necklaces, pins. Lots of women's stuff. A man's watch caught his eye. On the back was inscribed, "To Bobby, with love, Sue." This wasn't Jinko's watch. None of this was Jinko's jewelry.

Jinko is a crook.

The booze incident, this jewelry, and in a few minutes the DVD players... Three strikes, you're out.

Or in.

And yet...so what? Jered didn't know who the stuff belonged to. It wasn't his business. The only loyalty he had was to his own survival. And at the moment Jinko was a big part of that survival.

Jered started when the doorbell rang. He tossed the watch in the drawer and went to answer it.

The guy with the black beard must have been six foot six. Jered only came up to his shoulders. "Jinko here?"

"Uh, he couldn't make it. I'm supposed to help you."

The man gave Jered the once-over, and for the hundredth time he wished he had some beef on him. He felt like a wimpy T-ball kid next to a pro.

"Well?"

Jered didn't think Jinko would want the man inside, so he joined him out front, and the two of them headed to the garage. The man's car was already backed up, the trunk open and ready. Jered noticed him look around the neighborhood. Good idea. It was a quiet Sunday morning, but just the same, Jered waited until a car full of a Sunday-dressed family drove by before he opened the garage door.

The man headed for the boxes and took two back to his car.

Get the money first. "I..." Jered cleared his throat and tried to put some power in it. "Slow down. You owe Jinko five hundred. Money first."

The man stopped on his way back for a second load and smiled. "He got you trained, don't he?" He fished a wad out of his pocket and smacked it into Jered's hand. "Now help so I can get outta here."

Jered remembered that only ten machines were to be taken. When the man started taking another two, Jered stepped in his way. "Ten. Jinko said ten."

The man backed off, his hands raised. "Hey, I musta miscounted." His eyes flashed past Jered, then he pointed. "When'd he get those Palm dealies, those PDAs?"

Jered knew there was a stack near the paint shelf. "I don't know."

"I want some of those, too. How much?"

Jered had no idea. "You need to talk to—"

The man shoved past Jered and took one.

"I told you I don't know how much—"

The man pulled another bill from his pocket, glanced at it, and gave it to Jered. "Here's a twenty for your trouble. What Jinko don't know—"

"But he *will* know."

He shrugged. "Not if you don't tell 'im." He left the garage, shutting his trunk. "Nice doin' business wid you, kid."

Jered closed the garage door and stared at Andrew Jackson's face. He pocketed the money and headed for the house to take a shower.

Another twenty. For looking the other way. Easy work.

Jered sat on his cot and tied his shoes. His eyes kept looking at the stack of PDAs. There was a definite hole where one had been.

He got up and rearranged the boxes, overlapping the top row over the bottom so they weren't so perfectly lined up, so the hole was filled.

Better.

He had to get to work.

He was forty-five minutes late. Dishes were piling up.

"Where you been?" Vasylko asked. "Hop, hop. Do job."

Jered put on his apron and got to it, the five hundred burning through his pocket. Actually, the other pocket—with his fifty and new twenty—was doing a pretty good job of heating up, too. As he worked he looked for Jinko. He wanted to give him the money, but a part of him was nervous about meeting up with him again, dealing with questions.

He didn't have to wait long. Jinko came in from the dining room, spotted him, and came over. "How'd it go?"

"No problem." Jered wiped his hands on a towel and reached into his pocket. "Here—"

Jinko stopped him. "Come back to the storeroom."

They moved into privacy, and Jered handed over the money. Jinko counted it and put it away. "Everything go all right?"

Jered looked down. "Fine."

Jinko chucked him under his chin. "You're not very convincing."

It took all of Jered's strength to look at him, eye to eye. *Just tell him. Get it done with.* "That guy's big."

Jinko sniffed. "Big in body, small in mind. Don't worry about him. As long as things stay on the up-and-up, none's to worry."

Up-and-up? None of this is up-and-up. Blackbeard's a thief. Jinko's a thief.

And I'm a thief.

Jinko peeled off another fifty. "Here. For your trouble. Now get back to work, kid. You did good."

Hardly.

Seven

Find rest, O my soul, in God alone;
my hope comes from him.
He alone is my rock and my salvation;
he is my fortress, I will not be shaken.

PSALM 62:5–6

AVI KNOCKED ON THE WINDOW of the driver's side, startling Annie. "Aren't you coming inside, Mama?"

Annie had not even noticed that her daughter had gotten out of the car. Once she'd pulled in the driveway after church and had seen Cal's truck sitting there, she'd been consumed with what he would say. What she would say. Those questions had frozen her in her seat. How could she ever express the joy she'd felt at church? It had surprised even her. Oh, how she wanted Cal to feel such joy and hope and—

"Mama, come on. Come with me."

That snapped Annie out of it. After one of their fights, the atmosphere was always strung tight enough to snap at the slightest misstep. There was no way she'd send Avi in alone. Or first.

She got out of the car and held out her hand, more for her own comfort than her daughter's. As they walked toward the kitchen door, Annie tried to pray. She really did. But only one word repeated itself: *Help, help, help, help…* She hoped God would fill in the blanks.

Cal wasn't in the kitchen. She heard the TV in the living room. Annie found herself holding her breath and let it out. *This is ridiculous. I'm in my own home. He's my husband. We love each other.*

Avi opened the refrigerator. "Can we have lunch? I'm hungry."

Maybe if Annie made a nice lunch, she could bring Cal a plate, sit in front of the TV with him, and act as if everything was normal.

Maybe he wouldn't even ask about their morning. Maybe she wouldn't have to bring up church and God—

"Hi."

Cal stood in the doorway to the kitchen. Annie's heart returned to her chest. She hung her coat and purse on the rack. "Hot dogs okay for lunch?"

"Ooh, yeah. I'll get 'em out," Avi said.

"So how was it?" he asked.

"Nice. It was nice."

"But where'd you go? We don't have a church."

"We went where Merry and Susan go."

"And Sim," Avi said. "Sim was there." She pointed to the hot dogs. "I want mine cut up with a squirt of catsup on each slice, okay?"

"Sure. Okay." Annie washed her hands. She glanced at Cal. He was just standing there. It was hard reading him. Maybe if she explained more... "We saw the three of them standing in the parking lot; they asked us to go with them."

Avi got four hot dogs out of the package and put them on a plate for the microwave. She glanced at her father. "It was fun, Daddy. I got to use puppets to put on a show."

Cal ignored her and moved to Annie's side. She did not look at him. "Did *you* have *fun?*" His tone was mocking.

"Actually. Yes." All thoughts of sharing her joy died. It wasn't the time. "What are your plans for this afternoon?"

He took a step away. "I have a project I need to figure prices on: finishing off the Welsh's basement." He turned to Avi. "Go out to my truck and get my notebook, won't you, Av? It's on the front seat."

Avi did as she was told.

Annie put the plate in the microwave and pushed some buttons. Avi came back in. "Here's your notebook, Daddy. Did you need this other thingy? It was sitting—"

Annie caught a glimpse of a ticket before Cal grabbed it away.

"Let me have that," he said.

"When did you get a ticket?"

"The other day. I made an illegal left turn, that's all. No big deal."

The way he couldn't meet her eyes told her he was lying. But why?

He set the notebook on the table, folded the ticket in two, and stuffed it in his pocket. "They didn't get you to commit to anything, did they? Get you to give a chunk of money for some charity drive?"

It took her a moment to figure out he was talking about the church.

"No, no, nothing like that," Annie said. "They were very nice."

He took a seat and crossed his arms. "Because they do want something from you."

She didn't know what to say. "Why do you think that?"

He shrugged. "Experience."

She raised an eyebrow. "You have experience with a church?"

"Sure. I'm not a heathen, you know."

Heathen. What an odd word for him to use. "Did you go to church as a boy?"

He laughed bitterly. Then his voice rose as did his right arm. "Hellfire and damnation, fall upon you sinners!"

Annie took a step back. "It wasn't like that, Cal. Church this morning made me feel...full inside."

He snickered. "Oh, I can tell you exactly what you were full of." He reached out and touched her hand, his eyes concerned. "This is what they do, Annie-girl. They draw you into their fold, play a little music, say a few words they know everybody wants to hear, then make you feel like you owe them something. Like they've done you this big favor."

"It wasn't people who filled me up, Cal." How could she explain it?

He withdrew his hand and sat back.

She looked at him, then at her hands. The nail polish on her right thumb was horribly chipped. She took a cleansing breath. "I felt...God."

He shoved his chair back and stood, pointing a finger at her face. "They've brainwashed you! One time in a church and they've brainwashed you."

"They didn't—"

"You're not going back."

Annie straightened her shoulders. "We *are* going back. We're going every week."

He shook his head violently. "You're not going, and you're certainly not taking Avi."

"Avi loved Sunday school."

"Avi loves going to the hardware store. Avi loves cleaning her room. That girl's open and willing to go and do most anything, which is another reason why she's not going with you."

Annie rubbed her hands over her head. How could something so joyful be made so confusing? "You don't understand..."

"Obviously, you don't either, or you'd be able to explain it better."

She looked up. "It's too new to me. If Susan or Merry were here, they'd be able to find the exact place in the Bible to explain—"

He strode to the china cupboard and pulled out her Bible, waving it in the air between them. "That's the other thing. There will be no more Bible reading in the middle of the night." He headed to the kitchen door and went outside. Annie heard the top of a garbage can open—and bang closed.

No, he wouldn't—

He came back without the Bible and slammed the door. "There. That's done."

Annie sprang toward the door. He cut her off, holding her back. "You have no right to throw away my Bible. It's mine!" His grip hurt her arms.

"I have every right. I'm your husband. I'm protecting you from—"

She stopped fighting and stepped back. "Protecting me from God?"

"Protecting you from yourself."

She put a hand on his chest, pushed slightly, and turned away. She didn't want him near her. His attitude was like an infectious virus threatening a healthy organ. If she stayed close, he'd invade her entire being, bring her down, defeat her.

She left the kitchen. He called after her. "You'll thank me for this, Annie. You'll see I'm right."

Right? What was right anymore?

The phone rang at the bedside table. Annie didn't answer it. In the kitchen below her she heard Cal pick it up.

"No, you may not talk to her, Merry. She doesn't *want* to talk to you."

Annie sat up in bed. She did want to talk to Merry. Merry might be able to help. She reached for the extension, but when she picked it up, she heard two clicks. The line went dead.

She hung up the phone. Maybe it was for the best. Nothing was working out. Everything was a mess.

A few moments later there was a knock on the bedroom door. "Annie?"

She didn't answer him.

He tried the knob. "Why'd you lock the door?"

She turned onto her back, taking the pillow with her. "Isn't it obvious? I don't want to be disturbed."

"We saved you a hot dog."

"I'm not hungry."

The moment of silence brought relief. Annie had just closed her eyes when Cal said, "You going to be in there all day?"

"Just leave me alone, Cal."

"You're acting stupid."

She rolled back to her side.

"Avi and I are going to the park."

"You do that."

"We want you to come."

She thought of a good one. "We don't always get what we want."

He stomped down the stairs, his voice fading. "Pout all you want. I won't stop you."

Indeed you won't.

Cal pushed Avi on the swing.

"Higher, Daddy! Swing me over the top."

Over the top. That's what he felt. Why did Annie have to go to church anyway? Why did she have to mess up the perfectly good routine they'd established over many years of marriage? Why'd—

"Why are you so mad at Mama?"

He pushed the swing harder. "I'm not mad at her, Av. I'm frustrated." *I'm trying to save your mother from herself. From* them. *From* Him.

"You yelled. That's mad."

He wasn't going to argue the point with a ten-year-old.

"Church is fun, Daddy. You should come with us."

"No thanks."

"Why not?"

"Why?"

She couldn't answer that one. So there. End of discussion.

Annie heard the doorbell ring. Since Avi and Cal weren't home, she had no choice but to leave her pouting behind. It was Merry. And Ken.

When she opened the door, Annie scanned the street for Cal's truck. She invited them in, then shut the door quickly.

"Goodness. What was all that? I feel as though I'm in a spy movie," Merry said.

"Cal took Avi to the park. You can't be here when he comes back."

"Why not?"

She looked at Ken. She really didn't want to go into all this with him there. But she had no choice. "We argued. About church."

"What happened?" Merry took a step toward the living room, but when Annie held her ground in the entryway, she returned to her spot.

Ken held up a finger. "So that's why he was so upset."

Annie wasn't sure she understood his statement. "When did you see Cal?"

"This morning. That's why we're here. I gave him a speeding ticket when he was coming back from Eldora. He was going over ninety. He was real upset. I came to see how he was."

Annie's mind swam. "He was home all morning."

"Obviously he wasn't."

This didn't make any sense. "Why would he be in Eldora?"

"He said something about errands."

"The catchall excuse." Merry put a hand to her lips. "Oh, I'm sorry, Annie. I shouldn't speculate and imply—"

Annie went into the living room, needing to sit. "No, speculate. Speculate. I can't think of a single reason Cal would be in Eldora. On a Sunday morning."

"Maybe we should go," Merry said.

Only then did Annie realize they hadn't followed her into the living room but stood in the entryway as if eager to leave.

She stood. "Maybe you should." She opened the door for them.

"Call me?" Merry said.

Annie could only nod and shut the door.

What was going on?

She returned to the couch and clutched a pillow to her chest. The logistics of Cal's deception loomed large. In order for him to go to Eldora—twenty minutes away—do his "errands," and return to be home when she and Avi returned, he had to have left the moment they did. There hadn't been time for him to haphazardly decide to do errands. And what was open on Sunday mornings anyway? No. There had to be something in Eldora, that was a given. A draw. Something constant so that when he found himself with a free hour or so, he could go. Without hesitation.

She gasped at her first thought.

It was the only thing that made sense. They'd had an argument; he got upset. He'd run into the comforting arms of a mistress! That he would be satisfied with spending such a short time with her meant that his feelings were deep and the relationship long-standing. He was willing to drive forty minutes to see this other woman.

Annie pushed the pillow against her face and screamed into it. "No!"

There was no other explanation. None. Merry and Ken had figured it out, too. The fact that Cal had been upset on the way *home* from seeing his lover was proof that leaving her caused him grief;

coming home to Annie was not something he relished.

How dare he betray her like this! She'd always been faithful. Their marriage was good, their love real. How could he run into the arms of another—?

Because you've run into the arms of another Man. You're not just "his Annie" anymore. You're His *Annie.*

She let the pillow settle into her lap as her mind wandered over the past months—and before. Cal hadn't been himself for far longer than her conversion. She hadn't allowed herself to acknowledge it because she'd been doing her own searching. She'd justified the gap between them with the thought that all married couples go through times of restlessness, apartness, as if every so often a time of readjustment was needed.

Truth was, they'd both been searching. Annie's search culminated in the Praise Show and finding a true faith. Had Cal's search culminated in finding another woman? Had Annie been too caught up in her own changes to notice?

She bit the tip of the pillow. Out of anger. But also out of guilt. It was partly her fault. She'd caused him nothing but trouble with all this God-stuff. Talk about rocking the boat... After ten years of marriage, they'd created a nice life. Not perfect, but totally acceptable. And then she'd suddenly dragged Jesus into the mix, making waves, causing a storm. Cal hadn't asked for this. No wonder he'd run into the arms of another woman. What calm and comfort had Annie provided lately? Constantly challenging, changing. Wanting him to change.

Or were her looks to blame? Though she'd put on a few pounds, she was far from fat. She was also far from stunning or glamorous or a zillion other words she imagined described this mistress. Annie tended to do the quick and easy with her long hair, pulling either part or all of it up. And makeup? Two strokes of mascara and a little Chapstick were all she had time for. Yet Cal had never complained. He'd always liked her natural style.

Until he was confronted with the wows and wiles of someone who put being sexy on a front burner.

Oh, dear, dear, *dear.*

As far as her homemaking skills? She looked around the messy room. Why couldn't she ever get caught up? Annie shook her head. She couldn't even start letting her doubts gain wings in that direction.

Her jaw hurt from clenching, and she forced herself to relax and let the pillow live. Actually, maybe that was a good idea all around. Relax and let her marriage live. She was getting carried away. She had suspicions but no proof. She simply *had* to stop watching those soap operas with all their guilty husbands and vindictive wives.

Annie took a fresh breath and let the moment find new direction. Was Cal guilty? Was she? Either way there was room for improvement. She tossed the pillow down and stood. She'd make it up to him. Starting now.

Cal had no idea what he'd find when he got home from the park. Would Annie still be in bed, pouting? Would she be waiting for him at the door, arms crossed, ready for a fight? Or the third alternative: Would she apologize for her actions, they'd make up, and everything would be back to...?

He was going to say *normal,* but except for brief snippets of time, he wasn't sure what that was anymore.

He pulled into the driveway, and Avi scurried inside. *She* wasn't nervous about what she'd find.

Neither should he be. *Buck it up. Be a man.*

He slammed the door of the truck and headed in, trying to calm his stomach between here and there. He was only partially successful.

But when he got inside he was greeted with the smell of spices.

"Look, Daddy! Mama made pumpkin pies."

"I can smell them." He hung up his coat.

Annie took a step toward him. She'd put on his favorite green sweater that looked wonderful against her red hair. Speaking of hair, hers was down and curled. And was the blush on her cheeks makeup or natural? It didn't matter. She was lovely.

"I thought it would taste good after being out in the cold air," she said.

He searched her eyes and was relieved to see that in spite of everything, his Annie's eyes were as intoxicating as ever.

He extended a hand in her direction. She took it. "I'm sorry, Cal. I don't mean to upset you. Things will be better. The same as they used to be. I promise."

He pulled her close, covering his confusion with a hug.

What had brought this on?

What did it matter? Crisis averted.

Jered sank into a chair in the corner of the kitchen of Palamba's and closed his eyes. He'd never been so tired. It wasn't that he couldn't handle a nine-hour shift, but the shift, added to the lack of sleep because of the booze run, added to the stress of the DVD payoff...

He heard footsteps and his eyes shot open. But it was only Vasylko.

"You beat?"

"I'm beat."

"Why? You strong. You work long before."

"It's not the dishwashing; it's...I've been doing some extra work for Jinko."

Vasylko started to nod, hesitated, then finished the motion. He looked behind him. They were alone. "Be careful. Jinko nice man but..." He shrugged. "Not good for boy to get..." Not finding the right word, he interlocked his fingers.

Hooked up? *Does he know?* Jered sat forward. "Have you ever...helped him?"

The cook waved his hands. "No, no. I won't." He pointed to his eyes. "But I see. I see."

"Why don't you...turn him in?"

Vasylko nodded as if he'd thought about it, then fished a necklace from under his shirt. It was a cross. "I try to help with this."

A necklace?

"I talk to Jinko about cross. Show him the Way."

Jered wanted to laugh. He couldn't imagine Jinko ever listening to anyone talk about God-stuff, especially if it meant he wanted Jinko to stop dealing. And whatever Vasylko had said, it obviously hadn't worked.

Vasylko held the cross out. "You believe?"

"In God?"

"In Jesus."

If he told the cook he'd never thought about it much, he was afraid he'd get a sermon—in heavily accented, broken English, no less. He wasn't up for that. "Sure. Christmas. Easter. Sure."

Vasylko smiled. "More to it."

Jered stood. "Hey, I'm beat. I gotta go home and sleep."

The cook put a hand on his shoulder. "You go. 'Come to me, all you who are weary and burdened, and I will give you rest.'"

Sure. Whatever.

Tired as he was, Jered didn't go straight home after his shift. He drove to Valley View park on the edge of town. Since it was dark, cold, and after nine, no one was there. Which was fine with him. One thing he'd learned to do in the past three months was be alone. What surprised him was that he liked his own company. And even though he had his own separate space at Jinko's, being there, near Jinko, was not the same as being alone.

He left the truck and sat on a picnic table, zipping up a heavier jacket he'd found in the garage. Only one light was on in the parking lot behind him, but it was annoying. It ruined what he wanted to see. So he jumped off the table, found himself a small rock, and threw it at the light. He missed. He heaved another and another, until rock met glass.

And the night went dark.

But not dark.

Jered climbed back onto the table, his face raised. This was what he was looking for. Stars. Billions and billions of stars. The sky was a dome around him, an inverted bowl so rich in its blackness that it seemed it would have substance if you could only reach far enough and skim the curve with a hand.

As a kid he'd always liked the stars. He used to go to a deserted barn on the edge of town, climb up in the loft, and look out at the night sky—until the houses of Steadfast got too close and messed up the view with their lights.

People getting too close. That shouldn't mess things up, but it usually did. That or the lack of people getting close. Why couldn't it ever be just right? Why did the wrong people get close at the wrong times and the right people ignore him?

His dad, sure. But he was only the worst offender. There'd been others in his life. His mom started it, leaving when he was a baby. Why'd she have him if she didn't want him? He and his dad had done okay for a lot of years, until his dad started to love his stupid restaurant more than his son. Why did he do that? Jered couldn't think of anything *he'd* done to make his dad change so much.

Then there was Merry Cavanaugh. The town librarian. Steadfast was better for having her move to town. She'd cared about Jered. She believed in his music and had helped him look stuff up on the Internet.

Jered would have liked to get closer to Merry. Sure, she was older, but not that old. And she was alone just like he was. Her husband and son had been killed in a plane crash a couple years earlier, so she was ripe for some companionship, right? But maybe not. She'd had a shrine to them in her backyard. Sick stuff, holding onto the dead like that. Jered had done her a favor by tearing it apart.

And what about Sim? That annoying fourteen-year-old orphan intruder, coming into Steadfast to stir things up, make everybody like her and want to help her. She'd hung around with Jered, Moog, and Darrell, and had pretended to be tough and one of them, but it was all a ploy to get to Jered's dad. One time Jered had actually caught his dad playing Monopoly with her. He couldn't remember the last time he'd played a game with his dad. Not that he wanted to. Not that he wanted to...

See what happens when I try to get close to people? Jinko was right; people needed to look after themselves first. That was the only safe way to live.

Jered pulled his hands into the sleeves of the jacket. Jinko had drawn him close, was drawing him closer still with his deals and fifty-dollar bills. And maybe that was okay. That was business. That was survival.

His thoughts flew to Vasylko. Now there was a man it might be nice to know. Nice, funny. And Vasy listened. But Jered couldn't risk getting closer. Not with that cross stuff between them. He didn't need any Jesus-freak in his life, giving him a list of don'ts. And he certainly didn't need to draw God's attention by hanging around with one of His believers. Best to stay anonymous.

To God. And to the world. Hang out. Do what needed to be done to survive, but not get involved. Not let people get to him. Not care.

Jered wrapped his arms around his body, trying to stay warm. He stopped looking at the stars.

Jered slipped into the garage. Jinko's car was in the driveway, and the house was dark except for a light in an upstairs room. Jered kept the lights off, stripped down to his underwear, and was getting into bed when he noticed a shaft of moonlight hitting the shelf across the room. The shelf that held the PDAs.

They were stacked neatly, two rows high. Things had been rearranged. The empty spot glared.

He knows!

Jered grabbed his jeans and pulled them on. He had to get out of here, now! He stuffed his clothes in his backpack and put on his—

The light flicked on. "Where you been?"

Jered's heart slammed into his spine. Jinko stood in the doorway. He strolled in, his hands in his pockets.

"I went to a park. I was just sitting. Thinking."

Jinko headed toward the shelf, stalking it. "Good thing, thinking." He met Jered's eyes. "What were you thinking about?"

Jered let his eyes flit to the shelf and back. "I...I was thinking that I need to tell you something. Confess something."

Jinko stopped walking and faced him. He clasped his hands in front of him, with a sarcastic smile on his face. "Confession is good for the soul. Or so I've heard."

Jered dug his hand into the pocket of his jeans and pulled out three bills. He plucked the twenty. He held it out to Jinko but didn't move closer. "Here. This is yours."

Jinko put a hand to his chest. "Mine? For what?"

Just spill it. "For the Palm-thingy the tall guy took. He gave it to me to give to you."

For the first time Jinko looked at the shelf, then back to Jered. "PDAs are fifty, not twenty."

Jered looked at the bill. "Oh. Sorry. I didn't know."

"I guess you owe me thirty, don't you?"

Sure. Anything. Jered retrieved one of the fifties and gave it to him instead of the twenty. "Here. All paid up."

Jinko smoothed the bill, then folded it in half so it fit in his shirt pocket. "I guess we are. For now."

Jered's chest heaved. "Good. Good."

Jinko headed for the door. "Don't do that again, kid." He swung around. *"Comprendé?"*

Oh yeah. Jered *comprendéd* all right. Completely.

Annie opened her eyes. It couldn't be morning already.

It wasn't. The clock read 3:16. Wasn't that the same time she'd awakened yesterday morning when she'd gotten up to read the Bible?

The Bible!

She'd forgotten all about it. And Cal had thrown it away!

He told you no more middle-of-the-night Bible reading.

She suddenly felt sad. And mad. She looked at her sleeping husband, and her stomach stitched anew at the thought of him with another woman. She had the sudden urge to flail at him, wake him up, make him prove her wrong, make him pay for putting her in this position. She didn't want to even think about giving up God for Cal. She liked her Bible study. She liked church. She liked reading the—

You have no choice. Get things back to normal and then think about it.

Her marriage had to come first. God would understand. So if Cal said no more Bible-reading, there could be no more...

She wouldn't read it. She'd just get it. Rescue it. Leaving it in the garbage wasn't right.

She got out of bed and went downstairs. She slipped on her loafers sitting by the back door and was within a split second of flipping on the back porch light when she realized the light could be seen from the master bedroom. She hoped the moonlight would be enough.

Annie carefully turned the doorknob. When the door creaked she cringed. Why hadn't she noticed that it creaked before?

You weren't sneaking before.

She tiptoed outside, only tapping the door to its jamb so the cold air wouldn't rush in. They had two garbage cans. Which one? She lifted the lid of the first, angling her body so moonlight fell inside. A kitchen garbage sack lay neatly on its side, encompassing the can edge to edge. Had Cal shoved the Bible deep into the can? She'd only dig if she had to.

She opened the second can. No nice, neat sack. Newspapers and torn envelopes, a plastic jug that smelled of sour milk, and an empty Honey Nut Cheerios box. She'd have to dig.

Her fingers hit leather. The Bible had slid vertically, along the side. She pulled it out. The orange juice soaked napkin-message was nearby.

Thank You!

She replaced the lid and retraced her steps inside. She stood in the kitchen and rubbed a hand against its cover. A wave of wistfulness rolled over her. She was just getting into the Word. And now to have to set it aside...

But God held marriage sacred. If going to church and reading the Bible was breaking up their marriage, certainly He wouldn't want that. Certainly He'd understand.

Where should she put it? She needed a new hiding place where Cal would never look. A place where it would be safe.

Her eyes strayed upward. She knew the perfect place. But to get it there she'd have to be careful.

Annie went into the front room and grabbed a copy of *Good Housekeeping*. She slipped the pocket Bible inside and carried it in the crook of her arm. If Cal woke and stopped her...

She tiptoed into the bedroom, then into their walk-in closet. Her heart beat double-time, and her breathing nearly stopped in her quest to be quiet. She knelt beneath her pole of dresses and parted them, revealing the door to Avi's cubby. She opened it and quickly dropped the Bible inside, easing it between the wall and one of the oversized pillows that covered the floor. She shut the door, grateful it made no click.

"Annie?" Cal's voice was thick with sleep.

"I'm here."

"Come back to bed."

She gathered her nerves, stood, shoved the magazine under a pile of sweaters, and grabbed the top one. She exited the closet, pulling it over her head. "I felt chilled."

It was the truth. In more ways than one.

Eight

> *For God will bring every deed into judgment,*
> *including every hidden thing, whether it is good or evil.*

ECCLESIASTES 12:14

CAL HEADED FOR HIS TRUCK. He had a meeting with Bailey about the new restaurant.

As he passed the garbage cans next to the driveway, he remembered Annie's Bible and immediately thought of the previous day when he'd taken Avi to the park and Annie had been so pouty. She'd had plenty of time to retrieve it.

She wouldn't dare.

He put his hand on the lid, wanting but not wanting to look. He looked.

It was gone.

His heart pumped double-time. This was a pure act of defiance on her part. He'd said no. He'd forbidden her to read it. He'd ordered her to let go of her ridiculous God-obsession.

Forbidden? Ordered?

He put the lid back on and rubbed the space between his eyes. Those weren't words he and Annie used in their marriage. They had a good relationship. Sure, they could snipe at each other like two crows going after the same piece of food, but love was always present. Somewhere. Hiding sometimes. But still around. Also present was a certain degree of tolerance.

But words like *forbidden* and *ordered* had come up in his life before. Big-time. Eleven years previous they had been hurled at him by two supposedly Christian people. His entire pre-Annie life had been ruined by those two words.

It's God's fault.

Yes indeed, that was the bottom line. Cal had witnessed firsthand what happened when God got hold of people. He wasn't about to let it happen again.

Not with his family.

Annie braced herself. She'd just poured another cup of coffee when she heard the lid of the garbage can being set into place. She looked out the kitchen window. Cal stood by the cans, rubbing the space between his eyes. She fumbled her mug to the counter. *He knows I took it back!*

Hot coffee splashed on the front of her café uniform, but she pushed that fact into the back of her mind for the moment. She studied her husband's face. He was staring into space, his eyebrows nearly touching, a familiar look that indicated deep thought. What was he thinking?

He told me no more Bible. And he thinks I defied him. He doesn't know that I chose him. I chose him!

She suddenly wanted to be at work. Away. Anywhere but here, so close to Cal and this conflict that any second he could storm in and have it out with her. She didn't want another confrontation about the Bible. The Bible was a good thing. It was a God-thing. But it wasn't going to be an issue between them anymore.

Annie was tired of having issues: God—no God; another woman—no other woman. A simple life. That's what they needed to recapture. No surprises. No big stresses. Let their arguments be over Annie's penchant for being a clutter bug, or Cal's habit of shoving his dirty dishes under the couch. She could handle that. *That* was doable.

And yes, she knew she *could* improve in the wife department. The effort would be worth it. If she tried real hard...

It was a question of loyalty. She wanted Cal to choose her over anything and everything, just like she'd rechosen him.

Over God?

She emptied the rest of her coffee into the sink. Annie didn't see that she had much choice. It was the only way to make their life good again. Yet undoing the last few months wouldn't be easy. Where *should* she begin?

She got a reprieve when he got in his truck and drove away.

"What's got into you, boy? You getting paid by the dish?"

Jered looked up from the dishes to see Bonnie watching him. "I wish."

"Then take it down a notch. You're making the rest of us look bad."

Jered nodded but couldn't follow her advice. Not after getting caught stealing from Jinko. He *had* to work extra hard to prove to Jinko that he was worth having around. Jered couldn't lose this job. He couldn't lose his place in Jinko's garage. He couldn't lose Jinko's trust.

Jered looked around the restaurant kitchen. A lot of good the extra effort was doing him. He hadn't seen Jinko since he came in. Maybe it would have been smarter to hold off working so hard until he had an audience. Or maybe Bonnie would tell Jinko? He doubted it. Bonnie was nice, but she didn't seem the type to do people any favors. She did her job and went home. Period.

Vasylko called across the kitchen. "Hey, Jered. What you be Friday?"

"What?"

"Halloween. Jinko wants us dress for big day."

"You mean dress up?"

"Up. Yes. Dress up. Costumes."

"But we're back in the kitchen. No one sees us."

"On that night they do. Jinko like Halloween. He has big party—you see ads in paper?"

"I don't read the paper."

The cook shook a spatula at him. "Shame. Shame. You should read news."

The rest of the world could have been under attack by aliens, and Jered wouldn't know it. He hadn't seen a newspaper or even watched TV since he left home. "I'm not going to dress up."

"Why not?"

"I can't afford a costume."

"No worry. Jinko pay."

"For all of us?"

"Like I say, Jinko like Halloween. I am Elvis." He struck a pose. "Viva Las Vegas!"

I want to be Elvis. "What do I get to be?"

"Don't know. Ask Jinko."

He would. If he ever saw him. And had a surge of courage.

"Annie!" Donald pointed a spatula at her. "Rein yourself in, woman, or you'll be breaking my dishes—and paying for every one of them."

"Sorry." Annie was in a slam-bam mood and had been ever since she'd come to work. She couldn't do anything subtly. Every movement had an overdose of power behind it. As if she was mad. And she was. At Cal *and* herself. In a way, they'd both been unfaithful, straying from the home base of their relationship, changing the rules. But no more. She'd made a decision that was going to help her marriage.

Shouldn't she feel calm?

She brought Merry a bowl of vegetable soup, grabbing a tray of crackers on the way. When she set it down, it sloshed over the side of the bowl.

"Sorry." She wiped up the spill. "That seems to be my word of the day."

"So I've witnessed," Merry said. "What's up? I came in for lunch to give you support." She lowered her voice. "Did you talk to Cal about his trip to…?" She let her eyebrows finish the sentence.

Annie glanced around. No eyes were on her. "No. But I expect the worst."

Merry shook her head. "I'm so sorry."

She shrugged. "I guess I also hope for the best. I hope I'm wrong. Yet looking back on the past few months, Cal has been doing quite a few 'errands' in Eldora. I'm not sure I can blame him." She gave Merry another napkin. "I won't be coming to church with you again, Merry."

"Why not?"

"I can't let God break up my family."

"Order up!"

Annie left to get the food.

"Annie..."

She ignored her friend's voice. She didn't want Merry to argue with her. She couldn't let anything sway her from her new course.

She brought the burger platters to the couple in the corner. When she headed back to the counter, she pulled up short when Bailey and Cal came into the Plentiful.

Cal didn't even say hello but merely nodded at her. He took it upon himself to sit at a table for two in the corner.

Probably mad about the Bible being gone. *Oh, dear.*

She grabbed menus and headed toward them. She handed one to her husband and touched his shoulder. "Hey, hon."

He didn't look up. "Hey."

Then she gave a menu to Bailey, and her tension let loose. "Well now, Bailey. Isn't this a surprise? Since when do you go in for—what did you call it? 'Home cooking and no atmosphere' twice? In less than two weeks no less."

"Good morning to you too, Annie."

Behave yourself, Annie! You're trying to ease things over with Cal, not rile him more. She remembered to smile. Kind of. "What'll it be, gentlemen?"

Cal handed the menu back. "The usual for me."

Bailey perused the food choices with a look that said it was not a pleasant experience. She felt like ripping the menu from his hands. "Bailey? How about some nice fried gizzards, extra fat, gravy, and salt?"

He made a face and handed her the menu. "A chef's salad. House dressing on the side."

How boring of you.

She stood before them, waiting for Cal to say something. Anything. But he just played with the salt and pepper shakers.

"Okay then." She did a pivot and left.

Why was marriage so complicated?

❧   ❧   ❧

"You two have a fight or something?" Bailey asked.

Cal figured he might as well just say it. "It seems my wife has found God."

Bailey shook his head. "Uh-oh. Now you're in for it. There's nothing worse for a relationship than Jesus getting between a man and a woman."

"You have experience with this?"

Bailey shrugged. "After Sim and Claire came to town and hid out in the library attic, Merry got into the God-stuff."

"I didn't know. Is she fanatic about it?"

"Not really. But let me warn you, it's pretty hard for a guy like you and me to compete with the perfection of the J-man."

Don't I know it. "I take it you're not religious."

"If that means going to church, no. I believe God exists and all that, but from experience I also know He has a sick sense of humor."

"How so?"

"The whole Jered fiasco. I have a heart attack and need my son, and he ends up running away. I need and God takes."

"Been there, done that."

"Oh, really."

Cal bit his lower lip. He was way too close to telling Bailey about Treena. He hadn't even told Annie about Treena.

"Care to elaborate?" Bailey asked.

"Let's just say I've dabbled in the God-thing but decided to go it alone. It's easier to trust myself than to trust somebody I can't see and who might not exist."

"Whoo. You did have a bad experience, didn't you?"

Cal shoved the salt and pepper back where they belonged.

"Well, maybe you don't have to worry. It doesn't sound like God's dug real deep in Annie's life."

"Why do you say that?"

"She's acting as sarcastic as ever. God usually makes women gushy." His voice changed to a falsetto. "Don't you know that God loves you, Bailey? He has a plan for your life; I just know it." His voice went back to normal. "And they are more than willing to be a part of dictating that plan according to what they want. Nope, no sir. I'm not going to change my life for anyone. I'm fine right where I am. You and I are smart men, Cal. We have things under control. We don't need God."

"Amen to that."

No wonder Cal felt he could confide in Bailey. They were soul mates.

"You're not eating. You don't like the soup?" Annie asked Merry.

Merry shook her head and pushed the bowl away. "I've lost my appetite."

Annie changed her weight to the other foot, preparing herself. "Just say it. I'm not in the mood for beating around any bushes."

Merry wiped a drip of soup with a napkin. "I'm worried about you. You and Cal. Your marriage and... Surely you didn't mean it when you said you weren't coming back to church."

Annie looked at Cal, sitting in the corner. He glanced at her, then away. If only Bailey weren't with him, she would slip into the chair across from Cal and explain why she saved the Bible from the trash. It didn't mean she'd chosen against him; it was just an act of respect. It didn't mean she would read it.

Merry was talking. "...ignore all that has happened to you. I was with you at the Praise Show. I was there when you gave your life to Jesus. I was a witness. I saw the passion and light in your expression. It was real, Annie. And all your growth since then was real. You were changing and it—"

"Yes, I was changing. Changing too much. Changing so much that my marriage was threatened." She tapped the edge of Merry's table for emphasis. "God loves marriage. He wants it to be a strong institution. I can't lose Cal. Not for anybody. Not even for God."

"Order up!"

She left to do her duty, feeling Merry's eyes on her back.

Annie and Cal didn't have time to argue that night. Avi had a soccer game, and Cal was the coach. They celebrated the victory by going to the Dairy Sweet for hot fudge sundaes, and then Annie was consumed with laundry and helping Avi with her model of a Mayan temple for school. Cal spent time at the computer.

Time ran out to discuss anything, which in a way was fine. It had been a long day. Annie wasn't up to it.

It was exhausting being in the middle. God and Cal would have to stake their claims on her heart later. Right now she had chores to do.

Cal stared at the computer screen. Their savings account was pitiful: $1718. If not for the $1583 he'd deposited from the overpayment by the insurance company they'd have $135. Why couldn't they ever put anything away? It's not as if they were extravagant people. Yet, he *had* bought that new TV last spring...

Oh, well, he couldn't go back. And nobody but nobody watched TV on a twenty-seven-incher anymore. Couldn't a fellow have any luxuries? Didn't he deserve a few trappings of the good life?

But the timing was bad. He'd bought the TV before his father's health had turned, before Cal had been forced to take on the expense of a nursing home.

He thought about the ten-thousand-dollar inheritance Annie had received from her mother's estate. Why had he mentioned it to Bailey as money he could invest? Only five thousand was left in a CD. They'd had to use the rest to fix the furnace, Annie's car had needed new tires, then they'd paid off the previous year's Christmas bills. Whatever the details, half was gone, and more important, they'd agreed not to spend the rest but save it.

He looked at the window in front of him. It was whistling because it wouldn't close all the way. If he wanted to use their savings, he should put it toward replacing all the windows with thermal panes. Winter would be here soon, and the single panes were no match for the cold and wind.

He should *not* use the money to invest in Bailey's restaurant.

But the opportunity...

Cal hated being middle-class. Mediocre, can't-wait-for-the-pay-check middle-class.

Sweat equity. That's all he could offer Bailey. Can't get more middle-class than that. Sweat so the rich don't have to.

Cal couldn't imagine Bailey sweating. Or getting his fingernails dirty. How many times had he seen him pinch a piece of lint from his pants, or adjust the cuffs of his shirt below the sleeves of his sports coat?

Sports coat. Who in Steadfast wore suits or sports coats? Maybe George the banker, but other than that, you just didn't do it. Not unless you wanted to be set apart. Which, Cal realized, was exactly what Bailey wanted.

I could use a little setting apart myself.

No, he didn't want to wear suits or be worried if dust was on the toes of his shoes, but Cal wouldn't mind if people thought of him as something more than a handyman. Bailey called him a "building contractor." That was more like it. It was sure better than being known as a construction worker or, as Avi called anyone working with their hands, a "worker man."

His father had a lesser way of looking at his profession. "You still doing grunt work, Cal?" It didn't matter that it was his own business, that he had a steady stream of work. Pretty steady anyway.

He shut the computer off. What was the use? A grunt-work worker man. That's what he was, no matter how much money he pretended he had.

"Well, well."

Jered looked up from stocking the pantry shelves to find Jinko watching him. Noticing him. *Finally!*

He flattened a box that had held cans of refried beans. "Hi."

Jinko scanned the shelves. "Nice work. Vasylko says you've been working extra hard today."

Jered wished he could think of some excuse that didn't sound like he was trying to earn brownie points.

Jinko leaned against the counter and crossed his arms. "Feeling a bit guilty, are we?"

Jered adjusted a stack of cans. *Why can't I think of anything to say?*

Jinko pushed himself to standing. "Hey, I don't need to know your motives. I'm glad to get the work done." He put a hand on Jered's shoulder and looked him straight in the eyes. "And I reward loyalty. You know that, don't you?"

Jered was counting on it.

Jered sat at a back table and ate a plate of cheese enchiladas for his dinner break. Mondays weren't busy, but there was still a steady stream of customers.

He watched Jinko work the room. That man could talk to anybody and always found the right thing to say, treating all the customers like his best friends.

Jered had seen his dad do the dining-room shuffle at Bon Vivant, so he knew it was part of the job. But the way the two men handled the same job was... Jered ate some chips and tried to pinpoint the difference.

For one thing, the clothes. His dad's fancy suits versus Jinko's solid-colored shirts and pants—always dark: all navy, all black, all gray—went with the territory. If either man traded clothing, they wouldn't fit in. But it went beyond clothes.

He heard Jinko's deep laugh and watched him pat a customer on the back, lean forward to whisper in his ear, and laugh some more. The image Jered had of his dad talking to diners was of him standing at the head of their table, his hands clasped in front, his back straight. Like a snooty maître d'. Bailey Manson kept himself separate—as a restaurant owner and as a father. That was it. Jinko made contact. He connected with the customers and made them feel special, drawing people in.

Drawing me in. Jered suffered a shiver but didn't let himself think about why. He cut a huge bite of enchilada and shoved it in his mouth, chewing it along with his thoughts. There was another difference between his dad and Jinko. His dad was safe. Boring. Set in his ways. Blind to anything outside his immediate vision. He was an immovable force that couldn't—and wouldn't—be changed. Jinko was full of life, pulsing with it, shifting around as needed, always on the lookout for a new opportunity. A new opening. His eyes constantly scanned the room like he was trying to take it captive.

He noticed Jered watching him and winked.

See? He notices me. He appreciates me. He likes me.

Jered hurried to finish his dinner. He needed to get back to work. He didn't want to disappoint Jinko.

A few minutes later, as Jered stacked plates, he noticed Jinko leave the back way, slipping out without a word. It wasn't the first time he'd seen him disappear during the height of the evening. He always came back after a half hour or so, but it seemed weird.

Maybe he's just going out for a smoke. After all, that is *how we first met.*

Jered's curiosity got the best of him. He slipped out the back in time to see Jinko's taillights as he drove away. Where was he going?

Jered went back inside.

"In. Out. What you doing?" Vasylko asked.

Jered moved close. He didn't want the servers to hear. "Where does Jinko go?"

Vasylko nodded. "Ah. His slip-outs."

"Yeah. He does it a lot."

Vasylko dropped a chimichanga in a vat of hot oil. It sizzled violently. "Why don't you ask him?"

Jered shook his head. "It's none of my business."

"But you want to know, yes?"

Jered shrugged. He shouldn't have brought it up. He went back to the dishes.

Vasylko called after him. "You find out, you tell me, eh?"

Jered wouldn't promise a thing.

As usual, Jered got back to the house first after work. He was just turning out the light to go to sleep when he heard Jinko's car pull in. He moved to the window on the door and looked out. Jinko parked, then popped the trunk. He removed a huge crystal vase and a canvas bag. As he used his elbow to close the trunk he looked in Jered's direction.

Jered stepped away from the window. He closed his eyes then yelled at himself. Why was he acting guilty? He wasn't doing anything wrong looking out his own window.

You're not doing anything wrong, but...

There was a knock on his door. It was Jinko, still holding the vase and bag. "Come inside."

"I was just going to bed."

"Come inside."

Jered followed Jinko into the house. Jinko tossed his keys on the kitchen counter and set the vase and bag on the table. He turned the vase, admiring it. "Nice, isn't it?"

"I like the design stuff."

Jinko laughed. "That design stuff is hand cut with a diamond-tipped cutting wheel. This is Waterford."

"So?"

"It's the finest crystal in the world. Irish. This piece is probably worth eight hundred to a thousand dollars."

"You're kidding."

Jinko ran a finger along the vase's scalloped edge. "I don't kid about quality, kid."

"Where'd you get it?"

Jinko didn't even look up. "I stole it."

Jered coughed.

Jinko smiled. "Want to see what else I got?"

He was so casual about it. "Sure."

Jinko opened the canvas bag and pulled out a silver bowl, a glass ashtray, a glass paperweight with a blue flower in it, and a strange wood sculpture that didn't look like much of anything. He held the wood thing a moment. "This isn't worth anything, but I liked it." He looked at Jered. "So I took it."

"From where?"

"The place I robbed."

Jered swallowed. "You make it sound so easy."

He picked up the vase, caressing it. "Oh, it is, kid. You just need to have a system." He eyed Jered. "You want to hear mine?"

Not really.

Jinko smiled. "Course, if I tell you, I'll have to kill you."

Jered retreated a step. Jinko laughed and pulled him back to the table of loot, an arm around his shoulders. "Don't be so gullible. I wouldn't be showing or telling you all this if I didn't trust you. You're my loyal employee, right?"

"Yeah."

"Yes, Jered. Say yes. Yeah makes you sound stupid."

"Okay. I mean, yes."

"Better." He pulled out a chair. "Have a seat and listen to a master."

Jered took a seat opposite his boss, as far from the stolen goods as possible.

Jinko set the vase close. His hand continued to stroke it as he talked. "The key is to only take what people won't miss."

"How do you do that?"

"We are a people of possessions, kid. We don't just have one vase; we have six. We don't have one piece of silver; we have a dozen. We may have one on display, but the rest is stored in buffets, in closets, in drawers. I merely take what's out of sight. Out of sight, out of mind—until they look for it. By then, when they find the stuff gone, it's too late to ever figure out when they last saw it. There's no way to catch the evil thief then."

"How do you get in?"

Jinko shrugged. "I open the door. People don't lock their doors around here. Or if they do, a key's usually hidden close by." He pointed at Jered. "Point number two is not to push it. If I can't get in quickly, or if there's an alarm system, I walk away. I'm not that desperate."

Actually, the only reason Jered could imagine stealing was if he were desperate. Or hungry. "When do you do this?"

"During the evening when the owners are eating at Palamba's."

"Huh?"

Jinko sighed. "You really have to work on your vocabulary, kid." He spread his hands on the table. They were big hands. Powerful hands. "You've seen me chat with the customers, haven't you? Like tonight when I caught you watching me."

Jered didn't like the word *caught*. "I was eating dinner."

"And watching me. Don't deny it." Jered shrugged and Jinko continued. "I have a loyal customer base. I get to know them, know their names and what they do for a living. I hear about their vacations and their hobbies. Do they play golf every Saturday? Are they going to Bermuda next week?" He pointed to his eyes, then his ears. "Look and listen, kid. That's the essence of everything. People are aching, practically begging to spill their story. You just need to provide a willing ear. And brag?" He laughed. "I hear all about their promotions and their newest toys. And though I may not choose to steal the items they mention, I can make a pretty good guess about the other types of goodies they have in their homes."

Jered was figuring it out. "So when you slip out during the busy times?"

"I'm taking a quick trip to their houses and helping myself. In, out, done. Back in time to ask them how they enjoyed their meal."

Slick. "What do you do with all this stuff? I mean, won't people see it and recognize it?"

"Though we may be buddy-buddy during a meal, we don't run in the same circles." He relaxed in the chair. "And I'll just have to make sure I don't invite them over for dinner, won't I?"

"But what if a friend of a friend—?"

"It's covered, kid. Don't worry about it. And what I don't keep, I sell in KC for cash to buy my own baubles." He pushed the vase to the side and leaned over the table. Jered could see the pores in his nose. "Listen close now. The key to everything is image. I've made a lot of effort creating a certain image for myself." He swept a hand over his meticulous house. "Does this look like the house of a thief or the house of a successful man?"

A successful thief.

Jinko leaned back and slapped one hand on the table. "So. What do you think?"

"I...I think you have it down."

"That I do. I take that as a compliment. But the big question is, what are you going to do?"

"Me? Do?"

"About the knowledge I've just given you. Knowledge is power, kid, and I've just given you enough power to put me away for good."

"Oh, but I wouldn't—"

Jinko raised an eyebrow. "Wouldn't you? Wouldn't you turn me in and rid Eldora of an awful criminal?"

"I don't think of you as a criminal."

"That's what I am."

Jered was confused. "I don't know what you want me to say."

"I don't want you to *say* anything."

"Then I don't know what you want me to do."

Jinko flipped a hand as if they were discussing which movie to watch. "The only thing I want you to do is make a choice. Either you're for me or against me."

Jered jumped in. "I'm not against you, Jinko. Not at all. You've helped me. Tons."

"I saw potential in you, kid. I don't help just anybody. So are you in?"

His stomach flipped. "In?"

"In for a piece of the action?"

Jered shook his head. "Why do you need me? You've been doing fine on your own and—"

Jinko's face clouded. "I don't need you, kid. I'm doing you a favor. I'm being a mentor to a homeless kid who doesn't know his foot from his elbow. You stick with me, and I'll take you places."

"What kind of places?"

Jinko snickered. "You do have the questions, don't you?"

"I just want to know."

"Nothing wrong in that." He stroked his goatee. "Here's the deal. You help me out on a few projects, and I'll get you hooked up with a music producer."

It sounded great, but... "I did awful during Amateur Night."

"A fluke. I'm sure you can do better. With the proper coaching. With the proper management. With my help."

A coach, manager, help. How could Jered say no?

Jered set the glass paperweight with the blue flower on the box next to his bed. A present from Jinko. It was pretty. And heavy. Pretty heavy.

Pretty heavy stuff. That's what he was into now.

He turned over and tried to sleep.

Annie woke up, wide awake. She held her breath a moment to see if any sound had awakened her. The furnace hummed. Cal snored.

She turned over to go back to sleep.

She saw the clock. 3:16.

Again? How odd.

As she drifted back to sleep, she let a prayer escape. *Is this You, God?*

He didn't answer.

She was relieved.

Nine

Blessed is the man who makes the LORD his trust,
who does not look to the proud,
to those who turn aside to false gods.

PSALM 40:4

"I'VE GOT A QUESTION for you, Annie."

"Oh?" Annie put the phone in the crook of her neck as she made Avi a PB and J sandwich for her lunch box. She hoped Merry wasn't going to make her feel guilty about her decision to put her marriage first. It had been three days since she'd made the decision, and she was getting used to it, though it wasn't easy.

Every time Cal said he was going on errands, it took all of her will not to jump on him. Confront him. Yet to bring her suspicions about his infidelity out in the open would be a threat to their marriage. It was safer to do everything she could to make it just go away. If that was considered being chicken, so be it.

"How would you like to come to choir practice with me tonight?" Merry asked.

I'd love to collided with *I can't.*

Merry jumped in. "Don't worry if you're not a great singer. Great singers do not exist in the Steadfast Community Church choir—except for Maury Davidson. He'll be the first to tell you that."

Annie couldn't remember the last time she'd sung in a group that consisted of more than her and Avi singing to the car radio. "I *can* read music."

"Then you have one up on most of our tenor section. They are big into doing their own thing."

"How can that work in a choir?"

"It can't. Which might hint at the quality of our vocal offerings. But what we lack in expertise, we make up for in heart and soul. And volume."

It sounded wonderful. "I'd love to—" Then reality returned. "I can't."

"Sure you can."

"Cal will never go for it."

A moment of silence hung between them. Then Merry added, "My selfish impulse is to tell you to lie about where you're going, but that wouldn't be setting a very good example, would it?"

"Probably not."

"Could you ask him? We're just starting to work on our Christmas music. I'm sure you can fa-la-la with the best of us. Maybe you could appeal to his holiday spirit."

"Hmm."

"Think about it, okay? Seven-thirty. We need you—and you need us, Annie. It's not a huge commitment. Just singing with some friends. Okay?"

"We'll see." Annie hung up. She couldn't imagine Cal thinking of any church people as "friends." There was something seriously wrong with that.

Oh, dear. She would love to sing in the choir. But her resolve not to push Cal's God-button...

Merry's words repeated in her head: *"Appeal to his holiday spirit."*

Cal loved Christmas. She'd even heard him hum a few Christmas carols. Why should he object if she wanted to sing a few herself?

Choir was a possibility. If she handled it right.

Merry hung up the phone and closed her eyes. "Lord, please let Annie come to choir. It would be a way for her to reconnect. She's turning her back on You and on everything that has happened to her faith these past few months. She thinks it's a choice between her marriage and You, and it isn't."

She suddenly opened her eyes. "Is it?"

Merry prayed for a very long time.

❦   ❦   ❦

Jered was just getting out of the shower when Jinko knocked on the bathroom door. "I'll be done in a minute."

"Hurry up, kid. I've got something for you."

Another present? Jinko was one of the most generous people Jered had ever met. He put on some clothes and opened the door. Jinko stood in the hall holding a huge brown box.

"UPS just delivered it."

"What is it?"

"Your costume for tomorrow night."

"You bought me a costume?"

"Everybody dresses up—on me. I'm gaining quite a collection. Come on, I'll show you."

They went to the living room, and Jered opened the box. He wasn't sure what he expected—or was hoping for—but he had to admit he was disappointed. It was brown. And blah. And had a rope for a belt. "It's a monk's outfit."

"Robe."

Whatever.

"You look disappointed. Hoping to be a dashing pirate or a Confederate general or something?"

Jered felt himself redden. He smiled. "Well, yeah. Yes." He felt petty but had to say it. "Vasylko said he was going to be Elvis."

Jinko nodded. "Ah. The singer wanted to be a singer."

"It fits better than having me be a monk."

Jinko took the nubby brown costume out of the box and held it up to him. "Costumes either enhance what we are or let us explore a whole new identity. Or..." He retrieved a shopping bag that had been sitting beside the couch. "A costume can be functional, and in our case, hide what needs to be hidden."

What *was* he talking about?

Jinko gave him the bag. "You'll wear this underneath the robe."

The shopping bag was from a local discount store. Inside were a pair of black jeans, a long-sleeved black T-shirt, and a pair of black rubber-soled shoes.

"I see a theme here. You trying to make me your clone?"

"You wish. I'm supplying you with the proper attire for a real-life identity. Your new identity. A burglar."

A breath caught in Jered's throat. It wasn't that he didn't understand what they'd been talking about. He did. But to hear it put so bluntly...

Jinko spread the clothes neatly on the couch. "You wear your new duds under the monk's costume. I, myself, will be dressed similarly under my bright white-and-gold sheikh's costume."

"I've never seen you in anything but dark colors."

"Did you actually think my monochromatic style was a fashion statement? Dark is the color of night, kid. If I wore a white shirt, or one of those pastel golf numbers, I'd be seen." He pointed a finger. "You choose your moments to be seen. And I'll be seen tomorrow night. There. In the restaurant, playing the regal host. I'll be my most affable and charming—until the costume contest at midnight.

"I've hired a local DJ, Roxie Robins, to emcee the event. Being the exhibitionist she is, Roxie's sure to wear something skimpy, guaranteeing that all eyes will be on her during the contest."

"I've heard her. She's crazy."

"As a fox. As are we, kid. Because by midnight all the little trick-or-treating ghouls and goblins will be safely tucked into bed, passed out from an overdose of sugar. You and I will slip out, remove our costumes, drive your truck to our desired location, and get to work."

"My truck?"

"I'd rather not take a chance my car is seen. Not this time."

"But—"

"Which reminds me..." He pulled out a wad of bills and gave Jered a handful. "Go over to Skinner Auto and get your muffler fixed. Today. Tell them I sent you and it's a rush job. You need it done by tomorrow morning."

Jered got the connection. "It's too noisy?"

"Letting the world hear you coming and going when you're a punk kid is one thing. But when you're a burglar..."

"Quiet is king."

"You got it." Jinko put the rest of the money away. "Any questions?"

Only a million or so. "It sounds like you're going after something specific this time. What is it?"

"Coins, kid. A pricey bunch of coins. Good ol' Ed Cooperton just can't keep his mouth shut about them. Seems some rich uncle died and left him a bunch. I'm particularly interested in the Morgan halves."

"You know about coins?"

"Knowledge is power. Do a little research, gain a lot of money. Coins are easily sold. Got a dealer in KC that's aching for more. When Ed started bragging, I started planning."

"Can I see some of your coins?"

"*I* don't have any coins. I'm not a coin collector. I'm a coin seller."

The next popped out without warning. "Coin stealer."

Jinko shrugged. "First the one, then the other."

Jered's stomach began to churn. "Do you know where he keeps the coins in the house?"

"Of course."

"Is the house going to be unlocked?"

Jinko laughed. "My little detail man. Yes, kid. The house should be unlocked. Unless Ed's gotten smart in the past month—which I doubt." He carefully folded the monk's costume into its box. "Enough talk. Do what I told you to do. Tomorrow's a busy day."

As soon as Jinko left, Jered gathered the clothes and went out to the garage. He checked the sizes of his new black clothes. They should fit perfectly. Jinko was really something.

He put them on a shelf and took out the monk's robe. He'd wanted to be a singer. How about a few Gregorian chants? He slipped the robe over his head and tied the belt. He deepened his voice and sang a monkish, "Aaaahhhhmen."

He smiled at the effect in the garage. Funny how putting on a simple costume made him feel different.

His favorite Halloween costume of all time was when he was five or six and he'd been a cowboy—a singing cowboy like Gene Autry and Roy Rogers. He'd seen old reruns of their movies and loved every one. He'd had a vest with fringe on it, cowboy boots, a cowboy hat, and even a plastic guitar that played music if you turned a crank. His dad had wanted him to wear a holster, but he wasn't that kind of cowboy. He was a crooner, not a fighter.

And now I am a...a what?

The answer to that question was yet to be determined. He took the costume off.

Why didn't life ever turn out like he planned?

Cal provided the perfect opening for Annie to ask about choir. When he came in the kitchen door after work, he kissed her and asked, "What's up tonight?"

Now that you mention it... "Do *you* have any plans?"

He eyed her funny. "I asked you first."

Annie stirred the goulash. "I was thinking of going somewhere with Merry."

"Where?"

She hesitated, really wanting to lie. "Choir. They're starting to work on their Christmas music and..." The words poured out. Maybe if she kept them coming, he wouldn't be able to insert the *N*-word.

Her string of words didn't stop him. "No."

A glob of goulash fell from the spoon back into the pan. "I like to sing, Cal."

"Since when?"

"It's for Christmas. You like Christmas music."

He went through the mail on the counter, sorting it. "You're getting way too involved with Merry. She's a bad influence."

That didn't make sense. "Oh, yeah, she's a real bad influence. She drags me to bars, makes me stay out late, tempts me to flirt with every man I—"

His head whipped toward her. "She what?"

Annie hated herself for mentioning any sort of infidelity. "If she did any of those things, you could call her a bad influence. But since she doesn't, you can't say that about her." *But can I say those things about you?*

Cal flipped the pages of a new *Woodworking* magazine. "She's filling your head with nonsense. God nonsense." He turned to glare at her. "Where'd you put the Bible?"

She'd anticipated the question but had never come up with a good answer—and didn't come up with a good answer now. "It didn't belong in the garbage."

He slapped the magazine closed. "Better there than in this house."

Annie stared at him. His chest was heaving. How could a Bible threaten him so? The question surprised her by finding a voice. "What's going on, Cal? Why are you so afraid of a book?"

He turned back to the mail, tossing the junk in the trash. "I don't trust God. It's as simple as that."

Annie didn't know what to do. "What happened that made you so angry with Him?"

Cal's head shook back and forth, almost as if convincing himself that he shouldn't say more. But he did. Sort of. "I'm not afraid of anything. I'm not."

"I envy you."

He glanced at her. "What are you afraid of?"

She looked at the pot of goulash. To put it into words...

"Just tell me." His voice was suddenly soft. She always melted to that voice.

She put the spoon down and faced him. *I'm afraid I've lost you to a woman in Eldora.* She bypassed that fear and voiced another. "I'm afraid your partnership with Bailey is going to change things, change—"

His eyes brightened and he took her hand. "Oh, it will, Annie. Bailey's good at making money, at making things work. Getting hooked up with him will mean that I'll be able to get us a bigger place, a better life."

"We have enough, Cal."

He released her hand. "What's enough?"

She didn't have an answer to that one. She took *his* hand. "I'm not so afraid of the financial aspect of your dealings with Bailey as his other influence on you."

"I have no idea what you're talking about." He pulled away and sat at the table, taking his magazine with him.

How could she ever explain women's intuition? In spite of a few outward signs, most of her distrust of Bailey stemmed from feelings. She took the catty-corner seat. "It's just a feeling I have, but—"

He snickered. "Oh, that's productive."

She tried again. "Bailey's priorities are different than ours."

"His priority is to be a success. That's mine, too."

She sat back. How could she argue with that?

He flipped through the pages, snapping each one. "I'd be stupid to close the door on the opportunity Bailey's giving me, and for you to ask me to..."

She ran a hand across her forehead, trying to press her thoughts into place. "I'm not sure he'd be a good partner, that's all. He's out for himself. He seems very selfish." She thought of something else. "When was the last time you heard him talk about his son?"

"You judge him because he isn't all blubbery or obsessed about finding Jered?"

"If Avi ran away, we'd move the world to find her—and wouldn't stop until we did."

"Avi's ten. Jered was seventeen."

"He's still his son. He still left under bad circumstances."

"That's Bailey's business, not ours."

Annie stood. "But Bailey doesn't seem to care. That says something about him. If he doesn't care about his own son, will he care about you as a business partner?"

Cal ripped an advertising card from his magazine with extra fervor and kept ripping until it was in small pieces on the table. "How did we get to talking about Bailey anyway? We were talking about you being brainwashed by Merry, reading a Bible, going to church, wanting to get sucked up in a choir."

Annie's shoulders fell. Going to choir meant going to church. What *had* she been thinking? She couldn't have it both ways.

He looked down toward the magazine, but his eyes were focused past it, into the nothingness of the bare table. "All those things take you away from me, Annie. I want us to be close. Closer. Like we used—" He covered his eyes with a hand. "I'm feeling really stressed right now. I need you, Annie. I need you here with me. Don't go."

She took his hand. What choice did she have?

Cal went into the master bathroom and shut the door. Locked it. He put the lid down on the toilet and sat. He leaned forward, resting his arms on his thighs. His hands raked through his hair, finally becoming still over his face.

Why had he acted like such a wimp in front of his wife? Why had he revealed to her the essence of his secret?

"I don't trust God."

Had he ever put it so plainly? Even in private?

He peeked through his fingers. Trust was for the ignorant. The naive. The stupid. He'd been where Annie was once. He'd felt the excitement of believing he found life's answers. Jesus was a good salesman. He knew how to entice people to buy what He was offering. And He had loads of sneaky ways to close the deal. Lots of false promises of a good life. A better life. Happiness. Contentment. Peace.

Cal let out a bitter laugh. Buying into Jesus was like buying a new car. Sure, it was great at first, all shiny new with a fresh smell that spoke of something good and important. But after a while, when the newness wore off and you got a few dings in it, and your kid spilled an entire can of strawberry pop on the upholstery, it wasn't so special after all. Just ordinary. Affected by the bings and bongs of everyday life like everything else. That's when you realized your elation driving out of the car lot that first day was a farce, all a part of the sales con that got you to invest in something that wasn't really what it seemed.

Jesus wasn't what He seemed. Not at all. Jesus was big on making the sale but not great with the follow-through. Cal was just glad he hadn't completely bought into His line. He'd been on the edge of closing the deal when the whole thing with his dad and Treena had blown up. He'd only been going to church because of her.

He would have done anything for her.

A moan escaped, and he closed his eyes tight so the tears wouldn't come. Enough of this. It didn't help. Treena was a perfect Christian, an inspiration, the one who'd brought Cal to the edge of commitment. Except for one thing, she'd done everything right. One sin his father would never forgive. Nor obviously God. Because Treena was dead. A good Christian girl was dead. Where was God in that?

Cal started at a tap on the door.

"Daddy?"

He found his voice. "Yeah?"

"Mama says dinner's ready."

"I'm coming."

Avi stared at the bathroom door. Something was wrong. Before she'd knocked on the door she heard her dad laugh. But it wasn't a nice laugh. It was the kind of laugh people did when they realized things were really dumb.

But then her daddy had moaned, and it sounded like crying. What was he laughing about—and crying about—in the bathroom?

Suddenly, the door opened. Avi took a step back. For just a moment, before her father's face raced by surprise and found normal, she saw a look she'd never seen before: fear.

What does Daddy have to be afraid of?

He yanked her hair as he walked past. "Last one down has to paint the house."

"Daddy..." He was so funny.

But she ran fast anyway.

He let her win. As usual.

Annie sat next to Cal on the couch, his arm draped behind her shoulders. They watched some sitcom Cal liked. Annie couldn't have told you if the people on the screen were the main characters or just visiting. They sure talked about sex a lot.

She looked at Avi, sitting at their feet, coloring on the coffee table. She looked back to the TV and heard reference to something she and Cal didn't even talk about in private. This was supposed to be funny?

Avi looked up from her coloring and watched the TV. The mere thought that her innocent child was witnessing such discussions far beyond her years...

She stood and ruffled Avi's hair. "Let's you and I go make some cookies."

Avi didn't hesitate and slid the orange crayon in the box.

"Hey," Cal said. "I thought we were watching TV here."

Annie couldn't get into it in front of Avi. "Go ahead. Or come join us. I'll let you eat some cookie dough."

Cal scooted deeper into the cushions. "No thanks. But I want one when they're done."

Annie thought of the Little Red Hen story where no one wanted to help bake the bread, but everyone wanted to eat it.

Avi ran on ahead. "I get to crack the eggs."

A few eggshells never hurt anyone.

As Annie took the last batch of cookies from the oven she glanced at her watch. Seven fifty-five. She could have been at choir practice now. Meeting new people. Singing wonderful Christmas songs.

If only Cal hadn't been so adamant. His reaction had surprised her, both in its intensity and in the fact that she'd never seen him react like that—about anything—before. What else didn't she know about him?

But that's ridiculous. We've been married ten years. Whatever there is to know about him, I already know.

Or did she? She certainly hadn't known he was capable of having an affair.

Forget the what-if of going to choir. She'd made a choice. She had to stick with it.

She moved the cookies from baking sheet to paper towels to cool. Nothing was more comforting than the smell of chocolate chip cookies.

Avi was whipping up a froth of suds with one of the beaters in the sink when suddenly Annie's heart pulled. She was still amazed that at such odd moments the love for her daughter would grab her unaware, as if to remind her *don't take me for granted. This love is something special.*

This child was something special.

A love child.

Not really. Avi was a child conceived out of lust. Once, Annie had lived the life so readily portrayed on the sitcoms they'd just watched on TV. College had been a time for fun—with a little education on the side. Booze and boys. Usually in combination. One led to the other.

Rick hadn't been her first, but he had been her last before Cal saved her. Why did it often take a crisis to change behavior? She still didn't understand how she'd gotten pregnant. She wasn't dumb. She took precautions. But Avi was conceived and Rick was history.

Good riddance. He was a loser with gorgeous eyes. A whim. A conquest. Annie knew it was usually men who had such a cavalier attitude. But she'd had it, too.

Funny how a person's definition of love changed as they experienced it on different levels. She'd thought she'd experienced love before she met Cal but had soon realized all other loves were tin to the shiny brass of their relationship. The fact he had loved her *and* the baby growing inside her spoke volumes to his character.

The words she'd found in the verses of 1 Corinthians came to mind. Annie didn't remember many of them, but some had stuck: *"Love is patient, love is kind."* Above all, *"Love never fails."*

She felt a sudden need to read them all. But they were in the Bible upstairs, in Avi's cubby, so she couldn't easily... Besides, she'd made her choice to let the God-stuff go.

But the verses on love might really help right now.

She wiped her hands on a towel. "You want to finish up in here, sweet-apple?"

"I like to wash dishes, Mama."

Annie kissed the back of her head. "I always knew you were weird. Have at it, little girl. I'm going upstairs for a bit."

Annie walked quietly into the living room, wanting to check on Cal's status. Thankfully, he was asleep on the couch, some cop show playing out in spite of him. She tiptoed up the stairs. She didn't like sneaking, but there was no reason to stir up what didn't need stirring.

She slipped into the master bedroom and started to close the door. But a closed door raised suspicions. Best to keep it open. She went into the closet and retrieved the Bible from Avi's cubby. Then she went into the bathroom and shut the door.

She caught her reflection in the mirror and was taken aback by it—and it had nothing to do with the fact the mirror was old and a bit wavy. She didn't need a perfect mirror to see herself clutching the Bible to her chest like it was the Holy Grail. Her eyes were so intense. She rubbed at the crease between her brows. *Lighten up, Annie. You're not getting pulled into this again. You're just checking on a few pertinent verses.*

She sat on the toilet seat and opened the Bible. The page was marked. The words spoke to her now as they had the first time she'd read them: *"Love is patient, love is kind. It does not envy, it does not boast, it is not proud. It is not rude, it is not self-seeking, it is not easily angered, it keeps no record of wrongs. Love does not delight in evil but rejoices with the truth. It always protects, always trusts, always hopes, always perseveres. Love never fails."*

Why was this kind of love so hard?

She set the Bible on the floor and moved to the sink, leaning against it. How could she love like God wanted her to love when Cal didn't want her to acknowledge the God who would help her love him better? A mouthful. It didn't make sense.

"I shouldn't *be* in this position!"

There was a tap on the door. "You say something, Annie?"

"No, Cal...uh..."

"Avi woke me to say the timer's ringing."

"I'll be out in a minute." She took a step toward the toilet and flushed it.

Then she slid the Bible into the back waistband of her pants and washed her hands. When she caught sight of her eyes in the mirror they were heavy with uncertainty.

Ten

*Now it is required
that those who have been given a trust
must prove faithful.*

1 CORINTHIANS 4:2

As MERRY UNLOCKED THE DOOR of the Steadfast library, she looked at the poster on the door with new interest. It's not as if she hadn't looked at it every day for three weeks, but today...the face of Dr. Rudy Roswold smiled back at her as if sharing an idea. "Of course!"

Blanche and Ivan stood behind her, waiting to get in—as they did every morning within minutes of opening. "Of course what?" Ivan snapped.

Merry held the door open for them but pointed to the poster. "Are you two going to hear Dr. Roswold today at the courthouse?"

"Yes," Blanche said.

"No," Ivan said.

Blanche put her hands on the shelf of her hips and glared at him. "How dare you say no, you old kumquat. You, who reads every newspaper Merry gets in? Why wouldn't you want to hear about this man's experiences in Africa?"

He hung his coat on the rack by the door. "I like to read; I don't like to listen."

"You got that right. What did I say to you last night about this very subject?"

"I wasn't listening." He headed toward the periodical section with Blanche trailing after him.

"If you don't sit with me, I'll sit with Harold..."

Merry left them to bicker it out while she went to the phone on the counter. She hoped this worked.

What did she have to lose?

Merry waited at the door to the courthouse auditorium and kept checking her watch. She'd invited Annie to the talk but had not received a definite yea or nay. Annie would "try to come."

Merry hated seeing her friend on the fence with her faith. With happiness. When Annie hadn't shown up at choir, Merry had redoubled her prayers. Then this morning, when she remembered Dr. Roswold was known in Christian circles as a godly man and an inspirational speaker beyond his humanitarian side, she knew she had to make the invitation. She wasn't expecting any specific response from Annie, but hoped if *she* remained a faithful friend, Annie would come back to her faith.

She nearly clapped when she spotted Annie coming down the wide hall but was shocked by the drawn look on her face. She'd sounded kind of blah on the phone, but Merry had chalked it up to the normal stresses of a weekday morning. But now, seeing her in person, she knew it was something more.

Annie managed a smile. "Hey."

Merry slipped a hand through her arm. "You okay?"

"Do I look that bad?"

"Actually..."

Annie looked past her, into the room. "It's about to start."

They took their seats in the same row as Blanche and Ivan. Harold had offered to watch things at the library.

Annie set her purse under her chair. "Is Ken coming?"

Merry shook her head. "He had to work." She wished they had time to talk, but it was starting.

The mayor of Steadfast took the podium and introduced Dr. Roswold. The doctor spoke of his medical mission in Angola, showing slides of patients and townspeople. Most were malnourished, and many had limbs blown off from land mines. Yet there were also pictures of a few standing next to the minimal hospital, bandages on their broken bodies, flashing wide smiles full of hope.

Hope amid total darkness.

Annie's throat tightened so she could barely swallow. These poor people. She couldn't imagine living in such conditions, in such fear. And she also couldn't imagine being a person like Dr. Roswold, giving up a life of comfort in the States, a life of money and status, a nice home and the trappings of success. He was receiving none of the perks of being a doctor. Except the biggest one: helping others.

Loving others.

Annie was suddenly overwhelmed with the limits of her ability to love. God wanted her to love everyone, yet she couldn't even... If she couldn't even love her husband properly, how could she ever hope to love others in the world? She looked to her lap and squeezed her eyes shut, trying to stop the tears.

"Annie?" Merry touched her arm.

All Annie could do was raise a hand slightly. *I'll be all right. Maybe. Someday.*

But how? It was as if she was trapped between two worlds, two loves. Two ways of life. It was as if she was in a love triangle. *Love me!* said Cal.

Love Me! said God. And *love Cal. I want you to do both.*

Annie pulled in a breath. The difference was laid out plain and clear. Cal wanted her to love him and him alone. But God wanted her to love Himself—and Cal. Surely that was the better way. The right way. Surely it was possible.

The speaker was wrapping up. "I know you may feel overwhelmed right now. There is much to be done, and the needs are great. You might think, 'Oh no. Here's where he asks for money.'" He smiled. "And you'd be right. For that is how we can help from halfway around the world. But I'm asking you for more. I'm asking you for love. For that is limitless. As Shakespeare's fair Juliet said: 'My bounty is as boundless as the sea, my love as deep; the more I give to thee, the more I have, for both are infinite.'"

Dr. Roswold leaned on the podium, drawing them close. "We are asked to love much. We love our families, our friends, our country, our God, but we need to love even more. We need to love these people we will never meet, and help and pray for them as we are able." He stood erect. "Thank you for listening."

In the brief moment before the applause started, Annie made a decision. She would love both Cal and God. She would find a way. She *had* to find a way.

Lightness flowed through her, as if all that was heavy and burdensome was being collected in the passing and discarded where it could do no harm. She took a breath and actually felt it hit her lungs. She'd only felt such an infilling once before, on her knees, in a white tent, in a ball field...

She noticed baskets being passed for the collection. Without another thought she grabbed her purse from the floor. She didn't have any cash besides a few dollars. And that would not do. That would not be a valid representation of her love. She pulled out her checkbook and a pen then hesitated. How much should she give? Fifty? A hundred? Those amounts were pitiful tokens of the state of her heart.

Then another thought entered. Cal was always investing large chunks of money in get-rich-quick schemes. Wasn't this cause more worthy than any of those? Didn't this moment deserve a heady commemoration? Didn't it deserve a true sacrifice?

Annie readied her pen and let her hand take over. Let her heart take over.

Merry leaned close and saw the amount. "Annie! What are you doing?"

I'm learning to love. She ripped the check off and folded it in half. She kept repeating the words so she wouldn't think about the amount she'd just given away. *I'm learning to love. I'm learning to love.*

She was glad when the basket came by and she could drop the check inside. Afterward, her hand shook and she calmed it in the care of its mate.

What had she done?

You loved.

❧❧   ❧❧   ❧❧

Merry and Annie walked toward Annie's car. Merry wasn't sure what to say and didn't have a chance to say much. Annie was bubbling over with excitement about Dr. Roswold's hospital and what she'd just done—and her certainty that God had wanted her to do it. Her enthusiasm was wonderful and her generosity amazing. But also a bit of a concern. At such talks Merry guessed most people gave ten to twenty dollars. Perhaps they'd write a check for fifty, with the maximum contribution the rare hundred. But one thousand? She could picture Dr. Roswold's shock when he saw Annie's check. He'd probably wonder if it was for real. A joke.

The way Annie gushed, rehashing every point the doctor had made... Merry didn't doubt her sincerity and didn't want to quench her passion for giving. It was a good thing. It might even be a God-thing. Yet Merry's relief at seeing Annie return to God was tempered by the reality of what would happen when Cal found out.

Merry had once been on Cal's side of the faith issue, back before the crash that took the lives of her family. So she could guess how Cal would react—

"Yoo-hoo! Merry? Annie?" Blanche called from behind them. "Wait up."

Blanche pulled Ivan along until they all met on the sidewalk near the curb. "So?" she said, out of breath. "What do you think? Ivan thinks the people in the slides were actors."

"Surely not," Merry said.

He shrugged. "I said it was a possibility. But I put my five bucks into the basket just like everybody else."

Merry saw Annie's face go white. "Five dollars?" Annie said.

"I only had three, but that counts, too," Blanche said.

Annie edged her way to a nearby bench. "I need to sit."

"What's wrong?" Blanche asked.

"She's probably sick to her stomach from seeing those skinny, sickly people," Ivan said.

Blanche hit him on the arm. "That proves they weren't actors, you old pea pod."

"Not really. Haven't you ever heard of 'starving artists'?"

"Oh, you—"

Merry left Annie on the bench and herded the couple away. "Would you two go back to the library and spell Harold? I'll be there in a minute."

They both looked at Annie, their faces curious, but went on their way across the street, leaving Annie and Merry alone.

Merry took a seat next to her. Annie seemed oblivious, so she touched her arm.

Annie came to life. "Five dollars? And I gave a thousand?"

"It was a very generous gift."

"But what will Cal say?"

"I don't know. What will he say?"

Annie slid a hand through her hair. "He'll go ballistic. He's already anti-God, anti-me-having-anything-to-do-with-God. Even the thought of me going to choir was too much for him." She spun toward Merry. "Why did you let me do it? Why didn't you stop me?"

Merry wanted to defend herself but knew Annie didn't really blame her. They were questions born of panic. "You could probably put a stop payment on the check. You might even be able to catch Dr. Roswold and ask for it back."

Annie looked as if she was only partly listening. She was staring back at the courthouse, the fingers of one hand resting on her chin.

"Can I tell you a story that might help?"

Annie nodded. "Anything. Please."

Merry scooted back on the bench, creating a space between them. "You may not remember this. I don't talk about it much, but I was Cal."

"What?"

"The scenario you're going through now with you being the believer and Cal being against God? That was Lou and me. Lou believed. I didn't. And I had no wish to believe."

Annie's eyes lit with recognition. "I'd forgotten that. You're such a strong Christian now. I'd forgotten you were way different before the plane crash, before..."

"Before Lou and Justin were killed."

Annie nodded.

Merry looked across the square toward the library, which had become such an important place in her life. Her new life. Moving to Steadfast had been a good decision. She couldn't imagine living in Kansas City, living in the home her family had shared. The image of Justin holding up a picture he'd colored flashed in her mind. *"Looky, Mama! Do you like it?"*

She closed her eyes against it. Not now. This was not a time for wallowing in her memories. This was a time for snatching out a specific memory to help her friend.

"Are you okay?"

Merry nodded. She traced a capital *J* someone had etched into a slat of the bench. *Justin, Jesus...* "Lou loved the Lord with his entire being, and he tried—unsuccessfully—to get me to love Him, too. I wouldn't budge."

"Why not?"

She shrugged. Merry tried to pinpoint her reasoning. It was hazy. "I think it mostly had to do with pride. With control. To do what Lou wanted me to do would have been to give up something of myself. To give in. To lose. As a busy wife and mother, I felt little was in my control anyway, so I took what I could."

"That sounds a lot like Cal."

"That's why I'm telling you. Lou made a big charity gesture once, too. We had an old car, and Lou decided to donate it to a safe home for women who needed transportation. We were planning on trading it in for a new one, but because he donated it, we had to come up with a few thousand *more* dollars to pay for its replacement. Which meant I couldn't get the dinette set I wanted. It caused a lot of problems. A lot of arguments."

Annie pulled her hair away from her face and let it fall. "Cal wants to invest in a business with Bailey. That project is his dinette."

Merry nodded. "The problem is, there's always something to spend the money on and rarely extra money sitting around to give away. But that's why it means so much to God. Because it's a sacrifice."

"So I did good giving the thousand?"

Merry patted her hand. "You did good. But there are consequences."

"I'm not fond of that word..."

"I'm just glad you're focused on God again. You scared me a bit in the diner the other day, saying you weren't coming to church because you weren't letting God break up your family. You were choosing Cal over God."

Annie covered her face as if ashamed. "I was weary of the struggle. And with Cal having another woman—"

"You know that for sure?"

"Not for sure..."

"Remember, *if* he's guilty, he's the one in the wrong. Affairs are never justified. He should be groveling to you, asking your forgiveness."

Annie leaned her head back, looking at the sky. "And wouldn't I like to have him do that. It would give me the control back. I'd have the power." She lowered her chin and offered a small smile. "How I'd make him suffer."

Merry laughed. "How human of you."

"Yeah, well, I've got plenty of human traits racing full blast. I'm trying not to give in to them. I'm trying to do things the right way. That's why I took the blame for even the possibility of Cal's infidelity. That's why I'm trying so hard to save our marriage."

"Blame can be shared, Annie. And so can forgiveness." She tapped her leg with a finger. "I can guarantee you one thing."

"What's that?"

"You don't have to—nor should you—give up God and your faith for your husband. For anyone. Put Jesus first, and all the Cal-stuff will fall into place."

"When?"

"I have no idea."

"You're some help."

Merry remembered a saying that had helped her through waiting times. "God is never late and never early."

"You could've fooled me."

Merry sat back. "So what are you going to do about the check? I'll go with you to see Dr. Roswold."

Annie shook her head. "Let's leave it. I truly felt God leading me to do it. I'll let Him get me through the consequences."

How could she argue with that?

As they stood, Merry felt compelled to add one more thing. "Don't forget that God might have to do something drastic to get Cal's attention. He's a stubborn man, just like I was a stubborn woman."

Annie swallowed slowly. "I sure hope it's not a plane crash."

Merry's thoughts exactly.

As soon as she got home, Annie transferred one thousand dollars from their savings to her checking account.

It was a done deal. No going back now.

Since she had to work the dinner shift, she didn't have time to tell Cal about the donation. On such days, they virtually passed at the kitchen door—her going out, him coming in early from work to take care of Avi. A kiss on the cheek. *Bye, hon. There's a hamburger-and-rice casserole in the oven—and one thousand* less *dollars in the savings account.*

Forget that last bit. She hadn't said it, but she wanted to. Just have it out in the open so she wouldn't have to worry about it all night. Not that her resolve had wavered. It hadn't. She was proud to have followed God's direction. Now if only God would give her clear direction in how to reach Cal.

But as she served up plates and plates of the Mighty Meat Loaf dinner special at the Plentiful, she was dogged with the what-ifs of the unknown.

Actually, that wasn't true. She knew exactly how Cal would react. He'd blow up. He'd yell. He'd pace and shake the checkbook at her. And he'd ask, "What's gotten into you?"

And what would she tell him, plain and simple? "God. God's gotten into me, Cal. He wanted me to do it. We're supposed to love..."

That's where the unknown kicked in. How would he react to that? She could guess. But maybe, just maybe, since God was behind her donation, He'd pull off some kind of miracle within her husband

and make him back down and understand. If He could get Annie to give the money, surely He could get Cal to understand.

That was her prayer, oft repeated between coffee refills and small talk. *Make Cal understand.*

Please.

Cal stared at the computer screen. He'd just deposited the latest check he'd gotten for the Bon Vivant addition when he noticed the bank had made a horrible error. For some bizarre reason they had withdrawn one thousand dollars from the McFay savings account. Today.

Besides the newest check, there was only $718 left. That was it.

Impossible.

Cal picked up the phone, then realized the bank was closed. He'd call them first thing in the morning and let 'em have it. Then he suddenly had a horrible thought.

He switched screens, bringing up his checking account. Phew. It looked okay. He typed in Annie's account number.

A one-thousand-dollar deposit screamed at him.

His relief that the money had not disappeared into cyberspace—or in someone else's pocket—was tempered by his question of why? Why had a thousand dollars been transferred from their savings into Annie's checking?

You could bet a thousand dollars he'd find out.

You'd think that after ten years of being a waitress, Annie's legs and feet wouldn't hurt. But tonight they did. You'd have thought she was a rookie.

Was it because she was tense, worried about what she'd tell Cal about the thousand dollars? Or was it because she was eager to get home to help Avi get dressed in her princess costume for Halloween? Or were her legs anticipating the loads of walking they'd do tonight on the trick-or-treat run? Something had to give. Yet as she pulled into the driveway, she realized she would rather work another shift than go inside her own house.

Chicken.

She couldn't deny the title. One other thing she couldn't deny was her fatigue. The physical exhaustion combined with a dose of brain mush from praying during every free thought made her want to curl onto the backseat and call it a night.

She glanced at the backseat longingly at the same time she grabbed the handle of the door. She had to do this. Get the confrontation with Cal done. For her own sanity.

She got out of the car, repeating her mantra all the way inside: *Make Cal understand. Make Cal understand...*

Cal sat at the kitchen table, not in his usual spot—with his back to the door—but in Avi's spot that faced the door. Head-on. Nothing was on the table in front of him. No cup of coffee, bowl of ice cream, not even a magazine. His hands were clasped. And the way his eyes bored into Annie as she came in, she *knew* the jig was up. There was only one reason he was sitting at that table, at that time, in that way.

He was waiting for her.

She managed to slip in one final *Please, God* as she hung her coat and purse on the rack behind the door. She took a few steps toward the table and wiped her palms on her uniform. "Hi, hon."

His hands clasped each other more tightly. He took a breath that started in his toes, as if he'd been sitting there *not* breathing for a long, long time. He let it out.

Annie felt the need to fill the void. "Is Avi ready to go? I've already seen a few kids running to houses." She went to the pantry and pulled out two bags of candy and emptied them into the popcorn bowl. "She's going to need to wear a jacket under her costume. I know she'll object, but it's nippy out there."

He just stared at her. *It's a bit nippy in here, too.*

She couldn't take it any longer. She dropped her hands to her sides. *Maybe if I act innocent—or at least ignorant.* "Out with it. Why the glaring eyes?"

He blinked, letting his eyelids linger a moment in a closed position. When he opened them, three words came out. "One thousand dollars?"

The doorbell rang. Avi barreled down the stairs. "I'll get it!"

Annie grabbed the candy bowl and took a step toward the door. Cal's hand on her arm stopped her. "Answer me."

Avi came running back and took the bowl away from her. "It's a monster and a clown!"

"One piece each, sweet-apple."

Cal was still staring at her. Calmly volatile. She almost wished he would yell.

"It's the right thing to do, Cal."

"According to who?"

"I—"

He stood. "What are you up to, Annie? What are you going to buy? One thousand dollars is a lot of money."

All at once she realized how he'd found out. Their bank accounts on-line. He'd seen the transfer, but from his questions it was clear that Dr. Roswold's check hadn't cleared.

Still time to back out.

She shook her head at the thought and tried to recover the certainty she'd felt while talking with Merry. "It's already spent, Cal. During lunch I went with Merry to—"

He slapped the table, making her jump. "You and Merry went shopping and spent one thousand dollars?"

"Of course not! If you'd let me finish. Merry asked me to go with her to hear a speaker, and this man, Dr. Roswold, showed all sorts of slides and pictures of a hospital in Africa where he works and the poor children who need—"

"We have a child who needs. A child right here."

She gripped the back of a chair. "She doesn't *need*, Cal. She— we—have plenty."

He slid his chair back and stood. "Of course she has plenty. Plenty, because you and I work our tails off to provide for her. If those people in Africa need anything, let them work and—"

"Cal...it's not that easy. You know that. You've seen pictures, heard stories."

"Fairy tales to make hard-working people like us give up our money. I'd bet that out of every dollar donated, ninety-nine cents goes into some charity president's pocket. You want to toss a penny toward the needs of the world, go ahead. But it's a waste of money."

"Dr. Roswold isn't like that. He lives in one room at the back of the hospital. The donations he collects are for supplies and medicines and—"

"And his Swiss bank account."

He wasn't going to listen no matter what she said.

Cal gripped the back of his chair, and they faced each other, the table between them. "What were you thinking, Annie? One thousand dollars? A couple bucks—give that to a drunk on the street, I don't care. But our savings? I need that money for...for things and to invest in Bailey's restaurant."

So that's it. She bit her lower lip. "Maybe..." It was an odd thought. "Maybe this proves you shouldn't invest in his restaurant."

"All it proves is you're an impulsive, naive patsy, willing to give because some man makes you feel guilty, fills your head with false promises, and blatantly asks for it."

"Like Bailey did to you?"

His chin jutted back. She moved to the sink. "I'm sorry, Cal, but it's true and you know it. Bailey's getting you to invest your money, time, and dreams by making you feel guilty about our life, filling your head with false promises."

She poured a glass of water and took a sip. She faced him. "At least my donation to Dr. Roswold's hospital will be used to help people. Really help people."

Cal's breathing was heavy, his knuckles white as he gripped the chair. "You had no right to take that money without my approval."

"Have you cared whether I approve of you using money to invest in Bailey's project?"

"It's our project."

"And Dr. Roswold's hospital is God's project."

His smug look made her want to take it back. She'd been on the final lap, within yards of the finish line. Why had she blown a tire by bringing God into it?

His head was nodding. He let go of the chair and strolled, taking control of the room. "Merry. I should have known she'd be involved in all this. Don't you see what she's doing, Annie? She draws you into her church by telling you what you want to hear. She asks you to choir. Then she just *happens* to take you to hear a speaker who makes you feel guilty, pulling at your heartstrings by showing you the pitiful faces of a few starving kids, just knowing that our bank account will be ripe for the picking."

"It's not like—"

"She probably gets a cut."

"Cal!"

"She's like those people planted at auctions who get the bids going higher and higher. She's a decoy. A shill. A con woman."

"She's a good friend."

He shook his head. "She is good, I'll give her that." He started laughing. "Good ol' Annie. A sucker of the first degree! The good doctor and Merry are probably toasting you right now. It's not often they get someone to be a thousand dollars dumb."

He was wrong. He was so wrong.

Cal tucked his chair under the table. "You call the bank first thing in the morning and stop payment on that check."

Her head started shaking even before the words formed. "I can't do that, Cal."

"You most certainly can. If you don't do it, I will."

Everything was falling apart. "It was a good thing to give that money. A God-thing."

"Give me a break. And what do you know about God anyway? You've been thinking about Him a few weeks, and you think you know anything about how He works?" Cal pointed at finger at her. "I know God. I've known Him for years, and let me tell you this— He is not to be trusted, prayed at, or worshipped. He takes the good ones and leaves behind the mean ones. Where's the logic in that? I won't let Him do it with us. Not with my money, not with my dream, and not with my wife."

Annie felt as deflated as an old balloon. "He's not like that. He—"

Cal grabbed his jacket. "I'll take Avi trick-or-treating. You stay here. God'll keep you company."

The monk's robe was comfy, but the sleeves were a pain when it came to washing dishes. And it was hot over the other clothes. Plus, the work itself was hard tonight, the stream of dishes endless. All this made Jered wonder why he had to wear it at all. Except for a quick parade step into the dining room so Jinko could show off how fun-loving or generous (or whatever) he was with his staff, Jered had been confined to the kitchen. He finally couldn't take it anymore and started to take off the robe.

Bad timing.

Jinko happened to be entering the kitchen and nearly ran to his side, his white sheikh's robe sailing behind him. "What are you doing?"

"I'm hot. And the sleeves get in the way."

Jinko practically hissed. "Keep it on!"

Jered put it back on.

Jinko got in his face, his Arab headdress framing his anger. "You going to follow directions tonight?"

"Sure."

"You'd better be sure. I can't afford any screwups. You do exactly what I say and only what I say, *comprendé?*"

Jered was beginning to hate that word. "Yeah."

Jinko lifted an eyebrow. "Yeah?"

"Yes. Yes. Fine." He leaned toward Jinko. "Is that Ed guy here?"

Jinko shoved a finger to his lips in a call for silence.

Okay, okay.

Jinko stormed away.

Sheesh.

Jinko was right about Roxie Robbins. She was hot, she knew it, and dressed to flaunt it. She came to Palamba's dressed like a genie, but her costume was far skimpier and tighter than that TV genie ever wore. And at midnight she took control of the place, just like Jinko said she would.

"Hey, people! Are you ready?"

The crowd responded with whoops and yells.

"Then let's have ourselves a contest!"

Jered would have liked to watch, because there were some amazing costumes, but within seconds of Roxie's introduction, he felt Jinko's hand on his arm.

"It's time."

Jered didn't have time to be nervous. He and Jinko swept out the back way, yanking their costumes off as they walked. By the time they got in Jered's truck (with the new muffler), they were two men dressed in black.

Jered knew it wasn't time for small talk. He remained silent while Jinko told him where to turn. The final neighborhood was nice but not fancy. The houses were old, the bushes edging them big enough to hide behind.

"Pull up here, kill the lights and engine, and put on these gloves."

Jered pulled to the curb, wiped his palms on his black jeans, and put on the gloves. Could Jinko hear his heart beating against his chest?

Jinko flowed from one movement to the next like he was creating a long sentence without a period. He looked up the street and down, opened the door to the truck, got out, and walked across the lawn of the house on the corner, heading to the front door. All before Jered had time to fully register: *This is it.*

Jered scrambled after him, jerking his head around to make sure no one was watching. How would they even know? It was 12:15. Most houses were dark except for a porch light protecting jack-o'-lanterns from Halloween pranksters. He felt like a commando on reconnaissance, keeping low, zigging and zagging.

When he caught up with Jinko at the back door, he was greeted with a soft, "Calm down."

He'd try.

Jinko turned the doorknob. It was unlocked. He went in. Jered followed. He shut the door with a soft click. They stood still a moment, getting their bearings. Jinko pulled a skinny black flashlight from his pocket, aimed it at the floor, and turned it on. He moved to the front of the house. In the living room were two stacks of lidded white boxes, the kind Jered's dad used for old files. They were labeled "Uncle Jim's Stuff." Jinko took the lid off the top one. He put it back on.

"Help me," he whispered.

"What am I looking for?"

"Coins in individual plastic holders."

The first four boxes held books, photo albums, and a few pieces of clothing. In the fifth box...

Jered spotted them, a whole pile of coins—probably fifty—each one set in a cardboard holder that was slipped into a transparent square sleeve just a little bigger than the coin. "I found them!"

Jinko pulled a drawstring bag from the pocket of his jacket. "Hold this while I go through them."

"Why don't we just take all—?"

"Discretion, kid. Ed would notice. Give me a minute to see which ones are worth something."

Jinko held his flashlight's beam on the coins, tossing one coin in the bag and one aside. It seemed to be taking way too long. Jered kept checking the door, his ears straining to hear the sound of a car. He wanted out of there. None too soon, the coins were divided.

Jinko tied the bag shut, and Jered helped put the boxes back. They went out the way they had come. As they crossed the yard, Jinko whispered, "Walk!"

It was one of the hardest things Jered had ever done. They got in the truck and took off.

Jered took a corner too fast.

"Slow down!"

Jered slammed on the brakes.

"Park it! Let me drive!"

Jered complied and changed places with Jinko. The doors closed and Jinko sped away. "Sorry," Jered said.

Jinko was intent on driving. "My mistake. I should've known." His fingers gripped the steering wheel. Then he checked his watch. "Good timing. Now listen up."

Jered was all ears.

Jinko reached behind the seat and pulled out Jered's monk costume. "Get dressed. We're going back to work. We'll slip in the back as if we've only been out for a smoke. I'll go into the dining room first. You come in—or not. Wash some dishes if you want. Just act normal."

"I'll try."

"You'll do it!"

Jered nodded. He'd do it.

It was two in the morning, and they were finally done cleaning up. What was it with Halloween that made people extra messy?

Although Jered's body was exhausted from the work, it wouldn't shut down as the adrenaline from the burglary—and the fear of getting caught—kept pumping.

"You look sick," Vasylko said as he put on his coat. "You okay?"

"Long night."

"But good, eh?" The cook shook his hips. He made a ridiculous-looking Elvis, his belly far beyond even the King's late-life paunch.

"Yeah, yeah, the King lives."

Vasylko hesitated, then smiled. He pulled out his cross necklace—which looked amazingly appropriate with his white Elvis costume. "The King lives!"

Whatever.

Vasy went to his side, putting an arm around his shoulders. "You not right tonight. You worried. No need." He held up the cross again. "Jesus save you in all ways. He did me." They both looked up as they heard Jinko's voice. When Jinko didn't come in from the dining room, Vasy continued, "I have trouble in Russia. Jesus save me. Brought me here. He save you, too." He glanced toward the dining room. "I worry you and Jinko. Other boys...there was one. Same as you. He...gone."

This got Jered's attention. "Gone where?"

Vasy shrugged. "One night..." He clicked his fingers. "Gone. Never see."

"Maybe he quit."

"No." They heard Jinko's voice again. Vasy lowered his. "You careful. Don't want you gone." He slipped his hand in his pocket. "You need money, go home? Real home? I give you—"

"No, no," Jered said. "I'm fine. I'll be fine."

Vasy fingered the cross on his chain. "Jinko not going place."

"Huh?"

Vasy looked frustrated. "Going...place-es?"

"Yeah. Going places."

"His way not right way." He pulled the cross forward again. "This way, Jered. This way. This Man."

Jinko came in the kitchen and Jered was relieved. The conversation was far too heavy for his taste.

Vasy whispered in Jered's ear. "I pray for you. May God keep you safe, in His hand."

Jinko was all smiles. "Come on, people. Good job tonight, but get outta here. Work's over."

Jered certainly hoped so. He'd had enough for one night.

He'd had enough.

Jered tossed the monk's costume behind the seat and got in his truck. He waited his turn to exit the parking lot and had just started the engine when Jinko yanked open his door.

"Hey!"

"Out."

"Wha—?" Jinko pulled him out of the truck and led him toward his car. Was this when it was going to happen, just like Vasylko said? Was this when he would just be "gone"? "Where are we going?" Jered asked.

"We're going to finish the work."

"I thought we did."

They got in and Jinko started the car. "Stealing is only the first part. Now comes the selling. We're going to Kansas City."

"It's after two in the morning."

"Now. We need to be there first thing. We need to get rid of the coins before Ed Cooperton realizes they're gone. He and his wife will sleep late in the morning, and by the time they wake up, I plan on being on our way home, my pockets full of bills." He glanced at Jered. "Your pockets too, kid."

He breathed a little easier. Everything would be fine. Vasylko was wrong. There was no need to go home. Jinko cared about him more than his own father did.

Everything was fine.

Eleven

Buy the truth and do not sell it;
get wisdom, discipline and understanding.

PROVERBS 23:23

IT WASN'T A QUESTION of waking up at 3:16 again. Annie didn't sleep. How could she with Cal mad, with so much between them, keeping them apart? She prayed a lot and hoped God was listening.

As soon as the sun started coming up, she decided to go running. Maybe that would clear her mind. The sidewalks were dotted with a few smashed pumpkins from Halloween. Avi loved her pumpkin and made Annie take it inside every—

She saw a figure coming toward her and was surprised to see it was Claire Adams.

"Well, well," Claire said, stopping. "Our paths cross."

Annie caught her breath. "I've never seen you out here before."

"I don't run much. Just when I'm desperate."

"For what?"

"Inspiration. An opera house in Duluth wants me to design a mosaic for their atrium, and my mind's blank. What's your excuse?"

How could she word it? "I'm looking for inspiration of another kind. Cal and I had an argument about a donation I gave yesterday." She looked into the trees, seeing sky through the silhouette of leafless branches. "I tried to give something special to God and got shot down by my own husband."

Claire leaned her head back and laughed, then stopped herself with a hand. "Sorry. I'm not making light of your situation, but you do remember that I have a PhD in giving it all up for God and getting shot down."

Of course. Annie had forgotten.

"You remember last spring when God nudged me eight ways to Friday to give up my wealth and even my art in order to follow Him?"

"You ended up hidden in the library attic here in Steadfast. I met you when you came in for biscuits and gravy."

"Still a favorite."

"You even stayed with Harold for a while."

"Yes, I did." Claire stretched. "Care to walk and talk?" They headed down the street. "The point is, Annie, my sacrifice, my giving it up, is old news. What God was really up to was getting me to the point of saying a blanket yes to Him—before He even asked the next specific question. He wants all of us to give up anything that stands between us and total surrender to Him. In my case it was the need for fame."

"But now you're famous again," Annie said. "He helped you give it up but then gave it back to you?"

"He often does that."

Annie tried to apply it to her own situation. "So if God made me give up the thousand dollars, what happens now that Cal's stopped it?"

"Maybe the check wasn't the issue. Your willingness to give—to sacrifice—is worth a lot to the Almighty. 'God loves a cheerful giver.'"

"I don't feel so cheerful."

"You were at the time."

"But Cal...I'm supposed to stop the check this morning."

They walked to the next driveway in silence. "Then you have to abide by his wishes. It's not worth messing up your marriage about, Annie. Don't get into a power play. In fact, this might be a chance for you to do what God wants all wives to do, to submit—"

"I hate that word."

"Oh, the word's not the problem. It's gotten a bad rap, though as a divorced woman, I'm certainly no role model. But I've learned a lot since then, and if I had to do it over again..."

"Was your husband a Christian?"

Claire laughed. "He was a faithful hedonist."

Annie felt dumb. "I'm sorry, I don't know what that means."

"He worshipped pleasure—his own, mostly. Things made him

happier than people did. We were both big into 'accumulating.' He still is."

"That's what I don't get," Annie said. "God wants a wife to submit to her husband, even if he's wrong?"

"If he lives against God's moral or written laws, no go. But if he's just a putz? Yup. I think the hope is that the godly wife can win over the putzy husband by being an example of God's love."

"That's a lot of pressure on the wife."

"You're right there. But hey, we can handle it, can't we? I often think women are the stronger of the two sexes, at least in regard to places of the heart. And sometimes the roles *are* reversed, and the godly man is the one having to be the example."

Annie thought of Merry and her husband. "Okay. So I'll give in on this. Just so God knows my heart—that I wanted to give."

"You can count on it." They turned a corner near Susan's. "By the way, you did remember we're not having Bible study today. Sim and Cassie have a soccer game so the moms will be busy."

"I heard that."

Claire suddenly stopped walking. "I know what you need! An afternoon shopping with the girls. I'll ask Merry, and we could go to Eldora. There's some grout I have to pick up, so I have a reason for going there anyway. We could go out to eat and—"

It sounded wonderful. Girl time had been sparse lately. "You don't have to convince me. I know Cal's plans revolve around college football, so he'll be home to take care of Avi."

"Perfect. I'll call Merry and get back to you."

What a wonderful coincidence, running into Claire. At seven in the morning. On a backstreet. When Claire rarely ran.

Ha.

"Wake up, kid. Breakfast."

Jered opened his eyes. It took him a moment to remember where he was. Jinko's car. Going to Kansas City to sell the coins. He sat up and got untangled from the shoulder harness. He pushed the button that brought the passenger seat upright from a near horizontal recline. It sure beat sleeping against the window in his truck.

Jinko pulled into a Denny's and shut the car off. "Where are we?" Jered asked. The traffic on an interstate sped nearby.

"We're here. Kansas City. Thanks for the help driving, kid."

Jered arched his back. "Sorry. I was tired."

"Tell me about it."

The pull in Jinko's voice brought Jered fully awake. "Like I said, I'm sorry. I'll drive all the way home."

"Yes, you will." He got out and stretched. They went inside the restaurant. Jinko asked for a table in the corner. They used the facilities and looked at menus.

Jered had no idea how much money he had in his pocket. A few bucks at the most. And he was hungry. Really hungry. "Can you spot me for the meal? I didn't know we were leaving town."

"You left your wad of money at home?"

"Something like that."

"It's on me, kid. Have at it."

Gladly. He ordered steak and eggs and a Coke. Jinko had an omelet and coffee. Black. Jinko flirted with the waitress and she flirted back. He oozed charm and people responded—especially women. Jered wasn't sure if it was because women found him sexy (he supposed he was in a dangerous sort of way) or because he seemed full of power. And promises. Promises of what, Jered wasn't sure.

But it worked. When their meal came, the waitress winked at him, "I got the cook to make you an extra large omelet. Enjoy."

Jinko took her hand and winked back. "Oh, I will, dear Mandy, I will."

Jered looked at his own plate, which was covered with plenty of food. But still... "How come you get doubles?"

"Simple. I gave her what she was looking for."

"A tip?"

"That, too." He cut the entire omelet using sweeping strokes. "But that's not what she was looking for this early morning. Not all she was looking for."

Jered caught the waitress looking at Jinko. They exchanged a smile. "Oh, I get it. Sex."

"Crudely said, but essentially true. However, a more important element is involved. A more basic one. That of attention. I gave her attention. I noticed her. I used her name. That's what people want, kid. Proof of their existence by someone looking them in the eyes and using their names."

"You always call me '*kid*.'"

Jinko stopped in midchew. "You object?"

"Not really."

"It's a sign of affection. It goes beyond the use of your name. I like you, kid. Jered."

Jered felt his chest swell. "Kid is fine. Really."

"Then kid it is." He pointed to the food. "Now eat. Our meeting's in an hour."

People were sparse in downtown Kansas City on a Saturday morning. Jinko seemed to know exactly where he was going. For some reason this made Jered think of his dad, stuck in tiny little Steadfast. Bailey Manson didn't know his way around anywhere big. Certainly not around the world. Not like Jinko. Jinko was going places—

Vasylko's broken English came to mind: *"Jinko not going places. His way not right way."* The image of the cross came to mind, and Jered remembered a saying he'd heard: Jesus is the way, the truth, and the life.

Hmm. Where had that come from?

His thoughts moved from the light to the dark, to the kid who had worked for Jinko and was suddenly gone. What happened to him? Did Jinko take him on a trip to KC and—

"Here we are." Jinko pulled into a back alley. An old tan clunker was waiting. A grandpa type got out and stood by the passenger door. Jinko parked next to him and also got out. "Stay put," he told Jered.

No problem, though the man didn't look dangerous. Actually, he looked like the type who would be a greeter in Wal-Mart.

"Hey, Jinko. You sounded rushed on the phone."

"I am never rushed, Sid; you know that."

"My mistake. Whatcha got for me?"

As Jinko took out the drawstring bag, they moved close, blocking Jered's—and anyone else's—view of the coins. They lowered their voices. When they finally moved apart, Sid was closing the bag, and Jinko was folding a new wad of money into his shirt pocket.

Jinko got in his car, and Sid in his.

"That's it?" Jered asked.

"You want guns and police?"

"Of course not."

Jinko started the car. "Crime can be quite civil if you plan it right." They followed Sid out of the lot. "I'll get us out of KC, then you can bring us home while I sleep."

Home sounded good. Such as it was.

Driving gave Jered time to think. Just when he'd started to get comfortable in a situation, something stirred him up again. Vasylko was to blame this time. Why couldn't the cook leave well enough alone?

It's not like Jered was dumb. He knew Jinko was a crook. He knew stealing was wrong. But Jinko was a good guy, too. He could charm the light from a lightbulb. People liked him. He was a good businessman. And he cared about people. He'd taken in Jered from the street. He'd given him a job. He'd bought him clothes, given him a place to sleep. And he was going to help him with his music— which was more than his dad had ever done.

Jered could learn a lot from Jinko. He was a master at conquering life on his own terms. Jered looked at him now, asleep in the passenger seat. He didn't snore like his dad, his mouth hanging open like an idiot. He slept with his arms crossed, his head perfectly erect, as if he was in control even in sleep.

I want that.

But what about the kid who'd disappeared?

Jered shook his head. The missing kid was probably a runaway and had simply...run away. Jered could not believe this man seated next to him would ever hurt anyone. Jered had never even seen him mad. Well, not really mad.

Vasylko's voice reentered his head. *"This way, Jered. This way. This Man."*

Jered had to admit it was kind of fascinating to hear a man like Vasylko talk about Jesus like He was real. And he'd said Jesus had saved him from trouble in Russia. How? Was that real or just lofty la-di-da talk? Maybe, if given the chance, Jered would ask him about it. It might be a cool story.

But no. If he asked, he'd hear much more than he wanted about Jesus. He didn't want to go there.

Why not? What would it hurt?

Jered sat straighter in the car's seat, leaning against the steering wheel. He didn't need to hear about any Christ. He knew God didn't approve of his stealing. But did God want him to go hungry and have no place to stay? If God didn't want him to steal, then why didn't He give him what he needed?

So there.

When Jered shut off the car, Jinko stirred. "We're back," Jered said.

Jinko squinted and moaned his way to sitting. "But we're not home. We're at the restaurant. Why?"

Jered hadn't been sure about the decision. "My truck's still here. I thought that might look odd." He looked around at the other cars. "I was hoping we'd get back before people showed up for the lunch shift, but I didn't want to speed and have a cop stop us."

Jinko flipped the passenger visor down and looked at himself in the mirror. "Good thinking all around, kid. I'm impressed. I'll go in and see how things are going."

Jered handed him the keys. "Four hours' sleep isn't much to go on."

"I've survived on less."

Jered believed him. They got out and Jered fished his truck keys out of his pocket. "I'm going home to clean up. I'm supposed to be in at four."

Jinko was already walking toward the back door, talking without looking back. "See you later then."

Jered stood there a moment, staring at the closed door. The quiet alley. That was it? No thank-you? No "good job"? No share of the spoils? So much for giving Jered the attention he needed.

Then an odd thing happened. With his hurt feelings came the slightest hint of doubt.

But he shoved it away.

The check had been stopped, and the battlements between Cal and Annie had been lowered. As for the submission issue? Being an example? It worked, because Cal had been the one to suggest a check to Dr. Roswold's hospital in the amount of fifty dollars.

The important thing was, they were talking. And Cal was perfectly okay about taking care of Avi while she went shopping with Claire and Merry. He didn't even ask for details. That was fine with Annie.

On the way out, she passed Cal watching college football in the front room. "Bye, hon."

He pulled his eyes from the screen. "What time will you be back?"

"I don't know. Like I said, since we're getting a late start, I think we'll grab dinner somewhere. I'll be home by seven or so. No later."

She looked at the game. The camera scanned the cheering crowd. One man held up a sign that said: John 3:16.

3:16.

She took a step back, bumping into the couch.

Cal looked up. "What's with you?"

Annie put one hand to her chest and pointed with the other. "What's that sign mean?"

Cal looked at the screen. "'Go Huskers'?"

The camera had moved on.

John 3:16. That had to be a Bible verse. But how odd. What could it mean?

She had to find out. She headed upstairs.

"I thought you were leaving."

"I forgot something." She went into the master closet, opened the door of Avi's cubby, and retrieved her Bible. She listened for the game. She heard Cal exclaim over a bad call. She opened the book, found the verse, and read: "For God so loved the world that he gave his one and only Son, that whoever believes in him shall not perish but have eternal life."

She looked up. Why would they have that sign at a football game? Then she realized that wasn't the point.

She read the verse again. It was the essence of her faith. God loves us. God sent his Son Jesus. To have eternal life, we have to believe in Him.

She held the Bible to her chin as she thought through all the turmoil she'd experienced the past few weeks. Go to church; don't go to church. Follow Cal's wishes; follow God's. Yet through it all God had been speaking to her, trying to get her to remember the main point so well expressed in John 3:16.

She smiled and lifted her face. "Thanks. I got it now. I won't forget."

Now she could go shopping.

Claire opened the door of the restaurant for them. "I know you two will like this place."

"We're awfully early for dinner. It's only three," Merry said.

"You've heard of brunch? This is...linner. Between lunch and dinner."

"Or lupper," Annie said. "Between lunch and supper."

A handsome man with a ponytail greeted them. "Afternoon, ladies. Table for three?"

"You bet," Claire said. "And hurry, we're starving."

They were seated in a booth, and he handed them menus. "Enjoy. I'll get you some chips to stave off your hunger pangs."

"Good man," Annie said. They opened the menus, and Annie noted the name of the place. "Palamba's. That's an odd name."

Cal noticed he was speeding and let up on the accelerator. He didn't have to speed. He had all the time in the world. It was a new experience. He was used to sneaking off to Eldora to see his dad and slipping back to Steadfast within a time span of sixty to ninety minutes.

When Susan had called asking if Avi wanted to come to Sim's soccer game, it had been the perfect opening. Now, to have the entire afternoon... Such luxury. To celebrate, he planned to stop at his dad's favorite bakery and bring him a chocolate long john.

It was a good day.

Twelve

A false witness will not go unpunished,
and he who pours out lies will perish.

PROVERBS 19:9

JERED TOOK THE TRAY OF GLASSES into the eating area. He'd just come on duty, but there was always a lot to do between the lunch and dinner crowd.

He set the tray at the busser station and began setting the glasses on the shelves. But when he heard a certain laugh—

He caught the glass before it hit the counter. He whipped around and saw Merry Cavanaugh sitting at a booth with Claire Adams and Annie from the diner. What were they doing here?

Whatever the reason, he couldn't let them see him. He hurried through the rest of the glasses and was just about to head back to the kitchen when its door opened and Jinko stepped out. "Well, there you are—"

Jered rushed through the door, nearly knocking Jinko down.

"Hey, kid! Watch it."

"Sorry." He hurried to the dishwasher and started loading another tray of glasses. His hands were shaking.

Jinko came to his side. "Stop."

"I got work to—"

Jinko put a hand on his shoulder. "I said stop."

Breathe in, breathe out. Jered forced his shoulders to relax. "I saw some people I know. From Steadfast."

"Who?"

"The three ladies in the booth. I know them. They know me. They know my father."

166

Jinko took hold of his arm and pulled him toward the door. "Then introduce—"

Jered yanked his arm free. "No!"

Vasylko looked up from the stove. "Jered?"

He raised a hand to Vasy and moved back to the dishwasher. Jered kept his voice low and his eyes down. "I don't want them to see me. I can't let them see me."

Jinko took hold of Jered's upper arm and turned him around. He glared at him. "You're eighteen. Don't you think it's about time you show them you can make your own choices?"

It hit him funny and he laughed. Jered took a step back and slapped a hand on the stainless steel of the dishwasher. "Ah yes, look at me! I'm a dishwasher. What a success. What a wonderful choice!"

Vasy looked at him, fingering his cross.

Jered untied his apron. "I'm not feeling too good. I'm going home." He went out the back door.

Jinko ran after him. "Running away gets you nowhere, kid."

Exactly. Running had gotten Jered to the nowhere of where he was at.

Jered drove around. And around. Every time he got to the west side of Eldora, he was tempted to turn the wheel and head home. To his real home. Steadfast.

He'd show up at Bon Vivant, and his dad would look up from the reservation book and say, "Jered! You're home!" He'd get kind of teary and pull Jered into a hug. "I'm so glad you're back, son. I love you so much and I missed—"

Yeah right.

The reality that his dad would more likely glance up, say, "Be right with you," kept him driving around. And around.

Yet what was keeping him in Eldora? Was the iffy life he had with Jinko any better?

Jered felt used and confused. Why had Jinko included him in the burglary at all? He could have done it on his own, easy. And as far as the trip to KC? Except for driving back, Jered hadn't contributed a thing. So why was Jinko insisting he be involved? It didn't make sense.

Sure, Jinko gave him money, gave him a place to sleep. And sure, Jinko had talked about giving him a chance with a music producer. But the big question was why?

On the east side of Eldora, another thought came to him. A third alternative. Maybe he could leave town and head in the opposite direction. Away from Eldora, Steadfast, and even Kansas City. Maybe he should go somewhere completely new and start over. If Vasy could leave an entire country, couldn't Jered leave a state? If only he knew where Vasy lived, he'd—

No. Vasy was at work. And Jinko was at work. And Merry, Claire, and Annie were at work.

He was on his own.

Jered was suddenly weary, his eyes heavy. He knew the moment he let them close, he'd be asleep. He couldn't make any decision now. He was wiped out.

Tomorrow. He'd think about it tomorrow.

Jered flipped on the light inside the garage. His shirt was over his head within seconds, his shoes flipped into the corner. Bed. He needed—

All the bedding on his cot was gone. A bare mattress remained with a note attached: "You did good, kid. You've just earned yourself a real room. Upstairs, second door on the right. I've moved your stuff."

Jered looked at the shelf that had held his few possessions. It was empty. Even his guitar was gone.

Well then. He slipped his shirt back on, turned off the light, and went to the main house feeling like a servant who'd been invited into the master's domain. Jinko wasn't home yet; he must have made a special effort to get this done. He could have merely said, "You can move into the house," without doing the work himself. But Jinko had made it special by making it a surprise.

He'd also made it hard to refuse.

Though Jered had been in Jinko's house many times to use the shower, he looked at it with new eyes. This was his house now. His home. This was real. He wasn't homeless anymore. He wasn't a kid passing through. He had roots.

The second door on the right was closed, and Jered hesitated a moment before opening it. He knew it was a bedroom with a navy bedspread. He'd taken a peek inside on other days. But now that it was his room...

He turned the knob and pushed the door open without entering. Leaning in the crook between bed and wall was his guitar. His music was neatly stacked on a desk under a window. Something was on the bed.

Jered went inside to see but stopped short. Fanned neatly across the bedspread were twenty-dollar bills. Lots of them.

Jered swooped them up and counted. Fifteen twenty-dollar bills. Three hundred dollars.

He fell onto the bed, laughing, and tossed the money in the air, letting it float down upon him.

He wouldn't leave now.

He couldn't.

"Ah, come on, Merry. Just one more antique store."

Merry pulled at her hair. "Eek! Claire, we've created a monster!"

Annie pretended to pout. "I'm not that bad. I'm just having fun. That's legal, isn't it?"

"Last time I—" Claire did a double take and pointed ahead, as traffic passed at the intersection in front of them. "Annie? Isn't that Cal's truck?"

They all looked to the right as the white truck zoomed past. "It is! What's Cal—?" She slapped the back of the front seat. "Follow him, Claire!"

Claire didn't argue. She turned right at the corner.

Merry turned around to look at Annie, her eyes wide. "Annie, you don't think...?"

"What other explanation is there? As soon as he found out I'd be gone all day, he was probably on the phone making his plans. With her."

"But if he knew you were coming to Eldora, why would he risk it?"

Annie thought a moment. "I never told him where... He never asked, and I never told him where we were going. I just said we were going shopping and out to eat."

Merry snickered. "He couldn't think we were staying in Steadfast. That shopping expedition would have lasted a whole ten minutes."

"Let's not attempt to dissect the male mind. The point is, he's here," Claire said.

"Don't get too close!"

Claire eased up but said, "I doubt he knows my car. We're okay."

"Just give him room. I don't want to spook him."

Merry's voice was soft. "You really want to know?"

Annie's throat was dry. "It's not a matter of want. I have to know."

Cal's truck turned into a driveway—but not of a home. "Where's he going?" Claire asked.

"He's parking," Merry said.

"Pull to the side, up ahead," Annie said.

"What is this place?" Claire asked, craning her neck to see.

Annie read the sign that was nearly obscured by bushes: "Friendly Acres Retirement Village." She watched Cal go inside, then faced her friends. "I don't understand. His parents are long gone. He doesn't have any great-aunts or great-uncles. Avi and I are his only family."

"Maybe it's somebody he met somewhere?"

Annie shook her head. "Then why wouldn't he tell me? If he has an elderly friend...I love old people. I'd have come to visit with him."

Claire put her hand on the ignition. "You want to wait?"

"Do you mind?"

She shut off the car.

A half hour later, Merry exclaimed, "He's coming out!"

They all swung around in their seats to look. Cal was heading to his truck.

"Do you want me to continue to follow him?" Claire asked as she readied her keys.

Annie had already thought this through. "No. I want to go inside and see who he's been visiting. Maybe it will explain everything."

"But what if it's a fluke? A one-time visit?" Merry asked. "I don't want to play devil's advocate, but..."

"Then I'll further pursue the idea he's having an affair."

"Pray for the best, expect the worst?" Claire said.

"Get down!" Merry said. "He's driving out."

They all hunkered down in the car. "I feel like I'm in a mystery movie," Claire said.

Annie peeked out the window. Cal was gone. "And I plan to solve the mystery." She opened the door. "Anyone want to come along?"

"Mr. McFay? Yes, he was just—"

"I know that," Annie said. "I'm his wife." She put on her most charming smile. "It's just that I've never been here before, and I thought I'd help him out with the visiting duties, and..." *How can I word it?*

Claire did it for her. "We want to visit who Cal visited."

The receptionist's eyes scanned those of all three women. "All of you?"

"It's not against the rules, is it?" Merry asked.

"No, no. Mr. McFay can have as many visitors as he—"

Annie leaned on the counter. "Mr. McFay?"

"Your father-in-law. He's—"

Annie's knees buckled. She found herself helped to a chair in the lobby.

The receptionist left for a glass of water.

"Annie, what's wrong?" Merry asked.

"Cal's father is dead. He died before we got married."

"Apparently not," Claire said.

"Why would Cal lie?" Merry asked.

Annie stood. "I have to see him. Now."

❧❧❧   ❧❧❧   ❧❧❧

Fergis McFay sat in a wheelchair in the atrium. He had an oxygen tube in his nose and a tank on the back of the chair. He was sleeping despite two macaws squawking loudly in cages nearby. A few elderly people played cards. An employee, dressed in a teal uniform, watered plants. Annie, Merry, and Claire pulled three chairs close.

The receptionist tapped him on the shoulder. "Mr. McFay? Mr. McFay? You have more visitors."

He grunted, then opened his eyes. Immediately Annie saw that Cal had inherited his blue eyes from his father. He blinked a few times then looked around, panicked. "Where's my chainsaw?"

The receptionist patted his arm. "We'll find it for you." She looked to the ladies. "He has Alzheimer's. He lives in the past more than the present, but he comes and goes. Sometimes he's here."

"I need him to be here," Annie said.

Merry leaned close and whispered, "He doesn't know you anyway, Annie."

Good point. She thanked the receptionist and turned to her father-in-law. What an odd experience. To think someone was dead only to find them alive?

He surprised her by asking, "Who are you?" His voice was gruff. His eyes flashed.

"I'm Annie. I'm—"

He shook a finger at her and interrupted. "You're that white-trash girl, aren't you?"

"What?"

"The one Cal was going to save to impress me."

Annie looked at her friends. "Save? He married me."

Fergis flipped a hand. "Same thing." He looked at her midsection. "You still prego?"

Annie felt Merry's hand on her knee trying to give her comfort. It didn't work.

Suddenly, Claire chimed in. "Yes, she's pregnant. The baby's due in a few months."

What was she doing?

Fergis slumped back in his chair. He frowned and shook his head. "She's a fornicator having a bastard child." He spoke to Claire as if Annie weren't there. "And my son's going to marry her!"

"He's a good man," Claire said. "He loves her."

"No, he doesn't. He's just trying to impress me. Save the poor sinful girl, to atone for his own sins."

"He loved me. He *loves* me." Annie didn't like the desperate whine in her voice.

"He's trying to earn his way to heaven—and into my good graces. Dumb kid." His face changed, his arm raised. "'Put to death, therefore, whatever belongs to your earthly nature: sexual immorality, impurity, lust, evil desires and greed, which is idolatry. Because of these, the wrath of God is coming!'"

He put his arm down and leaned over the side of his wheelchair, searching for something. "Now, where is my chainsaw? I have that grove to clear. Someone took it." He glared at Annie. "Did you take it?"

She shook her head.

Merry helped her to standing. "Let's go, Annie."

"Annie!" Fergis said. "My boy was going to marry her, but I forbid it! I forbid it!"

Annie felt herself being hurried away. The next thing she knew, they were in the car, and Claire was driving on the highway home. *Home. Just get me home.*

She curled up on the backseat and closed her eyes. If only she could close her ears and stop the words being repeated in her head.

When Annie came in the kitchen door, Cal called out from the living room. "That you, Annie-girl?"

It's me. Annie. Your fornicating charity case.

She let her purse drop to the floor. She kept her jacket on and went into the living room. The television was on. She moved across the room like a floating zombie. She turned it off with a finger. The effort was difficult.

"Hey! I was watching that."

She turned to face him.

"Sheesh, Annie. What's wrong? You look like you've been run over."

She drew in a breath. "I have been run over. Run over by your lies."

He showed a glimmer of panic. "What are you talking about?"

She sank into the rocker but did not rock. "I met a man today." She purposely didn't say more. Let him suffer that fear for just a moment. It would serve him right. "His name is Fergis McFay."

Cal popped off the couch. "When? Why did you visit my father?"

Annie had to laugh. "When? Why did *I*...? You're asking the wrong questions, Cal. How about the big one: Why did you tell me your father was dead? Why have you been hiding his existence all these years?"

He fell onto the couch as if his muscles had left him. "I wanted to tell you so many times..."

"Why didn't you?"

Cal leaned forward, setting his elbows on his thighs. He ran his hands over his face. "I didn't want to admit I lied. I didn't want you to think badly of me."

She couldn't remain seated. She had to pace. "But a lie strung out for years becomes worse."

"I know; I know..."

She spun around and faced him. "Where has he been all these years?"

"In Eldora. He had his own house until recently. His health..."

"So that's why you've been making these trips to Eldora?"

"He's kind of needy right now."

"You're not having an affair?" She hadn't meant to say it. Was it good she'd said it?

His jaw dropped. "Why would you think...? No!" He stood and took her arms. "No, Annie. I love you. You alone. I would never be unfaithful."

She'd known that. Deep down, she'd known that. She dropped her forehead against his chest, and he wrapped his arms around her.

"I'm so sorry, Annie. My father is a difficult man. He didn't approve of me marrying you since you were pregnant with another man's child."

Annie stood erect and stepped back. "He called me a fornicator and Avi a bastard."

Cal reached for her, but she stepped away. They needed to finish this.

"My father calls himself a Christian. But he's first and foremost a judge. Everything has always been black and white to him. And I was never good enough. Nothing I did was good enough, even though I tried and tried to be the kind of man he wanted me to be."

Cal looked so pitiful, but Annie didn't go to him. Not yet. "He said you saved me, you saved the poor pregnant girl to impress him."

He hesitated a moment, then shrugged. "He was big into doing good deeds."

"I was a charity project to get brownie points with him?"

"Annie, I chose you over my father. I married you even when he said not to. That's why I said he was dead. I didn't want you to have to endure his mean ways. I was trying to protect you."

"I don't need protection. I'm a big girl."

Cal's voice softened. "You don't need protection now, but you did then. You needed me." He took a step toward her, and she didn't move away. He stroked her hair away from her face. "And I needed you, Annie-girl. I love you."

She let him hug her, and after a few moments she hugged back.

Cal lay in bed, Annie asleep against his chest. He was glad that was over. He was glad the secret was out. Now Annie could come with him to visit his dad. And Avi had a grandfather she didn't even know about. Who knows? Maybe a granddaughter would soften his father.

But Cal's relief was short-lived. One secret was out in the open.

If only they all were...

Thirteen

People who want to get rich
fall into temptation and a trap
and into many foolish and harmful desires
that plunge men into ruin and destruction.

1 TIMOTHY 6:9

ONE MONTH LATER

"CHESTNUTS ROASTING *on an open fire...*"

Bailey tossed the wad of Christmas lights on the couch. *Bah. Humbug.* He strode to the stereo and ejected Nat King Cole. Who was he trying to kid? Putting up a Christmas tree was meaningless without Jered around.

He looked toward the box containing their collection of Santas. It was always Jered's job to arrange them on the mantel.

He noticed a Santa's foot sticking out the top. He retrieved the toppled jolly man. The stuffed Santa had a lopsided beard from the time Jered, at age five, had decided to give it a trim with fingernail scissors.

Bailey moved toward the kitchen, toward a pair of scissors so he could make it right. Fix Jered's mistake. Why hadn't he done it before?

But in the doorway he stopped. He looked at the Santa with the deformed beard. He ran a finger along its ragged edge.

He backtracked and set him on the mantel, front and center. Then he hauled the rest of the boxes back to the basement.

This one Santa was enough this year.

This one particular Santa said it all.

"Chestnuts roasting on an open fire..."

"Jered? Come here."

He glanced up from untangling the string of Christmas lights. They were all white, not like the cool multicolored ones he and his dad always had. But he couldn't be picky. At least Jinko had a tree—such as it was. Just a tabletop thing Jinko said he could buy. Kind of pitiful, but better than nothing. Yet not a single Santa in sight. Jered had always loved to set up their Santa collection.

"Jered! Get up here!"

He tossed the lights on the couch. "Coming." He went upstairs to Jinko's den and found him at the desk. A newspaper was open to the want ads. One ad was circled in red ink. Jinko pegged it with a finger.

"This. This is it."

The print was too small, and Jered couldn't read it without picking it up. But since Jinko wasn't offering... Jered had learned not to grab. "What's 'it'?"

Jinko snatched the paper, shoving it under Jered's nose. *"It* is a place to get rich. A coin auction here in Eldora."

Jered took the page and read the ad. Coins. Money. That sounded good. But an auction? "We steal from houses, not people."

Jinko smiled. "Semantics, kid. Big gains always include big risks."

Jered shrugged. He wasn't about to argue—or ask too many questions.

"That's *it?* I come up with a stunning way to make some big cash, and all you can do is shrug?"

"I'm sure it's doable."

Jinko tossed the paper on the desk. "I'll *do* it without you, if that's what you want. I'm only trying to look after you. I don't think you realize where you'd be without me."

Yes, but... It was a complicated point.

Jinko tapped the ad. "If you don't want to be in on it, I'll find someone else." His eyes did their own advertising.

Jered shoved his hands in his pockets. How could he refuse? "I'm in."

"Good choice."

Jered took a step toward the hall. He turned back. "You want to come help me decorate the tree?"

"Christmas is your deal, kid, not mine. Knock yourself out."

Ho ho ho.

"Chestnuts roasting on an open fire..."

Annie loved this song. The mellow voice, the warm feeling of hearth and home. It was so nice to have an addition to their family gatherings this year. Since Cal had shared his secret father, they'd all been back to see Fergis many times. Avi, too. It was a little hard for her to understand how come she suddenly had an instant grand-father, but the old man and the girl hit it off immediately. Avi had even gotten Fergis to laugh. Kids. The wonder drug.

And Thanksgiving a week ago had been nice with another place set at the table. Family. Things were the way they were supposed to be. Mostly.

"Annie? Can you come here, please?"

Cal was in the kitchen. She set aside the Christmas stocking she was cross-stitching for her father-in-law. She'd have to work on it double time to get it done.

"What's up?" she asked.

He was at the computer, but it was off. A newspaper sat on top of the desk, open to the want ads. One ad was circled in red ink. Cal pegged it with a finger.

"This. This is it."

The print was too small, and Annie picked it up. "What's *it?*"

"It is a place to get rich. A coin auction in Eldora."

Annie read the ad. Coins. Money. That sounded good. But an auction? "What do you have in mind?"

Cal took the paper back. "We buy coins and sell them on-line. We can make a mint, pun intended. Plus, I have another idea if they have the *right* coins."

Oh, dear. What with the extra expense of Fergis's care and Christmas presents to buy, she really didn't feel they should invest in anything right now.

He huffed at her. "No reaction? I come up with a great way to make some real money, and all you can do is stand there?"

"I suppose it sounds doable. But should we really spend—?"

Cal tossed the paper on the desk. "I'm only trying to look after you, Annie. And there's Avi and Dad to consider, too. With my regular job, plus Bailey's project, plus this opportunity..." He wrapped an arm around her waist and pulled her close. "I'm trying real hard to provide well for us."

How could she argue with him? Actually, she was trying hard not to argue about anything. Their marriage was delicate at the moment. They were still rebuilding since the truth about his father had come out. Through that incident, Annie had finally realized how important it was for Cal to feel like a success.

No matter how many "I'm proud of you's" she said, he wouldn't accept his own worth unless he felt he was financially successful. If only he'd be willing to find his true worth, in Christ Jesus. Unfortunately, little progress had been made in that direction.

"If you don't want to be in on it, I suppose I could go alone."

Annie shoved her hands in her pockets. How could she refuse? "I guess I'm in."

"Good choice."

They were going to an auction.

She went back to her needlework. It *was* good Cal wanted to include her in his new project. But what about her being able to include him in her interests? She'd gone to choir the past month and had even taken Avi with her. The church was getting ready for a big Christmas pageant this Sunday. She was glad Cal hadn't made too much of a stink. She'd even started taking Avi to church. Yet week after week Cal stayed home. They were back to living separate lives. She hated that. She wanted to be able to interconnect with him. Especially about God.

She pricked her finger.

Ouch.

⊰⊱   ⊰⊱   ⊰⊱

Annie took her running shoes onto the front stoop and sat to put them on. The concrete was cold against her seat. It had snowed last week, but most of it had melted. She hated the thought of days when she wouldn't be able to run because of the weather. Her extra pounds were coming off quite nicely.

"Looky, Mama." Avi stood beneath the living room window, a string of lights looped around her shoulders. "Daddy has lights on two bushes already."

"Looking good, family," she said.

Cal set the ladder to string the lights on the eaves. "Where you going?"

"Running."

"We were planning to get the tree after we're done here."

"I'll be back." She blew them each a kiss and headed out. Actually, this was not a random run. She had a mission.

She headed toward Merry's and found her and Ken stringing Christmas lights on Merry's porch.

"Hey, hey, Annie. Two more hands," Ken said. "Come help."

"Actually, I've *come* seeking some help of my own."

"Uh-oh. Sounds ominous."

Merry pointed to the porch swing. "Care to sit?"

"Absolutely."

She and Merry took a seat on the swing. Ken hung back on the top step. "Is this girl talk? Would you prefer I go?"

"No need. I'd like you to stay and give me a man's perspective. This involves Cal."

Annie let Merry create the rhythm of their movement. It reminded her of life in general: forward, back, forward, back. "You know that Cal and I have fallen into a kind of rhythm regarding God or no-God in our lives."

"How's that going?"

"Okay, I guess. Once we got the Fergis secret out in the open, things have been pretty good. Kind of. We're back to the status quo anyway. But I'm thinking it's the chicken way out. Sure, we don't argue about faith much anymore, but that isn't necessarily a good thing." She angled her body toward her friends. "It's not as though we're divided about paper or plastic, country or classical. This is important stuff here."

"Eternal stuff."

"Exactly!" She knew Merry would understand. "I want to see Cal up in heaven, for my own sake as well as his. I know Jesus is the way—the only way. 'I am the way and the truth and the life. No one comes to the Father except through me.' But what if something happens to Cal before he makes the right decision? Time is not endless. People do run *out* of time."

"Indeed they do," Ken said.

Merry looked at her lap, and Annie knew she was thinking about her lost family. Lost to this life but alive in heaven with the Lord.

Annie touched her knee. "How do I make Cal choose Jesus before it's too late?"

"That's *the* question." Ken leaned against the railing. "You can't *make* him do anything, Annie. You know that, whether it's making Cal take out the garbage or making him cut his ties with Bailey's newest brainchild."

"You know about Bailey's business idea?"

"Doesn't everyone?" He continued. "You certainly can't make Cal know God and choose Jesus as his Savior. You are not your husband's Holy Spirit."

Annie looked down. "That's not what I want to hear."

Ken nodded. "I know."

She looked across the yard. A pile of leaves was doing a whirlpool dance in the street in between the remnants of snow. "If only Cal could understand that I can't limit God to a portion of my life. It would be like asking oxygen to leave some of my cells alone. If that were possible, the cells would die. I'd die."

Annie tilted her head back and took a deep breath. The swing adjusted to the change in the distribution of her weight. "I just want him to have what I have, to know what I know, to feel what I feel." She looked at Merry. "It's for his own good."

"Which is probably one reason he resists."

Annie shrugged. "So now what?"

Ken moved directly in front of the swing. "We step up the prayers. God wants Cal more than you do, Annie, more than any of us do. But the deal that has to be struck is between Cal and God. It's got to be Cal's decision."

"Sometimes I hate free will."

Merry laughed. "It's both costly and priceless, isn't it?"

"Would you like me to talk to him?" Ken asked.

She jumped on the idea. "That would be great." Then reality set in. "But what would you say? Not to doubt your abilities, but I'm not sure getting talked to by anyone is what Cal needs."

"Then what does he need?" Merry asked.

Only God knows. Annie shook her head. She stood, making the swing gyrate at its loss. "I better go. Thanks for listening. Again."

"Anytime."

"And keep praying for my stubborn, arrogant husband who—"

"Who is a child of God," Merry said.

Annie expelled a breath. It was good to be reminded of the bottom line.

Cal sat on the bed and hung up the phone. He'd just called the auction's number to get a detailed listing of the coins to be sold. It was all set. Tomorrow he and Annie would go to the auction, buy up some coins to sell on-line, and more important, see if he could find three particular coins.

The idea had come to him as soon as he'd seen the ad. The timing was perfect. His "other idea," of which he hadn't told Annie, came about because he'd run into his old college poker buddy Scott Wheeler when he was in Eldora one day. They'd spent a good ten minutes reminiscing. The subject had turned to coins when they'd started talking about their old hobbies. Did Cal still do a lot of fishing and did Scott still collect coins? No and yes.

Scott mentioned he was down to missing only three half-dollars to make his collection of Barber halves complete—which would make its value shoot up to nearly five thousand dollars. From his wallet, he'd pulled a list of the three coins and had asked Cal to be on the lookout for them. Said he'd pay top dollar. Cal had written them down.

If those three coins were being sold at the auction, Cal could temporarily use some of Annie's inheritance money to buy them, then sell them to Scott for a nifty profit and be a little closer to having some real money in the bank.

But what if Scott's at the auction, too?

No problem. Cal would get other coins to sell on the Internet. *Cal's Coins...*

He heard Annie's and Avi's voices singing from downstairs: *"Joy to the world, the Lord is come..."* They were finishing up the tree and the other Christmas decorations and were really getting into it—especially this year. He'd never heard so many Jesus songs. Whatever.

Not that he was a Scrooge. He loved Christmas. But he had to admit he loved it better before Jesus had become a part of it. Santa, presents, tons of food—that was the focus of the Christmases they'd had the last ten years. He'd had enough of the Jesus-Christmas growing up. Jesus crammed down his throat.

Cal thought of Thanksgiving and the sight of Annie and his father talking about some Bible verses. His stomach grabbed. During his dad's few moments in the here and now, he talked to Annie about God-stuff. How rude was that? Didn't they recognize God was the problem? That God was the one who'd made the secret a necessity? Maybe his dad was too stubborn to see, but certainly Annie could understand that God caused the rift in the first—

But she doesn't know the whole story.

He shook his head against the thought of telling her more. She'd recently been privy to one hidden portion of his past. She couldn't see the rest. She'd never understand that even if his motives weren't initially pure, everything had worked out.

Avi started a new song, *"Deck the halls with boughs of holly..."*

He wished Avi and Annie hadn't decided to take part in the Christmas pageant. All those rehearsals. And the big to-do was Sunday. They were begging him to go and had even wanted him to bring Dad.

No way. They could fa-la-la-Christ-is-born all they wanted; he wouldn't be a part of it. And he certainly wouldn't subject himself to his father's judgment about the singing, the costumes, whatever would *not* be acceptable in Fergis McFay's eyes.

He heard Avi's voice. "Come down, Daddy. We're going to put the baby Jesus in the manger."

He sighed. No sir, certain boundaries had to be maintained for the good of the family. His family. "Go ahead. I'm busy right now."

Pooh.

Avi sat on the bottom step and cupped her face in her hands. She looked at her mother, who was arranging a red candle on the TV. "He's not coming to the Christmas thingy Sunday either, is he, Mama?"

"Did you expect him to?"

No. But that didn't mean Avi couldn't hope. And pray. She'd never prayed before she started going to church and to Bible study with her mama over at Sim's house. But she prayed now. Quite a bit.

And it worked. Most of the time anyway.

She prayed she'd get a good grade in spelling, and she'd gotten a sparkle-star. She'd prayed that Andy Simon would quit bugging her at recess, and soon after, he started bugging Sally Mason instead.

Once those prayers had been answered, Avi started praying for bigger things. When she'd really wanted to go to Cassie's birthday party, she prayed her stomachache would go away, and it had.

She'd even prayed "God bless" for her new grandpa. He was a funny old guy, and sometimes it was hard to keep track of what he was talking about, but it was neat to have a grandpa like her friends did. They'd even had him over for Thanksgiving. He let her push him in his wheelchair. He had a pocket in the side for magazines that was full of cracker crumbs.

But most of all, she prayed for her dad, that he'd stop being so mean about God. And especially Jesus. It's like the *J*-word was a slap to him. Every time they said Jesus' name, his eyes got small and his jaw tensed up like it did when he was ready to yell at Avi for being naughty.

Talking about Jesus wasn't being naughty. It was good. *He* was good. Why couldn't Daddy see that? Why couldn't he come to church with them, or at least come to the Christmas pageant? Avi was going to be an angel with a real halo.

But her dad wouldn't see her.

And that made her sad.

Vasylko greeted Jered when he came into work. "Hey, boy. Is tomorrow big night?"

It took Jered a moment. *Amateur Night.* Jered hung his coat on a hook. "Nah."

"You not try since first time." He made a chicken noise. "Eh?"

"I'm not chicken. I've been practicing hard but—"

"Then why not sing?"

Because Jinko says the time isn't right. "I will. Soon."

"You better. Dreams die if not fed."

Jered tied his apron and got to work. He believed what Vasylko said, 100 percent. He was working on it. During the last few weeks, he'd finally had time to feed his dream. By most accounts his life had gotten easier. By moving into Jinko's house, he now had a real room, a living room, and even Jinko's piano to mess around on.

And Jinko kept feeding him with hope, with talk that one of these days when Jered got good enough—what *was* good enough?—he'd invite some big record producer to hear him. He even talked about having a private audition, away from the craziness of Amateur Night.

The time was never right. Yet how could Jinko judge his progress anyway? He never had time to listen. He was always hurrying in and out, rarely at home, and he never asked Jered to play for him. Jered was beginning to think the whole thing was a ploy to get him to help with the stealing.

It reminded Jered of a movie he saw once when he was little: *Oliver.* A guy in the movie named Fager or Fagin or something taught kids how to pick pockets. Jinko had taught *him* how to steal and had even let Jered do a few "appointments" on his own. He got a higher cut for those—as he should, since he was taking the risk— and truth was, the whole thing *did* give Jered a rush. He felt guilty about that.

Jinko still handled the fencing of the goods up in KC. Fine with Jered. He didn't have connections. But there was a good possibility Jinko was ripping him off, selling things for more than he let on and keeping the difference. Whatever. Wouldn't Jered do the same?

All in all, it was a good life. A good living. Not conventional or boring like his life in Steadfast. If Darryl and Moog knew what he was doing, they'd freak.

One Saturday when Jered was feeling brave (and dumb), he'd decided to drop in on his old buddies and flash a little cash. He'd driven to Steadfast and spotted the two of them parked as usual in the lot behind the hardware store, drinking beer. But when he saw that a new guy had been added—someone he didn't recognize—he didn't stop. Obviously, his friends had moved on without him. Replaced him.

He was dispensable. Again.

The only place he didn't seem dispensable was in Jinko's house. Jinko needed him and he needed Jinko. And just to make sure Jinko didn't come home one day and order him out, Jered was extra careful to keep things clean and tidy. Once, Jered had moved a statue on the coffee table to the mantel because he wanted to put his music on the table to practice. When Jinko had seen it, he shoved the music aside and replaced the statue. He even turned it a hair to the left, as if it had one spot, and one specific spot in the house, and Jinko's world wouldn't spin right until it was in place.

But now the auction. The whole thing made Jered nervous. So what if it might be a bigger haul? They were doing fine. Why risk it?

Big gains always include big risk.

Maybe that was true but—

Vasylko called to him over the din of the dishwasher. "Hey, Jered. I forget ask. You have good Thanksgiving last week? Turkey? Gobble-gobble?"

Actually, he and Jinko had hit a house over on Spring Street that day. The owners were out of town. With family. Sharing a special meal.

Vasy was waiting for an answer. Jered turned the question around. "Did *you* have a nice day?"

"Of course. I make girlfriend big turkey. We go all-American. We have yums and everything."

"Yums?"

"Orange potatoes?"

"Yams. Sweet potatoes."

"Yams, yums. They were *yum.*" Vasy took up an order of enchiladas and handed it to a waiter. "Vasylko has much to be thankful." He wiped the side of his head with his upper arm. "Jered too, eh?"

A snicker escaped.

"No?" Vasy asked.

Jered shrugged and finished filling a tray of plates.

Vasy stirred the vat of beans. "Holiday. You should be home. With family." He looked around the kitchen. Oddly, they were alone. Vasy stepped away from the stove and came to Jered's side. "Jinko is no family. You go home, Jered. Go where people love you."

Jered grabbed another tray to fill with dishes.

Vasy's hand squeezed his shoulder. "I pray for you."

Annie lay on the couch, in the dark except for the twinkling lights of the Christmas tree. If she squinted her eyes, each light widened and spread into a prism. Beautiful.

She loved Christmas. Especially this year when it seemed fuller and more complete. She mourned how many years she'd been content with half a Christmas—a Christmas without Christ. It's as if she'd previously held a succulent orange in her hand, content with the feel of it, the smell of it, never realizing the real treasure was inside and could only be found by peeling away the pretty layers. And oh, the taste of Christ Jesus! Nothing could compare.

She turned on her side, snuggled into a pillow, and looked at the Nativity scene on the coffee table before her. She'd decided on this position rather than the mantel because she wanted this symbol of the true meaning of Christmas to be in the center of the room. Unavoidable. Practically in Cal's face.

Surely he'd at least glance at it while he was watching TV, and maybe it would stir some long-forgotten corner of his heart. And that place would soften, and he would capture the wonder of the season and understand how deeply her own life had changed since this Babe, this Son of God, this Savior had come into her life.

Or not.

She closed her eyes against tears. *Oh Lord, please help him see!*

She heard a sound in the entry and opened her eyes to find Avi standing there. "Hey, sweet-apple."

Avi looked at the tree and took a deep breath. "It's pretty."

"It's perfect." Annie scooted her back against the cushions and opened her arm, inviting her daughter to join her on the couch. Avi tucked herself in, like one spoon fitting into another. Annie covered her with an arm, loving the smell of her hair.

"I love you, Mama."

"I love you, too."

A near-perfect moment. Only one person was missing.

Fourteen

O Sovereign LORD, my strong deliverer,
who shields my head in the day of battle—
do not grant the wicked their desires, O LORD;
do not let their plans succeed,
or they will become proud.

PSALM 140:7–8

ANNIE SPREAD CHERRY PRESERVES on a piece of toast as Cal came into the kitchen, folding some papers in half. "Why aren't you ready, Annie?"

She took a bite and glanced at the clock on the microwave. "The rehearsal isn't until this afternoon. I have plenty of time."

"What rehearsal?"

I've told him... "The dress rehearsal for the Christmas pageant. Avi and I have to be there at one and—"

Cal tossed the papers on the table. "Oh, this is great."

"What?"

"You know very well what. You're not going."

"We have to go. It's required."

"Required?"

She took another bite. "I don't know what you're so upset about. I told you about this dress rehearsal weeks ago, when Avi and I first started going to choir." She pointed to the calendar next to the refrigerator. "It's on the calendar."

He threw his hands in the air. "Well then. Maybe I should write myself onto the calendar so I can have a moment of your precious time."

"Cal..." He was being ridiculous. And hadn't she wanted them to have special time yesterday while they were putting up the Christmas decorations? He'd *chosen* not to be involved. "We can do something tomorrow, after the pageant. Go to Eldora and have a nice dinner or—"

"You can forget about me going to any pageant." He grabbed his ski coat and shoved his arms in the sleeves with a *swish, swish* sound.

"But Avi's an angel and—"

His face was flushed. "You can forget about me going to anything *you* want, when you can't even follow through with your promise to go with me."

"What are you talking about?"

He rolled his eyes. "Proof of how I rate. You can't even remember a commitment you made to me yesterday."

Annie sucked in a breath. "The auction?"

"Yes, the auction. It starts at ten."

"The auction is today?"

"You know very well it's today."

Annie popped out of her chair. This couldn't be happening. "I did *not* know it was today. I would never have agreed to go if I'd known. There's no way I can go to the auction. The rehearsal..."

He picked up the papers and shoved them into the inner pocket of his coat. "Let's get down to it, Annie. There's no way you'll go anywhere I want you to go or do anything I want you to do."

"Cal, don't be—"

"Right? Don't be right?"

"That's not what I was going to say."

He took a step toward her, and it took all her will not to compensate by taking a step back. He moved his face to within inches of hers. Confusion filled his eyes. "Ever since this Jesus... You're not my wife anymore."

"What?" She took that step back.

"You're not the Annie I married. You've changed."

"For the better. I'm really trying to be the best—"

"Best for whom? Certainly not best for me."

This was absurd. "Cal, faith shouldn't come between us. It should bring us together. Jesus is helping me be all I can be. Not that I'm perfect—I have a long way to go—but I'm trying really hard to—"

"To break us up. To make me feel the fool. To gang up with my father against me."

"No!"

He strode to the china cabinet and flung open the door. He pointed to the stack of plates. "I don't know where you're hiding your Bible, but I know you have it. I know you've been reading it."

He had to stop talking like this. But yes, it was still hidden in Avi's cubby, and she was reading it. "The Bible is good, Cal. It's changed everything for me."

He huffed. "Don't I know it."

"It's a guidebook. It's—"

He snickered. "A guidebook for judging people."

She struggled between wanting to crawl into a corner or fling herself at him, arms flailing against his chest. "I don't understand you, Cal. This God hot button you have. Your father believes. He's a little adamant about a few things, and he was wrong ten years ago being so judgmental about me, but we're getting to know each other now. Things will be okay." She took a fresh breath. "If only you'd share—"

He slammed the cabinet door shut, making the glass rattle. "Don't pretend you know my father because you've spent a few hours with him and fed him pumpkin pie! He and God..." Cal held his hand out like a stop sign. "It's not even Dad's fault. He's just a misguided, bitter man. God turned me against God. It's *His* fault and *His* doing."

"What did—what do you think He did?"

"I will not get into this. This is not about then; it's about now."

"But then affects now."

He shook his head. "Now is the only time that's important."

"That's not true."

"It is true!" His voice vibrated in the room. He paced up and back, up and back, then stopped in front of her. "It's moment-of-truth time, Annie. Now."

"What are you—?"

"It's time you choose."

Her heart grabbed. "I don't understand." *But I think I do. Oh Lord, I think I do. Please don't let him say it. Please—*

"You need to choose between me and God. Between me and your precious Jesus."

A nervous laugh escaped. "Cal. Don't be silly."

His face broke, then contorted, becoming almost fiendish. "I am *not* being silly! This is life and death. The life and death of us, of our marriage. I can't live with another man in your life. I cannot share you with the Father, Son, and Holy Spirit. I *won't* share you!"

How had their discussion about schedules gotten to this?

"Choose! Choose now, Annie. Him or me!"

It was a scene in a movie. It *had* to be a scene in a movie. It couldn't be happening. She tried to keep her tone light. "Surely you can't be giving me an ultimatum."

"I most certainly can. I'm tired of living separate lives. I do my thing; you and God and Avi do yours. I'm left in the cold, Annie. You've left me out in the cold."

She reached for his hand, but he pulled it away. "I don't mean to, Cal. More than anything I want to share my new life with you. And I truly tried setting God aside, but He wouldn't stay put. I know there's a way for me—for us. You don't know how many times I've wanted to try to explain to you—"

"I don't need your lectures."

"It wouldn't be a lecture."

"It *would* be a lecture. With you telling me how bad I am, telling me I need Jesus, that I need a Savior."

Her voice was soft. "You do." She quickly added, "I do. We all do."

"But some more than others, right?"

Actually... No. Annie couldn't think that way. She was no better than Cal. She was happier than Cal, more content. But that was because she *had* admitted how bad *she* was, how much *she* needed a Savior. It wasn't a contest between husband and wife; it was a parallel road. Or it could be. She desperately wanted Cal to be beside her on that road, walking with her, holding her hand. Now and...

"I want to be with you in heaven, Cal."

He stared at her a moment, then laughed. "There is no heaven."

His certainty scared her. "Of course there is. And if we have a relationship with God, if we believe Jesus is who He said He is—"

Cal flipped his hands by his ears. "Yada, yada, yada. Christian bunkum."

"It's not bunkum. It's truth. It's God's promise to us. It's hope. It's life. It's—"

"A pack of lies."

She felt her own anger rise. "You are the most stubborn, arrogant, egotistical, proud—"

He applauded. "Keep it up. Calling me names does wonders for a marriage."

He was right about that one. *Lord, help!* She took a breath and let it out through her teeth. "I'm sorry about not being able to go to the auction with you. I didn't understand it was today. If I had I wouldn't have—"

"Chosen me." He dug his keys out of his jeans pocket. "It appears my ultimatum has been accepted and answered. You *have* made a choice between me and God."

"No, I—"

"Yes, you have. And God won." He yanked the kitchen door open. "You've made your choice, Annie. Just don't be surprised when there are consequences."

"Cal."

He slammed the door behind him. It took her a good minute to move. What had just happened? A single word repeated itself: *No, no, no, no, no...*

When she tried to walk to a chair, her legs buckled, and she collapsed into a heap. Her downward momentum continued until she was resting her arms on the floor, her face buried within their folds.

How could God have allowed this to happen? She was truly sorry she'd agreed to go to the auction, but it was an honest mistake. And there was no way she and Avi could miss the dress rehearsal. They'd made a commitment...

What about your commitment to your husband? You are *choosing God over Cal.*

No. Not really. The majority of her time was here, with Cal.

But was it? God was with her all the time, so even when she was with Cal, she wasn't completely with him.

How can this ever work?

She allowed herself to turn on her side, drawing her knees into a fetal curl, resting her head on an arm. The floor was cold. A tear slid past her hair to the floor. She let it go unimpeded.

God, I'm trying to do the right thing, find the right balance. I'm trying not to be a fanatic believer like his father. I'm trying to be loving, to be a good wife, but I don't know what to do.

Words came to her like a ticker tape, and she recognized them as coming from Jeremiah: *"Call to me and I will answer you and tell you great and unsearchable things you do not know."*

She managed a soft laugh. *Unsearchable things?* She'd take it. At the moment she felt as if she knew nothing. Nothing at all. If only God would tell her some unsearchable things, things that went beyond what she could even fathom, much less search for. Things He wanted to tell her.

"Mama? What are you doing on the floor?"

Annie scrambled to stand and turned away so she could wipe her face.

But Avi came around to see. "You've been crying."

"Daddy and I had a little argument."

"I heard. Did he knock you down?"

Annie put a hand to Avi's head and drew it to her side. "No, no, sweet-apple. Your daddy wouldn't hurt me. I was just tired. I don't like it when we argue."

"Me neither."

Annie hated that their daughter had overheard. She forced a smile. "Are you excited about the rehearsal and getting to wear your costume?"

"Daddy doesn't want us to do it. Maybe we shouldn't."

Annie took her shoulders and drew her front and center, leaning down to her eye level. "We should do it, Avi. It's a wonderful pageant and a wonderful way to celebrate Jesus' birth." *But it will cost us.*

Avi let out a sigh heavy with relief. "Good. 'Cause I like my halo."

It was amazing how kids could get back to basics. "Go watch some cartoons. I'll make pancakes, okay?"

Annie got out the skillet. She hoped Cal was successful at the auction. Maybe that would make him forget their argument.

And his ultimatum.

Cal paid for gas, a cup of coffee, and a package of chocolate donuts. Some breakfast.

Why did Annie purposely make him mad? She knew the auction was today. Why had she told him she'd go if she had no intention...

It was an honest mistake.

He tore open the package and popped a donut in his mouth whole. No. It was part of a pattern. A pattern where God was deliberately shoving Cal out of the picture, out of his own marriage.

I can't let Him win. God had won before, luring Cal close before He took Treena away. Cal wouldn't let it happen again. He would fight for Annie. Win her back. Make her see that their old life was a good one, the only life for them.

But was it?

Grinding the gears, he pulled onto the street heading to Eldora. He had to calm down. He couldn't do anything about the Annie situation right now. He had other work to do. Work that would gain them the financial security they needed, that would show him as the great provider. Work that would prove what a wonderful man he was.

He sat a little straighter in the seat. He *was* a wonderful man. If Annie knew what was good for her, she'd realize that.

She'd better.

Cal got his bidding number and gave his ID info at the check-in desk. He was now officially a player. It was going to be a great day. He was entering a nobody and would leave with the means of making himself a somebody. Exciting stuff.

He wandered by the tables of coins and joined the other bidders in making a close inspection. The individual coins were in small plastic cases so the oil from fingers wouldn't further discolor them. Some people used magnifying glasses to check the degree of detail. Cal had no idea what to look for but figured the newer it looked, the better.

He watched as they checked their faxed inventory sheets, making notations on them. He found his in the pocket of his ski coat and followed suit. He'd done his research on the Internet and had painstakingly written down the typical prices for each piece.

He looked for the Barber halves that would make him rich. Another man was looking at them, a man with a ponytail and a goatee. He was wearing a long black leather coat and looked as if he could be a country singer—or a hit man. An odd combination.

The man looked up. "Mornin'."

"Mornin'."

He handed Cal one of the coins. "You interested in these?"

Cal wasn't sure it was wise to say, but he said it anyway. "I think so."

The man's expression changed, as if Cal's status had been upped because of his answer. "You must be a die-hard collector."

"Yeah, well..."

"Do you have a Barber set?"

No, but I know someone who does. He'd forgotten about the possibility that Scott Wheeler might be at this same auction. He did a quick scan of the room. No Scott.

The man repeated his question. "You have a set?"

"Yes," Cal said. "I just need three to make it complete."

"I'm impressed," said the man. "Once it's complete it will be worth four, five thousand?"

"Sounds about right."

The man pointed to the chairs. "Want to sit?"

"Sure."

They moved to the seats. The man sat beside a teenager who was drinking a Mountain Dew. "Did you get anything for me, kid?"

The boy stood. "No. Sorry. What do you want?"

The man turned to Cal. "What's your pleasure? I'm buying."

"Coffee would be great. Black."

The kid hesitated and stared at him. The man whapped him on the thigh. "Two coffees."

"Yeah. I mean yes. I'll be right back."

The kid left. "That your son?"

"Nephew."

They got comfortable and hung their jackets on the back of the chairs. The boy returned with the coffees.

"Thanks."

The man extended a hand to shake. "I should introduce myself. I'm Chuck Wallin. And this is my nephew, Joe."

Cal shook his hand, then the boy's. The boy looked a little nervous. "Nice to meet you. I'm Cal McFay."

Cal McFay? Was this guy related to Annie McFay, the waitress at the Plentiful? He looked familiar. The image of a white truck with some kind of sign on the side came to mind.

Jered was about to ask when he realized he couldn't. He didn't want anyone to know who he was or that he had ties to Steadfast. That's one reason he was relieved the auction was in Eldora. He never would have gone if it had been in his hometown.

But it was okay. He wasn't Jered Manson. Not here. Not on this day. He was Joe Wallin, nephew of... He looked at Jinko, trying to remember what name he'd given himself. His mind was blank. He'd have to be careful not to call him *any* name.

The good thing about being a kid around two men was that nobody expected him to join in the conversation—nor did they want him to. He could sit back and listen at will. *Children should be seen and not heard*. Or they should *hear*. Listen. Like a bug on a wall.

The trick was not getting squished.

Cal knew his ego was out of control, but he couldn't seem to stop himself. It was so easy to talk to Chuck, and for some reason, he felt the need to brag.

Brag about coins he didn't even own.

By the time the auction started, Cal had implied he owned a set of Barber halves, a bunch of silver proof sets, Morgans and Wheats in plentiful quantities, and even some gold coins. Each time he added a coin to his nonexistent inventory, Chuck treated him better, with more respect. After the argument with Annie, Cal figured he was ripe for some respect and due a double helping.

The auctioneer clipped on his mike and said welcome. The coffee felt like a bad idea in his stomach.

"Here we go," Chuck whispered.

Cal wasn't sure how it happened. But, accompanied by the backslaps and congratulations of his new friend Chuck, he'd been high bidder on the three Barber halves Scott needed. Plus, he'd spent another twenty-five hundred dollars on additional coins. Nearly all of Annie's inheritance was gone. He wasn't even sure he'd gotten a good deal, but in the midst of buying one lot after another, what he *had* gotten was attention. He was a big shot. He was somebody. He was a player.

As he wrote out a check to pay for his coins, his hand shook. *What will Annie say?* kept floating through his mind.

He felt a hand on his shoulder. "Congratulations again, Cal."

"Thanks, Chuck."

"You going to celebrate?"

That was the last thing he felt like doing. He shook his head. "I think I'll head home."

Chuck elbowed him. "Do a little private celebrating with the wife, eh?"

Cal looked at his watch. Annie and Avi were at their rehearsal. Just as well. He needed some time to regroup. "Actually, she's gone for the afternoon. I'm going to take it easy."

"Gaze at your spoils?"

Cal took his receipt. "Sure."

"Hey," Chuck said, drawing Joe close. "I have a great idea. Since the wifey's not home, how about we go to your house and share a few? Toast your success. You got a couple beers?"

It might be nice. Chuck was a good guy. And since Annie was gone... "I think I can scrounge some up."

The kid spoke for the first time. "I don't know about that. I...uh..."

Chuck leveled him with a look. "You have better things to do, Joe?"

Joe blinked twice. "Uh, no. I guess not."

"Then let's get going. We'll follow you."

Once they were on the highway to Steadfast, Jinko pounced. "What was all that hemming and hawing about? Getting into his house is imperative. Getting invited to his house so we can see its setup and even see where he puts the coins is a bonus we can't pass up."

Jered hated to say it, but he had to. "I know his wife."

Jinko swerved toward the shoulder then back. "What?"

"He said his name was Cal McFay. As far as I know, only one McFay family lives in Steadfast. Which means his wife is a waitress at the Plentiful Café. She knows me—or she knows who I am."

"Great, just great." Jered could hear Jinko breathing. Finally, Jinko said, "But Cal didn't recognize you."

"I've never met him. Just her. And only when I've come into the café to eat something. Nowhere else."

"So maybe she won't know you."

She'll know me. Annie remembers everybody's name.

Jinko repeated himself. "So maybe she won't know you."

Jered shrugged and tried to think of something positive. "Cal said his wife wasn't home. Annie isn't home."

"True. We may have lucked out." Jinko tapped a finger on the steering wheel. "We get in, scope out the place, drink one beer, then get out. It'll be fine."

"Maybe." Jered looked at Cal's truck a quarter mile in front of them. "But maybe we should just turn around and go home. He might not even notice we're gone until it's too late. And he'll think we remembered something else we had to do. It'll be over. He'll never see us again."

"You turning chicken on me? Wanting to run and hide before things even start?"

Exactly. "I don't like the idea of tooling around Steadfast in the daytime again. Even though Cal doesn't know me, other people do."

"When we get to town, duck down."

"But won't Cal think it's strange?"

"So what? You spilled your drink on the floor of the car or something. You really think he's going to ask even if he does notice?"

Probably not.

"We're doing this, kid. We've come too far to turn back. We're on the edge of the payload of payloads. Fate placed us next to the big bidder of the day, the one who not only bought the three most precious coins at the auction, but who now has a complete set. Any man who spends nearly five thousand dollars at a coin auction has got to have ten times that much at home."

Bonnie came through the kitchen door of Palamba's. But instead of picking up her order or entering it into the computer, she came directly to Vasylko's side.

The cook glanced up from the fajita steak he was grilling. He noticed her face was pale. "What wrong?"

She eyed the door. "Two cops are here wanting to talk to Jinko. And Jered, too."

And Vasylko knew—he *knew*—what it was about: judgment day. "They not here."

"I told them that. But they have a few questions. Should I talk to them?"

Vasylko didn't think Bonnie knew anything. And Jinko had left him in charge. "I talk."

"But it's getting busy."

"Not busy yet. Have them come here. I take minute."

"Are you sure?"

"I sure." But he wasn't sure. Wasn't sure *if* he should talk to the police or *what* he would say. And he didn't much like police. The ones in Russia... But this was America. Things were different here.

The rules were different. Better. *God, help me do the right thing.*

Bonnie led two men into the kitchen. Vasylko was glad they were wearing overcoats and not uniforms. Even with that, they got enough looks from the other employees. And he was sure Bonnie was already spreading the news.

"I'm Detective Robinson and this is Detective Spencer. Thanks for agreeing to speak with us, Mister...?"

"Vasylko Andropov."

The shorter one with the mustache—Spencer—took out a notepad and pen. "Can you spell that?"

"No problem. Hold please." He served up the steak fajitas and wiped his hands on a towel. He motioned to the back door. "We go outside?"

"Fine."

Vasylko grabbed a jacket on the way out. He spelled his name, gave an address and phone number, then said, "Okay, shoot."

"Where is your boss and Jered Manson?"

"They took day off."

"Do you know why?"

He shoved his hands in his pockets against the cold. "They in trouble?"

"Perhaps." He eyed Vasylko a moment. "Does that surprise you?"

"No."

"Can you explain?"

How should he word it? "Jered good kid, wants to be musician. Jinko help him—or say he help him."

"Help him how?"

"Get audition. He give Jered place to stay."

"Why?"

Vasylko wished he could say it was because Jinko was such a nice man, but he couldn't. It was the time for the truth. "Jinko made him...owe him. Jered owe him."

Robinson's eyebrows rose. "For giving him a place to stay?"

"And job. Jered wash dishes."

Spencer tapped his pencil on the pad. "So Jinko promises Jered a break in the music business, provides him with a place to stay and a job...for what? I'm guessing it wasn't done from the goodness of his heart. What did Jered have to do for him?"

This was the hard part. Vasylko dragged a toe on the concrete. "Jered help him."

"Do what?"

Vasy glanced up, then down. "Whatever Jinko want."

"Sexual favors?"

"No, no! Not that." At least not that he knew of. "What I see I only guess. I don't *know.*"

"None of us know. That's why we're investigating. To find out."

"What this about?"

"We've had a couple burglaries. One of the victims ID'd Jered Manson's truck. A patrol car spotted it at Jinko's address. A neighbor said the boy has been living there with Mr. Daly. We traced him to this restaurant. We obtained a search warrant and this morning found some of the stolen property in the truck."

Vasylko's shoulders were heavy.

"Is this what you suspected?"

He nodded.

"What did you see?"

It was time for the truth. For Jered. The boy would be in trouble, but a little trouble was better than the big trouble that was sure to come. Vasylko told them about the odd shipments of liquor and the suspicious comings and goings of Jinko and Jered during business hours. "Jered good kid."

"Not anymore."

Vasylko put a hand on Spencer's arm. "No. He good kid now. He just tempted."

"Temptation is the way of the world, Mr. Andropov. It's what we deal with every day."

Vasylko nodded. It was an unfortunate truth. "You arrest them?"

"We want to bring them in for questioning."

"Maybe they explain."

"Let's hope so."

The policemen left, but Vasylko lingered outside a moment. The day was overcast. It looked like snow. He closed his eyes and took a deep breath. *Father, help them. Be with Jinko and Jered. Make it work out Your way.*

"You going to be okay, Mama?" Avi asked.

Annie sat on the couch and put her feet on the coffee table. "I'll be fine. Sorry I made us leave the rehearsal early, sweet-apple. You could have stayed."

"It's okay. They got to my angel part. I know what to do. Besides, I didn't want you to come home alone, all sick." She spread an afghan over her mother's legs.

"You're a good girl, you know that?"

"I'm going up in my cubby, okay?"

"That's fine."

Annie closed her eyes, mentally following the sounds of Avi's footsteps on the stairs, down the hall into the master closet, to her cubby. Contentedly tucked away. Good.

If only she could find a bit of that contentment for herself. Ever since her argument with Cal that morning, Annie's stomach had been acting up. She'd tried to dismiss it as the flu or something she ate, but she knew it was stress. This morning's argument was serious, with a lot at stake.

"Choose now, Annie! Him or me!"

At the moment she didn't know if she could choose between coffee or tea. Her mind was a jumble and her stomach agitated like a washing machine. She put a hand on her midsection, trying to calm it.

Suddenly, she heard Cal's truck pull into the driveway. Her stomach offered a new surge. He was home! The auction was over. The auction she should have attended.

Father, please help me get through this. Help me only say what You want me to say. I'm so weary... Help me not make things worse.

Annie waited for her husband.

Cal sat in his truck a moment. In front of him, in the driveway, was Annie's car. She was home. Why was she home?

He looked behind him and saw Chuck park on the street in front of the house next door. He and Joe got out and started walking up the driveway. Cal's mind swam. What could he say to stop them from going in, or more important, to stop them from saying how much he spent at the auction? Maybe Chuck would instinctively keep his secret. Chuck seemed to be the type who would keep a few secrets of his own from his wife. If he had one.

As Cal retrieved his coins and exited the truck, he realized he knew nothing about Chuck or Joe. While he'd gone on and on about his fictitious coins, Chuck hadn't offered a single detail about his life. Or his coin collection. And Cal hadn't asked. Why hadn't he asked?

Chuck caught up with him and slapped him on the back. "What are we waiting out here for? I'm ready for that beer."

What could he do? Cal went up the steps to the back door. "Come on in." He scanned the kitchen and was relieved Annie wasn't there. Maybe someone had picked her up for rehearsal.

Suddenly, she appeared in the doorway to the living room. "Hi, hon." Her eyes moved past him to the others. "Who have we...?"

Cal didn't understand the look on his wife's face. He turned around to look at Chuck and Joe. Joe's face was pasty, and he hung in the space of the open door as if to come farther inside would be moving into danger.

And for the first time, Chuck seemed a bit unsure of himself. He took a step back. "Sorry. We don't mean to intrude. We'd better be going."

Annie walked into the kitchen. "Jered? Is that you?"

Cal shook his head. "This is Chuck and this is Joe. I met them at the coin auction."

She took a step toward the boy. "Jered, your dad's been so worried about you! Where have you been?"

Cal didn't understand.

Annie poked him in the arm. "This is Bailey's boy. Jered."

Cal's entire morning played back like a foreign film in need of subtitles. "But you said your name was Joe. Chuck said you were his nephew."

As Cal talked, as Joe/Jered stared at him with his mouth moving but not saying a word, Chuck calmly shut the kitchen door. And locked it. When he turned around he had a grin.

And a gun.

"How about that beer?"

Fifteen

Therefore pride is their necklace;
they clothe themselves with violence.
From their callous hearts comes iniquity;
the evil conceits of their minds know no limits.

PSALM 73:6–7

JERED STARED AT THE GUN. Cal stared at the gun. Annie stared at the gun.

"Put that thing away," Cal said.

Jered seconded that notion. If he'd known Jinko was going to use a gun, he never...

"Alas," Jinko said with an exaggerated sigh, "I wish I could. But I can't. Now, if you'll sit, we'll get down to business and be on our way."

"What business?" Cal said.

"The coin business." Jinko motioned toward the table with the gun. "Sit. If you please."

Cal and Annie sat. Jered stood behind Jinko, not knowing what to do. Should he sit, too? At the moment he felt more on the McFay's side than Jinko's.

"Jered, go to the front door and lock it. Then check the house. See if anyone else is here."

Annie piped up. "No one else is here. Just us."

"We'll see."

Jered left and did as he was told. It was a nice house, if a little messy. Jinko would have a fit if his house ever looked this way. His eyes lingered on the Christmas tree. A full-sized one. Not the table-top size Jinko had.

No one was around. He came back to the kitchen. Jinko had pulled out a kitchen chair and had a foot on it as he leaned on his thigh.

"Anyone?"

"Nope. There is a little girl's room. But she's not here."

"Where's your daughter?" Jinko asked.

Annie answered. "Cal has a child by a previous marriage. She's at her mother's this weekend. We keep a room for her."

Jinko turned to Jered. "Is that true?"

He shrugged. "I dunno. I never paid much attention to the little kids around town."

"Oh, no. You were too busy becoming a famous musician."

Jinko's voice was full of mocking. Jered didn't understand—or like it.

"How *is* your music coming, Jered?" Annie asked.

"Not too—"

Jinko's foot hit the floor. "Quiet! This is not old home week."

"What do you want?" Cal asked.

As Jinko talked, he practice-aimed at various things around the kitchen. "We want your coins, Cal. Namely, your Barber collection."

"I..." Cal shifted in his chair.

"What's a Barber collection?"

Jinko rolled his eyes. "You really need to educate the little woman, Cal." He turned to Annie like a frustrated teacher. "It's a collection of Barber half-dollars dated from 1892–1915. Today at the auction your husband purchased the final three coins to make his collection complete."

Annie looked at Cal. "What is he talking about?"

Cal's eyes flitted from his wife to Jinko then Jered. Something wasn't right.

"I...I bought a few coins. At the auction. Like I told you I would do."

"He spent nearly five thousand," Jinko said.

"What?"

Cal touched his wife's arm. "I got everything I was looking for. It was a very successful auction."

"But five thousand dollars? You had to dip into *my* inheritance. You got after me for wanting to donate to a charity, then you go and blow our money on a few coins? I never dreamed you planned on spending that kind of—"

Jinko laughed. "Although I'm enjoying the sitcom confrontation, you can duke it out later. Right now, we just want the collection, then we'll be on our way."

Annie put a hand to her forehead. "A collection? Cal, what have you done?"

Cal felt like a mouse in a maze, boxed into a corner. Why had he bragged about coins he didn't own? If it weren't for that bragging, these two thieves wouldn't be here, holding his family at gunpoint.

Family? *Avi! Where is Avi?* Bailey's boy had searched the house and hadn't found her. Was she at a friend's? Annie had been pretty smart to say Avi's bedroom belonged to a stepdaughter who was away. At least Chuck wouldn't be looking for her.

But where was she?

Chuck hit him on the side of his shoulder with the gun. "Hey, coin man. You can do the checkbook hustle later. Just get the coins and we'll be going."

This was a nightmare. Maybe if he confessed right away, before it went any further... He scraped a spot of dried food from the table with a fingernail. "I may have exaggerated a bit."

The look Annie gave him was every bit as biting as Chuck's.

There was no way out. None. He took a deep breath, fueling his confession. "I lied, okay? I said I had a collection of Barber halves and a bunch of coins, and I don't."

For the first time, Jered spoke. "You don't?"

"No."

"There." Annie turned to Chuck, and Cal saw hope in her eyes. Her voice was pleading. "See? He doesn't have what you want. You can leave now. We promise not to say a word to anyone. Please go. Please."

"I'm afraid we can't do that, little lady."

"Why not?"

"Because I don't believe your husband. A man doesn't spend five thousand at an auction unless he owns coins and knows a lot about coins."

Wanna bet? Now Cal really felt like a fool. "I don't have any other coins. Honest."

Chuck laughed. "'Honest,' he says? Honest? Either you lied at the auction or you're lying now. One or the other. Neither is the action of an honest man."

Cal slapped a hand on the table. "I don't have any other coins! Search the house if you want and you'll—"

"No!" Annie's eyes were wild. Cal watched as she forced calm into them. "I will not have two strangers rummaging through my house."

Chuck looked around the kitchen. "Looks like someone's been rummaging already. You wouldn't win any awards for housekeeping, lady."

"The name's Annie, and I'll thank you to hold your comments about my housekeeping to yourself."

"A cluttered house indicates a cluttered mind," Chuck said.

"Jinko is a neat freak," Jered said. "You should see his—"

Cal caught the slip. "Jinko?"

Chuck/Jinko whapped Jered's chest with the back of a hand. "Shut up, kid! Shut up."

Jered put a hand to his mouth. "Oh. Sorry. Sorry."

"That's an interesting name, Jinko," Annie said. "Is that your real name or a nickname?"

Jinko shook his head, incredulous. "I am not going to go into the roots of my name. This is neither the time nor the place." He pointed the gun at Cal. "Now. Where are the coins?"

Annie's insides churned and threatened to do something nasty. Amid all the talk, all the tension, one word kept coming to mind: *Avi!* All she could think about was their daughter up in her cubby. *Stay there, sweet-apple! Stay there. Lord, help her stay put and keep quiet.*

Was it proper to thank God for her ability to come up with the lie about the room belonging to a stepdaughter? The lie had been pure instinct—a mother's instinct to protect her child. *Lord, forgive me, but keep Avi safe.*

She couldn't believe Cal had brought this on. Bragging about something he didn't even have. How stupid. And spending her inheritance on coins when he knew so little about them? When he'd talked about the auction, she'd never imagined...

He was over the top. The fact he would stoop to such a thing made her even more determined for him *not* to invest in Bailey's restaurant. Bailey was a bad influence, making her husband focus on money and wanting more.

Bailey. She looked at Jered, Bailey's son, right here in their kitchen, nonchalantly sitting on their counter like a teenager waiting to be fed a snack.

No, that wasn't quite accurate. She studied him until he looked in her direction, then away. Even though his legs were dangling, his body was tense, his hands gripping then ungripping the edge of the counter. His eyes flitted from Jinko to the floor and back again. Rarely did he look at her or Cal. How had he gotten hooked up with a gun-wielding criminal? What other crimes had they committed together? Obviously Jered's music dream had never panned out. But how had he moved from point A to point B?

Jinko and Cal were rambling on about coins. She knew she should listen, but she couldn't concentrate. How would this end? How *could* this end when there were no coins? What would appease Jinko and make him leave? She looked around the room, trying to think of any valuables she could offer him. They had a nice set of china that had been her grandmother's, but Jinko would laugh at that. Rightfully so. Antiques were probably not easily turned over for cash.

Cash. Cash would do it. But of that, they had none. So what could she offer them?

She offered up a plea: *Father, I'll give up anything to make this go away. Anything!*

Jered wanted out of here. He was trying to act casual, act the tough guy, but it was hard. He wasn't in the same class as Jinko. Jinko acted like waving a gun was old hat. He *must* have done it before. Jered thought of Vasy's comment about the boy who'd disappeared. If Jered had known Jinko had a gun, he wouldn't have come today. He would have left long ago.

But was that the truth? He'd had plenty of nudges to get him to leave Jinko. Plenty of hints of the danger. Plenty of chances. And yet Jered stayed. What was wrong with him?

He rubbed his forehead, then realized it might be taken as a gesture of weakness. He forced his hand back to the edge of the counter. If only he knew what he was supposed to do, how he was supposed to act. This was Annie, a woman who'd served him countless burgers and fries, always giving him a cherry in his Coke since the first time he'd asked. She was a nice lady. Why'd that Cal guy have to belong to her?

Speaking of... He wasn't impressed with Cal. He reminded Jered of his dad, all talk and brags and acting like a big shot. Served him right to get in trouble for it.

But what Jered didn't get was why Jinko was hanging around. Why not just grab the coins Cal had bought at the auction and take off? Didn't every minute they spent in the house increase the chances of getting caught? If he could get Jinko alone, he might risk asking him that same question. Might. Maybe.

He wouldn't have to.

"Here's what I want you to do," Jinko said to Cal. "I want you to call up your friend who *does* have the Barber collection and tell him what you bought for him. Invite him over and tell him to bring the collection with him, saying, as partial payment, you want to witness him popping those last three babies in their proper place. Then we'll help ourselves and be on our way."

"I don't want you messing with Scott, too."

Jinko extended the gun at arm's length, aiming at Cal. Then

Jinko cocked his head. "No, this is better," and moved the aim toward Annie. "I've heard the most powerful threats are not made toward ourselves, but toward those we love. Am I right?"

Cal's eyebrows nearly touched. He extended a hand. "Put it down. Don't point it at her—at anyone, okay?"

"That's up to you."

"I'll call him. I'll call Scott."

Jinko lowered the gun. "Do it."

Cal's eyes wouldn't focus on the small typeface in the phone book, and he'd left his reading glasses in the truck. Was that a three or an eight?

"If you'll excuse my pun—what's the holdup?" Jinko asked.

"I...I can't read the small print."

"Jered, hop down and help the man."

Jered did as he was told and dialed the number, handing the receiver to Cal.

"No funny stuff. Keep it light. One friend helping another."

Cal cleared his throat and wished his heart would stop ricocheting off the wall of his chest. He tried taking some deep breaths, hoping his voice wouldn't sound stressed.

The phone rang and rang. And rang. "No one answers."

"Wait for the answering machine to pick up. Everyone has an answering machine."

That wasn't true. Cal knew quite a few people who hated the things and had shut them off. The phone kept ringing. Cal shook his head.

Jinko grabbed the phone away and listened himself. "We'll keep trying. You'll call every five minutes."

"It's coming up on nighttime. A lot of people go out Saturday night."

"Yeah," Jered said. "On Saturday nights it gets really busy at the restaurant. We—"

Jinko's glare cut him off.

Jered looked to the floor.

Restaurant? Jered worked at a restaurant? With Jinko? It couldn't be in Steadfast, that's for sure. So where? In nearby Winstead? Morrow Grove? Or maybe Eldora? If Cal had a chance to talk to Jered alone, maybe he could find out.

But then what? What if he did know where they worked? Cal's mind couldn't focus.

But apparently Annie's could. "What do you do at the restaurant?"

"Enough of that." Jinko stepped between them to stop any further conversation. "Be quiet so Cal can call again." He motioned to Cal. "Dial."

Cal wasn't sure whether he hoped Scott would be home or not. Everything was getting way too complicated.

He had the awful feeling it was only the beginning.

Avi had been holding her breath. She let it out, then took another one as quietly as she could. Her heart pounded. Bad men were in her house! They had a gun! And they had her parents!

She curled onto the pillows scattered over the floor of her cubby. She'd heard the clomp-clomp of the bad man's shoes as he came up the stairs looking to see if anyone else was at home. She heard him come into her parents' closet. She was glad the door to her cubby was hidden by her mama's dresses and not her daddy's shorter shirts.

She remembered Mama talking about trading the clothes around in the closet so Avi wouldn't have to deal with them, but Avi had said she didn't mind parting the dresses to get to her special place. It was kind of like parting the clothes to get to the magical land through the wardrobe in her Narnia books. Parting dresses was much more exciting than simply opening the little door and climbing in.

Her daddy and a man were talking about coins in the kitchen below. She had a jar full of coins on her dresser she was saving for her parents' and Grandpa's Christmas presents, but the bad men could have all of it, if only they'd leave her family alone.

Mama had lied about her, saying she was a stepdaughter gone to stay with her daddy's first wife. At first she hadn't understood and had even wondered if Daddy had a first wife he hadn't told her about. After all, he'd kept Grandpa a secret. But then she figured out that the lie her mother told had probably saved her from being found. That made her feel better about everything. If Mama would lie for her—and Mama hated lying—then Avi knew she'd do anything to keep her safe. She would protect—

Avi noticed the corner of a book hiding between the door wall and the stack of pillows. She pulled it out. It was Mama's pocket Bible. She'd seen her reading it often—but always when her daddy was gone. Nothing had been said, but Avi understood it was safer to do God-things beyond her Daddy's knowing.

It made her sad, but she went along, though sometimes she forgot and sang a God-song or said something she'd learned at Sunday school in her daddy's presence. At such times she'd see his face pinch up, but she also noticed he wasn't as hard on her as he was on Mama about such things. There were advantages to being Daddy's little girl.

Mama had been hiding her Bible in the cubby a long time and had asked Avi if it was okay. It made her feel kind of special that Mama trusted this special book to her special place. At least she had another book to read.

She got comfy and opened the pages.

Merry hung up her coat behind the library counter. "Thanks so much for filling in for me, Harold."

"How did rehearsal go?"

"The fuzzy caps for the kids playing the sheep kept slipping down over their faces, and Jimmy Mayer fell into the manger, breaking it, but other than that..."

"Pray for a miracle tomorrow?"

"That might be nice."

He straightened the stack of bookmarks. "I'll be going then. See you at the pageant."

Merry settled in and was just changing her mental gears from singing to library business when she suddenly got the notion to call Annie to see how she was feeling. Was she truly sick, or was it stress?

Merry wondered how many stomachaches she'd caused Lou over the years.

The phone rang four times until the answering machine picked up. That was odd. If Annie was feeling bad enough to leave rehearsal early, she should be home. Shouldn't she?

Merry would call again later.

Merry, I'm here! Help us, please help us!

Everyone in the kitchen stared at the answering machine on the kitchen desk and listened as Merry left her message: "Hope you're feeling okay. I'll call again later. Bye."

The click of the disconnection and the subsequent *click-whirr* of the answering machine were like a knife to Annie's heart. A chance missed. If only—

"I don't know about you," Jinko said, "but I'm hungry. Who's the cook around here?"

Annie raised a hand. *Food soothes the savage beast.* Cooking would be good. Cooking might help. Cooking would keep her busy. "What would you like?"

"I defer to you, little lady." Jinko gave her a bow, which would have looked noble if it weren't for the gun in his hand. "What were you planning to make for dinner before we stopped by?"

Stopped by? She did a mental inventory of her kitchen. Monday was grocery day, and it was only Saturday. "I'd planned on ordering pizza."

"Yeah. Pizza would be good," Cal said.

"I'll take pizza," Jered said.

Jinko rolled his eyes. "Oh, sure. Let's invite a stranger into the house so you two can pass him a note or yell for help. Nix the pizza. What else do you have?"

She pushed back from the table, then stopped. Should she have asked permission? Jinko *did* tense up. Annie pointed at the refrigerator. "I need to look in the fridge and pantry." He motioned for her to move. She took a look. "How about chili? I make a great chili. And I could make some cinnamon rolls—not from scratch, but I could take some tube-rolls and add brown sugar and cinnamon and—"

Jinko held up a hand. "I don't need the recipe. Chili and rolls it is. Go for it. And plenty of it. I get mean when I'm hungry." He grinned and caressed the gun. "And you don't want to see me mean."

Avi smelled cinnamon rolls. Her stomach growled, but how could her mama get her some food without the men seeing? *Would* Mama get her some food? Or had they forgotten about her?

She turned back to the Bible. She'd flipped through it, reading the verses her mama had highlighted with a yellow pencil. But one stood out in the Psalms. (Avi had mistakenly called them the Palms once in Sunday school, and kids laughed. She'd never make *that* mistake again.)

She kept reading the verse over and over. She nearly had it memorized: *"Keep me as the apple of your eye; hide me in the shadow of your wings from the wicked who assail me, from my mortal enemies who surround me."*

Her mama called her sweet-apple because she was the apple of her mother's eye. And now, in this Bible, the writer was asking God to keep him like the apple of His eye—God's eye. Was she the apple of God's eye, too? She hoped so.

It was getting cold. There was no heat in the cubby, which was why she didn't usually stay in here long in the winter. She pulled a blanket over her shoulder, picturing it as a wing that God would use to keep her safe. Safe from the wicked men who surrounded her.

She repeated the verse again and tried not to think of cinnamon rolls.

I have to get these to Avi.

While Jinko and Jered ate seconds and thirds of chili and rolls, Annie picked at her food. She was consumed with the desire to check on Avi and get her some food. But even more than that, she was tortured by the thought that their daughter was afraid. She ached to give her a hug.

Annie suddenly got an idea and was immediately glad it was winter and she was wearing her bulky green sweater. In one motion she stood and grabbed the bread basket. "I'll get us more rolls." Over at the counter she tucked two rolls under her sweater, blousing it over her hips, forming an inward gutter all around. She took a deep breath and brought the basket to the table. "Excuse me, but I need to go to the bathroom."

Jinko looked up from his chili. "Where is it?"

"Upstairs."

"There's no bathroom down here?"

She shrugged. "It's an old house."

Jinko held up a finger, delaying her. "Jered, go upstairs and bring down any phones." He blinked and turned to Cal. "You have a computer anywhere besides in here?"

"No."

"Cell phones?"

Cal pointed to his jacket.

Jinko nodded to Jered and he retrieved it. "Now go get any other phones. Then stand at the bottom of the stairs guarding the front door and wait for her."

Jered took a roll with him. "Let's go."

Annie let Jered go up first. He came down with the phone from their bedroom. "Is this the only one?"

She nodded.

He sat on the bottom step while she went up. She tried not to run, but once in the master bedroom, she scurried to the closet. She tapped on the cubby door, then opened it. Avi was wrapped like a cocoon, her eyes wide.

"Mama!"

Annie put a finger to her lips and pulled out the rolls. Avi took them eagerly. "You stay in here no matter what, okay? They're bad men, but we'll be okay. They don't know you're here."

Avi nodded. "It's cold."

Annie's heart broke at what her daughter had to suffer. She grabbed her pink quilted robe from a hanger, one of Cal's bulkiest sweaters, and a pair of sweatpants. Then her fuzzy slippers and a pair of socks. All would be way too big for Avi, but they were warm.

Annie glanced toward the door. Time was up. "Do you have water?"

Avi nodded. "My sipper's here."

"Good. Now stay put. I'll be back." She reached in and hugged her, kissing her on the cheek.

As Annie backed out, Avi held out the pocket Bible. "I found it here. I've been reading it."

Annie's throat tightened, and she thanked God for giving her daughter comfort from a hidden Bible.

"Here," Avi said. "You take it."

"No, you can keep—"

Avi shook her head adamantly. "No, Mama. You take it."

The certainty in Avi's voice made her stop the argument. Annie took the Bible. As she closed the door, Avi whispered, "I'm praying, Mama."

Annie held back tears. She stuck the Bible into the back waistband of her jeans. Then she detoured to the master bath, flushed, and ran the water. She looked at her reflection and was surprised *not* to see fear. Not fear. Determination. These men would not win. They would not. They would not harm her family.

"What took you so long?" Jinko asked.

Annie sat on her chair. "I'm sorry, but it takes as long as it takes."

Cal searched his wife's face for a clue as to what she'd done upstairs. Was Avi up there? Had she seen her? Or had Annie truly gone to the bathroom?

Their eyes met and she offered him the slightest nod. Then a wink. Cal wasn't sure exactly what it meant, but he was encouraged. She seemed to have things under control.

No thanks to you.

"Jered, help clear the table."

He didn't argue but took dishes to the counter where Annie rinsed them.

"Thanks," she said. "I appreciate the help."

Jered was embarrassed to feel himself blush. You'd think he'd never gotten a compliment before.

Actually...that wasn't far from the truth. His dad wasn't big on "Thank you's" or "Attaboy's." But he was big on "You missed a spot" and "Can't you move faster?" Sometimes Jered liked to play psychologist and think about where he'd be right now if his dad had said thank you once in a while. Been nicer. Cared about anything other than his stupid Bon Vivant.

On a trip back to the table he looked at Jinko. He owned a restaurant, too. From what Jered could see it had tons more customers than Bon Vivant ever had, but Jinko wasn't obsessed with it. Jinko thought of other things.

Like stealing.

Okay. So Jinko wasn't perfect either. At least he paid Jered some attention. At least he understood Jered's dream of a music career and was doing something to help with it.

He stopped in midstep as a thought hit him. *Or was he doing anything?*

Jinko noticed him standing there. "What's with you, kid? Get zapped by a stun gun?"

Jered shook his head. Now was not the time or place to ask Jinko about the record producer and exactly when Jered was going to get an audition. Besides, Jinko would probably answer how he always answered: *Soon, kid, soon.*

Merry was getting ready to lock up the library for the evening when she called Annie for the second time. Again no answer. She must be feeling better or she'd be home. Maybe they'd gone out for the evening.

Taking Avi with them?

Merry shook the unknown away. She left another short message: "Hope you're feeling better. See you tomorrow."

At least she hoped she'd see Avi and Annie tomorrow. The Christmas pageant needed them.

❧   ❧   ❧

"See you tomorrow!" Annie's throat caught at Merry's words on the answering machine.

Tomorrow wasn't just any Sunday. It was the Christmas pageant! If Annie and Avi didn't show up, Merry would come looking. And if she did, maybe Annie could get her a message. Somehow...

"What's tomorrow?" Jinko asked.

"Just church."

Jinko shrugged. But Cal gave Annie a lingering look. Had he remembered the pageant? Was he thinking the same thing she was?

If only they had some time alone.

Cal was weary of calling Scott Wheeler. It was ten o'clock and was obvious—to everyone but Jinko—that Scott was out for the evening. Besides that, Cal's nerves were frayed to the point of breaking. Jinko hadn't left Annie and Cal alone for even a minute, so he'd had no chance to talk to her or to ask where Avi was.

They'd spent the entire evening watching TV, all four of them together in the living room. Jinko and Jered were sprawled on the couch, and Cal sat in his recliner. Annie sat in her rocker and read some book with an odd title: *My Utmost* something-or-other.

Cal didn't hear a word of the sitcoms. He was trying to figure out how to get the gun away from Jinko without it going off. He'd never been around guns. Could it go off with the slightest nudge?

Cal watched as Jered laughed at the TV show. He had asked if they could turn the Christmas lights on. In many ways Jered seemed like a kid. Did Bailey have a tree? It was a hard call. Either Bailey had nothing in the way of decorations or he'd overdo it, for show. Cal couldn't imagine him being in between.

Poor kid.

What an odd thought. Bailey was a good guy, a successful man. Why would Cal feel sorry for his son? Cal studied Jered some more. He had his feet on the coffee table, his right foot in constant motion, coming precariously close to one of the wise men. If only Cal could call Bailey and tell him.

The weird thing was, Cal wasn't completely sure Bailey would be happy about the news. Especially considering the fact that Jered was hooked up with a criminal and was holding Cal's family hostage. None of this made sense. Why would Jered be hanging around with the likes of Jinko?

The sitcom ended and the news began. Soon it would be time for bed. How would they work this? Would they stay up all night, right here in the living room? Maybe when Jinko slept and Jered was keeping watch, Cal could get the gun and—

"*Our top story. Two Eldora men are wanted for questioning in some burglaries. Jinko Daly, the owner of Palamba's restaurant, and Jered Manson, a dishwasher at the establishment, are wanted by police for questioning regarding the burglary of the Stetson and Dillon households. Just two nights ago, Aaron Stetson realized a pair of silver candlesticks had been—*"

Jinko was on his feet with Jered close behind. Jered pointed at the screen. "They know about us! They're after us!"

Cal smiled and snickered. Maybe there was a God. Maybe there was—

Jinko slammed the side of the gun against Cal's face.

Siixteen

Keep me from the snares they have laid for me,
from the traps set by evildoers.
Let the wicked fall into their own nets,
while I pass by in safety.

PSALM 141:9–10

CAL'S HEAD EXPLODED—but thankfully, the gun did not.

"Cal!" Annie jumped up. Jinko pushed her back into the rocker.

"Shut up! Quiet!" Jinko's eyes were locked on the TV news. He grabbed the remote and upped the volume.

Cal's cheek burned, his ear rang. And his heart raced. He touched his face. There was blood. The gun had broken the skin.

Annie was fairly bursting to stand and help him. "Let me get the first aid—"

Jinko glared at her. "I said shut up! He's fine."

Cal nodded at her, patting a hand in the air, calming her. She sat back a bit. Good. He didn't need her riling Jinko.

Cal tried to think past the pain. He couldn't give in to it. Things were getting dicey. He had to concentrate...

The news said that Jinko and Jered had done this—or something like it—before. Jinko was obviously a pro and had somehow lured Jered into it. And now they were wanted by the law. Would this make their present situation better or worse?

"How did they find out it was us?" Jered said.

Jinko flashed him a look and he was quiet.

"*...vehicle spotted near the crime scenes has been traced to Jered Manson and was found parked at the residence of Mr. Daly. Daly and Manson have not been seen today and took the day off from work.*

Eldora police have contacted the police forces in neighboring towns and are looking for Daly's car: a black 2001 Mercedes with license plate DX-1823."

"They know your car!" Jered took two steps toward the front door. "They'll see it outside. We have to go!"

Jinko held up a hand. "Hold on. Let me think."

Suddenly pictures of Jered and Jinko flashed on the screen.

"That's my high school graduation picture! How did they get that?"

"Your dad's been looking for you, Jered," Annie said. "I'm sure he gave it to the police months ago."

Jered fell onto the couch, his head in his hands. "Everyone will see. The whole town of Steadfast will think I'm a criminal."

"You are a criminal, you twit!" Jinko yelled. The picture of Jinko was a promo shot in front of his restaurant.

Annie looked a little dazed. She raised a hand weakly. "I was at Palamba's a couple of weeks ago." She looked at Jinko. "I can't believe you run that place."

"I saw you," Jered said. "I saw you and Claire and Merry."

"Why didn't you say something? Come out and say hel—"

Jinko swung the gun at her and she flinched. "Because he's a runaway, lady. Because he didn't want people from this stinking town knowing where he was. Okay?"

She nodded and glanced one more time at Jered, but he looked away.

"We gotta go," the boy whined. "We gotta go now."

Jinko's head shook back and forth. "I'm not leaving empty-handed. What we have to do is think." As the news broke for a commercial, he began to pace between the television and the coffee table. "We need to get rid of the car. For now. After we get the coins, we'll use one of theirs."

Cal's mind ran with possibilities. Whatever he could do to end this thing... "I could drive it somewhere, leave it, and walk home."

Jinko rolled his eyes. "And take a detour to the police station?"

Well, yeah. It was worth a try.

Jinko ran to a living room window and peered out. "Why do you have your cars in the driveway? Don't you have a garage?"

"We do, but it's full of my tools and wood and stuff. We've gotten in the habit of just leaving our cars out."

Jinko let the curtain drop. "Not anymore. You have five minutes to make room for my car. Then we'll do some rearranging and get it inside."

It would take way more than five minutes to clear a space. While Annie was a clutter-bug inside, Cal was just as bad in the garage. "I'm not sure five minutes is enough time."

Jinko got in his face, making him rock back in the recliner. "Make it enough time."

"Sure. I guess."

"Now go. Jered, go help him."

The boy shook his head. "I don't want to go outside. My face was just on TV."

"It's dark. Go. And no funny stuff, Cal, or your wife is dead."

With a look to Annie, Cal did as he was told. *Hang in there, Annie-love. We'll get through this.*

"Close the garage door behind us," Jered said.

Cal hated taking orders from a kid—a punk kid, no less—but he closed it. The place was a pit.

"Jinko would have a fit if he saw this mess," Jered said.

"How did you ever get hooked up with him?"

Jered picked up a couple two-by-fours. "We need to get going. Clear a space. Just like Jinko said."

Cal made a decision. "Let's move everything against the back wall. Stack it. But we can only go out about two feet, or his car won't fit."

They worked side by side, Cal's head throbbing every time he bent over. He didn't have much time to pump Jered for information, so he tried to sort out the questions he wanted to ask. He narrowed it down to two. "Are you afraid of Jinko?" *Should we be afraid?*

Jered carried a box of caulk to the back. "Not really. I mean, I wasn't."

"You weren't, but you are now?"

Jered seemed to realize what role he was supposed to be playing. His voice hardened in his version of tough man. "Yes, I am now. And you should be, too. He'll use that gun if he has to. Don't cross him."

"You've seen him use a gun before?"

Jered showed Cal his back and dragged a duffel bag of tarps across the floor. "He'll use it, okay? Don't make him mad. Just do as he says."

It was an unsatisfactory answer, but Cal doubted he'd get a better one. "Why did you run away from home? Your dad's been looking for you. He's been worried."

Jered arched his back and laughed. "My dad? Worried about me? No way. Mad at me? Sure. Disappointed in me? Always. But worried? Never."

"But he's been looking..." Actually Cal wasn't sure how much Bailey had been looking for Jered. Maybe it was best to leave it alone.

Jered did a double take at a blueprint that was opened on the workbench. He moved toward it. "This is for Bon Vivant."

"Yes."

"Is my dad adding on?"

"I finished it right before Thanksgiving."

Jered stared at the plans, then suddenly snatched them up, tore them, wadded them, and threw them across the room.

"What did you do that for?"

The kid stood over the trashed plan, his chest heaving, his hands pumping fists. "He wasn't worried about me! He went on with his life as usual. He wasn't upset about me being gone. He added on to his precious restaurant like nothing had happened. My being gone didn't affect him one bit."

Cal hated how this looked and hated even more that what Jered said sounded true. Why *had* Bailey continued with the addition project? How could he have done that? Cal thought back and realized if he hadn't known from other sources that Bailey's son had run away, he wouldn't have suspected it, wouldn't have even known Bailey had a son. Something was terribly wrong with that.

Jered kicked a torn page. "We need to keep going. Jinko's counting on us. I don't want to disappoint him."

It was an odd statement. Not the statement of a boy afraid of his partner but of a boy in search of a father figure.

All things considered, Cal couldn't blame him.

Annie and Jinko sat in the living room. Jinko flipped channels, trying to find more info about the burglaries.

Talk to him.

Annie immediately countered the thought with a question: *About what?*

But she knew very well *what.* She was in the midst of what could be a life-and-death situation. She had one goal: to save her family from further harm.

And save Jinko and Jered, too.

Huh? The thought was so foreign, so out of place for the situation, that she knew it came from God. And as such, she had only one choice. She must obey. But she was scared. What if she made Jinko madder than he already was? What if he yelled at her, whipped his gun against *her* face, stopping her words? What if—?

I'm here. Trust Me.

With a deep breath she set *My Utmost for His Highest* on the floor. It was an amazing book about faith, but she needed to pull out the big guns. She slipped her pocket Bible out of her back waistband and set it on her lap. *Lord, give me the words—Your words.*

"Don't be afraid," she said to Jinko—but also to herself.

Jinko flashed her a look. "I'm not afraid. You're the one who should be afraid."

Her stomach flipped. "No thank you."

He did a double take. "Excuse me?"

She rocked up and back, holding the Bible with both hands. She found that her stomach had miraculously settled. "I said no thank you. I will not be afraid. I choose not to be afraid."

He laughed. "You choose?"

"Yes, sir."

"And what makes you so brave?"

Inside, she laughed at the perfect opening God had supplied. She held up the Bible. "This. God."

He squinted at the title. "That's not God. That's the Bible."

"It's God's Word. His words."

"Yeah, yeah, you got nothing."

He was wrong, and she found herself smiling. "I have everything through Him. That's why I'm not afraid." She ruffled through the pages and opened at random. Her eyes zeroed in on a verse: *"To live is Christ and to die is gain."*

What was that supposed to mean?

Jinko turned his attention back to the TV. "Save the Bible-thumping, lady. That's mystic mumbo jumbo. Do me a favor and keep it to yourself."

Annie looked down at the Bible.

She shivered.

Jered and Cal came in the back door. Annie looked at the clock on the TV. It had been ten minutes, not five like Jinko had ordered. She hoped he wouldn't notice, wouldn't punish.

They came in the living room, and Annie sought Cal's eyes. He nodded, calming her. His face was horrible to see, rivulets and smudges of blood, drying. His eye and upper cheek were swollen.

Jinko was still flipping channels. Jered pointed at the television. "Anything else on the news?"

"Nothing," Jinko said. "The garage ready?"

"Anytime."

Jinko hit the remote and tossed it on the recliner. "Jered, you move their car, I'll move the truck, and Cal here, can move our car into the garage."

"I don't think the two of us should go outside," Jered said.

"So you'd let both of our hostages get in vehicles? Think, kid."

Jered appeared to be thinking, but clearly he wasn't getting it.

Jinko sighed. "We need one of them in here—like the wife—because if she's left behind, then Mr. Macho Man won't try anything, knowing we'll hurt her if he drives off. Hurt her far more than a whap to the face." He turned to Cal. *"Comprendé,* Macho Man?"

Cal nodded. "I get it."

"Good." Jinko turned to Annie. "We'll only be outside a couple minutes, tops. Behave yourself."

She continued her rocking, but her mind swam with what she could do in those two minutes. *Call the police? Get Avi more food and drink? Get Avi out?*

She followed the men into the kitchen. Unfortunately, as Jinko walked past the phone, he backtracked a step, unplugged it from the wall, and took it with him outside, along with the extension from upstairs.

That left helping Avi.

Annie gave her keys to Cal and let her fingers touch his. Their first contact. It helped more than she expected. To be in close proximity to Cal for so long yet unable to touch him... Then the men were outside.

Annie waited at the door until they were occupied, then she bolted to the pantry, grabbed a jar of peanut butter, a box of crackers, and a six-pack of juice boxes. She ran up the stairs, through the master bedroom, and flung open the door to the cubby.

"Food! I have food!"

Avi looked pained. "I have to go to the bathroom."

Oh, dear. "Go!" Annie whispered. "Go fast. They're all outside."

Avi stumbled out of the cubby, tripping on the slippers and long sweatpants. Annie carried her to the master bathroom. "Hurry, sweet-apple. Hurry!"

She heard three engines swell and purr. There was no window in the bathroom, so she couldn't see. Annie heard a foreign-sounding vehicle drive toward the back of the house. They had Jinko's car in. She only had seconds.

"Done, Mama."

"Don't flush."

"What?"

Annie grabbed Avi and ran her back into the closet, giving her an extra squeeze and kiss. "Love you, dear one. Stay safe."

"Are they staying all night, Mama?"

"It appears so."

"Why are they doing this?"

Annie heard one engine shut off. "Shh!" She waved good-bye to her little girl and shut the door.

She ran back to the bathroom and flushed just as she heard footsteps come in the kitchen door.

"Hey, lady?" Jinko yelled. "Where—?"

She forced herself to be calm and walked down the front stairs. "I had to use the facilities." She met them at the bottom of the stairs. "Speaking of another need, I really would like to go to bed. It's been a long day."

Jinko looked around the first floor, then walked to the kitchen and back. "There are only these two doors, right?"

"Right," Cal said.

"Is there a basement?"

"Unfinished."

"Walkout?"

"No. Only tiny window wells."

Jinko pointed at Jered. "Go check." He looked up the stairs.

Annie really wanted to be with Cal so they could talk. And she needed to be in the master bedroom so she could be close to Avi. *"You do not have, because you do not ask God."*

Lord, make it work. She raised a finger. "Sir? I'd really appreciate it if we could sleep in our own room."

Jinko snickered. "You want me to allow you to sleep together?"

"Us being together is easier for you, too. Only one room to watch."

"Hmm." He pointed to the couch. "Jered, you sack out there and I'll—"

"But there's another bedroom. Can't I sleep—?"

"I need you on the first floor. Here. Near the doors." Jinko turned his head right, then left. He pointed to the small buffet in the entry. "Help me move this." Jered took an end, and they moved the buffet in front of the door. "Now go stack some canned goods by the back one. Good and wobbly so they'll fall if anyone tries to leave."

"We won't try to leave," Annie said. *Not with Avi here.*

"You bet you won't."

They waited by the stairs until Jered completed his work. "All done."

"Good. Then sleep. I'll get the romantics settled and move a chair outside their door. I'll take first watch. Then it's your turn."

Jered sprawled on the couch. Annie hated seeing his shoes on the furn—

"Take off your shoes, you twit," Jinko said.

Jered shucked them off, placing them in a neat twosome at the foot of the couch.

Jinko motioned up the stairs. "Shall we?"

Annie started to shut the bedroom door, but Jinko extended a hand to stop its swing. "The door stays open."

She shook her head. "I'm sorry. But I cannot put on my bedclothes with a strange man able to watch."

"Deal with it."

"No."

"Annie!" Cal couldn't believe her gumption.

She turned to her husband, crossing her arms. "I'm a modest woman, Cal. You know that. And I will not have him gaping at me—at us—while we sleep. Or as we *try* to sleep, because there is no way I can sleep with him looking in on us. That's it. End of discussion."

Jinko laughed, shaking his head. "Your wife's a pistol, isn't she, Cal? How do you keep her reined in?"

"I..."

"The truth is you don't, right?"

He felt himself blush and shrugged. Now was not the time to argue. Let Jinko think what he wanted.

Jinko went to the bedroom window and peered out. Checking on the feasibility of an escape route? Cal knew it was a straight shot down, with a flower bed below. No branches close. No roof to hop onto.

When Jinko tried opening it, Cal remembered something. "It's painted shut. I've been meaning to fix that."

"Good thing you didn't," Jinko said, moving to the door. "Well then, little lady. I guess you can have your privacy." He tipped an imaginary hat. "Sleep well."

Cal shut the door, and Annie hurled herself into his arms. Nothing had ever felt so good. "I'm so sorry, Annie. So sorry," he whispered.

"Shh, shh. It's okay. It will be okay."

Shouldn't he be the one saying that?

She suddenly pulled back. She was smiling, and he couldn't imagine why. Then she pulled him into the closet, a finger to her lips. She pointed to the cubby and he understood. Avi was in there!

She crooked a finger at it, indicating he should open it. Then she pointed to herself and tiptoed into the main room to stand guard.

Cal carefully opened the door and found their daughter huddled in a bunch of their clothes and blankets.

"Daddy!" she whispered. Her face registered shock at the sight of his face. Tears were on her cheeks. Avi, who never cried. It killed him...

With a motion he silenced her, then gave her a hug. "Oh, darlin', it's all right. Everything will be all right." He pulled back to look at her, wiping a tear with his thumb. "You okay?"

She nodded then pointed to a stash of food. "Mama brought it up."

When did she do that?

Cal heard a chair being set outside the bedroom door. The old house had thin walls. "We're going to bed," he told Avi. "We'll be right there." He pointed to the bedroom. "But you stay put until we get you. Understand? You don't come out. Ever."

She nodded. "When will they go, Daddy?"

"I don't know, darlin'. Hopefully in the morning."

"What do they want?"

"Money. Coins."

"Then give them some."

If only I could. He couldn't explain. He didn't want to explain. "Shh, now. Go to sleep. Love you."

"Love you too, Daddy."

❧   ❧   ❧

Bailey Manson sat forward on his couch, the remote dangling in his hand. Had he really heard his son's name on the news? Surely not. Surely it was a horrible mistake.

Please make it be a horrible mistake.

There was a knock on the door. Who would be stopping by at such a late hour? It couldn't be good.

The knock continued. "Bailey? It's me. Ken Kendell."

Officer Ken Kendell. Bailey's nerves tightened. "Coming." He opened the door.

Ken looked at him sheepishly. "Sorry to bother you, Bailey." He glanced past him to the television. "You saw? You heard?"

He didn't want to do this through an open door. "Come in."

Ken entered.

"Sit."

Ken sat on the Morris chair—or rather, perched on its edge. Bailey wanted to tell him to sit back and relax, because as long as he sat at attention, the news could not be good.

"What's this about, Ken? Surely Jered can't be involved."

"It looks that way. Like the news said, his truck was seen at the crime scenes and then spotted at the home of Mr. Daly."

"Who is this Daly?"

"He owns a restaurant and bar in Eldora. Palamba's."

Bailey made a face. "It's a dive."

"It's hardly a dive. It's a nice place. They have great burritos."

"Oh, please..."

Ken shifted on the chair. "The Eldora police have interviewed some of the employees, and they say Jered's okay. Healthwise, that is. In case you're interested."

Bailey felt his cheeks flush, more from the fact he hadn't thought about asking if Jered was okay than Ken's comment. "I can't believe he's involved in burglaries. He's not a perfect kid, but he's not a bad one either."

Ken shrugged. "Circumstances can make people do odd things. He did need to find a way to survive..."

"He needed to come home. If he had stayed here, none of this would have happened. He had everything he needed here."

Ken stood. "I just wanted to stop by to see how you were doing."

He threw his hands in the air. "How do you think I'm doing? My son's name is splashed all over the nightly news, telling the world he's a suspected criminal. Do you know what that will do to my reputation?"

Ken's left eyebrow rose. "Sorry it's inconveniencing you, Bailey."

He realized his error. "It's not *inconveniencing* me; it's—"

"Embarrassing you?"

Bailey ran his hands through his hair. "Ugh. Sorry. I'm upset. My mind's not working straight." He took a fresh breath. "Is this Jinko dangerous?"

"We must assume so."

Bailey suddenly felt tears threaten. "Please—" His voice cracked and he swallowed. "Please keep me informed."

"Will do."

Bailey let Ken see himself out.

Jered couldn't get comfortable on the McFay's couch. His wallet was in the way. He removed it and was just about to toss it on the coffee table when he opened it. He removed the bent snapshot of him and his dad, taken years ago at the opening of Bon Vivant. They were both smiling, and his dad's arm was around his shoulder.

Another time, another place, another life.

His eyes glared at the darkened television. His name had been on the news as a criminal. He prayed his dad worked late, missing it. Either way, other people in Steadfast *had* seen it. Moog and Darryl, Sim, his other friends at school. He shivered at the thought of them talking about him, laughing at him. *"Can you believe Jered's a big-time thief?"*

If *they* were surprised, he was absolutely shocked. How had all this happened? How could running away to pursue a dream end up with his name announced as a criminal on television? He'd wanted people to know his name for good reasons, not this.

He wasn't a thief. He wasn't.

But you stole. Over and over you stole.

He flipped over on his side and pulled the afghan onto his shoulder. It was almost as if the past seven weeks had been separate from reality, like he'd been caught in a bubble, doing the same thing over and over again, never being able to run straight and hard against its surface to break through to the real world beyond.

Not entirely true. How many times had Vasylko offered him money to get home? How many times had Vasy warned him, told him what he didn't want to hear?

He opened his eyes and saw the Christmas tree before him. If he squinted his eyes, the lights stretched and throbbed. Very cool. Did his father have a tree? Was the Santa collection on the mantel surrounded by that wispy white stuff that looked like snow? Was there a present under the tree for him?

He looked past the tree to the door. *Leave! Now!*

He raised onto an elbow and listened. The house was silent. The McFays were in bed, and Jinko was sitting outside their door. Jered let his eyes wander from the front door, up the stairs to where Jinko sat. With one step Jinko could leave his place by the bedroom door and look down the stairs. Jered couldn't get out that way.

But how about the back?

He thought of all the cans he'd stacked as a noisy warning if their hostages tried to escape. Would those same cans keep him captive?

I can be careful. I can move them. I can leave.

Jered set the afghan to the side and sat up. He listened to the other sounds of the house. The furnace was going, and at just that moment, the refrigerator started up, giving him more cover. It was now or never.

He picked up his shoes and tiptoed to the kitchen. He took his coat off the hook and wrapped his shoes inside. Once outside, he could run hard, carrying the bundle like a quarterback carrying a football toward a touchdown.

That ready, he stooped next to the door and studied the can sculpture a moment. It was like that kid's game he had called Jenga, where you built a tower and then had to carefully remove the pieces, trying not to make it fall. He figured out the first move and safely removed a can of pork and beans. Next came a can of corn.

He forced himself to take a breath and flexed his fingers like a safecracker. If he took the green beans down next, would that make the peas—?

"Going somewhere?"

Jered fell backward, missing the can tower with his foot by an inch. He thought fast, then picked up the can of corn. "I thought of a way to redo this to make it better." He glanced at Jinko as he picked up the can. "If we put it over here..."

"Nice try, kid."

Jered put the beans back on, not daring to look at Jinko. Not when his face was always so readable. "There. Isn't that better?" He stood, then noticed his jacket bundle. He stepped in front of it.

Jinko pushed him aside. "And what's this?" He unwrapped the package until his shoes fell to the floor.

There was nothing Jered could say. Nothing.

Jinko shoved the parcel into Jered's arms. "You don't want to know what would have happened if you'd gotten out and I'd caught up with you."

"I...I'm sorry."

"Save it." He shoved Jered toward the front room. "Get back to sleep. I'll wake you in a few hours to take over." Jinko shoved the barrel of the gun against Jered's chin. It was cold and hard. "You try this again and I'll use the gun. If not on you, then on your father. I know where he lives. Remember?"

Jered hurried back to the couch, his spine tingling as if he was being chased by something evil and dangerous.

There was no way out. None.

Seventeen

Do not be afraid; do not be discouraged.
Go out to face them tomorrow,
and the LORD will be with you.

2 CHRONICLES 20:17

ANNIE OPENED HER EYES. It was the middle of the night. Within seconds the reality of their hostage situation returned. It had not been a dream.

But what had awakened her? It had sounded like a click. The click of a door? Had Jinko peeked in to check on them?

She held her breath. Nothing at first, then she heard whispers in the hall. She slipped out of bed and moved to listen.

Jinko was talking. "You awake enough to do this, kid?"

"Yeah, I'm awake." Jered's voice was heavy with sleep.

"You'd better be. You sit and guard them. Can you handle that? I'd leave you the gun, but you've proven yourself untrustworthy, so I can't."

Annie's ears perked up. *What was that supposed to mean?*

"Just yell if you need me. *I* won't let you down."

So there was dissension among the thieves. Had something happened while she'd been sleeping? And if so, how could she and Cal take advantage of it?

She sat on the floor by the door to think, pulling her nightgown over her legs and feet. Jered was guarding the door. A sleepy Jered. Jinko was going to sleep on the couch. The exterior doors were booby-trapped. The window was painted shut.

She looked at the bedside table where the phone usually stood. If only she could call for help, get someone to rescue them.

Rescue me, O Lord.

The phrase seemed familiar. Wasn't it a verse? She retrieved her Bible from the dresser and went into the bathroom for light. She pulled the door so she wouldn't wake Cal and took a seat on the toilet lid. The phrase repeated itself in her mind. *Rescue me, O Lord.*

If only she had a big Bible with a concordance in the back so she could look up the word *rescue*. *Help me, God. Help me find this verse.*

She forced herself to think logically. The words were a personal plea. They weren't "Help *us*, O Lord"; they were "Help *me*." One man or woman talking to God. Where were there a lot of one-on-one conversations between a person and God?

Psalms. King David was always talking to God, and the Psalms were like his personal prayer journal. It was worth a try.

But there were so many Psalms. One hundred and fifty of them. For no particular reason she started from the back. She scanned the verses looking for the phrase. Then suddenly, word matched word: *"Rescue me, O LORD, from evil men; protect me from men of violence, who devise evil plans in their hearts and stir up war every day."* Psalm 140, verses 1 and 2. It was a match! It was real. The phrase coming to her was not a coincidence.

But what was she supposed to do with it?

She read the words again. It was a good description of their plight. They needed to be rescued from evil men of violence with evil plans in their hearts. It was a plea for help.

If only someone could read it. See it. Understand.

Merry.

If only she could copy it in a note and get it to Merry. Annie's mind swam with the logistics of it. When she and Avi didn't show up at the Christmas pageant, there was a good possibility Merry would come by to check on them. Could Annie get a note under the front door so Merry would find it on the step?

The door was blocked by the buffet. And if Merry could find it, then Jinko might find it and get mad. The verse was clear in its implications.

Then don't write it out. Reference it. Let Merry look it up.

That was better. If she could just get Merry to see "Ps 140:1–2," that would be enough. And Jinko would never have a clue that a message was being sent. But how could Annie get Merry to see the reference?

She stood and leaned against the sink, trying to stir up an answer. She looked at the mirror and noticed a speck. Absently she scraped it away with a fingernail, leaving behind a smudge. She took a towel to wipe it clean. Then it hit her.

A smudge. Writing. Mirror. Glass. She ran a finger across the mirror, glorying in its trail. Avi wrote on glass all the time with her Window Writers. On her windows—on her windows that faced the front of the house! Avi's windows were full of pictures. Pictures and various words like *Hi* and *Avi*.

She would have to risk it.

Annie stood on her side of the bedroom door and thought a moment. She needed an alibi for opening the door, for possibly being caught in the hallway.

A blanket.

She grabbed the throw blanket from the bottom of their bed. If caught, she would say she was worried about Jered being cold and was getting a blanket for him.

Armed with that, she leaned her ear against the door and listened. She heard a soft snore. Jered was asleep!

"Father, protect me. Be with me," she whispered.

She wiped her palms on her nightgown and put one hand on the doorknob. She turned it, leaning into the door so the latch wouldn't click. It didn't make a sound. She opened the door an inch and peered out. Jered was slumped in the chair, his back against the wall of the hallway. His head was back, his mouth open, his arms crossed.

But his legs were extended like a blockade before her. She'd have to step over him.

She lifted her nightgown above her knees so it wouldn't brush against him. She took a long step over his legs, supporting herself on the wall. His snoring stopped, then started, and she froze, one toe touching the carpet on the far side. He did not wake up.

She decided a stream of motion was necessary for her own sanity and probably wouldn't make any more noise than her choppy movements. Besides, every moment counted.

She tried to take a deep breath without making any noise. It wasn't easy, but once her lungs were fueled, she finished her motion over Jered's legs and scurried down the hall to Avi's bedroom. She pushed the door shut enough to camouflage her presence and moved to the window. A pail of Window Writers sat ready. She looked at Avi's window pictures. The purple was the most easily read. She picked it up and wrote backward, so it could be read from outside: M.C. Ps 140:1–2 A.M. She liked the addition of their initials and also hoped that Annie's adult lettering would stand out among Avi's.

It was all she could do. *Make it enough, Lord. Make it enough.*

She took up the blanket and headed back to her room. She had just stepped over Jered when the snoring stopped.

His eyes opened and he sat up. "Huh?"

Annie's heart threatened to burst through her chest. She smiled and put a finger to her lips. She unfolded the blanket and whispered, "I thought you might be cold."

He accepted the blanket. She went inside and closed the door.

Mission accomplished. It was in God's hands now.

That fact offered enough comfort for her to go back to sleep.

What was Annie up to?

Cal had awakened when she'd first gotten up and had nearly gone to her side when she'd slid to the floor outside the door, pulling her nightgown over her feet like a little girl. She'd looked so childlike in the moonlight. So beautiful and vulnerable and—

No. That wasn't right. The reason he hadn't gone to comfort her was that she *hadn't* looked vulnerable. She looked strong and determined, her forehead tight as she concentrated on her thoughts. And sure enough, within a few moments, she had grabbed her Bible and slipped into the bathroom. It wasn't picked up for mere bathroom reading. She had a purpose.

Purpose. That was the main element dividing them lately. The more Annie got into God, the more focused she was. She wasn't focused in a fanatical kind of way—as he'd expected her to be—but in a quiet assured way, as though she was a person who'd been given direction, was merely waiting for further instructions, and moreover, was confident she'd get them.

Annie had closed the door of the bathroom so only a slit of light marked her place, her presence, her side of life versus his. It was appropriate. She seemed to live in the light until it nearly glowed about her, while he lived in the dark, watching from afar, content to stay safe under the covers of life and watch.

It's not that he couldn't join her. He could. Nothing would make her happier than if he said, "I want to know about the change in you."

He didn't need to ask. He knew about the Jesus-change. Or at least knew about part of it. Been there, done that. It wasn't his fault the whole feeling of elation, of anything being possible, of hope, hadn't stuck. God had done a good job of ruining any chance of that. So now...he was who he was. Period.

What he was, was a coward. When Annie had come out of the bathroom and taken up the blanket, he'd nearly said something, nearly asked, "What are you doing?"

But he hadn't. The sight of her on a mission was mesmerizing. But the clincher had been when she closed her eyes and whispered, "Father, protect me. Be with me." Not "Cal, protect me. Be with me." Father. God. Proving she trusted Him more than him.

That hurt.

But why shouldn't she? What have you done for her lately? Lied about your father, piddled away the family money, and now her inheritance. If it weren't for you, they wouldn't be in this mess and Jinko wouldn't be threatening your family.

And so he'd stayed in bed and held his breath as his brave (crazy?) wife stepped over the sleeping kid and tiptoed down the hall to do...something. He couldn't imagine what was so important she'd take such a risk. And when she returned—obviously successful in whatever her plan was—he'd let the moment to ask slip by.

He didn't want to be shown up by God again. He wasn't sure he could take the humiliation.

He tried to sleep.

Jered was on a stage, his guitar resting on his knee. The music was beautiful, and the man in the front row was nodding and taking notes. And somehow Jered knew it was a record producer, and in a few moments his entire life would—

"Wake up!" Someone shook his shoulder. Why would the producer shake him?

But it wasn't a music mogul. It was Jinko standing over him. "Some guard you are."

The vapor of his dream was sucked into a vacuum to be tossed in the trash. This was reality. "I must have dozed off."

Jinko snatched up the blanket. "Where did you get this?"

"Annie gave it to me."

Jinko's face made it seem like a bad thing. He pounded on the bedroom door. "Up, people! Up!"

Annie cracked open the door. "We're up. We're going to take showers. Why don't you put the coffee on?"

Jinko put a hand to his chest. "You want *us* to put the coffee on?"

She shrugged. "Then wait. We'll be down shortly." She shut the door and locked it.

Jered looked at Jinko, waiting for his reaction. Annie had turned from scared to one gutsy lady. What had brought that on?

Jinko drilled the blanket into the chair. "I need coffee."

Annie had her ear to the door. She smiled as she heard the men go downstairs. Locking the door had been a risk, but a risk she had to take.

She turned to Cal and whispered, "Get Avi out!"

Cal hurried into the closet and quietly opened the cubby. "Come on, darlin'. Come out."

"Is it over?" she asked.

"No, sweet-apple. Not yet. They're downstairs. I locked the door and said we were taking showers."

After a round of hugs, Avi squirmed in her oversized clothes. "Can I take these off?"

"For a little while." Annie pulled the sweatshirt over her head.

Avi stretched. "It feels good to stand." She pointed toward the bedroom. "It's morning?"

Annie felt awful. How would *she* fare in a confined space with no natural light, no window, no contact with the outside world? "I'll get you some breakfast later. Do you want a hot shower?"

Avi nodded. "Can you just hold me first?"

Avi and Annie didn't say much as they sat together in the chair by the window. Their touch became their words, their synchronized rocking their sentences. As soon as Cal was done with his shower, Annie herded Avi toward the bathroom.

She noticed the laundry basket of clean clothes she hadn't put away. Sometimes it paid to be messy. She pulled some out for Avi. "We can only let the shower run twice. Daddy's done the first one. So now you take a quick shower and leave the water running. Then I'll take a turn." She flicked the end of her daughter's nose, then let her finger return for emphasis. "No singing."

Annie got Avi settled, then went back to the bedroom. Cal sat at the end of the bed, drying his hair with a towel, staring at her. "What?" she asked.

"You think of everything, don't you?"

"What are you talking about?"

"You're handling this as if the whole thing is a mystery novel, as if Avi having to stay hidden in her cubby is simply part of a carefully crafted plotline."

She kept her voice low. After all, she was supposed to be in the shower. "Where's this coming from? You want me to continue to cower, be afraid?"

"It would be more normal. Understandable."

Annie couldn't believe he was doing this. Not now. "Who cares about normal, Cal? Those men have us hostage. One of them has a gun and—"

"Because of me."

Since he'd said it... "Because of you. But even that isn't important at the moment. What's important is moving past our fear, staying calm, using our heads, and letting God handle it."

He snickered. "Gee, maybe He'll send down a legion of angels to save us."

"He could, but He probably won't."

"You bet He won't. He doesn't save anyone."

Cal had made such comments before. Annie was weary of them, and the situation had taken away her ability to let them go unchallenged. "Enough, Cal. It's time you explain what happened to make you so bitter."

"I told you. My dad—"

She shook her head. "There's more than that. I know it."

"Go take your shower."

The shower could wait. "Now. It's now or never." He studied her a moment, and she could tell he was considering it. She took his hand and sat on the bed beside him. "Tell me. Please. The time for secrets has passed. I want to understand. Everything."

And I want you to understand.

The thought surprised him. The notion to tell her about Treena had been near the surface many times in their lives, especially since the secret about his father had been uncovered. But now...sharing a life-and-death situation pushed the timing front and center. *It's now or never* had meaning at such times.

He turned her hand over and ran a finger along her palm. "I knew God once. Jesus. I prayed, went to church, the whole schmear."

"When was this?"

"Before I met you." He held her hand between the two of his. "I was engaged to another girl once."

Annie's right eyebrow rose. "I...I didn't know—"

"We don't have much time. Let me say this."

She nodded and was silent.

"Treena was devoutly religious. In a good way. Unlike my parents' fire and brimstone, she's the one who made me think about a Jesus who loved, who forgave. I loved her so much I would have done anything for her. I even agreed not to have sex until we were married, because that's what she believed was right."

He looked up at her. "But then there was one night. We'd taken a blanket and watched the sunset. We'd fallen asleep, and when we woke up and snuggled close... We made love almost before we'd truly woken up." He looked at their hands. He was holding Annie's captive, but she wasn't trying to get away.

"She got pregnant. But in a way, it was okay—at least from my point of view. We were planning on getting married anyway. Treena had more guilt about it than I did. I knew we'd messed up, yet since we were making it right, everything would be fine. Even her congregation was being good about it. It was a time when I really started thinking that her God-way was the right way and it might just be *the* way for me."

"Cal, that's wonder—"

He held up a hand. "But then my parents got into the picture. No loving let's-work-through-this. Only vile words, judgment. As if they were perfect. It really got to Treena. Shame took over, and it started to break her."

The memory of her struggles and sorrow racked him still. "I hated seeing her that way. But my parents made her feel so sinful..." He sighed. "They took a girl who was oozing love and joy and made her a sobbing shell."

He let go of Annie's hand. He had to say this next thing alone. Completely alone. "I tried to make her see they were wrong. I chose her. I loved *her*. We had an argument at my apartment over it. Treena drove away. She crashed. She died."

Annie's words were a whisper, "Oh, Cal..."

He shook his head. He didn't want comfort, didn't deserve comfort. "God took my love and my baby. That's why I want nothing to do with Him or His believers." He hoped Annie didn't counter his feelings with any "It's God's will" or some other baloney.

"Why didn't you tell me?"

Cal heard the shower. They'd left Avi in too long. He had to finish. Get this done. And yet, this was the hardest part. "Soon after Treena's death, you came along, a girl who was pregnant and in need of a husband, and I jumped in to save you—and your baby. I had a huge need to do something right."

She put a hand to her neck and he saw her tense. He waited for her words: *I was a rebound? A charity case? Something to make* you *feel good?*

All deserved. All expected.

"Go on," she finally said.

"This is why I never told you before now. I couldn't. I never wanted—never want—you to think... I fell in love with you. The circumstances of your situation might have caused me to be interested at first, but I never would have married you—or adopted Avi as my own—if I hadn't loved you." He kissed her hands. "I do love you, Annie."

The door to the bathroom opened and Avi peeked out. "Mama, I'm done." The shower was still running. Annie stood. "I have to get in the shower."

She left him.

He deserved worse.

Annie had never taken a shower so fast in her life. She washed her hair and was rinsing it in double time, realizing they'd left Avi in too long. Jinko would only be so tolerant. Besides, the water was getting decidedly tepid.

She regretted the necessity of speed. Of all times in her life, she needed a long, hot, lingering, soul-searching shower. Cal's story of Treena had opened so many locked drawers that she didn't know which one to rummage through first. She was glad he had finally shared with her but also saddened that it had taken something as drastic as their present situation for him to do so. Why couldn't he have told her this years ago?

Because he knew you'd react like you wanted to react. With anger and hurt. She and Avi were a project to make him feel virtuous? He'd *come* to love them? The fact she had been able to remain silent was God's doing.

Her own guilt's doing.

Hadn't she used Cal for her own purposes? Alone and pregnant, hadn't she latched on to his willingness, his kindness, with an intensity that was born more of need than love?

He'd grown to love her, and she'd grown to love him. That was the bottom line. Love *had* conquered all. Conquered much. Could it do so in their present situation?

Time was up. She shut off the water.

A heavy knock on the bedroom door made Cal jump and Avi give off a little yelp. Cal put a hand to her mouth.

"What's taking so long? Open this door!" Jinko yelled. "Now!"

Without prompting, Avi slid under the bed. Cal scanned the room and shoved her dirty clothes under the clean ones in the basket. He opened the door.

Jinko strode in. "I give you an inch... Where's your wife?"

Cal nodded toward the bathroom. "She's finishing up."

"Enough of that." Jinko banged on the bathroom door. "I want you downstairs. Now!"

Annie opened the door. Her hair was wet, a comb in her hand. "I'll just be a minute."

Jinko pointed to Cal. "*You,* come with me. It's time you called your coin friend."

"But it's early."

Jinko lowered his chin. "You want to wrap this thing up soon or not?"

Good point.

"Scott!" Cal had never been so relieved to hear anyone's voice.

His friend sounded half asleep. "Who is this?"

"It's Cal McFay. In Steadfast."

"Cal? It's Sunday morning."

"I know. Sorry." He looked at Jinko who spurred him on with a hand. "But I was excited and tried to call you last night."

"We were out. Excited about what?"

"Your Barber collection. The three coins you needed. I got them for you."

"Where?"

"At an auction in Eldora."

"I didn't know about any auction."

"It was in the paper."

A pause. "We've been at Madge's parents' this last week. Had the paper stopped. Why didn't you call me? I would have gone."

Because I wanted to buy them first and make a profit. "I didn't think of you until I got there and saw what they had. But I have them now, and they're all yours."

"How much?"

At the last minute, Cal removed the profit from the price. He had to make sure Scott came over so *this* could be over. "I'll sell them to you for what I paid for them."

"That's great, Cal. I really appreciate it."

Cal let out the breath he'd been saving. "Can you come over—?" He caught Jinko's expression. "Can you bring the Barber set over, then I'll give them to you?"

"Why do you need—?"

"I've never seen a complete set. It would be cool to see you press the last three coins into their proper spots to make it complete."

"Yeah...well, all right. It's the least I can do, considering. What time?"

"Now would be good."

Scott laughed. "How about after lunch. Two?"

"Sure. I guess." Cal gave Scott his address and hung up. "Did I do all right?"

Jinko wiped up a drip from his coffee mug. "You did great—*if* he comes through."

"Oh, he will. He will."

I hope he will.

After getting Avi settled in her cubby—sneaking her a coloring book, crayons, and her Barbies—Annie came into the kitchen. "How about omelets? I make a mean omelet."

"Fine with me," Jered said. "I'm starved."

"All that 'sleeping' works up an appetite, eh?" Jinko winked. "Omelets would be fine."

As Annie got out the pan, the phone rang. They all froze. "Should I answer it?" she asked.

"It might be Scott, calling back," Cal said.

She turned to her husband. "You got ahold of him?"

"He's coming at two."

"Enough chatter," Jinko said. "No, you will not answer it. To everyone but our coin man, you are not at home."

The machine picked up. Merry's voice filled the room. "Where are you, Annie? You okay? We'll wait as long as possible. But hurry up."

The Christmas pageant.

"What is she talking about?" Jinko asked.

"Like I said before: church. We always sit with Merry. She's obviously been waiting."

But hopefully she'll do more than that...

Merry sat among the choir and readied herself for the next song. The Christmas pageant was grand. Except for one flaw: Where were Annie and Avi? Merry had called multiple times but had only gotten the machine. The only explanation was that the McFays were out of town. But why? And why now? Had something happened to Cal's dad? Surely Cal couldn't have been so mean as to forbid them to be in the pageant.

Father, wherever they are, take care of them.

As she ended the prayer, she knew she had to do her part, too. After the pageant, she'd stop over to check on them. Just in case.

Bailey slept in because he hadn't slept well. He'd hoped that with the morning light he'd find clarity. Actually, he'd hoped with the morning light the whole Jered-the-thief fiasco would be gone.

No such luck.

He put on his robe, went downstairs, slipped on his loafers, and trudged into the fresh frosting of snow to get the Sunday paper. On the way back to the house, he opened it and read the headline: *Local Boy Wanted for Questioning.*

He pulled the paper to his chest and scanned the neighborhood from the porch. Most of his neighbors' papers were gone, already safely inside, being perused over Sunday breakfast. He'd be the laughingstock. He was ruined.

He hurried inside, closed the door, and felt a sudden need to talk to someone. Get some support. Maybe he was overreacting. He hoped he was overreacting.

He ran through his list of possible confidants. The list was lacking. There was Sanchez, his chef at Bon Vivant. And perhaps the head waiter, Stanley. But he quickly discarded the notion of opening up to them. He was their boss. He had to maintain a gap of authority—however misplaced it might be.

Cal!

Although he hadn't known Cal but six months, in many ways the handyman was Bailey's first real friend. Besides, there was another advantage to talking with Cal—Cal didn't know Jered and didn't know the details of their father-son history. Cal would be on Bailey's side.

Somebody had to be.

He got dressed and headed out. To Cal's house.

Eighteen

"Do not be afraid of them,
for I am with you and will rescue you," declares the LORD.

JEREMIAH 1:8

MERRY AND KEN PULLED IN FRONT of the McFay residence and shut off the car.

"Both vehicles are here," Merry said.

Ken tapped his thumbs against the steering wheel. "Wherever they've been, at least they're home now. But I still can't believe Annie and Avi would miss the pageant."

"Whatever it was, it must have been important," Merry said. "All Avi could talk about was being an angel and wearing a halo." She took a breath and put her hand on the car door. "Let's go find out what happened."

They got out of the car and headed up the walk. Ken retrieved the Sunday paper, tapping it against his hand for emphasis. "This is odd. It's nearly noon."

Merry shook her head. "Annie isn't one to sleep late, and even if they've just gotten home, you'd think they would have gotten the paper." She looked at him. "Wouldn't you?"

Ken looked at the house as if seeing it for the first time.

As they went onto the front stoop, Merry felt a chill and sensed it had nothing to do with the weather. "Something isn't right."

Ken rang the doorbell.

Ding-dong!

Annie's heart stopped, then started double time. Finally, someone was here!

She took a step from the stove toward the front—

"Stop!" Jinko hissed and held up a hand. "Nobody move. Be perfectly quiet."

The doorbell rang again. Was it Merry? *Please be Merry! Please see my message on the window.*

Cal glanced toward the kitchen door. *Yes!* The next logical step would be for Merry to come around back and peek in the glass of the kitchen door. She'd see them and then—

Jinko must have also seen the direction of Cal's eyes because suddenly he said, "Everybody down! Get in the corner away from the window and the door."

Reluctantly Annie left her spot by the stove. She left the burner on. Maybe if the cheese sandwiches started to burn, and Merry saw the smoke...

The four of them huddled on the floor in the crook of the kitchen, Jinko on the outside, his gun raised. Within a minute there was a knock on the kitchen door. Annie could imagine Merry cupping her hands against the glass, looking in. What would she see? Unfortunately, nothing unusual. If only Annie had already set the table for four—*that* would have looked suspicious.

Another knock. "Annie? Cal? You in there?"

It *was* Merry! Annie had the urge to cry out. Scream. That would get her attention.

Her face must have revealed her intentions because Jinko touched the gun to her cheek and whispered, "Don't even think about it."

Cal took her hand and squeezed. They exchanged a look of helplessness.

They heard Ken talking. "Maybe they went for a walk? A run?"

"It's below freezing," Merry said.

"Let's get back to the car."

Silence. They were gone.

That's it? They gave up so easily? Annie wanted to stay where she was forever, curl up in a ball, and let someone tell her when it was over. She was tired of thinking, of trying to find a way out. Let someone else do it for a while.

Let Me do it.

Gladly. God could have it with her blessing.

Merry and Ken got back in his car, but Ken didn't start the engine.

His action spoke volumes. All Merry said was, "I know. Me, too."

She leaned low and peered out the window at the McFay house. The sun hit the front windows...

She saw drawing on the ones upstairs. "What's that in Avi's window?"

Ken looked in the direction she was pointing. "Some kid's drawings. And...well...writing?"

Merry squinted. Amid the child's doodling was some adult penmanship. *M.C. Ps 140:1–2 A.M.*

Ps?

Postscript? Psst? Ps...

Psalm! Ps was the abbreviation for the Psalms! She read the line again, the singular letters forming a message. She sucked in a breath. "Ken! There's a message up there! For me!"

"Where?"

Merry leaned over him. "See? M.C. stands for Merry Cavanaugh. Ps 140:1–2 is a Bible reference. And A.M. is Annie McFay. She's written me a message."

"Why would she do that?"

Goose bumps took Merry's arms captive. She grabbed her Bible from the backseat and turned pages frantically. She pegged the verses with a finger and read aloud. "*'Rescue me, O Lord, from evil men; protect me from men of violence, who devise evil plans in their hearts and stir up war every day.'*" She looked up. "Rescue me. Evil men! It's a call for help!" She looked at the house. "Someone has them hostage!"

Ken stared at the house, his head shaking. "I may be a cop, but come on, this is Steadfast, Kansas. People aren't held hostage here."

Merry bit her fingernail. The entire scenario flew in the face of the it-can't-happen-here, it-can't-happen-to-me philosophy.

But what if it was true? She read the verse again but was interrupted when another car pulled to the curb and parked directly across the street from them. It was Bailey.

He saw her and got out. Ken rolled down his window. "Bailey, get in." He motioned to the backseat.

"What?"

"Get in!" Merry added.

He did as he was told. "What's going on? You look like you're going to burst."

She turned around to face him. "We think someone is holding the McFays hostage."

Bailey laughed. "What are you talking about?"

She told him the entire story. The phone calls, the pageant, knocking on the door, the cars being home, the newspaper, and finally, the message on the window.

At the end of her recitation, Bailey fell back against the seat. "They're in there now?"

"I believe so."

He sat quietly a moment. "Why didn't Annie just write 'Help!' on the window?"

Ken took over. "She'd be afraid the men would see it and get angry."

Merry pointed to the window. "The way she did it is brilliant."

"But how did she know you'd come by?"

"She didn't. But she had a good idea I would when they didn't show up at the pageant." She thought of something. "Why are you here?"

Bailey looked at Ken, then away. "I wanted to talk to Cal about something."

Ken mouthed a word to her: *Jered.* Suddenly, Merry remembered. "Jered! Oh, Bailey, I'm so sorry. I saw it in the paper this morning, but with all this... Do you really think he's involved in burglaries?"

Bailey picked a piece of lint off the car seat. "I don't want to think about it." He waved a hand in front of his face, as if that could handily wipe the reality away. "So. What do we do about this? About here. Now."

Ken started the car. "I'll go call it in. Get some help out here."

"Isn't that a bit drastic?" Bailey asked.

"Maybe. But I'd rather feel foolish and find them sleeping in than ignore it and have someone get hurt."

Merry nodded. "Poor Avi. She must be so scared."

Just as Bailey couldn't think about Jered being involved with bad men, Merry couldn't think about Avi being held captive by one. Or some.

There were too many unknowns. Ken pulled away. It was time to get some answers.

"Jered, go check out front and see if the busybody is gone—and don't let yourself be seen."

Duh. Jered moved to the front of the house, hugging the walls of the hallway. The front door didn't have a window, but he tried the peephole. He hoped he wouldn't find someone looking back at him.

He didn't. But what he saw was almost worse. Directly across the street was his father's car, but it was empty.

He tried to see to either side of the stoop, but the peephole had its limits. He moved to the living room and carefully pulled aside one of the drapes. He didn't see anyone.

Where was his dad? And why had he come over? Did he know Jered was there?

"Jered!" Jinko's whisper was harsh.

Jered hurried back to the kitchen, his mind swimming.

"Is she gone?"

"She's gone." He took a fresh breath and made a decision. "The coast is clear."

Kind of. Sort of.

Dad? Where are you?

Annie checked her watch. It was almost one. She wanted to cry. It had been an hour since Merry had stopped by, which meant she hadn't seen the note and help was not on its way. Though she'd managed to slip Avi some food, her daughter couldn't stay in the cubby forever. Annie wanted it over. Soon.

Their only hope was for Jinko and Jered to get their coins and leave. Scott Wheeler was due within the hour. *If* Scott brought his Barber coin collection, and *if* Jinko managed to take it from him quickly and cleanly, then they would get in their car and—

Annie's head whipped toward the garage. Jinko's car—the getaway car—was hidden in the garage, blocked by Cal's truck and Annie's van. Even if Jinko did manage to steal the coins from Scott, he wouldn't be able to get away without more fruit-basket-upset with the cars. And she couldn't imagine Jinko giving up his Mercedes for one of their clunkers.

She glanced at Jinko, eating his second sandwich. Did he realize this? He seemed to have everything under control, and yet, if he did, had he figured out how they were going to leave? Above everything else, she wanted them to leave.

Suddenly, her stomach wrenched. The only safe way to buy Jinko and Jered time to escape would be to kill everyone in the house. *No, that can't happen. No, Father, don't let that happen!*

Jinko looked at her. "What's wrong with you?"

Annie couldn't show her fear. She couldn't. *Calm, Lord, give me calm.* She actually managed a smile and turned to Jered, "Now that we have time, tell me about your music. Merry told me you want to be a composer and a performer."

Jered was so shocked by the question he nearly choked. "I'm working on it."

Jinko made a *harrumph* sound, and Jered's stomach grabbed. He stared at him, hoping he'd interpreted the sound wrong. Jinko took a drink of coffee.

"Don't you believe in Jered's music?" Annie asked Jinko.

So Jered hadn't interpreted it wrong. Jinko's harrumph *was* a sound of contempt. Of making fun. Of unbelief. "Yeah. I want to hear too," Jered said. "Don't you believe in my music?"

Jinko looked up from his plate. "Watch it, kid."

Something swelled inside Jered that forced its way out. Maybe it was brought on by the sight of his dad's car. Maybe it was brought on by the fact his name had been announced as a criminal on the evening news. "I need you to answer me. Don't you believe in my music?"

Jinko dabbed his mouth with a napkin. "No. No, I don't."

Each word was a slap. "But you've been promising me a private audition with a producer. You've been setting it up."

"Actually, I *haven't* been setting it up." He curled his fingers under and checked his nails. "You're not good enough, kid. I've heard you sing. I've heard your so-called compositions. Mediocre at best."

"That's rude," Annie said.

"Hey, the truth is often rude. But that still doesn't make it any less the truth."

Jered couldn't breathe. "So you've been stringing me along, pretending you were going to help me, making me help *you?*" What little pride he had shriveled and died. He shoved back from the table. "You've been using me!"

"Take it down a notch, kid. You benefited, too; don't act like you didn't. You've gotten paid."

"I don't care about money."

"That's a lie."

"I don't care about money as much as you do, Jinko. I was helping because of the promised audition. And...I wanted you to be proud of me. The money was nice, but I don't care about it. Not really."

Jinko reached out, as if to touch Jered, but he pulled farther back. "Hey. Kid. I am proud of you. I've never had anyone learn as fast as you've learned. You were by far the best."

A puff of air could have knocked Jered over. The others. He'd known there were others. The kid who disappeared, for one. He'd *known.* But to hear Jinko say it...

"They didn't have the persistence you do, kid. Nor the courage. They'd handle a few *opportunities,* then chicken out. Leave town. You're the only one who stayed. That's why I let you move into my house. As a reward for your loyalty. I told you that."

Jinko *had* told him that. Loyalty. Not love. Why hadn't he seen the distinction?

Now it was too late. He was involved in a hostage situation. The cops in Eldora knew about some—if not all—of the burglaries. They'd traced his car to Jinko's. They'd said his name on TV. He was going to jail. His life was ruined. Forget the music. The dream was dead.

Jered bolted from the room.

Annie stared at Jinko. Though she'd known he was a thief and a wicked man, she hadn't thought he was evil. Until now. "How could you lie to that boy? How could you promise him something you weren't going to do? And now, how could you crush his dream like that?"

Cal put a hand on her arm, trying to calm her. "Annie. Shush. This is none of our busi—"

She pulled her arm away. "But it is our business!" The last twenty hours had taken away her ability to be subtle. She pointed toward the front of the house. "That boy is one of Steadfast's own. He's Bailey's son. You, of all people, should be defending him."

"I don't even know him."

Her voice rose. "He's a kid in trouble. You don't need to know him!" She turned to Jinko. "I want to talk to him, and I really don't care if you give me permission, but I'll ask for it anyhow. Can I go?"

Jinko patted his gun and nodded toward Cal. "I have my insurance policy, so go for it, lady. Right the wrongs of the world. Make the little boy feel all better."

She found Jered on the front stair, his head in his hands. She sat sideways on the step below him, put a hand on his knee, and let it linger there until he glanced up. "I'm so sorry, Jered. Don't let him get to you."

Jered sniffed and looked toward the wall, wiping his eyes using the shoulder of his shirt. "I believed in him. I thought everything would be all right with him helping me. Though it's been kinda messed up, I thought he was leading me to good things. Better things."

"He's leading you in the opposite direction, Jered. He's working on the side of evil. He took you, an innocent boy—"

Jered snickered. "I'm far from innocent."

"Agreed," Annie said. "None of us are. But you weren't involved in bad things before, not to the depth you are now, were you?"

"No. Never."

"Then he's led you astray. Evil does that. Good leads you to better your life, and to better the lives of others. Evil only looks out for itself and leads to dark places."

He looked at the railing. "The whole world's dark."

Annie realized an opening had been made. She glanced toward the kitchen and heard Cal and Jinko talking. She stood and slipped the pocket Bible from the back waistband of her jeans.

Jered saw the Bible. "You've been carrying that around with you?"

"You never know when you might need it." She couldn't pinpoint any particular verses but knew the gist of what they said—what she had to say now. "Listen, Jered, we often make our own hard times. God gives us free will to make choices. Some good and some bad."

"You got that right."

"Some are just dumb or misguided choices, but some are dipped in evil." She nodded toward the kitchen. "I think Jinko is more than a misguided man. I think he's evil. He does evil."

"But he can be real nice—"

"You think evil shows itself with claws and growls? It's a lot more successful when it's nice to us, doing us favors, being the essence of charm." His eyes showed that he got the connection. "But the good thing is, even in the darkest, scariest times, even in the times when we want to kick ourselves for getting into such a mess, God is with us. He'll help us win against the evil, resist it. He'll lead us through. This book is the map and prayer is the vehicle."

"God may help you, but He won't help me."

She put a hand on the Bible. "That's not true. He loves you, Jered. You, Jered Manson, are a child of the Father. And He wants you to take a stand against this evil you've been associated with. He's offering you a choice."

Jered shook his head. "There's no way out. We're wanted by the police; Jinko's in the kitchen with a gun. You don't know what I've done. I've taken lots of things from lots of people. I know God doesn't like that. No one has to tell me that. So how can He want anything to do with me? It doesn't make sense."

"It may not make sense, but it's a truth—*the* truth. God loves you and will forgive you if you confess to Him and ask for His forgiveness. Jesus died on the cross for just that reason, for just this moment when one of His own realizes he needs Him and wants Him in his life." She realized the verse that had dogged her sleep for days was the only one she could remember now. She found the page and showed him. "Here. This is the essence of it all. Read it."

Jered held the Bible. His reading voice revealed more intelligence than his previous actions. "*For God so loved the world that he gave his one and only Son, that whoever believes in him shall not perish but have eternal life.*" He looked up. "Eternal life?"

"Up in heaven. There is more than this life, Jered. It doesn't end here. But it can start here." Annie was a little nervous but decided to go the final step. "Are you that person, Jered? Do you realize how much you need Him and His forgiveness? Do you want Him in your life forever and ever?"

Jered angled away from her. He bit his lower lip. Then his face crumpled. Tears came but he didn't wipe them away. "I...I want everything to change. I want things to be better. *I* want to be better. I'm tired of my old life. I want to start over."

She put a hand on his head. "Oh, Jered. Jesus is the King of starting over."

Jered covered his face with his hands and cried. Annie got on the step next to him and took him in her arms. It was a good start. A very good start.

Where are they?

Cal kept looking toward the front of the house where Annie and Jered had gone. He didn't like being alone with Jinko. Not that his wife could protect him from this man, but somehow her mere presence seemed to calm things. Why was that?

You know the answer.

Cal took his plate to the counter. He would not admit God was the source of his wife's calm. God didn't calm down; He stirred up. Look at Treena. Look at his dad...

He rinsed the plate. He was glad he'd told Annie about Treena. It was good she knew why he was against God. Maybe it would cause her to ease up a bit.

Fat chance.

Cal wasn't sure anything could make his wife's faith waver. Their current situation was a perfect example. While Cal spent time wondering why this was happening, Annie seemed able to forgo the need for such answers and just deal with the problem at hand. And so well, too. Except for a few flashes of anxiety, Annie was a stone wall of faith and control. Her inner strength was a puzzlement.

And an inspiration. Admit it.

"Here," Jinko said. "Take my plate. I'm done." He leaned back, expecting Cal to obey.

I'll show you what you can do with your plate.

"Cal..."

Cal snatched up the plate. He hated this. Hated it.

Hated Jinko.

He finished the dishes, his mind swirling with acts of revenge. Jinko would pay. Cal would make sure of it.

Merry parked her van a half block from Annie's house. She shut off the engine. "I hate being this far away."

"Ken wants us to be safe," Bailey said from the passenger seat. "He didn't want us coming *this* close."

Touché. "Yet if it weren't for me wanting to stop by Annie's—"

"He wouldn't be putting his life in danger."

Actually, she'd thought of that. After losing one husband to early death, she wasn't too pleased she'd fallen in love with a man whose profession could be dangerous. She offered up another quick prayer for everyone's safety.

And she quit complaining. It did no good anyway. She leaned on the steering wheel and watched Ken do a three-point turn in someone's driveway so he could pull in front, where they'd first parked. He got out of the cruiser, did a double take at seeing them, then gave them a stern stay-put signal.

Ken looked up the street and waited until a second cruiser took a position behind Bailey's car. That officer—Ted Cody—got out and slipped between houses, heading toward the back door. After he was in place, Ken headed to the front door.

But at that moment, a blue truck pulled up, the driver looking from one police cruiser to the other. He pulled ahead of Ken's vehicle, nearly blocking the driveway. Ken quickly backtracked. The man rolled down his window and they talked.

"I wish we could hear," she told Bailey.

Ken finished talking to the guy in the truck, got in the cruiser, and pulled out, even with Merry's van.

"What's going on?" she asked out the window.

"I'm going to let Scott Wheeler go up to the door and see who answers. He said Cal called him up this morning, saying he'd purchased some special coins for him at an auction. Wanted him to come over. This might be what the men inside are after, because the coins fill out a collection. Cal asked Scott to bring it along because he wanted to see it—which Scott thought was strange. I told him to leave it in his truck so he'll have to go back for it. Hopefully, he'll see something—or someone—and be able to tell us what's up."

"Isn't this dangerous?"

"Mr. Wheeler's the one who suggested it, gave me his whole résumé about how he's ex-Army and could handle it. I told him not to go inside. He's supposed to ask Cal to come out to his truck to see the collection." Ken glanced back, toward the house. "We want to see if Cal's okay. Annie and Avi, too, hopefully."

The man was waiting on the front walk, looking at Ken, then back toward the house nervously. If anyone was looking out the windows, he'd know something was up. They had to act. Now.

Ken pointed toward the McFay's door. It was a go.

❧❧❧   ❧❧❧   ❧❧❧

The doorbell rang.

It was only a few minutes after two. Annie was thrilled Scott was prompt. She couldn't stand the waiting anymore. Especially not since she'd devised a plan.

She'd positioned herself upstairs—saying she needed to use the bathroom—in the hopes that once Scott got here, Jinko and Jered would be occupied...

She heard Jinko's voice coming from the kitchen. "Open the door, Cal. And no funny stuff. Just bring him back here."

With Jinko and Jered in the kitchen, she had a chance. On his way to the door, Cal glanced to the upper hall and their eyes met. She put a finger to her lips and ran toward Avi's room.

Annie heard Cal push the small buffet aside and open the door. The men greeted each other. That was of no concern to her now. She looked out the front of the house and was shocked to see the edge of two police cruisers. And was that Merry's van down the street? And Bailey's car, directly across?

She nearly laughed with relief. Her window message had worked! She pulled Avi's curtains aside, all pretense at subtlety gone. With the purple marker she wrote in huge letters: HELP! 2 MEN. 1 GUN. WE OK. Since she had time, she decided to add: JINKO DALY & JERED MANSON.

She spotted Ken behind a tree, reading what she wrote. She waved at him. He waved back, nodding. He ran to the police cruiser, opened the door, and called someone.

The cavalry was on its way!

Annie's attention was drawn back into the house as she heard Cal's voice rise. "I need you to bring it in, Scott. Why won't you bring it in?"

"I..."

Scott's voice sounded funny, and Annie guessed he was trying to follow Ken's orders—which were probably strict instructions not to go inside. Wise advice. On the other hand, if Scott *didn't* bring the collection inside, then Jinko and Jered would never leave. If only she could do something, say something...

Lord, what should I do?

Jinko did the doing. She suddenly heard him. "That's enough of this! Get in here! Now! And shut that door!"

Annie ran to the hallway in time to see Jinko burst out of the kitchen and yank Scott inside. But before he could get Cal and Scott out of the way enough to close the door, Scott shouted outside, "Help!"

That's when Jinko hit him on the side of the head with his gun. Scott fell to the floor.

Avi jumped, knocking her lamp over.

Someone had yelled, "Help!"

But it wasn't her dad. Who was it?

She righted the lamp and heard loud voices and a big thump!

Her mother yelled, "Stop it! Why did you do that?"

Avi bit her fingers. Her parents were in big trouble. She couldn't stay hidden any longer. She couldn't.

She opened the door to her cubby.

Nineteen

Dear friend, do not imitate what is evil but what is good.
Anyone who does what is good is from God.
Anyone who does what is evil has not seen God.

3 John 1:11

BAILEY COULDN'T BELIEVE IT. Everything happened so fast. Annie at the window, the man from the truck being jerked inside while yelling for help. The two police officers reacting by pulling out their guns, then Ken retreating to his cruiser to call for more backup.

Yet all Bailey could focus on was one name that Ken had repeated during his call, a name written on the window: JERED MANSON. Jered. His Jered. His son was inside! Everything they'd said on the news and in the paper was true.

Jered was a criminal.

How had this happened? How had his little boy...?

Bailey was out of the van, though he couldn't remember opening the door. So was Merry. They both stared at the house.

"Get back!" Ken yelled. "They're armed."

They moved to the far side of the van and hunkered down. Behind them neighbors opened their front doors, checking out the ruckus.

"Back!" Ken yelled. Doors closed and heads appeared in windows.

Merry bowed her head. "Lord, protect them! Make this turn out all right."

All right? How could this ever be all right?

He must have snickered.

"You find my prayers funny?"

Bitter laughter spilled out, and he fell back on the curb, sitting.

"I find this whole thing funny. Ridiculous. To think that my son, who had trouble following directions to make his bed, could have grown up enough to organize burglaries or have guts enough to take people hostage..." He rested his elbows on his upraised knees and ripped his hands through his hair. "This whole thing is absurd."

He felt Merry's hand on his shoulder. "Maybe he's not really involved. Maybe he's a victim, too."

He could only hope. "Jered's never been a bad kid."

"Of course he hasn't. He probably just got in with the wrong people."

Yes, that was it. It was someone else's fault. It was certainly not... "It's not my fault."

"No one's saying it is."

He looked at her. "But people will think badly of me. They'll talk about me." He shook his head and looked to the ground. "I'll never live this down." Merry removed her hand, and he felt her eyes. He looked up. "What?"

"*You'll* never live this down? What about Jered living through it? What about Annie and Avi and Cal and that poor man who just screamed for help living through it?"

"Well—"

"You're worried about your pride? You're worried about being embarrassed when people's lives are at stake?"

"No, of course—" It had just slipped out. He didn't mean it.

"Believe it or not, *you* are not the victim here, Bailey Manson."

"I know that. I—"

Her eyes glared. "If I could stand up and walk away from you right now, I would. As it is, I'll ask you to leave me alone and keep your thoughts to yourself so I can pray. Pray for the victims. Pray for God's help. You might try it, Bailey. I'm sure God would be thrilled to hear from you."

She scooted over a few feet and bowed her head.

Merry's prayers rattled the space between earth and heaven with their ferocity and interweaving themes. *I'm so sorry! Why did I just do that?*

wove with *Keep them safe! Protect them all! Give us wisdom!*

She wanted to open her eyes and look at Bailey to see how he was doing, but she couldn't. She was afraid she'd find him squashed like a bug on the pavement. For that's what she'd just done—verbally squashed him.

Forgive me, Lord. Forgive me. Help him.

She'd known Bailey was an egotistical snob. She'd known that the first time she'd met him strutting around Bon Vivant as if *he* was allowing *her* the privilege of eating there. If the food wasn't so delicious... And she'd witnessed the whole scenario when Jered ran away after Bailey had his heart attack. Father and son, disagreeing on priorities. A battle of wills and dreams. But for Bailey to sit outside a house that held people in danger and think about how the situation affected *him*...

"Blessed are the merciful, for they will be shown mercy."

Merry let a breath in, then out. Jesus' directive was clear. Bailey was an annoying man with a wrong attitude. But more than anything right now, he needed mercy. Kindness. Love.

Why me, Lord? Let someone else do it.

At the moment, there *was* nobody else. She nodded her agreement along with her amen and opened her eyes. Bailey sat on the curb where she had left him, staring at her van just a few inches in front of him. His chin was set, no sign of shame or remorse in his body.

But Merry knew that didn't matter. God had called people to love the unlovable.

Even Bailey Manson. Hard as it was.

She scooted close. He did not look in her direction. She put an arm around his shoulders and gave him a little squeeze. She felt his muscles relax.

'Nuff said.

They'd gotten Scott Wheeler to the couch. He had a gash on the side of his head from the butt of Jinko's gun. Cal was getting some ice and a towel. Annie knelt at Scott's side, stroking his face. "It'll be okay. We'll take care of you."

He moaned and occasionally opened his eyes, but they rolled more than focused. Annie looked at Jinko, who was peeking out the front window. "Why did you hit him?"

Jinko shrugged. "He yelled."

"Because you yanked him inside."

"He wouldn't bring the Barber set in." He gestured toward the front. "He brought police with him. He deserves what he got."

Jered ran to his side. "There's police outside?"

"Looks to be two cruisers, but I'd bet more are on the way." He smiled. "Actually, it appears we're getting quite an audience. Faces in every window. We'll be on the news again, kid."

Jered backed away. "I don't want to be on the news! I'm tired of this whole thing. I want to go home."

The gun pointed at his face. "There's no going home. I thought you knew that."

Jered looked as if he was going to cry, and Annie wanted to comfort him. He was in so far over his head.

Jered stepped back, next to the Christmas tree, pulling his eyes away from the gun. He fingered a gold star ornament. "We can stop this thing now, Jinko. I'll give back everything I've ever taken. I'll tell them I'm sorry and—"

Jinko laughed. "And you expect them to say, 'Well, okay. Everything's all better now'?" His voice hardened. "It ain't going to happen, kid. Even I know about consequences. I just happen to like to play to the edge of those consequences. Test them."

The star fell to the carpet. "But I don't!"

"But you did. By teaming up with me you did."

Jered retrieved the star and put it back on a branch. Then, oddly, he froze. A moment later he pointed up the stairs. "There's a little girl upstairs!"

Cal heard Jered's words and came running, ice in hand. It was chaos, with Jered pointing from the entryway, Avi calling out, and Jinko running up the stairs, with Annie trying to push her way past him.

"Get away!" Annie was like a madwoman, pushing, shoving,

pulling at Jinko, heedless of the gun. She reached the landing first and scooped Avi into her arms. "You leave her alone!"

Jinko stood, halfway up the stairs, the gun pointed. He had a bleeding scratch on his face. "Get down here! Now!"

Annie shook her head, cradling Avi's head with her hand. "Not until you get away."

Cal tossed the ice onto the floor, pushed past Jered, and ran up the stairs to his family. Jinko put a hand on his arm, but he shoved it away. He *had* to get to them. Touch them. Be a unit with them.

He reached the top of the stairs, and he and Annie hugged Avi between them. Cal whispered into the mix, "Why didn't you stay hidden, darlin'?"

"I heard someone scream. I needed to help."

"Aaaw," Jinko said. "Isn't that sweet?" He descended the stairs and pointed to the living room with his gun. His voice changed from condescending to harsh. "Enough family time! In the living room. All of you."

Annie carried Avi downstairs, steadied by Cal's hand. As they moved past Jinko, Cal felt Annie shiver. She moved to the far corner, to her rocker. Cal stood beside them. Everything had changed. It was a new ball game. Much more was at stake.

Annie kissed Avi's forehead. "So what now?"

Jinko moved to the edge between entryway and living room. He made a fist with his free hand and brought both hands to his forehead, letting out an awful roar. "You lied to me!"

The intensity of his words was a sock to Cal's stomach. Up until now Jinko had been fairly controlled. But now, it was as if something had popped. They had to get Jinko calmed down or—

Jinko whipped his head toward Jered. "Did you know about this?"

"No. No! How would I know?"

"You were the one who searched the place. You looked upstairs! Why didn't you see her?"

"It wasn't his fault," Annie said. "There's a little storage area off our closet Avi likes to play in. She was inside when you first came in. She stayed inside."

Jinko was silent a few moments, breathing in and out. Cal had no idea what to say to make it better. If only Avi had stayed where he'd told her to stay...

The moment was broken by Scott moaning.

"Cal, get that ice on his head," Annie said.

He took a step toward the fallen ice, but Jinko stopped him. He aimed the gun right at Annie. "You are not in charge! Do you understand that, lady? You are *not* in charge."

She held Avi closer, rocked forward, then back. "And neither are you."

Cal's knees nearly buckled. *Annie! What are you doing? Be quiet! Don't provoke...*

All eyes were on Jinko. He stared at Annie. Cal didn't dare look at his wife, but he assumed she was staring right back. Where did she get her strength? Or was it stupidity? All that could be heard was the *swish-creak, swish-creak* of the rocker against the carpet.

Finally, Jinko spoke. "You know what, little lady?"

"What?"

His eyes gave her a full body scan. "I like you. You've got guts. Fire. After this is over, I'm going to remember where you live and come visit you, and we can get to know—"

Cal lunged at him, but Jinko shoved him into Jered's arms. Cal shook the kid's hands away.

"Don't *ever* do that again!" Jinko said.

Annie's voice was plaintive. "Cal..."

He forced himself to calm down, forced his hands to relax.

They heard another car drive up, and Jinko moved to the window. "More police. Looks like the sheriff. Oh, this is great. Just great." He tossed the drapery aside, causing it to catch on an angel figurine sitting on the television. It fell to the floor.

"The angel!" Avi said.

Jinko flashed her a look. "Keep that kid quiet!"

Annie pulled her close and shushed her.

Jinko began to pace in a tight there-and-back pattern. "We're running out of time. We need to grab the coins Cal bought at the auction and whatever else, then get out of here."

"Out, how?" Jered asked.

"Let me handle that." He handed Jered the gun. "Take this."

"I don't—" Jered nearly dropped it.

Jinko roughly wrapped his hands over Jered's, pressing the gun into his fingers. "Hold this on them. Don't let them move—or the whole lot of you will never move again. *Comprendé?*"

Jered's face was petrified. "What are you going to do?"

Jinko took the stairs two at a time.

The gun was so heavy! Jered had never held a gun, and he didn't like the feel of it. Could it go off if he jostled it the wrong way?

He decided the best thing to do was to keep his finger off the trigger. Just hold it. Point it. Hopefully that would be enough.

They heard Jinko upstairs, banging, tossing, breaking things. That wasn't like Jinko at all. It made Jered nervous.

"If he's looking for more coins, there are none," Cal said quietly.

Jered cleared his throat. "Why should we believe you?"

"Because we're telling the truth." Cal pointed to Scott. "Can I get this ice to him?"

Jered shook his head violently. "Jinko said not to move."

Annie spoke, her voice calm, as always. "Then *you* give Scott the ice pack. You do it."

That was a possibility. But first, Jered had to get Cal out of the way. He pointed to the recliner. "Sit."

Cal sat.

Keeping his eyes on Cal, keeping the gun on him, Jered retrieved the bag of ice and brought it to Scott, who took it weakly but managed to press it against his wound.

The little girl was whimpering. He hated when kids cried. "You okay?"

She looked up from her mother's shoulder and nodded. "I'm sorry I came out."

Her mom pulled her head close. "It's okay, sweet-apple. It's okay. You were a good, brave girl to stay in there alone so long."

Jered thought of something. "How did she eat?"

"I snuck her food," Annie said.

The little girl sat up. "I'm hungry."

"Not now, okay?" Jered said. "Later. But not now."

She nodded and rested her head against her mom.

Jered had no idea what to do next. Things were nerve-racking enough without Jinko going crazy upstairs. Jered hoped he was finding a way out.

"I wish he wouldn't break things," Cal said. "He doesn't have to break things."

"He can do what he wants," Jered said.

"Your dad's outside," Annie said.

Jered's heart bounced. "I know."

"You saw him?"

"I saw his car."

"He's there with Merry. They're in her van in front of the neighbor's."

Jered had to see. He moved to the window, then remembered he was supposed to be holding the gun on the McFays. It was awkward doing both. He parted the drapes just enough.

"To the right. The tan van," Annie said.

Jered saw a bit of the van just beyond the police cruisers and the cops that were hunkered down behind them talking on walkie-talkies. He didn't see his dad though—

There! Was that him poking his head up? *Dad? Is that you?*

His excitement flipped to shame. His dad was a witness to all this...this mess he'd gotten himself into. Now he'd never be proud of him. Now he'd never want Jered back.

He thought of the birthday card he'd taken from his house when he snuck in to get his guitar. He'd looked at it often—and memorized its words: *Happy birthday, son. May all your dreams come true.*

Dreams?

They were gone. All gone.

He turned back to his hostages. "I don't want to hear any more about my dad. We're living separate lives now. I can't live the kind of life he wants me to live."

"So this is the kind of life *you* want to live?"

Annie had a point. Jered changed his weight to the other foot. "Jinko says we have to live for ourselves. If we're worried what other people are thinking or feeling, we'll drive ourselves crazy." He hesitated. He wasn't sure about this next part. "We have to believe we're better than the rest."

Annie shook her head. "That is completely, 100 percent wrong."

"It's not. Jinko says—"

"Jinko says whatever it takes to make you do what he wants you to do. Jinko says whatever it takes to justify stealing from and hurting other people, using them for his own gain and pleasure."

"Now is not the time to debate philosophy, Annie," Cal said.

"It most certainly is. Jered's on the edge of a huge decision and—"

"No, I'm not."

"Sure you are. What did you and I talk about on the stairs, just this morning?"

Was that just this morning? Jered didn't want to go into it. Not in front of the husband. "That was then. I was mad at Jinko. You caught me at a weak moment."

"No, God caught you. You said you wanted to start over."

Cal's head whipped toward Jered, then back at Annie. "You talked to him about God?"

"Of course."

"Where was I?"

"In the kitchen with Jinko." She waved a hand. "The whens of it aren't important. What's important is that you've already made a choice, Jered. God knows you're thinking about Him. You can't go back."

Jered was surprised to find he was glad about that. Though he had no idea how to glue what happened earlier onto this moment, this crisis, he was glad it wasn't for nothing. It counted.

Annie glanced upstairs and lowered her voice. "Let us go, Jered. Let us go out the back door and run to the police and be safe."

"Cans are in the way." *I already tried that.*

"So we make noise. We'll do it fast and be gone before Jinko can react. Besides, you have the gun, and I know you won't use it."

She has me pegged. Jered pointed to the man on the couch. "What about him?"

The man opened one eye. "Just get me outta here."

Jered looked up the stairs. Jinko had moved from the back of the house to the front. As long as he was noisy, he was busy. *But what about me?*

Annie answered as if she'd heard. "You can come with us."

"But I'm wanted by the police."

"I don't know what you did or didn't do," Annie said. "But who would you rather deal with: the law or Jinko?"

Cal sat forward on the recliner, his eyes flitting from upstairs to the conversation. "If we're going to do this, we need to—"

"If you're going to do what?"

Jinko!

Jered instinctively moved to the far side of the room, away from the stairwell. He stood next to Annie. Only when Jinko started down the stairs did he remember the gun. He raised it, pretending to be doing his job.

Annie started rocking again. "If we're going to get something to eat—Avi's hungry—we need to do it soon." She began to stand. "I'm going to make her a—"

Jinko took a step toward her, and she—and Jered—flinched. He stopped, then stared at Jered a moment. "What's gotten into you, kid? You're acting like a scared rabbit."

Jered cleared his throat, hoping his voice wouldn't come out in a squeak. "I was thinking—"

"Well, stop it. Let me do your thinking for you." Jinko grabbed the gun away from him.

He was only too ready to let it go. Annie shook her head, and he realized that what Jinko just said was wrong. Jered had to think for himself. Make his own choices.

Jinko pointed at Scott. "Why does he have an ice pack? Who gave him an ice pack?"

"I did," Jered said. "He needed—"

"*He* needed? It's not what they need, kid; it's what we need, what we do, what we decide. If you're so keen on their needs, why don't you go out to the kitchen and make the kid a sandwich? You could even ask her about what kind of jelly she wants."

"Grape," the girl said.

"Shut up, kid."

"Don't talk to her like that," Annie said.

"I'll talk to her any way I like. I'm the one in charge here. I'm the one—"

The phone rang.

They all looked in the direction of the kitchen.

Maybe it's the police. Maybe it's my dad. Aren't you going to answer it, Jinko? Just answer it and get this thing over.

The answering machine picked up. "Jinko Daly? This is the police. Pick up. We want to talk to you."

Jered stared at Jinko. *Come on...pick it up.*

Jinko pointed at Jered. "Get it."

"Me?"

"I'm not leaving this room. Get it."

"What do I say?"

"Say hello, kid."

Annie dealt with two conversations at the same time. On the one hand, her ears strained to hear all that Jered said into the phone; at the same time, she was having her own conversation with God.

"No, this is Jered. Jered Manson."

Father, I know You're here among us.

"Everybody's fine. Or pretty much fine."

We need Your guidance and direction.

"Uh...Jinko has a gun."

Jinko took a step toward the kitchen. "You tell him Jinko will use that gun if he doesn't get what he wants."

As Jered repeated the line, Annie pulled Avi even closer and exchanged a look with Cal. *Lord, protect us. Keep us safe. Make this end soon.*

"Uh-huh. In the living room—"

Jinko rushed into the kitchen. "Give me that! Move in there."

Suddenly, Jered stumbled into the entryway. He blushed and put his hands in his pockets.

Annie's first reaction was that she felt sorry for him. Jered wasn't on Jinko's side anymore. But was he on *their* side? Another fact hit her. *The man with the gun is in the other room! Busy. On the phone.*

She glanced at the front door. Cal followed the direction of her gaze. He looked behind him toward the sound of Jinko's voice. Then he looked at Scott and shrugged. Would it be possible to make a run for it?

Jered took a few steps toward them, shaking his head and waving a hand. "Uh-uh. No way. Don't even think about it." He whispered and pointed toward the kitchen. "He's right *there.*" He made a motion with his index finger and thumb, like a kid pretending to shoot.

Annie leaned back against the rocker and let up on her grip of Avi. She hadn't been aware that she'd leaned forward and was holding Avi as if flight was imminent.

"We can't, Mama."

Annie kissed her head. "I know."

"But what *can* we do?"

"Pray, sweet-apple. Pray."

Avi nodded against her chest.

They heard Jinko say, "Call me back in five minutes," and hang up. He appeared in the living room and gestured upstairs. "Everybody up to the master bedroom. I need you contained and away from a door."

"But Scott..." Cal said.

Jinko pointed the gun at the man on the couch. "Scott has no choice. Now go. And once you're up there, shut the door. Jered, you hang out on the stairs and guard them."

Cal helped Scott to his feet and up the stairs, letting Annie and Avi go first. Although the move was taking them farther away from a door to escape, Annie was glad to be together, and she was especially glad for the requirement of the closed door. It would give them a chance to talk. And any place *away* from the gun was an improvement. *Thank You, God!*

The bedroom was a pit, drawers open and rifled through, boxes in the closet tossed on the floor. Annie knew they had nothing of value for Jinko to find. But what bothered her more than the mess or losing a few trinkets was what Jinko's rampage revealed of his character. Up to now he'd been pretty controlled. Calm. The destruction upstairs showed his other side.

They settled Scott on the bed. "Can I get you anything?" Annie asked. "Aspirin? A cold compress?"

"The compress would be great, but I don't know if I should take medicine."

Annie and Cal didn't know either. They decided against it.

"Can I go in my cubby?" Avi asked.

Annie was going to say yes—after all, it was a place that would give Avi comfort—but then Cal answered, "Not now, darlin'. We need to stay close. Together. In case we have a chance to get out."

"We can bring some of your pillows and toys out here. Make you a little cushy place in the corner. Does that sound good?"

Avi nodded to her mother wholeheartedly. She and Annie made it happen. Within a minute, the little girl had a comfy pile of blankets, pillows, and books in the corner by the window.

Ignoring the mess, Annie moved the bedroom chair that usually sat in that space to the far side of the bed, near Scott. She offered it to Cal, but he insisted she take it, while he sat on the bed next to his friend. They formed a tight triangle.

"I'm so sorry I got you into this, Scott."

Scott touched his head. "Me too, Cal. Who are those guys?"

"I met them at the auction. They saw what I bought and followed me home."

Annie waited for him to add the part about bragging about coins he did not have, but he didn't say more.

"I thought it was odd you wanted me to bring the collection here."

Cal shrugged. "Their idea."

"But then seeing the police out front when I drove up..."

Speaking of... They all remained silent a moment and listened. They could hear Jinko on the phone in the kitchen below. "I need to get to my car, but it's blocked into the garage. So this is what we're going to do. I want whatever police cars are out there to park your cars perpendicular to the street, one after another, real tight."

Cal illustrated Jinko's words by making a slicing motion with one hand forming a cross over his other, demonstrating the cars' position in the street. "They won't be able to go after him," he whispered.

Jinko wasn't through. "I'll toss the McFays' car keys outside so their cars can be parked nose-in toward the file of cruisers, in front of them and behind. And then I want their keys put in my vehicle. Also in my vehicle you will place a bag containing fifty thousand dollars. Only then will we get my car out of the garage and—" Jinko paused. "Hey, I don't care if you find it acceptable or not. I'm the one calling the shots here. And by the way, just to make sure you don't take any potshots at us, we're going to bring a hostage with us."

Annie grabbed Cal's knee. "He's going to take a hostage?"

"Shh!"

Jinko yelled, "Don't talk to me about time! I'll give you five minutes to say yes, or the next sound you hear will be the sound of someone dying."

Twenty

Everything belongs to you,
and you belong to Christ,
and Christ belongs to God.

1 CORINTHIANS 3:22–4:1, NLT

THE PHONE RANG DOWNSTAIRS. Annie and Cal held their breath.

Jinko answered it. "You made a good choice. I'll toss the keys out now and give you an hour to make it happen."

Annie's stomach fluttered. "It's going to happen."

"I know." Cal swallowed hard. "And soon. I'll be going soon."

Annie's heart flipped at her husband's words. "Cal..."

He looked straight ahead, then at her. "I'm going, Annie. You know it."

She knew it. Scott couldn't and Annie shouldn't. And Avi...surely Jinko wouldn't even consider that.

They sat still a few moments, the only sound Jinko's and Jered's murmurings from the living room and Avi singing quietly in the corner as she played with her bride paper dolls, "'Seek and ye shall find, knock, knock, and the door shall be opened, ask and it shall be given, and the love come a-tumblin' down.'"

Suddenly Cal pulled Annie to her feet. "We need to talk." He led her into the closet. They immediately found each other's arms and let the contact do the talking a few moments.

"Cal, I don't want you to do this."

"And I don't want to do this. But we heard him. He's going to take a hostage. It has to be me. There's no other way."

She pushed back from him. "There has to be. I don't want you alone with him. Who knows what he may do to a hostage once he's safely away."

Cal looked past her. "Hopefully, he'll just drop me off out in the country somewhere. There's no reason for him to kill me. The police know his name. They know his car. Killing me would just get him into more trouble, and he doesn't need that."

Suddenly her legs were weak. She buckled and slipped to the floor, with Cal's arms slowing her fall. They hugged and rocked in the same way she had rocked Avi.

"I love you, Annie," Cal said.

"I love you, too."

"And I want you to know how proud I am of you."

She had to look at him. "Proud?"

He looked uncomfortable with the words. "During this entire thing, you've become so strong, so calm, so—"

"It's not my doing, Cal. God did that. God gave me the strength to find the calm. It's His calm."

He shook his head. "Don't start. Not now."

She shoved him away. "Yes, exactly now. We don't have time for games or power plays. For weeks now, months, we've either been arguing or tiptoeing through each other's worlds, skirting past each other, being careful not to intersect. I've hated it. Haven't you?"

He shrugged.

"No! Don't shrug at me. This is important!" She lowered her voice. *Lord, please...* She took Cal's hands in hers and studied them. Such strong hands from such a strong man. A stubborn man.

"You once gave me an ultimatum. Choose you or God."

"Yeah, well, you pretty much made your choice. You haven't been the same."

"No, I haven't. But instead of seeing the change as bad, I wish you'd see how good it is."

"It's not good. I don't want you ending up broken and confused like Treena, or worse, judgmental and mean like my dad. It's tearing us apart, Annie-girl."

"But it doesn't have to. I've been aching to...to..."

"Convert me."

"No." She tried to calm her breathing. "This has nothing to do with converting. 'Converting' is calculated, high-pressure."

"And your point is?"

She let out a breath. "If I've been pushy, forgive me. I'm still try-ing to figure out how it's supposed to fit together. In the process I may have been too...passionate."

He snickered. "Tell me about it."

Oh, dear. Had she done everything wrong? Not talking or talk-ing too much? She tried to make amends. "Like I said, this has nothing to do with converting; it has to do with sharing, with loving another person so much that you ache for him to understand what you have. You want him to see the light."

Cal shook his head. "I've seen the light and found it much too glaring and harsh."

Unfortunately, from what he'd said before, he wasn't exaggerat-ing. How could she ever dispel a lifetime of opinions and experiences? She felt tears threaten. "I don't know how to reach you, Cal."

"Maybe I'm unreachable. Have you ever considered that?"

Actually...

He raised his knees and rested his arms on them. "The way you've gotten so caught up in God scares me."

She reached toward him, but he pulled away. "It shouldn't. It should make you want what I have. I tried to do it your way, to ignore God. But I couldn't without feeling as though I was being disobedi-ent to Him."

"I will *never* be that obsessed about anything."

"I'm not obsessed, Cal. I'm committed."

He sighed. "Don't you see that I want you to be that committed to me?"

"I *am* committed to you."

"Not like that." One hand clasped his other. "Sometimes, when you aren't looking, I study you and see this peace in your face, this utterly contented look, as if you are fantasizing about the most deli-cious food or the most beautiful place on the earth."

But He is my food. And faith is a beautiful place to live.

"You look so...so utterly satisfied."

She wanted to burst out with, *That's exactly what I am! He is my total satisfaction! He is everything to me!* But she didn't. It was almost as if a restraining hand had been placed on her arm. *Take it easy, Annie. Don't scare him away from Me. This isn't about you. This is about him. About him and Me.*

She pulled her legs beneath her and sat on her knees facing her husband. She tried to set aside all that was Annie to allow God to give her the words Cal needed to hear, not the words she needed to say. Finally, it seemed right. "Please hear me, Cal. I'll try to say this right. God has become my personal God, but He's not my exclusive God. He doesn't care for me any more than He cares for you or Avi, your dad, Treena, or even Jinko downstairs."

"Don't talk about Jinko."

"The point is, God doesn't change; we do. He is constant, stable, perfect, ever present, and ever ready to bless us."

"I don't feel very blessed at the moment."

"Me either. Hard times test us. But again, *He* hasn't changed. He *won't* change. He's the same right this minute as He was last week when I felt His presence in church during an especially gorgeous song, as He was when my stomach was on the edge of giving out when I was sneaking Avi food. Our circumstances change, our emotions change, we are faced with ever-changing choices, but He doesn't change."

"Why doesn't He make Jinko and Jered go away? Why did he let Treena die?"

She opened her mouth to answer, closed it, then opened it again. "I don't know."

He laughed. "Oddly, I find your ignorance refreshing."

She had to remind herself this wasn't about her. "We may not understand the whys. And it's human nature to want things to be happy and fun all the time. But we're not the whole picture. I'm realizing that more and more. Though God cares about us as individuals, loves us as if we were His only children, He has the world to consider. What each of us does affects many, many people. What might seem bad to us may, in fact, be something glorious for someone else."

Her stomach stitched, surprising her. She swallowed and continued. "God can bring good out of bad. And sometimes..." A new thought interrupted. It loomed over her, present but not present, like an apparition waiting to be noticed.

"Sometimes...?" Cal asked.

The thought became clearer around the edges, and as it did, Annie mentally wanted to turn away, not see. And yet she had to see. She had to understand. *Lord, what are You trying to tell me?*

"Greater love has no one than this, that he lay down his life for his friends."

What?

She closed her eyes as words spun through her mind, their tendrils caressing her previous thoughts and wrapping around her fears.

Obedience means sacrifice.

Her eyes flung open.

She put a hand to her chest, trying to find the breath to express it out loud. "Sometimes..." She closed her eyes. "Sacrifice is involved."

There. She'd said it.

"What are you talking about?"

What *was* she talking about? "I don't feel very good."

Annie ran from the room.

Cal knocked on the door of the bathroom. "Annie-girl? You okay?"

She sat back from the toilet where she'd lost her lunch. She wiped her mouth. "I'm fine. I'll be fine." She flushed but remained on the floor, leaning back against the tub.

"Let me in."

"Go be with Avi. I'll be fine. Just give me a minute."

She was relieved when he didn't pursue it. She *did* need a minute. More than a minute. Many minutes to recover from the violence her body had just gone through, but mostly to recover from the directive that had brought on the violent reaction.

Or was it a directive? Perhaps it was just an opportunity? A suggestion?

Or a premonition?

It revolved around obedience. What had she said to Cal earlier? That she'd felt disobedient to God when she'd chosen Cal over Him?

Choose Me for *him. To reach him. Obedience means sacrifice.*

She pushed herself to standing, her breathing suddenly labored.

Her head shook in short bursts, her hands pumped fists at her side. God couldn't want this. He couldn't.

You know Me. Cal doesn't. He needs more time.

She whipped toward the door as if Cal were standing there. It was true! She knew God. She was His. She knew where she would spend eternity. Her salvation was assured. A done deal.

But her husband...was he going to heaven?

Maybe. *"I am the way and the truth and the life. No one comes to the Father except through me."*

This was not a wishy-washy, gray issue. You couldn't *happen* into heaven; you couldn't get there on the coattails of a relative. Heaven was a gift and a choice. A conscious choice. Even though Cal seemed far away from God now, he'd been heading on the right road once. Treena had opened his eyes to a loving God. But had Cal committed to Jesus back then? Had he accepted Jesus as Savior? Did he believe Jesus was who He said He was?

"I don't know!"

She put a hand to her chest, trying to calm its beating. They'd never talked about it. *Why haven't we talked about it?*

A wave of panic overtook her, soon followed by a wave of calm: *You don't know the state of Cal's salvation, Annie, but I know. Listen to Me now. You know Me. Cal doesn't. He needs more time. Don't put him at risk.*

Thoughts crashed into reality; concept became action. Soon Jinko Daly would take one of them as a hostage in his car. He'd drive past the danger of multiple police officers. One of them would be alone with a frightened, stressed man on the edge who had little to lose.

One of them could die.

"I need to go."

They were four little words that could change everything.

But then four more words appeared in her consciousness: *You don't have to.*

These four words added to the others forced her to take a deep breath and let it out. God would not *make* her take this chance—this opportunity. Choice was of vital importance to the King of kings, the Lord of lords. It was a question, not an order: Could she put her life on the line for her family? Should she? Would she? God's ultimatum was powerful, yet full of mercy: *Will you do this for Me? For Cal?*

She heard Jinko's voice calling from downstairs. "Everybody down here! Now! It's time."

Bailey grabbed Ken's arm, making him jump.

"Don't do that!"

"Sorry."

Ken pointed toward Merry's van. "You two have to stay back. You can't be here. It's dangerous. In fact, we need Merry to move her van back another couple hundred feet."

Bailey looked toward his own vehicle, sitting across the street from the house. In the line of fire. He was surprised to find it meant nothing to him. Or at least not as much as it had yesterday. "Have you heard from Jered?"

"Not since our initial call. Since then we've only talked to Jinko Daly. As far as we know Jered's okay."

"I can't believe he's involved in all this. I can't."

Ken's attention was drawn by another officer. "Get back, Bailey. Let us do our job."

Merry was waiting for him at the van. "What did he say?"

"He says we have to move the van back."

"What about Jered?"

"Let's move the van."

Getting out of the van after moving it, Merry and Bailey were assailed by reporters who had congregated at the corner of the McFay's street. Stu Noxley of the *Steadfast Beat* led the pack, his pad and pen ready. Bailey noticed his shirt was coming untucked. He looked like a "before" picture in a masculine makeover.

"Give us the scoop, you two. Any shots fired yet?"

"Stu!" Merry said.

He waved a pencil toward the other reporters. "It's a fair question. It's what we need to know."

"No, no shots have been fired. Hopefully, things will be settled peacefully, with no one hurt."

A woman with royal blue reading glasses balanced on her nose nudged Stu aside. "Is it true your son is one of the criminals, Mr. Manson?"

"He's not a criminal."

"But he's inside. He's in the house. He's holding the McFays hostage."

"He's inside, but—"

"If he's not a criminal, why is he there?" asked a man with an awful toupee.

Bailey tried to think of an excuse for Jered. "He knows Annie. He's met her lots of times at the Plentiful."

"The Plentiful?"

Stu explained. "The Plentiful Café. On the square. Annie's a waitress. They serve the best cinnamon rolls in—"

"So your son's been stalking her?"

"What?"

"Was your son infatuated with Annie McFay—a married woman?" asked a reporter who was wearing a skirt that was one size too small. Her camera was poised and ready.

This is ridiculous. "He was doing no such thing! He barely knew her, and I don't think he ever met Cal."

Toupee-man tapped his pen on his pad. "So if he didn't know them, and isn't a criminal, why is he in their house?"

Good question. "No comment." Bailey got back in the van and locked the door.

Merry followed. "Sorry about that, Bailey."

Her cell phone rang, startling them both. She talked briefly, then said, "Thanks, Claire. We'll be right there." She hung up, then put her keys in the ignition.

"What's Claire want?"

She started the van.

"Merry, where are you going? I need to stay here."

She pulled away from the curb, the reporters moving out of her way. "We need to go where we can do the most good."

"Where's that?"

"Wherever I take you. Now shush and let me drive."

Merry felt only slightly guilty for kidnapping Bailey to the church. Maybe the sight of people praying for the McFays—and even for Jered—would help him get through this.

And maybe not. But if not, Merry was more than willing to hand Bailey over to the Almighty. Let Him handle the man. And a hearty good luck to the Father, Son, and Holy Spirit, too.

When she pulled into the church parking lot, Bailey grabbed the door handle with the same note of panic she'd imagine him having if Merry had pulled into the parking lot of a McDonald's. There was no way he wanted to be associated with such a place.

Tough.

"What are we doing here?"

"Meeting some people." She turned off the van.

"I don't do church, Merry. You can meet without—"

She palmed her keys and faced him in the seat. "We're not here to do church, Bailey. We're gathering here to pray. Pray for Annie and Cal, for Avi and Jered. Pray for their safety. Surely you can't object to that." She leveled him with a look. "Can you?"

He wiped his palms on his pants. "Can't I just stay here?"

She opened her door. "Suit yourself." She got out and started up the walk. The back of her neck prickled with the thought of his eyes on her back. Part of her wanted to stay behind and beg, and part wanted to get into the church ASAP, slam the door on him, and lock it. She was not about to force God on anybody, especially not the egotistical likes of Bailey "Full of Himself" Manson.

When she got all the way to the door without him following, she gave her van one final glance.

He's all Yours, Lord. Do with him what You will.

I can't believe she actually left me here!

Bailey put his hand back on the door handle. He could walk

home, lock the door, close the blinds, and hole up until this entire thing blew over.

The big question was: What exactly did "blow over" entail? Jered surrendering to police? Jered being rescued, proving it was all a big mistake and he was actually a victim in all this?

Or Jered being wounded—or worse—in a shootout?

He put a hand to his brow and shook his head. *No, please. Not that.*

His eyes shot open. Had he just prayed?

He looked at the church and thought of the people praying inside. His eyes moved upward to the roof and to the sky above, realizing he was looking for evidence of prayer waves making their way to heaven like smoke in a chimney. Were the melted patches of snow on the roof places where prayer had come through, burning its way toward heaven and God's ears?

Ridiculous.

Yet comforting, too. And while he was on the subject, how *did* prayers get from a person's head to God? Telepathy? Some celestial e-mail? Could God "hear" what was only being thought? Had God heard his *No, please. Not that?*

Bailey jerked when a knuckle knocked on the window beside him. It was Claire Adams. He rolled the window down.

"What are you doing all alone out here, Bailey?"

"Uh..." Brilliant answer.

She opened the door for him. "This is Merry's van. I take it she went ahead inside?"

He had no choice but to get out. "Yes."

"Then let's get going." She shut the door behind him and put an arm around his shoulders. "It will be all right, Bailey. Prayer changes things."

He certainly hoped so.

Jinko pulled the curtains aside and looked out the front window. "They're changing position. They're moving the cars just like I asked." He turned back, smiling, like a CEO who'd gotten his way from unwilling subordinates.

Annie sat on the couch next to Cal. She'd purposely placed Avi in his lap. They held hands. In just a few moments, Jinko would take one of them outside at gunpoint. Cal thought it would be him. But Annie knew better.

Cal will never go for it. He'll never agree.

That was a given. Cal would never let her put herself in danger. It was against his code of honor, his code of husbandhood, his code of being a man.

It didn't make sense. It wouldn't make sense to anyone but Annie and God.

And just because Annie understood God's reasoning, didn't mean she wanted to do it. She closed her eyes and pictured the scene of Jesus in the Garden of Gethsemane hours before his crucifixion. Suddenly, she needed to read it, hear His words in her head. She pulled the pocket Bible from the back of her waistband.

Jinko rolled his eyes. "If you think you're going to put a hex on me, lady, it won't work."

"Don't be ridiculous. This is a book of love and truth, not hexes." She didn't wait for his permission but opened it to one of the four Gospels, knowing they all would mention the moment in history she was looking for. She found it first in Mark, chapter 14:

They went to a place called Gethsemane, and Jesus said to his disciples, "Sit here while I pray." He took Peter, James and John along with him, and he began to be deeply distressed and troubled. "My soul is overwhelmed with sorrow to the point of death," he said to them. "Stay here and keep watch." Going a little farther, he fell to the ground and prayed that if possible the hour might pass from him. *"Abba,* Father," he said, "everything is possible for you. Take this cup from me. Yet not what I will, but what you will."

Her eyes swam with tears as she read and reread Jesus' plea, as His plea became hers: *Abba, Father, everything is possible for You. Take this cup from me. Yet not what I will, but what You will.*

Her resolve was on the fence, and she knew it was weak. At any moment it could fall toward the side of safety, and she'd chicken out. Only by His strength would it fall toward the side of *His* way and *His* will.

She held the Bible to her chest. *Lord, I'm willing but so horribly weak and scared. You're going to need to help me. I want to obey. Be with me. Be with us all.*

Jinko dropped the curtain, turned toward them, and clapped his hands once. "Okay. Let's do this thing. Up."

As Cal started to set Avi on the couch beside him, Annie popped to her feet. "I'm ready."

"Annie?" Cal said.

"Take me."

"Take—? No way! Sit down!" Cal tugged at her hand, but she stepped out of his reach.

"I'm volunteering. Take me."

Cal set Avi on the couch none too gently in his effort to stand. "Annie, sit down! Now!"

She shook her head and moved beside Jinko. "I'm going, Cal. It's me. It has to be me."

"What are you talking about?"

Jinko put his arm around Annie's shoulders and pulled her close. She shuddered, remembering his earlier sexual innuendo. There was more at stake here than even her life. *Everything* was at stake.

Jinko kissed the side of her head. "It seems the little lady has overridden your choice, Macho Man. And I approve. Oh yes, I approve."

Cal's breathing came in short bursts. "But I don't! She can't go. She can't!"

"Mama?" Avi sat on the edge of the couch, as if ready to fling herself into her mother's arms.

Annie's heart tore in two. "It will be all right, sweet-apple. It will be just fine."

Cal took a step toward them. "You are *not* going!"

Jinko raised his gun and cocked it. His face lost all pretense of charm. Had his eyes gotten darker? "She most certainly is going. And you're going to be a good boy. Go back to the couch, take your daughter on your lap, comfort her like a good daddy," he grinned wickedly, "and let your wife do your job."

Oh, dear. Jinko had made it a question of Cal's manhood. That's not what it was at all. She had to let him know the reason. If obedience was sacrifice and she wasn't going to live to tell him later, she had to let him know now. She had to!

The words burst out. "You need more time, Cal. You need more time to choose Him, really choose—"

"Shut up!" The gun rested against her cheek while Jinko's other hand groped her backside. He whispered in her ear, the words slithering into her consciousness. "Not another word, my love. Not another word."

She shivered. *Oh, Father, I can't do this. I can't.*

Cal stood by the couch. Every muscle in his body was tensed to lunge at Jinko. Avi clung to his legs. *At least they have each other. They will always have each other. No matter what happens.*

Jinko yanked her toward the door. "It's showtime."

Twenty-one

"Now my heart is troubled, and what shall I say?
'Father, save me from this hour'?
No, it was for this very reason I came to this hour.
Father, glorify your name!"

JOHN 12:27–28

JINKO MOVED EVERYONE into the kitchen so they could make their move out the back door. The coin-guy, along with Cal and the little girl, sat at the kitchen table. Jinko had his arm wrapped across Annie's chest from behind.

It was time.

Don't go!

The inner words were like a slap and made Jered step away from the kitchen door instead of toward it.

"What are you doing?" Jinko yelled. "Tuck in behind me, and we'll go out together."

Annie turned her head toward him. "Don't come with us, Jered. Stay behind. Don't get involved any deep—"

Jinko jerked her hard and put the barrel of the gun to her ear. "Shut up! Jered's a part of this, and he's coming with us." Jinko flashed him a look. "Get up here. Now!"

Jered moved in behind him.

With a foot Jinko kicked the cans away from the door. "Now get my keys out of my pocket, kid, and when we go outside, run to the garage and back my car out."

"I'm driving?" Jered imagined them dodging police cars.

"You'd rather hold the gun on her?"

He shook his head. No guns. He didn't even want to touch the gun again.

"Then do as I say." Jinko opened the kitchen door. Nobody moved. It was getting dark. When did that happen? Time meant nothing.

Jered saw Jinko's fingers regrip the gun. A stream of sweat slid down his forehead, and for the first time, Jered noticed that Jinko smelled ripe. Or maybe he was smelling his own fear.

"Hold on just a minute," Jinko said. "Go look out the front and tell me what they're doing."

Jered was happy to be anywhere but at the open door. He went into the living room and edged the curtains aside. "They're hunkered behind the cars, pointing their guns this way."

"Of course they are. What did you think they'd be doing? Playing canasta?"

Jered didn't know what canasta was, but now was not the time to ask. He got the picture. And it wasn't good. He went back to the kitchen. "Now what?"

Jinko's deep breath was not comforting. "We go. Now."

Cal's voice was sickening. "Annie..."

"Mama!" The little girl was crying.

She looked back at them and tried to smile. "I love you both. I'll be okay."

Cal's voice hardened. "She'd better be okay, you creep! If you hurt her in any way, I'll come after you, no matter how long, no matter—"

Jinko seemed to ignore him, but Jered couldn't. Goose bumps crawled up his arms. He didn't want an angry husband coming after him. Cal wasn't kidding around. If anything happened to his wife... Nothing better happen. Nothing *would* happen. Jinko would simply use her as a shield to get away. Then he'd let her go.

Right?

Please. Please make it okay.

Jinko slid his arm around Annie's waist and pulled her toward him like he was hugging a pillow. She looked so little in his grip. So weak. Yet in many ways, Annie had proven herself to be stronger than the lot of them. She was one amazing—

"Now!"

They took a step toward the door. Jered wanted to throw up.

❧   ❧   ❧

Jinko stepped onto the stoop, his gun at Annie's head. The weight of it rested against her temple, and his grip around her waist using his left arm pulled her close under her ribs, making it hard to breathe.

As they moved down the back steps, Annie looked toward the police. Lit by the streetlights she saw Ken Kendell, Ted Cody, and other officers she didn't recognize. Just as Jinko had asked, the police cruisers were parked perpendicular in the street in front of the neighbor's with Cal's truck pointing into them on the far side, and her van making the last point of the cross, closest to them.

A cross. *Jesus, help us.*

It was all the prayer she could manage as things moved fast. Jered slid out from behind their body screen and ran toward the garage. He tripped and sprawled. He was as nervous as she was. He got to his feet and went inside. She heard an engine start, then the ignition grind a second time.

"Stupid kid," Jinko said under his breath.

He held her on the edge of the driveway. Jered zoomed in reverse, zigzagging precariously close to the house. The red of brake lights blinked as the car jerked to a stop.

Jinko pulled her toward the backseat on the passenger side, but he couldn't open the door and keep hold of her and the gun. "Jered! Open the door for us."

Jered hopped out of the driver's side and came around the front of the car. With his wild eyes he looked like a scared little boy, and Annie found herself wanting to comfort *him*. The door was locked.

"Go around!" Jinko yelled at him.

Jered ran around to the open driver's door and fumbled for the unlock button. He was nearly in tears.

"Come on!"

He came around again and opened the door. But just as Jinko was shoving Annie in the back door, someone yelled, "Jered!"

Annie looked out the back window and saw Jered sprinting toward the police cars, his hands raised.

Jinko pushed her the rest of the way inside.

She fell across the seat.

He tried to close the door, but her legs blocked—

The gun went off.

Bang!

Cal leapt from the kitchen chair. A gunshot?

"Daddy?"

Scott stood. "Cal? Was that—?"

He set Avi down. "Stay here, Av! Don't move! Either of you."

Cal rushed out the open door in time to see Ken run toward Jinko's vehicle, his gun drawn. Other officers followed close behind, their eyes riveted on whatever was happening in the car.

"Cal! Get back inside!"

At Ken's order, Cal took two steps back, feeling like a rope being tugged in two directions.

Another office yelled, "Drop the gun, Daly! Get your hands up!"

"Daddy?"

He turned to see Avi standing by the table. He had to make her safe. Cal scooped her up and ran to the stairs, depositing her on the fourth step from the bottom. "Go up to your cubby and don't come out until I come get you."

"But Daddy—"

"Go!"

She ran up the stairs. It felt good to have her safe.

But what about Annie?

He heard all sorts of commotion at the side of the house. He sprinted for the kitchen door just in time to hear Ken call for an ambulance.

Jinko was up against the car being cuffed.

Annie! Where was Annie?

The back doors of the car were wide open, and Ken and Ted leaned in on either side. Ken changed position, and Cal saw blood on his hands.

His wife's blood?

No, no, no, no! Cal staggered toward the car. The officer taking

Jinko away alerted the others. "Husband. Get the husband."

Ted came around the car door and grabbed Cal by the arms, holding him back. Cal's eyes searched for Annie. He saw her limp hand leaning against the back of the seat. Her lifeless hand.

That's when he screamed.

At the sound of her father's scream, Avi sucked in a breath. Then, with a burst, she shoved open her cubby door and scrambled out. She stood in her parents' closet and did a 360, needing to see what was happening outside. But there was no window.

She heard loud voices and running feet. Was that a siren? Her daddy had screamed. Was he hurt?

No. The gunshot came before.

Mama!

She had to see! Forgetting her promise to stay put, she ran to her bedroom and looked out the front window. Everybody was running around the driveway to her right. She tried to see to the side by pressing her face to the glass but couldn't.

The siren got loud and an ambulance pulled up front. Two men in white got a bed with wheels out of the back. They ran toward the place where she couldn't see. Didn't walk. Ran.

"Mama, Mama, Mama. Please be all right, Mama." Her lips kissed the glass with each word. "PleaseGodpleaseGodpleaseGod..."

Suddenly, she saw the men bring the bed-thing back. They were still running. Her mama was strapped onto it. There was blood all over.

Avi pressed her hands to the window.

Then she screamed just like Daddy.

Jered wanted to scream but feared if he did—within the confines of the police cruiser—his scream would whip around and swallow him whole. He wanted to close his eyes but couldn't. The sight of Annie McFay being wheeled to the ambulance, blood all over...

"Hey, kid!"

Jered jerked toward the voice. Jinko sat in the cruiser parked beside him. Neither car could move until they got the McFay cars out of the way. The windows were up, but Jinko didn't let that stop him. He yelled to make Jered hear.

Jered looked away. It was all Jinko's fault.

"It's all your fault, kid!"

That last part caused him to look back. He shook his head.

Jinko nodded toward the ambulance. "Your fault!" His smile was pure evil.

The truck and van were moved, and a cop got in Jinko's cruiser and must have told him to shut up, because he didn't say any more. He just winked as he was driven away.

"It's all your fault."

Was it?

Another cop got in Jered's car and started the engine. "Time to go, boy."

"Where we going?"

The cop scathed him with a look. "Jail."

"But I wasn't a part of this. Not really. I ran. Didn't you see me run? I escaped from Jinko, too."

"Save it. You can tell your story to Ken soon enough."

"But—"

"You have the right to remain silent..."

Jered recognized the Miranda rights from a zillion cop shows. He shook his head. "No, no..." He didn't want to hear it. He didn't want it said to *him.*

The cop looked back at him. "No? You *don't* understand these rights?"

"Well, yeah. Yes. I understand but—"

The cop's voice was hard. "You don't realize the creek you're up, do you, boy?"

"But I—"

"You want a lawyer? We'll get you one."

He wanted his dad. But no way could he call him. No way.

"I want a lawyer."

◆◇◆◇◆◇◆◇◆◇

Cal burst through the kitchen door toward the front of the house. "Avi!"

"Daddy!" His daughter appeared at the top of the stairs.

"Come on! We need to get to the hospital."

She ran down and catapulted into his arms. He held her close and flew to the truck.

She whispered in his ear, "I saw blood, Daddy. I saw blood."

"I know darlin'. I know."

I know!

When the prayer group heard the siren, they looked up from their prayers. But they did not drop hands. In fact, they held each other's hands even tighter.

Merry's heart found her throat. The siren had to be related to the McFays. There weren't that many ambulance runs in Steadfast. A few scattered heart attacks, an occasional car accident, but not much more.

This is much *more.*

Merry stood, placing Bailey's hand in Susan's safekeeping. "I'm going to call the hospital."

"We'll keep going. Together, people," Claire said. *"Our Father, who art in heaven..."*

Merry went into the narthex, flipped her cell phone open, and called the ER. Stella, her friend from the Bible study, answered. "What's with the siren, Stella? Fill me in."

"An ambulance was called to the McFays'. A gunshot wound."

Merry put a hand to her stomach. "Who is it?"

Stella's voice broke. "Annie. Oh, Merry, it's Annie."

"Is she...?"

"She's alive, but barely. Gunshot wound to the abdomen. ETA a couple minutes."

"I'm on my way."

❧   ❧   ❧

Bailey stood, shell-shocked. Merry was gone. She'd stormed into the prayer group, said Annie had been shot, and was gone to the hospital in the span of seconds, taking the nurse, Susan, with her. He hadn't even had time to ask any questions.

Claire's hand touched his arm. "The hospital didn't mention Jered, Bailey, so I'm sure he's fine."

He took a step toward the door, then back, then toward the door again. "I don't know what to do."

Claire, Sim, Harold, that old couple from the library, and all the others who'd been praying gathered around him, offering comfort.

But there was no comfort. Annie was shot; Jered was involved and might even be hurt. And he hadn't been there. He'd been here, praying.

A lot of good it had done.

He pulled away from the circle. "I have to go."

"Go where?" Harold asked. "We don't know if Jered is at the hospital or—"

Bailey pushed open the door. "I have to go somewhere. I can't stay here doing nothing."

"It's not nothing, Bailey," Claire said from the doorway.

Whatever. "Who's driving me? Or do I have to walk?"

"Cal!"

He looked up when Merry and Susan burst into the ER entrance. He'd never been so glad to see anyone. Apparently, Avi felt the same because she jumped off Cal's lap and ran to Merry.

Merry pulled Avi's head against her rib cage. "Oh, baby. Shh, shh. It'll be all right."

Cal knew they were hollow words, but he grabbed on to them as truth. He'd take what he could get.

Merry looked at Cal over Avi's embrace. "Any word?"

"Nothing." He pointed to the back. "Somebody came out and said they were taking her to surgery."

"I'll go see what I can find out." Susan tweaked the end of Avi's nose. "You stay here with your daddy and Merry, okay?"

Cal sat and Avi found his lap. Merry remained standing. "Susan's a nurse. She'll make it okay. I know it."

Cal wished he felt as confident.

Avi found his hand. "Can we pray, Daddy?"

Praying wouldn't do any good. It hadn't done any good for Treena. He remembered being huddled in a similar waiting room, praying prayers that were never answered.

"Please?"

He didn't need it, but Avi did. He took her other hand. Immediately she bowed her head and began, "God, please make Mama better..."

In spite of himself, Cal found himself agreeing with everything his daughter said.

Claire dropped Bailey off at the ER and went to park. He ran in and asked the lady at the ER desk about Jered.

"Your son's not here, Bailey."

They both looked down the corridor as they heard a commotion going on in a nearby room. Was Annie in there?

He turned back to the woman. "Then where is he?"

"I don't know, but he's not here."

Worthless woman. Bailey turned to leave. She called after him. "You might try the police station."

Her words made his legs weak, but he didn't stop moving. And he didn't look back. He couldn't bear the humiliation. As he passed the waiting room, he spotted Merry, Cal, and a little girl. Cal was staring ahead like a zombie.

Bailey looked at the exit. They hadn't seen him. Claire hadn't come in yet. He could slip out and not have to deal with them.

Now. Not have to deal with them now. *But you will have to deal with them.*

The little girl squirmed in her father's arms, breaking Cal's daze. He looked up and saw Bailey.

Bailey had no choice but to acknowledge him. He'd come so

close to getting out of the building...

"Bailey," Merry said. "What—?"

"Bailey." Cal's voice sounded like it had been torn in two. He held out a hand. "I'm so glad you came."

Awkwardly, Bailey took Cal's hand and gave it a pat. He sat across from the other three. The seats were the essence of uncomfortable. And tacky? Orange vinyl.

Cal hugged his daughter closer, her head resting on his chest. He stroked her hair behind her ear over and over. And over. The repeated gesture would have driven Bailey crazy, but the girl didn't seem to mind.

Bailey realized he should say something. "How's Annie doing?" He didn't ask who shot her.

Cal glanced at Avi. "She's being taken care of."

"Where was she shot?"

Merry looked alarmed. "Bailey..."

Certainly the girl knew her mother had been shot?

Cal put a hand to his daughter's ear. "In the stomach. The side." He nodded and went back to the hair-behind-the-ear thing. "But she'll be fine. She'll be fine."

The girl nodded against his chest. Bailey noticed Cal had blood on his jeans. The implications made his stomach roll.

Bailey shifted in his seat. He couldn't get comfortable. Besides, he had to go. He had to find...he had to know... "Have you seen Jered?"

"The police have him."

"He's under arrest?"

Cal's eyes cleared and narrowed. "He held us hostage, Bailey. Your son held us hostage."

Claire came in, breathless. "How's—?"

Bailey stood, took her arm, and pulled her toward the door. "I have to go. I hope Annie's okay, Cal. I really do."

For Jered's sake I really *do.*

Claire pulled next to Bailey's car, still parked in front of the McFay's house. "Are you sure you don't want me to go with you to the police station?"

Bailey already had his door open. "Positive. Thanks for the lift."
He did *not* need an audience to confront his son.

In spite of living in Steadfast his entire life, Jered Manson had never
set foot in the police station. Not that he shouldn't have. He'd done
some mighty mischief with Darryl and Moog that should have
brought him here, but for some reason, it never had. They used to
laugh about that.

This isn't mischief now.

No, indeed, this time was different.

As Jered was led inside by the cop, he spotted Jinko being led
beyond the office part through a door. Toward the cells?

Unfortunately, Jinko spotted him, too. Though he was wearing
some plastic-looking cuffs, he whipped his head around. "You keep
your mouth shut, kid! Not a word! Not a—" The cop cut him off by
giving him a final shove through the door. It closed behind him with
a solid *ca-click*.

Was Jered going in there, too? Would he be put in a cell with
Jinko? He couldn't...that couldn't...no way could he...

"In here."

The cop led him beyond a counter and a desk to an office.
Suddenly it became very important to Jered that it had a window. He
could see out. He was not being brought to a dark, horrible place
where he'd rot away and—

"Sit." As the cop sat behind the desk, Jered saw a name tag that
said CODY.

"What's going to happen to me?"

"Good question. And I'd say it pretty much depends on your
answers." He raised a hand. "But don't say anything yet. Not until
your lawyer gets here."

My lawyer. There was something damning about those two
words. Good people didn't need lawyers. Innocent people didn't need
lawyers. Bad people hired them to find loopholes and get them off,
so they could hug in the courtroom after the verdict was read and
have smug looks on their faces because they pulled one over on the

system. Jered couldn't remember the last TV show or movie where a lawyer defended an innocent person.

But you're not innocent.

Jered ran his hands through his hair, started biting his fingernails, then finally put his hands under his thighs, needing to hold them captive. At least they hadn't put cuffs on him. That was a good sign, wasn't it?

Maybe they ran out of cuffs.

At least I'm not back in a cell like Jinko.

Maybe they only had one cell.

At least... At least nothing. He was in big trouble, and no amount of excuses could get him out of it.

The front door opened, and a man wearing a red polo shirt came in, carrying a briefcase.

"Willy. In here."

The man came into the office. He held out his hand to Jered. "Hi, I'm Willy Bradford. I'm your lawyer. And you are?"

Jered shook hands but stared, his mouth unable to work. His lawyer? A lawyer named Willy?

Officer Cody answered for him. "He's Jered Manson."

Willy looked up. "Bailey's son, right?"

"That's him."

Willy sat next to Jered, opened the briefcase, and removed a yellow pad and pen. "Have you called his father?"

"No."

"Call him."

Officer Cody looked at Jered. "How old are you?"

"Eighteen."

He looked back to Willy. "The kid's legal. I don't have to call him."

Yeah, he doesn't have to call him.

Willy put a hand on the edge of the desk. "Come on, Ted, call the boy's dad."

"Maybe he doesn't want me to. He never asked me to."

Willy's right eyebrow rose. "You want us to call your dad, Jered?"

"Uh..." *Yes. No. Maybe.*

He didn't have to answer because at that moment his dad came in the front door.

At the sight of him, the "no" answer loomed large. Jered turned toward the wall and slumped in his chair. *Don't come in here. Please don't come in here.*

"Over here, Bailey."

Jered didn't see his dad standing in the doorway; he *felt* his presence there. Maybe this scene would play out like the movies too, with the dad pulling the long-lost son into his arms, forgiving everything.

"What have you done, Jered? What have you *done?*"

Nice seeing you, too, Dad.

Jered crossed his arms and didn't look at him. He never, ever wanted to look at him again. "Get him out of here." He hated how his voice cracked. "Get him out!"

"Out? What are you talking about?" his dad asked.

Willy stood and Jered risked a glance. He blocked the sight line between them. "You'll have to leave, Bailey."

"Leave? I just got here. I'm not going to—"

Officer Cody stood too, taking a step toward his dad. "Your boy is eighteen. He doesn't have to see you unless he wants to. And he doesn't."

"Of course he wants to see me. I'm his father."

Jered turned his eyes back to the wall. He couldn't see this, couldn't hear this.

"Out, Bailey. This is between Jered, his lawyer, and me. Go sit in the waiting area. You can see him later."

"But—"

Jered heard a bit of scuffling and the door close. Maybe a jail cell would be an improvement. His dad couldn't get to him in a jail cell.

The two men returned to their seats. "Well then," Officer Cody said. "Some reunion, huh?"

Jered risked a look.

The officer leaned on his desk. "You don't have to talk to your father, Jered, but you've got to know he's been worried about you. We all have. We've been trying to find you for months."

"I wasn't lost."

Officer Cody sat back. "Hmm."

Willy spoke next. "Can we get on with this?"

"Have at it."

Willy turned to Jered. "Have you said anything? Implicated yourself in any way?"

"Uh..."

"No. He hasn't said anything. And I haven't asked. We were waiting for you."

"Good, good." Willy pointed at Jered. "You be quiet a moment, all right?"

Jered nodded. *Gladly.*

Willy turned to Officer Cody. "Fill me in."

It was like he wasn't even in the room. Officer Cody and Jered's lawyer talked back and forth, throwing out words like *accessory* and *complicity.* Willy had told him not to say a thing, but he was fairly bursting with wanting to talk. Wanting to explain. Surely once they heard how Jinko had duped him and drawn him into the crimes...

You could have said no.

Jered found himself shaking his head and stopped the motion. Could he have said no? Step one had led so smoothly to step two. Then three and four. A ton of steps leading to this moment, sitting in this chair, being charged with...with what? It all depended on... "Is Annie okay?"

The two men stopped talking and looked at him. It was like they'd just remembered he was there.

Officer Cody spoke first. "I don't know."

Willy put a hand on the desk. "We need to know, Ted. Call the hospital."

The cop picked up the phone and finally got the right person. "I'm checking on the status of Annie McFay. She was brought in with a gunshot—" He listened a moment. "Okay. Thank you."

It seemed forever between his hanging up and the next words. "She made it through surgery. But she's critical."

"She's okay?" Jered asked.

"She's in critical condition."

"But she's not...?"

"Lucky for you."

Jered shook his head. "You know I didn't shoot her. Jinko shot her. I wasn't even there. I'd run away from Jinko, toward you guys, toward the car. I'd given myself up."

"But because you ran, she got shot."

Jered's memory grabbed on to Jinko's words shouted between cruisers: *It's all your fault, kid.* "But I didn't..."

"I'm sure you didn't mean to, but because you bolted, everything turned crazy. That's when she was shot."

Tears popped up unannounced. "I didn't mean..." He seemed unable to finish a sentence. Why couldn't he finish a sentence?

Willy put a hand on his arm. "Cut the guilt trip, Ted."

"Hey, I was there. You weren't."

Jered stood. "I think I'm going to be sick."

He got to the men's room just in time.

Jered was washing his hands when he heard a commotion outside the restroom.

"But I'm his father!"

"Go home, Bailey. Now's not a good time."

A few more words. Then his father's voice faded.

Willy came inside. "Tenacious man, your father."

Jered realized the water was still running. He shut it off and dried his hands.

Willy leaned against a sink and crossed his arms. "I'm glad we have a chance to talk privately. You're in big trouble, young man."

Jered tossed the paper towel in the trash. "What are they going to charge me with?"

"That depends on whether Annie dies."

Jered shook his head. "She can't die."

"This isn't the movies, son. Actually, she can." He put a hand on Jered's arm. "Annie's a nice lady. Let's pray she's okay."

"I don't know how to pray."

Only after seeing the odd look on Willy's face did Jered realize Willy hadn't meant the "pray" phrase literally. Jered scuffed a toe against the floor. "I mean..."

"No, you're right," Willy said. "We do need to pray—really pray. As far as you not knowing how? I'm probably not the best... My secretary's always asking me for names of clients and victims to put them on a prayer list of some sort. She's always after me to join in. But hey..." He shrugged and smiled. "Far as I know, there's no art to it or she wouldn't keep asking *me*. I think you just do it. Say whatever you want."

"And God hears?"

"So it seems." He put a hand on Jered's shoulder. "It certainly can't hurt. And if it would make you feel better, I'll even venture to let off a few myself."

Jered squeezed his eyes tight against tears and suddenly wished he were with someone who knew about God and Jesus and prayer: Annie or even Vasylko. He thought of Vasy and his cross necklace, Annie and her hidden Bible. They'd tried to tell him that Jesus was a way out; they'd tried to warn him. But now it was too late.

They heard voices outside. Officer Cody stuck his head in the door. "You two coming out?"

"Just conferring with my client, Ted. Give us a minute."

"You can use the office, you know."

"We're fine."

The door closed. Willy took a deep breath. "Well, this certainly has turned into an interesting conversation—but a good one."

Jered had trouble swallowing. "What happens now?"

"I try to work something out with the police—*if* you're willing to come clean and tell them everything you know about Jinko."

"So I'll get off—"

"Not off. There are consequences to what you did, Jered. But they'll go easier on you if you cooperate."

"I don't know..." Jered thought of Jinko's stern eyes, his strong hands. *"Keep your mouth shut, kid."*

"Every bit of information will help."

Jered caught a glimpse of himself in the mirror. The reflection seemed to belong to someone else. What had he become? Where was the real Jered?

And then he knew what had to be done. He had to find him. Find the real Jered Manson.

"I'll talk. I'll tell them everything."

Twenty-two

Whether it is favorable or unfavorable,
we will obey the LORD our God, to whom we are sending you,
so that it will go well with us,
for we will obey the LORD our God.

JEREMIAH 42:6

CAL SAW THE GLIMMER OF SUNLIGHT through the blinds of the hospital room. Was it morning? He rested his forehead against the hospital bed, his hand grasping Annie's. The sheets smelled of disinfectant. Of other times. Times when he'd sat next to Treena and—

Annie's hand stirred, and he looked up.

She moaned softly.

He stood. "Annie?"

She opened her eyes but didn't look in his direction at first. She looked straight up and blinked.

"Annie-girl, I'm here."

She turned her head. He could tell she recognized him even before she spoke. "Cal?"

He started to cry and drew her hand to his lips. "It's me. I'm here. You're here. It's going to be all right."

She took a deep breath, then winced. "Mmm."

"They have Jinko and Jered. They caught them."

Her next breath seemed to catch. She let it out. "Avi?"

"Av's fine. Everyone's fine." He swallowed. "You're fine."

She flinched as if the pain had finally caught up with the fact she was awake. "I was shot."

"Yes, you were. But they got the bullet out." He wasn't about to mention the damage to her stomach, a kidney, or the intestines.

308

She didn't say anything. The only sound in the room was the *beep-beep* of machines monitoring her vitals.

Suddenly she smiled. "You have more time. You have more time now."

"What?"

Her eyes fluttered. She was still groggy yet looked utterly content. "It worked out. You have more time."

"You said something like that at the house. I don't under—"

Her eyes closed.

He stared at her frail frame. *Come on, Annie! Live!*

It was not a prayer. It was an order.

He felt a hand on his shoulder. It was Susan dressed in her nurse's uniform. She was on duty. That made him feel a little better. "Officer Kendell wants to talk with you." She cocked her head toward the public areas of the ICU.

He shook his head. The last thing he felt like doing was rehashing the last two days.

"I'll stay with her while you're gone."

Not ideal, but doable. He kissed Annie's forehead and left. He found Ken in the waiting room. "Don't you have enough to do talking to Jinko and Jered?"

"How's Annie?"

"Fine. Fine."

Ken took the hint. "I'll make this as quick as possible. I promise."

Cal let the chip fall off his shoulder. Questioning was inevitable. And so was punishment.

Annie didn't know if she was dreaming or thinking real thoughts. It didn't matter. They were one and the same. One word kept repeating itself, in different ways, in different tones, in different melodies. *Time. Time. Time.*

And as the word wrapped itself around her being, one thing became very clear: Cal had it now, and she didn't.

But that was okay. It was okay.

❧   ❧   ❧

Jered was in a jail cell—a cell next to Jinko's. Unfortunately, since there were only two cells, it wasn't as if Jered could ask to be moved. At least a wall divided them. Listening to Jinko was bad enough. Seeing him would have been torture.

Listening would have been easier if Jinko had yelled at him or threatened him openly. But Jinko didn't do that. He whispered. And so his words, devoid of the full power and tone of voice Jered knew, took on an otherworldly quality, as if it wasn't Jinko talking at all, just a disembodied voice seeping through the cracks in the walls, trying to capture his soul.

"You better not have talked to them, kid. They're the enemy. I'm your friend; I took you in and cared for you. You don't need them. You and I have to stick together. I'll take care of you. It's us against them. Remember what side you're on."

That was the big question. The big choice. What side? Whose side was he on?

He turned over in his bunk and put the pillow on top of his head, trying to block out the voice. Didn't Jinko ever sleep? *I don't want to take sides. I don't want to choose. I just want to close my eyes and have it go away. I told them all I know; I'm empty. There isn't any more. I'm done.*

Exactly. You're done.

Jered's eyes shot open and the voice—that wasn't Jinko's—continued. *Your life is done. You've blown everything. Why go on?*

He shook his head against the words. He'd done a good thing. He told the truth. Willy said everything would be better now because he'd come clean.

Clean? You think that's clean? You'll never be clean. You're dirty, kid. Tainted and defiled. Saying a few words won't make you clean. You are stained beyond cleaning.

He squeezed his eyes shut. This didn't jibe with what Annie, Vasylko, and even Willy had said. He could pray. God would listen. And he could be forgiven. Somehow Jesus dying on the cross took care of the forgiveness part. He wasn't sure exactly how...

Give it up, Jered. Let it go. Let your life go before you mess it up even worse. Think of how peaceful it will be not to have to deal with any of this anymore. It will be like you're sleeping, dreaming. It's the only way to truly get away from this, to escape—

Jered bolted upright in bed. "Jesus, I'm sorry! Help me!"

He heard Jinko's laughter. "Dream on, kid. Jesus can't help you now. Nobody can help you but me. I'm your only hope."

Jered drew a breath from a new, open place inside, then let out the words his conscience had been waiting—aching—to say: "Shut up, Jinko! Just shut up."

When Jinko didn't respond, he smiled. *This moment of silence brought to you by Jesus Christ.*

Hallelujah amen.

Jinko didn't remain silent too long, but Jered didn't care anymore. He suddenly had the strength to *not* listen, to block out the rantings of this man. Such a desperate, pathetic man. Messed up. Jinko was going down, and no smooth line of bull could make it otherwise.

Jered lay on his back, his hands behind his head, looking at the ceiling. He knew he was smiling, and he also knew it didn't make a lot of sense. Not according to any sense he was used to anyway. There was no reason he should feel calm and confident. And yet that's exactly how he felt.

For he was not alone. He was not desperate. He was not a vulnerable kid, ripe for the picking by someone like Jinko Daly. He was a boy—a man—with a mind of his own. A will. A free will. And though that will had gotten knotted, opening himself up to Jesus had untangled it, letting it flow free with each breath. The past was a dark place. The future was full of light. He stood in a hallway between the two and could step either way.

The door to the cell opened. Officer Kendell came in. "Jered. You have a visitor."

He sat up in his bunk. "Who?"

"Merry. Merry Cavanaugh."

He jumped up. Merry, the only person to ever believe in his music.

The door was unlocked, and Ken led Jered to a lunchroom. "You'll have to meet here. We're letting Jinko and his lawyer use the office."

Jered didn't care where he met Merry.

She stood when he came in. "Jered." She took a step toward him, then hesitated, looking to Ken. "Can I hug him?"

"Sure." Ken pulled out a chair and started to sit.

"Ken, I'd like to talk to Jered alone."

He stood. "He's under arrest, Merry."

She extended her hands to take in the room. "No exits, no windows. If he promises not to hold me prisoner with a coffee mug, can you trust us?"

He pushed the chair back. "I'll be right outside the door."

"Thank you." She looked at Jered and smiled a sad smile. "Now, how about that hug?"

Jered didn't want to let her go. He couldn't remember the last human contact he'd had and didn't realize he missed it—needed it— until he experienced it now.

She pulled away. "Let's sit."

They sat catty-corner to each other. She patted a hand on the table. It was an awkward moment. "So," Merry said.

"You don't have to say any more."

She nodded. "You going to be okay?"

It was his turn to nod. "Actually, I think yeah. Yes. I'll be okay."

She cocked her head. "Now this is a Jered I didn't expect to find."

"You expected a weak loser kid?"

"No, no, of course not. But I thought you'd be upset, scared, or else sullen and defensive. Not..."

He didn't help her define it, hoping she could pinpoint the change in him. If Merry saw it, maybe it was real. "Not...?"

She studied him a moment. "I see a sureness in you I've never seen before. A serenity."

He smiled. *Serenity.* He liked that word. A lot.

She looked at him a moment longer, her eyes searching his. Then she laughed. "You found Jesus, didn't you?"

Jered put a hand to his chest, bowled over. "You can see that?"

"So it's true?"

He nodded. She was out of her seat in seconds, giving him another hug. "I'm so happy for you, Jered!" She sat back down, pulling her chair close. "When? How?"

He wished he could pinpoint an exact moment, but it was a series of moments. "It's been building a long time. A cook at Palamba's told me stuff, then Annie talked about the forgiveness part, then my lawyer...even Jinko helped a bit."

"Annie?"

"While we were holding her hostage."

Merry sat back.

"How is she doing?" he asked.

"Holding on. But her condition is critical."

He thought of something else. "Is the little girl okay?"

"Avi's with Sim right now. We're all pitching in. She's fine."

Sim. A name from another lifetime. "Sim lives here?"

Merry brought him up to date on Sim, Claire, Harold, and even on Moog and Darryl. It felt wonderful to talk about old times. Better times? He wasn't sure about that, for they had been pretty messed up. Messed up enough to run away from them. From those times to this one...

They shared a quiet moment. "You haven't asked about your dad."

Jered picked at a piece of dried food on the table. "No need."

"Don't say that. Of course there's a need. You need him now and he needs—"

"He needs a son who isn't a disgrace, who won't mess up his dreams."

She leaned over the table. "Jered, he's been worried about you. Searching for you."

Jered snickered. "Now he's found me." He thought of their brief meeting the day before. "I've already seen him."

"You have?"

"Sure. We had a nice reunion where he expressed his deep love and approval by saying, 'What have you done, Jered? What have you done?'" He swiped one palm over the other. "That pretty much says it all."

Merry ran a hand over her forehead. "He's waiting outside. He wants to see you."

Jered shoved his chair back and stood. "I don't want to see him."

She took hold of his hand, trying to pull him back. "Do it for him."

Jered looked down at her. His laugh was bitter. "Why should I?"

She withdrew her hand, looking at the floor. Then she looked up. "Because Jesus would want you to."

He found his head shaking no. "That wasn't part of the deal."

Her left eyebrow rose. "So it's okay for Jesus to forgive you but not okay for you to forgive your dad?"

He crossed his arms, not wanting to hear.

Merry stood and touched his shoulder. "Talk to him, Jered. Jesus loves you just as you are. Do the same for your dad."

He found he couldn't agree out loud, but he did find the strength to nod.

Bailey had never been more nervous. It was ridiculous. He was the father. He was the authority figure. He was the one in control. His son was weak, the one who messed up. A loser.

But he's your son.

Merry led him toward a back room. She paused outside the door and whispered in his ear, "Behave yourself, Bailey. Love him, don't condemn him."

He opened the door. Jered was sitting at a lunch table. Though Bailey had seen him the day before, he hadn't had time to fully take in his son's physical changes. His hair was shorter, and his clothes seemed less baggy than the style he'd worn when he lived at home. Positive changes, both of them.

But we're meeting in a police station. He's under arrest.

So much for positive changes.

Bailey heard the door shut behind him. With little imagination it sounded like the ominous click of a jail cell. He took a few steps toward the table. Jered did not run into his arms. He didn't even stand. In fact, his eyes were decidedly hard. Bailey found support by grabbing the back of a chair. "Hi, Jered."

"Hi."

Well then. Now what?

Suddenly, what Bailey should say battled with what came out of his mouth. He should have said: *It's good to see you.*

"Not the most auspicious way to return home, now is it?"

Jered's face did not change. "Things happen. Choices are made."

That's a very grown-up attitude, Jered. Although I hate the choice you made, I'm glad you're owning up to it.

"I can't believe you let yourself get involved with a criminal."

Jered shrugged. "He didn't seem so bad to begin with."

I know how easy it is to get caught up in things. I've made a few mistakes myself. I'm just glad you're back.

"I saw that Willy Bradford is representing you. From what I've heard, he's a mediocre lawyer at best. I know a lawyer in Kansas City who—"

"Willy's fine, Dad. It's taken care of. I've confessed to everything."

That's the way to go, son. Whenever you make mistakes, stand up tall, tell the truth, and take your licks like a man.

"I wish you wouldn't have done that. Now the whole world will know."

Jered's face sagged, and his lower jaw started to quiver. Suddenly, he pushed back from the table and went to the counter, leaning forward against it, showing Bailey his back.

Bailey watched as his son took a few breaths in and out. Finally, he turned around, his face in control—and older somehow. Or at least more mature. A certainty was there that hadn't been previously. "I messed up, Dad. And I'm sorry. No one forced me to do anything. What I did affected a lot of people." He looked down. "I just hope— I pray—that Annie comes through this okay. She's a neat, neat lady who taught me a lot. She's had a big effect on my life."

She is a nice lady. And I hope she's okay, too.

"*She* taught you a lot? When was this?"

"While we were holding them hostage."

Bailey's laughter drowned out all the should-have-saids. "In a couple days, *she* had a big effect on your life? What about me? Some thanks I get for raising you and dealing with you year after year."

Jered's eyes blinked as if Bailey had thrown something too close. "*Dealing* with me, Dad?"

Bailey wagged a finger at him. "Don't argue semantics with me. You know what I mean. You were not an easy teenager to have around."

"And you were not an easy father."

"I did my best."

"So did I."

"No, you didn't. You ran away. You didn't stick around and...and..."

"Fight?"

Bailey threw his hands in the air and began to pace. "Sometimes you drive me absolutely crazy. Sometimes I'm sorry—"

"I'm sorry too, Dad." The softness of Jered's voice made Bailey stop all movement and words. He was mesmerized by the intensity in his son's eyes. It wasn't a frantic intensity but a calm one. As if he knew the secret to making everything all right.

"What's gotten into you, boy?"

Jered gave a little laugh. "You'd never believe it if I told you."

"Give it a shot."

Jered looked to the ceiling as he took in his breath. "I've found Jesus, Dad."

Oh, please...

"And you know what? I'm finding that God's the only Father I need right now."

"That's incredibly rude."

Jered shrugged. "I can't please you. I know it. So I'm going to stop trying." His chin was strong. "Jesus loves me. Just as I am."

This is ridiculous. "I must say, you've set a new world record. You hear about inmates finding religion while they're in jail, but you've managed to do it in just a few hours. Maybe they'll give you a medal."

Jered's jaw tightened, and for a moment, Bailey feared his son would hit him. Instead, Jered calmly walked past him toward the door.

"Where are you going? We're not done here."

Jered didn't respond but opened the door leading to the hall. Ken was outside. "I'm through in here."

The look Ken gave Bailey before he led Jered away made Bailey's skin crawl with humiliation. How dare his son treat him that way? He ran to the doorway. "That's so like you, Jered. Running away again!"

Jered and Ken disappeared around a corner, leaving Bailey alone.

Merry had waited around for Bailey to have his talk with Jered and had heard his gracious last words to his son. She'd had it with him. Was it impossible for Bailey to talk with Jered without blowing up or being hurtful?

He stormed out of the police station, muttering under his breath. She rushed after him. He got in his car, but she stopped the swing of his door with a hand. On impulse she grabbed his car keys.

"Hey! What did you do that for?"

She had no idea. "Just hold on a minute, Bailey. Just—"

"Leave me alone, Merry. I've had enough for today."

She palmed the keys and crossed her arms. "You are the most selfish, narrow-minded—"

Suddenly he slumped over the wheel. His chest heaved.

Was he crying? Was he feeling remorse?

Pray.

For Bailey? That's the last thing she felt like doing. He was the most infuria—

The thought widened. *Get everyone to pray.*

And then she knew.

She plied his hand off the wheel and pulled.

"What are you doing?"

She found unusual strength, forcing him to exit the car. "Come with me, Bailey. Come on. Out."

"Where are we going?"

She pushed him toward her van. "I hate to keep kidnapping you, but it's for your own good. For everyone's good."

She unlocked the passenger side and waited until he got in, then got in herself.

"I'm *not* going to another prayer meeting," he said.

Wanna bet?

Merry held the door of the library while the regulars exited. She locked the door after them.

"You can't close the library in the middle of the day, Merry," Ivan said. "People will complain."

"They'll live. And if said '*people*' would be willing to listen, I'll be more than willing to tell them why I closed. The lives of two of our citizens are at stake."

"I think it's exciting," Blanche said. She took Ivan's arm to negotiate the front steps. "The Plentiful won't know what hit it. Steadfast won't know what hit it."

Harold offered his arm to Merry. "This *is* rather unorthodox."

"A crisis demands the unorthodox."

They reached the street, and Merry detoured toward the library's parking lot.

"Hey, Merry." Ivan pointed across the square. "The Plentiful's this way."

"Just a minute. I have to make a pickup." She pointed to her van, to Bailey, sitting in the front seat. He'd refused to get out.

Ivan cocked his head to see against the sun's reflection on the windshield. "What's he doing in there?"

Blanche swatted his arm. "Being as stubborn as you, you old green bean."

"We're doing this for *his* son," Ivan said.

Merry approached the door, and the others followed. "Which is why we're picking him up."

Bailey's arms were across his chest. His head shook no. He locked the door.

Merry used her key to unlock it and held it up as evidence that he wasn't going to win this battle. "Four against one, Bailey. You might as well come out."

"Surround him!" Blanche scurried toward the driver's side, taking the stance of a sumo wrestler.

"Stop that," Ivan said. "You look ridiculous."

Blanche stood erect. "Then get him out."

Harold opened Bailey's door, and Merry offered her hand. "Come on, Bailey. It will help. You know it will."

"Prayer didn't help last time. Annie got shot. Jered's in jail."

"It most certainly did help. They're both alive."

Bailey took one last look at the people around him. Then he took Merry's hand.

As the group entered the Plentiful Café, Bailey wanted to crawl into a hole. Merry was crazy. This just wasn't done.

Dottie looked up from her coffee rounds. "Hey, Donald! We're being invaded."

Donald peeked through the pass-through. Merry went over to him and quietly discussed something. All talking had stopped.

Donald spoke. "Sure, Merry. For Annie, anything." He dinged the bell to get everyone's attention. He swept a spatula toward the room. "Listen up, people. Merry here has something she wants to do."

Merry had the floor. She looked across the room at the nine customers. Not bad for the middle of the afternoon. Bailey recognized no one. "I'm sorry to interrupt your eating, but at this minute, a few of our fellow neighbors are going through a crisis. I know most of you and recognize the rest. I know we can count on you to help."

"It's Annie, isn't it?" said Ed Burroughs from the hardware store.

Blanche stepped forward. "You bet it's Annie. She's in the hospital fighting for her life."

"She was shot," said Oscar from the motel. He pointed at Bailey. "By his son."

Bailey stepped forward. "Jered did *not* shoot Annie!"

"The news implied—"

"That's not what I heard."

Merry spread her hands. "Enough. If the news said that, it was wrong."

People settled back into their seats. Bailey felt Harold's hand on his shoulder. He tried to unclench his fists.

"Jered is the other Steadfast son who needs our help."

"But he was one of the bad guys."

Donald pointed his spatula at them. "The kid ran away. He probably got hooked up with the wrong people. He's still our kid."

"He's still our kid." Bailey suddenly felt weak in the knees. How could a short-order cook feel more compassion for Jered than he did?

Ivan pulled out a chair for him. "Sit, Bailey. You don't look well."

Merry glanced in his direction but kept going. "We're here because we want to ask all of you to pray for Annie and Jered. Both are fighting for their lives. Pass the word and get your churches to pray, and your families. Friends. Everyone. In fact, I'd like to share a prayer right here where Annie worked. Right now."

Oscar raised a hand. "You can't pray in here. It's a public place."

Donald slapped a hand on the counter. "I am so sick of this PC hooey. We can pray wherever we please. And if you don't like it, leave."

Oscar looked at his coffee cup but didn't move.

"Well, then," Merry said. "That's the spirit. Now. Let's bow our heads…"

Bailey couldn't believe it as these people prayed for his Jered, with Harold even adding a prayer for Bailey and Cal. They didn't hate him. They weren't condemning him.

It's not about you. It's time to stop hating. Stop condemning.

As the group moved toward the communal "Amen," Bailey found himself praying along with them. And it felt good. Freeing, even.

Would wonders never cease?

Merry pulled next to Bailey's car in the parking lot of the police station. "Here we are."

Bailey wanted to say something profound to express all that he was feeling. But there were no words. Except three.

He couldn't look at her. He didn't trust his emotions. But he did manage to say, "Thank you, Merry."

"You're welcome. You'll see. Prayer changes things. It does. Everything will be all right."

He felt a surge of real hope. "Annie won't die? Jered will be set free?"

"I don't know."

"But you said—"

"Everything will be all right. God may not decide to answer our prayers like we want Him to, but He will answer them. The good thing about prayer is knowing we're doing everything we *can* do. We need to let that give us comfort."

"But what if—?"

She put her hand on his. "It's His now, Bailey. It was always His, but with our prayers, we're relinquishing our hold on it. We've done what we were supposed to do: 'Pray without ceasing.' Try to find peace in that, okay?"

Peace seemed very far away. But not as unreachable as it had been before. "I'll try."

Susan hung up the phone from talking to Merry about the prayer chain that was sweeping Steadfast. Merry certainly had guts, starting it up in the Plentiful. But why not? Susan could visualize the prayers spreading across town, much like those Internet stories spread across the world in a matter of hours. One tells two tells four... What a glorious thing.

She did her part, calling Stella down in the ER to spread the word, then gathering the other nurses in ICU for their own prayer circle as the beeps of the machines kept rhythm.

As soon as the prayers were on their way to heaven, she knew the very next person she had to tell was Annie. Surely the news would buoy her and give her hope. Susan saw Dr. Hillerby coming out of Annie's room. "How's the patient, Doctor? I have great news for her."

Dr. Hillerby took her aside and put a hand on her shoulder. His touch sent shivers down her spine. "I'm sorry, Susan. I know she's a good friend. But her vitals are weakening. The internal damage was extensive. We've done all we can. There's always a chance, but...but now it's up to her."

And God. Susan put one hand on the baby kicking inside her and grabbed the sill of the window looking into Annie's intensive care room with the other. She looked at her friend, then back to the doctor. *No, this can't be. The prayer chain...* "Does she know? Does she realize?"

Dr. Hillerby shrugged. "Patients usually sense it."

Annie turned her head in Susan's direction. Their eyes met through the glass.

Susan offered a weak wave. "This can't be," she whispered. "It can't! The prayers have just started. They'll work; I know they will."

Dr. Hillerby patted her back. "I'm going to call Cal, get him and Avi back over here. Now's your chance to go in and see her."

As a nurse this wasn't the first time Susan had witnessed death, but she suddenly felt like a rookie. "I don't know what to say."

"Share your heart. And let her share hers." He squeezed her shoulder. "I'd better make that call. Now."

Time was that short?

He left her, and Susan wanted to run. Hide. Be anywhere but here. *Tell me when it's over.* But she couldn't. What was happening next was not about her. It was about Annie. And as painful as it was going to be, she had to keep that focus.

Annie was still looking at her. Her fingers moved slightly, a come-here gesture.

Susan didn't have time for any more preparation. As she went to her friend's side, as she somehow found a smile, she prayed another, more desperate prayer: *Father, heal her. Save her! Please, hear our prayers! Make us a miracle!*

Twenty-three

Enter through the narrow gate.
For wide is the gate and broad is the road that leads to destruction,
and many enter through it.
But small is the gate and narrow the road that leads to life,
and only a few find it.

MATTHEW 7:13–14

CAL RAN THROUGH THE HALLS of the hospital, dragging Avi behind him.

"Daddy! Slow down!"

He scooped her up and kept running. He had to get to Annie! He had to see her now!

He was out of breath when he reached Intensive Care. He stopped short outside Annie's room. Susan was inside. And Dr. Hillerby, and two other nurses.

Oh no! It's too late!

Susan saw him and rushed toward them. She took his hand. And Avi's.

"Susan, no...no..."

She was crying. But smiling, too. "That's right, Cal. No! She's not dead. Something happened, something wonderful. I was sitting with her and—"

"Daddy?"

He pushed past Susan, pulling Avi with him. The doctor looked up. He was grinning. The other nurses parted, giving him access to his wife.

She was awake. She was smiling. "Cal." Her voice sounded stronger than last time. She looked at Avi. "Sweet-apple."

Cal lunged for her hand, kissing it, pulling it to his chest. Avi slipped between him and the bed. She tentatively touched her mother's arm. "Mama? You okay?"

"I will be." She glanced at the doctor. "I know I will be."

They all looked to the doctor for confirmation. "We're not completely out of the woods, but her vitals are strong, suddenly strong even. If they stabilize... We'll be taking her in for some more tests." He shook his head. "I called you in because...it's a true miracle. I'd only be half a doctor if I didn't acknowledge what went on here."

"It's the miracle of prayer," Susan said.

The doctor put the chart away and spoke to Cal. "I'll give you a minute alone, but then we have to do those tests. And let our miracle lady rest."

Everyone left Cal and Avi alone with Annie. He couldn't stop looking at her. There was a bit of color in her cheeks and a light in her eyes that hadn't been present before.

"Oh, Annie, I—"

"God did this, Cal."

He nodded. "You're a strong—"

"No. I'm weak." She put a hand on Avi's head, stroking her hair. "I was on the verge of death, Cal. I felt it. And I could see it in Dr. Hillerby's eyes. Susan's eyes."

Cal looked away. She was right. The doctor *had* called him, saying the end was near.

Avi looked up at her father. "Daddy, you said she was dying. You said we had to hurry. But she's not."

Annie squeezed his hand. "I'm not."

"I prayed, Mama. I prayed hard."

"I know you did. I prayed, too." She swallowed hard and grabbed a fresh breath. "I have to tell you what happened. Susan was in here, sitting with me. We were praying together. She told me the whole town was praying."

Cal couldn't imagine.

"Even Bailey. Everyone was praying for me and Jered."

Cal shook his head. "Not that kid. He doesn't deserve—"

"Yes, Cal. That kid does deserve—and need—our prayers." She closed her eyes.

"Take it easy, hon. Don't tax—"

Her eyes opened. "Then let me say this. Let me get this out."

He nodded.

"While Susan was sitting with me, while we were praying, I felt a warmth inside." She waved a splayed hand an inch above her torso. "It flowed through me like blood through my veins. It seemed to strengthen me. And I felt better." She touched the area of her wound and laughed softly. "I even checked to see if the wound was gone. But it's still there."

"But you're better, Mama."

"I'm better. And God did it." She locked her eyes on Cal. "He did it. Medicine had given up on me. God changed the logical outcome. That's what a miracle is. Admit it."

Miracles didn't happen.

She squeezed his hand with more strength than he thought possible. Her voice was intense, enunciating every syllable. "Admit it."

Susan came in. "We have to take you for those tests now, Annie."

Cal kissed his wife, and they wheeled her away.

Merry hung up the phone, pumped a fist in the air, and shouted, "Praise the Lord!"

Blanche looked up from her station at the library's computers. "Goodness, Merry. Is there news?"

Merry hurried around the counter, searching out Harold and Ivan. A few other patrons looked at her expectantly. "That was Susan. Annie's going to be okay!"

They hugged each other, laughing and talking at once. Ivan grabbed Blanche and did a swirling two-step.

Merry quieted them. "But what makes it even more wonderful is how far she came. We didn't know this, but while we were praying Annie was on the verge of dying. The doctor had even called Cal and Avi to her bedside."

"Oh my," Blanche said.

Harold held a book of Greek tragedies by Euripides to his chest. "Annie on the edge of dying? You calling us to pray and getting the prayer chain going? The timing can't be a coincidence."

Merry hadn't thought of that and remembered her sudden inclination to pray. To get everyone to pray. She shivered and felt Harold's hand on her arm.

"It's a miracle, Merry."

For Annie. And Steadfast.

Once Merry had dropped him off, Bailey didn't go home. Couldn't go home. He'd sat in his car stunned by all he'd seen at the Plentiful. Only after praying had he finally gained enough courage to enter the police station. He closed the door quietly behind him.

Ken looked up from his desk. "What do you want, Bailey?"

He moved close so the other officers wouldn't hear. "I'd like to see Jered. Please."

"I don't think that's a good idea. You upset him."

Bailey fingered the file tray on the desk. "I know. I'm sorry. I was wrong."

Ken sat back in his chair and rocked, looking way too smug. "Well, well. I heard about the prayers at the Plentiful. It's hard to be cocky and pray—and accept prayer from others—isn't it, Bailey?"

Nearly impossible. The ringing of the phone saved him from having to admit that to Ken.

Ken answered it. "You're kidding! Bailey's here. I'll tell him." He hung up. "Yes, indeed, amazing things happen when people pray. That was Merry. She just heard that Annie's going to be all right. She was literally snatched from the edge of death by what even the doctors are calling a miracle."

Bailey's throat tightened. "That's great."

"You bet it's great." Ken cocked a thumb toward the cells. "Great for your son, too. It might be the answer to both prayers."

All Bailey could do was nod. *Thank You, God.*

Ken stood and got out his keys. "You want to be the one to tell him?"

Me? Surely not me. But Bailey nodded and pulled in a breath, trying to find calm. He'd come to humble himself before his son, but now he would get the chance to share the greatest news with him. He didn't deserve it.

"You can use my office. I'll go get him."

Officer Kendell came into view. "Visitor, Jered."

Jered was lying on his bunk, his arm covering his eyes. He peeked beneath it. "Who is it?"

"Your dad."

Jinko yelled from the next cell. "Aaaw, twice in one day, kid! He must *really* care about you." His laugh was mean.

Jered covered his eyes again. "I'll pass."

The cop unlocked the cell door. "Come on."

"I said no—"

"Now!"

Surely they couldn't make him... He sat up. "Don't I have a choice?"

"No."

Jered jumped down and filed out. Officer Kendell led him to his office. His dad stood by the window and changed his weight from left to right and back again, then raised a hand slightly in a wave. Jered had never seen him so nervous.

Jered took the guest chair. He didn't know where to look, what to say. And who knew what his dad would say? He braced himself for some cut.

Bailey took a step toward him. "Good news. Annie's going to be okay."

It took a moment for that to sink in. He covered his face with his hands. *Thank You! Thank You!*

"Hey, it's okay, Jered. It'll be okay."

Upon hearing the kind words—coming from his dad—Jered put his hands down.

His dad looked away, toward the window.

Suddenly, more than anything, Jered wanted his father's eyes back on him. He wanted his full attention. He wanted him to say more "it will be okay" words. "I'm...I'm sorry, Dad. I know I've caused you a lot of pain and—"

Then a miracle happened. His dad shook his head and put a finger to his lips, stopping Jered's words. His eyes teared up. "I'm the one who's sorry. I haven't been a good dad. I've been self-centered, thinking about the business, not supporting your music. I...if only—"

Jered raised a hand. "Don't start with the if-onlys. We can't change things and God's forgiven us, so..." He realized it was the second time he'd mentioned God in his dad's presence. Bailey Manson didn't *do* God.

His dad looked at his hands. "People have been praying for you, Jered."

"Who?"

"People all over Steadfast. Merry started it, at the Plentiful, no less. Then word spread. We were praying for you and for Annie and—"

"We?"

His father's eyes sought the safety of the window again. "I prayed, too."

Jered let a moment pass, gathering courage. "Why haven't we prayed before, Dad? Why didn't I grow up going to church?"

His head whipped around. "So I suppose that's my fault too, right?"

"It's not mine."

His dad's shoulders dropped as if they'd sprung a leak and deflated. "Truth is, I never thought about it." His eyes were pitiful. "And up until the last year or so, we'd done all right, hadn't we, Jered?"

"It was okay."

"But?"

Jered wasn't comfortable with this conversation, yet felt compelled to continue. And tell the truth. "You and I did it alone, but what if we'd had God around? It would have been better, don't you think?"

His dad didn't answer.

Officer Kendell filled the doorway. "Time's up, Jered." He stood to leave, but his dad's hand on his shoulder stopped him. He turned around.

"Can I hug him?" his dad asked.

"Sure."

Then suddenly, his dad's arms were around him, and he was a little boy in need of a father again. And his dad hugged him tight, like he needed a son.

Both in need of the Father. Both in need of the Son.

Cal hoped his father would have a few moments of coherence on the phone. Just long enough for him to understand that Cal wasn't coming to visit for a few days.

"Cal? That you?"

"It's me, Dad. I just wanted—"

"I saw you on TV! I saw Annie. Is she going to be okay?"

"She's going to be fine, Dad."

"I knew my prayers would work!"

"You've been—?"

"Whole group of us been praying. Annie being all right—it's God's doing, that's what it is. It's..."

He'd trailed off. Did his father set the phone down? "Dad?"

Suddenly, "Did you take my chainsaw? I've been looking for it all day, and I need it to clear the grove."

Cal sighed. "I'll look for it, Dad. I'll see you in a few days."

"You bring it with you, now. Don't forget."

"I won't." There was a lot he'd never forget.

"How do you like my new room?" Annie asked.

Cal settled into the chair beside her. The regular hospital room was a big improvement over the ICU she'd been in for the past week. "Where'd all these flowers come from?"

"People. There were so many I had Susan take some to other

patients." She adjusted her bed to a better angle in order to see him. "We need to talk."

He took her hand, mindful of the IV. "We can talk later, Annie. We have all the time—"

"No!" She pulled her hand away.

He sat back. "Don't get riled, Annie-girl."

She fingered her water sipper, calming herself. "If this experience taught us anything, Cal, it's that we don't have all the time in the world. At any moment, with any decision, our lives can change forever."

He retrieved her hand and kissed it. "I almost lost you. If only you'd let me go with Jinko."

Finally. To the point she wanted to make. "I had to go, Cal. I had to be the one to risk my life."

"That's ridiculous. As the man of the family—"

"This isn't about gender. Or even the position in a family. This is about eternity. This is about being with each other in heaven."

"Don't talk about heaven. You're alive. You—"

"But don't you see? We have to talk about heaven. No, I'm not dead. God let me live. That truly is a miracle and a testament to the power of prayer. But someday we will die and..." *Lord, give me Your words! Now, of all times, give me Your words.*

But Cal jumped into her hesitation. "I do *not* want to talk about death. Nor will I be treated like a child. Of course I know we're going to die."

"But do you understand what happens next?"

"They have a funeral."

If she were home, she'd probably walk out of the room right now to flee the frustration and the argument. But she couldn't flee. *I have you right where I want you, Annie—where I need you. Tell him.*

She began again and was relieved to hear her voice was steady. "Do you believe in heaven?"

"Sure. Angels. Halos. All that stuff."

She didn't let herself get distracted from the main point. That would be for another time. "Do you believe in hell?"

He shrugged. "I guess I've never thought about it much."

Ah, ignorance, the bane of the world. "Hell exists just as much as heaven does. After we die we go to one or the other. So choose. Now. Which will it be? Heaven or hell?"

"Annie, this is ridiculous."

"Choose!"

"Fine. I choose heaven."

Step one completed. "How do you get to heaven?"

"You die."

"Cal, please. For me."

"Okay, okay. You do good things. Good people go to heaven; bad people go to hell."

"Wrong. Try again."

"What do you mean, try again? I'm right. I know I'm right."

"Are you willing to stake your life on it—your soul's eternal life?"

He stood and went to the window. He fingered the bloom of a pink rose. "Annie, I don't want to get into all this Jesus-stuff. I really don't."

Anger propelled her words. "Then it's a good thing I was the one who was shot. It's a good thing you didn't go, because you *aren't* ready. You *do* need more time to rip off your blinders, pull your head out of the sand, and knock that girder off your shoulder."

He rushed to her bedside. "Shh! You're going to get the nurses in here."

At that moment Susan stepped into the room, grabbed the door-knob, and shut the door. But she was smiling, and she winked at Annie.

It was a conspiracy.

Annie took Cal's hands in hers. "Dear man that I love, I risked my life because I know that I'm going to heaven when I die, and I couldn't risk your *eternal* life by letting you face that danger. We each have a choice to make, Cal. Heaven or hell. You say you've chosen heaven. Fine. There is only one way to heaven. By accepting Jesus as your Savior."

"That's a narrow viewpoint."

"'*Narrow is the gate.*'" She couldn't remember the rest of the verse. "You mentioned good and bad people. What you need to understand,

Cal, is that there is good and bad in all of us. We are all sinners."

"Now you sound like my father."

"That part of what he says is true. What you learned when you were with Treena is true. Find that truth again. Now. Before it's too late."

He looked overwhelmed. He sank into the chair and rested his head against the mattress.

She stroked his head.

She comforted *him*.

"That's the last of them," Cal said to Avi.

She dried the last dish and put it on the counter for him to put in the cupboard. At her request, they'd had macaroni and cheese for dinner. Not his favorite, but something he could make.

"I'm going up to my cubby, Daddy. Want to come?"

"Me?"

"Sure."

"I'm too big."

She looked disappointed and went upstairs alone. He plopped onto the couch, picked up the remote, but didn't turn the television on. The last thing he wanted to hear was TV chatter.

But without it...the house was so quiet.

He found himself on the stairs, seeking out Avi.

The light in the master closet was on, the door to her cubby ajar. "Knock knock," he said, tapping the wall.

She shoved the door open, her face bright. "You came to visit!" She moved back. "Come see, Daddy. Come in and see."

It's not that the door wasn't wide enough. It was a good two feet by three feet, but Cal had never once considered entering his daughter's domain.

Until now.

He crawled inside as Avi frantically moved books and dolls aside, making room.

"Here, lean back here," she said, fluffing a pile of pillows.

"So this is where our extra pillows went."

"Mama said it was okay."

He flicked the end of her nose. "It is. I'm just giving you a hard time." He got settled in. Actually, it was kind of neat. The slant of the roof made standing impossible, but Avi had made it quite comfy. She had the walls decorated with drawings. One caught his eye. It was a cross section of their house with two men on the first floor with Annie and him, and Avi huddled in her cubby upstairs. To think of her up here, by herself, afraid...

"Want to see my newest drawing?"

"Sure."

She presented him with a picture of the three of them—plus an older man with glasses and an oxygen tank. His father.

"That's our family."

He kissed the top of her head. "It's very nice. But what's this?" He pointed to the band of blue with a bunch of disembodied faces looking down.

"Those are the angels protecting us, and that big one is Jesus. It's God looking down. Mama said He's always with us. Watching us. Taking care of us." She looked right at him. "He healed Mama. We prayed, and He did it for us. Right, Daddy?"

The evidence was clear enough for a ten-year-old to see. Wasn't it about time he...?

"You're right, Avi. You're completely right."

Avi nodded. Case closed. Then she took down the picture of the bad guys and taped up the picture of their family.

"There," she said. "All better now."

There. All better now, indeed.

Epilogue

If you have any encouragement from being united with Christ,
if any comfort from his love, if any fellowship with the Spirit,
if any tenderness and compassion,
then make my joy complete by being like-minded,
having the same love, being one in spirit and purpose.

PHILIPPIANS 2:1–2

ONE YEAR LATER

BLANCHE SHOVED THE BOX of myrrh into Ivan's hands. "It's official. You are the first wise man who's an old rutabaga."

"Just because I wanted more sequins on the box." Ivan straightened his turban. "A king should have lots of sequins."

Annie approached them, a cassette tape in her hands. As the director of the Christmas pageant this year, her nerves were a bit frayed. "Get along, you two. Blanche, go see if Bailey has his frankincense. And I think Cal and Ken were looking for their shepherd staffs."

Blanche sighed deeply as she was walking away. "What would you do without me?" She swung around to Ivan. *"Don't* even think about it."

Avi ran up to Annie, holding her angel wings, which were decidedly broken. "Mama, look!"

Oh, dear. "Take it to Susan. She'll fix it."

She watched as Avi ran to the corner where Susan worked at a sewing machine, making last-minute repairs. Sim played with baby Caleb close by.

Annie spotted her original target. "Harold!" He had been invaluable as her assistant director. For who would know more about good drama than a former teacher of Shakespeare? "I was looking for you. I need you to—"

He took hold of her upper arms. "I need you to calm down. Everything will be fine. Wonderful." He nodded toward the choir, who were getting dressed. She watched Claire straighten the stole of Merry's robe. They saw her and offered a thumbs-up.

"See?" Harold said.

Annie wasn't convinced. "What we need is a miracle."

Harold slipped his hand through her arm and turned them both to the right. "See that?" he said, pointing. "That's a miracle."

Bailey was helping Cal adjust the headdress of his costume with as much care as he would if they were appearing on the cover of *GQ*. Who would have thought these two would ever set foot in a church, much less participate?

God.

"You get my drift, Miss Annie?" Harold said. "You ready to let go and let God?"

"You shamed me into it, Harold."

"Whatever it takes."

She remembered why she'd wanted to find Harold. She handed him the tape. "Here's the cassette to make the recording for Jered in jail. You have someone to work the recorder?"

"Yes, dear. And here's hoping that next year Jered will be right here, helping us."

"With good behavior, that's the plan. I'd love to see him involved with the music."

Cal spotted her and left Bailey's adjustments. He put his arms around her waist. "Are you ready?"

"I hope so."

He rubbed the crease that appeared between her eyes in times of stress. "We're all prayed up, Annie-girl. Let it go."

The significance of his simple words was not lost on her.

He leaned close. "Have you ever been kissed by a shepherd?"

She fingered the edge of his headdress. "Not today."

Cal took care of it.

And God took care of the rest.

The Beginning...

Suddenly a great company of the heavenly host appeared with the angel,
praising God and saying, "Glory to God in the highest,
and on earth peace to men on whom his favor rests."

LUKE 2:13–14

The publisher and author would love to hear your
comments about this book. *Please contact us at:*
www.letstalkfiction.com

VERSES FOR *THE ULTIMATUM*

Dear readers:

Sometimes people ask how much of my life shows up in my books.

Too much sometimes.

Last spring, when I first wrote this manuscript, I was in...a mood. Let me revise that: a **Mood.** The problem was that I was way too busy. My to-do list consisted of thirty-four items—and these were not five-minute tasks like sweep the floor. The pressure weighed me down and made me a frazzled and frayed female. "Don't Tread on Me" should have been tattooed on my forehead.

I got to the point where I figured that I might as well include item numbers thirty-five, end world hunger, and thirty-six, ban commercials from television, because the chances of my checking off the last item—on time—seemed just as impossible. As far as making time for God? I had Him penciled in on Tuesdays from 2:30–2:31 A.M. It didn't help that our youngest was graduating from high school and the whole empty-nest thing loomed large...

But, by gum and by golly, I got the manuscript turned in. On time. Check one off the list.

Or not.

A few months later, when I received the editorial review of the manuscript from my editor (where she gives the author extensive notes regarding the bigger issues to address), I was faced with a problem. Though Julee was tactful, basically the whole manuscript was a moody mess (my term, not hers). The husband Cal was nasty and totally unlikable, Annie was constantly picking fights (and winning, of course), and the issue of faith? It was generally a beat-'em-over-the-head-with-God book. I could have sold the sermons on cassette for a good profit.

However, curiously, the Jered-Jinko storyline—the criminal story-line—was okay. Not a problem there. But the story about the family? The police should have been called to handle the domestic disputes. The topper was that I even had Annie die in the end. Deathbed scene, the works. Talk about a downer! Yet the odd thing was, I didn't shed a tear in writing it. That should have told me some-thing (like I was just plain weary of her and glad to see her gone?).

Needless to say, when confronted with these awful truths, I was stunned how the stress of last spring had adversely affected what I was writing. All my books stem from self-experience, but this one was over the edge. In truth, it was disconcerting. Even a bit scary.

But God is good, and Julee is patient (and my list of thirty-four to-dos had all been completed—numbers thirty-five and thirty-six still pending). I give whampum thanks to both of them for giving me the opportunity to redeem this book from the pits of negativity and (hopefully) lift it up to some semblance of true faith and inspiration for the reader. Our God is the God of second chances, and I certainly got one with this book. Big-time.

Your turn. Don't waste the chances He offers nor the lessons He gives you to learn. And take my advice, make your life easier by put-ting Him on the top of your list.

And keep Him there, no matter what.

Many blessings,

Nancy Moser

Discussion Questions

1. People come to Christ in different ways: Some can name one defining moment, others come to Him a little at a time, while still others can't remember a time when they weren't His. How did it happen to you? Or if it hasn't happened yet, what's keeping you from fully committing to Him?

2. Cal and Annie don't understand each other. Do you have a family member who doesn't understand your faith—or do you find it hard to understand someone else's deep faith? What are the best ways for a believer and an unbeliever to connect?

3. Have you ever pushed too hard to share your faith? What were the results?

4. Jinko Daly lured Jered with charm and false promises. Do you think evil is more insidious if it's blatant or subtle? Why? When have you experienced either or both types?

5. As the years passed, it got harder and harder for Cal to tell Annie his secrets. Do you have a secret that should come out? What's keeping you from clearing the air? Should all secrets come out?

6. Bailey was a proud man. What were the consequences of his pride? How should a person deal with unhealthy pride—in themselves or someone else?

7. Annie suspects Cal of having an affair. Do you think she handled her suspicions correctly? How might things have turned out if she'd reacted differently?

8. God often has to do something drastic to get our attention. How has He gotten your attention? Or has He?

9. Jered's dream was to be in the music business. Do you think he had what it takes to succeed? What's your dream? What are you doing to make it happen?

10. Annie was willing to sacrifice her life for her family, which reveals a powerful love. But her reason for doing so—to give her husband more time to know the Lord—shows an even deeper commitment to her faith. How would you have reacted if put in this situation?

MORE FICTION TITLES FROM
Nancy Moser

A STEADFAST SURRENDER

Claire Adams has wealth, power, and potential. She needs nothing and thinks she has everything... until God offers her the chance of a lifetime in Steadfast, Kansas.

ISBN 1-59052-143-9

THE SEAT BESIDE ME

Follow five passengers and the people beside them on a tragic plane flight. Some live; some die. Why them? Why not you?

ISBN 1-57673-884-1

THE MUSTARD SEED SERIES

The Invitation ~ BOOK ONE

Julia, Walter, Kathy, and Natalie have little in common, until each receives an invitation from an anonymous sender: *If you have faith as small as a mustard seed…nothing will be impossible for you. Please come to Haven, Nebraska.* At first, they all resist. But soon all four find themselves embarking on a journey that takes them beyond their wildest imaginings and tests their faith to the breaking point. Before it's over, each discovers that faith can move mountains—if you open your heart to the One who has called you.

ISBN 1-57673-352-1

The Quest ~ BOOK TWO

Julia, Walter, Kathy, Del, and Natalie are once again joined in a quest for faith and a battle against the forces determined to stop them, as they implement the decisions and direction they received in *The Invitation*. When the heat is turned up and the enemy unleashes his greatest opposition, the Havenites learn that it's not enough to *know* what's right; with God's help, one must *do* what's right. No matter what the cost.

ISBN 1-57673-410-2

The Temptation ~ BOOK THREE

The saga continues as the Havenites live out the commitments made in *The Quest*. Julia, Walter, Kathy, Del, and Natalie, each successful in their individual pursuits, think all is going well—and therein lies great danger. As complacency attacks the characters' focus on God, they start believing their achievements have risen from their own savvy and power. As they come together for a reunion, the characters face Satan's chaotic interference and learn the true nature of temptation. They must recover their courage to live out their plea to the Lord: "Lead us not into temptation, but deliver us from evil..."

ISBN 1-57673-734-9